LOST IN HIS ARMS

"Let me get something to warm you," Rick said.

His thoughtfulness surprised Jennie for she hadn't been sure what to expect from him. The last time they'd kissed he'd been cold and aloof afterward, but now he seemed so—so nice. She watched as he unrolled the bedroll and then as he strode purposefully back to her to wrap it about her trembling body.

"Thank you," Jennie murmured, grateful for the protection not only from the cold, but also his searing regard, for the touch of his eyes upon her had been as arousing as any physical caress. When his arms didn't release her, she looked up at him expectantly.

"You're welcome." His words were a growl as he nestled her close.

Then, with slow precision, his mouth took hers in a devouring, passionate kiss that swept away all her inhibitions . . .

Books by Bobbi Smith

Dream Warrior

Pirate's Promise

Texas Splendor

Capture My Heart

Desert Heart

The Gunfighter

Captive Pride

The Viking

Arizona Caress

Island Fire

Heaven

Arizona Temptress

Published by Kensington Publishing Corporation

ARIZONA TEMPTRESS

BOBBI SMITH

ZEBRA BOOKS
KENSINGTON PUBLISHING CORP.
http://www.kensingtonbooks.com

ZEBRA BOOKS are published by

Kensington Publishing Corp.
119 West 40th Street
New York, NY 10018

All Kensington titles, imprints, and distributed lines are available at special quantity discounts for bulk purchases for sales promotion, premiums, fund-raising, educational, or institutional use.

Special book excerpts or customized printings can also be created to fit specific needs. For details, write or phone the office of the Kensington Special Sales Manager: Attn. Special Sales Department. Kensington Publishing Corp., 119 West 40th Street, New York, NY 10018. Phone: 1-800-221-2647.

Zebra and the Z logo Reg. U.S. Pat. & TM Off.

First Printing: March 1986
ISBN-13: 978-1-4201-3150-5
ISBN-10: 1-4201-3150-8

First Electronic Edition: November 2013
eISBN-13: 978-1-4201-3281-6
eISBN-10: 1-4201-3281-4

10 9 8 7 6 5 4 3 2

Printed in the United States of America

This one's for Mary Jane Pellarin and Sandy Jaffe who've been supportive from the very beginning and for Mary Martin, Rochelle Wayne and Dianne Schwartz who were always there when I needed them.

Author's Note of Thanks

I'd like to thank all the wonderful people in Arizona who helped me with my research:

Cindy Coffman, of Gold Canyon Ranch—who braved the wilds of Willow (Peralta) Canyon with me.

Tom Kollenborn—who kept me enthralled with his tales of the Superstitions.

Ellen and John McCrea, of the Arizona Book Cache Bookstores—who were always there to lend a hand when I had a question.

Bobbie Suncelia—who helped immeasurably with the detailed research.

Prologue

Arizona Territory, 1840s

Since the beginning of time, the mountains had stood tall in their awesome majesty. Cruel and unforgiving, they rose abruptly above the desert floor; the harshness of their face showed the world only a shadow of the ruthlessness contained within their heart.

They watched and they waited, ferociously guarding the secrets of the ages, and they sneered contemptuously at the pitiful attempts by mortal men to discover their hidden treasure. Jagged and deadly, the rock-strewn cliffs stood as warriors, ready to do battle with those foolish enough to trespass, and they presided over the demise of those reckless adventurers with imperious disdain.

"Hurry! We must hurry!" Don Rodrigo Peralta hissed the order in low, desperate tones to his men as he stood guard over the long line of plodding, heavily laden pack mules.

"They can go no faster, Don Rodrigo. The gold is heavy," one of the workers offered in explanation.

"I know, Pedro. You are doing your best." Rodrigo sighed as his gaze raked searchingly over the boulder-strewn mountainside. What was it? What made him feel that all was not quite as it seemed to be?

Watching the entourage of pack animals and men pass by, his expression was both proud and worried. They had done well during their mining venture here in the Superstition Mountains, and he knew his father, Juan, would be pleased with their success. All that remained to be done was to transport the gold home to Sonora.

"Rodrigo! Why do you look so worried?" Antonio Peralta rode up beside his brother. "The hard part is over. The mining is done and we are going home!"

Rodrigo smiled at him. "You're right, of course. I'm being foolish, I guess, but I get the feeling that we're being watched."

Antonio frowned. "Indians?"

He shrugged. "I hope not, my brother."

Antonio was silent as he surveyed the craggy, barren peaks surrounding them. "It seems quiet enough. We'll be fine once we get out of the mountains."

"I'm sure you're right." Rodrigo looked around trying to catch sight of his son. "Have you seen Ricardo?"

"He is riding farther back. Do you want to speak with him?"

"No. I hadn't seen him in a while and I was growing concerned. You know how tricky this trail is and this is his first trip to the mine."

"And probably his last." There was a deep abiding bitterness in Antonio's answer. "The war with the United States has ruined us. When the treaty is ratified by the Americans, we will be forbidden from taking what is rightfully ours!"

"That's true. That's why Father insisted we bring back as much gold as we could this trip."

He nodded, his mood brightening. "I don't think he'll be disappointed. We've done well."

"Indeed." Rodrigo agreed watching as the caravan of two hundred gold-ladened mules continued on past him down the winding trail.

The trek out of the mountains went slowly for them and each mile they moved seemed a victory. The footing was treacherous following the path marked by the topped Saguaro cacti, the drop-offs sheer and steep, but they struggled onward, intent only on going home.

As they crossed the crest of Freemont Saddle and descended into Willow Canyon on the final leg of their journey out of the mountain range, eighteen-year-old Rick Peralta searched the length of the pack train until he found his father and uncle.

"Pedro tells me we'll be out of here in just a few more hours!" He was excited at the prospect of heading back home after the long weeks of hard work in the mines.

"It won't be long now." Antonio grinned at his boyish enthusiasm. "And I'm sure all the senoritas will be glad to have you back."

"They won't be nearly as happy to see me as I will be to see them." Rick smiled widely.

"I'm sure that more than a few are pining away for you," his uncle teased, knowing of his reputation with the ladies.

"My intentions have always been most circumspect." Rick said, trying to reply to his uncle's baiting with dignity, but his eyes were twinkling.

"Perhaps some of the senoritas wish they weren't." Antonio chuckled. "We shall just have to wait and see."

"Ricardo." Rodrigo interrupted the playful banter between his brother and his son. "I want you to stay to the back and make sure there are no stragglers. Once we reach the desert, we will regroup and move out as fast as possible."

"Yes, sir," he answered respectfully.

"And Rick?"

"Yes, Father?"

"Have your rifle ready. If the Apache are near, they'll attack as soon as we're in the open. Keep watch."

"Do you think they're close by?" Rick was suddenly alert.

"I'm not sure, but I don't want to take any chances. The

9

mules are too heavily burdened to move quickly in an emergency, so we have to be prepared just in case."

"Right." Rick hurried toward the end of the slow-moving column of men and animals.

Rodrigo watched his son ride away and his pride in him was obvious. "He will be a fine man. It's a pity Ana didn't live to see him grown." He grew melancholy at the thought of his long-dead wife.

"She would have been pleased. You've done a good job," Antonio complimented. "Someday, I will have a son like Ricardo."

"But first, you have to find yourself a bride!" He laughed at his brother, the perennial bachelor, and kneed his horse to action. "Come. Let's go home."

It was late afternoon when the procession finally left the rocky protection of the desolate, jagged range, and spirits were running high as all the men thought of the homecoming that awaited them when they returned to El Rancho Grande with this great wealth of gold.

Rodrigo's feeling of foreboding had faded as they had moved out onto open ground, and he was as eager as his men to begin this final segment of the trip back to Mexico. Their hopes and dreams were never to come to pass.

The Apache attacked savagely; their intent deadly.

Startled, caught off guard by the bloodthirsty assault, the Mexicans, who moments before had been contemplating the joys of home, were mown down, their horses scattered; their richly ladened mules stampeded.

Caught in the thick of the others' panicked retreat, Rick had presence of mind enough to stop and try to fight back. Bravely, he stayed at Antonio's side until the pressure from the hostiles became too great and they were forced to draw back. Regrouping with a few other survivors in a shallow, barely protected canyon, they prepared, with grim determination, to pay the Indians back for their bloody ambush.

The Apache, however, were not to be denied complete

10

victory. Relentless in their pursuit, they gave them no time to plan a counterattack. Doggedly they hounded them, until the light began to fail with the coming of night. Drawing back, the Indians waited. Morning, they knew, would come soon enough.

As the day faded into night, Rick and Antonio grew desperate. They had little food, some water, and their ammunition was running dangerously low. Knowing that their only chance for survival was to escape under the cover of darkness, Rick, Antonio, and the men who were with them left their horses behind as decoys and began to make their way back into the mountains, hoping to gain some protection in the rugged wilderness.

But the Apache knew every crevice and boulder and they were waiting when the sun's light broke the horizon. With unerring precision, they cut them down.

Antonio had been leading Rick along the crest of a mountainous peak when the brave who had been stalking them attacked. Shoving Rick aside, Antonio took on the Indian alone.

Thrown clear by his uncle's timely, self-sacrificing move, Rick slipped and fell over the edge of the cliff. Landing unconscious on a slanting ledge, he rolled from sight below the trail.

When he regained consciousness some time later, it was over. The entire entourage had been wiped out.

In shock, lost and more alone than he'd ever been in his life, Rick clawed his way from his precarious perch and wandered the uncharted canyons in search of help. The horrors of the massacre would stay with him the rest of his life, but no memory would affect him more dramatically than the discovery of his beloved uncle's tortured and mutilated body. Rick fashioned a grave as best he could in the stony ground, covering Antonio with rocks to save him from the scavengers that ravaged the countryside. Of his father, he found no trace.

His discovery of an uninjured horse was the only thing that saved Rick from certain death. Leaving the horror of the mountains behind, he quickly headed back toward civilization and the sanctity that was El Rancho Grande.

When Rick had left his home he had been an innocent boy in search of adventure, but when he returned, he was a man: a man whose soul had been scarred by the blood-curdling memory of the Apache's vicious slaughter in those looming, desolate mountains.

Chapter One

Arizona Territory 1850s

"Ah." Jennie McCaine groaned sensuously as she settled her slim, sore body into the hot, steaming bath water. "Thank you, Hildago. This feels wonderful. We must have ridden fifty miles today."

Hildago Teran smiled appreciatively as she busied herself picking up the clothing that Jennie had so haphazardly discarded in her haste to soak in the scented water. "You love ranch life and you know it."

Jennie returned her smile as she leaned back against the side of the tub. "Sometimes I wonder—like right now." Shifting stiffly once more, she sighed in relief as she finally found the most comfortable position.

"Well, you relax for awhile in that hot water. I guarantee, it'll ease what's bothering you," the older woman teased.

"Lord, I hope so." Jennie closed her eyes as she rested in the soothing heat. "Oh, Hildago," she added almost as an afterthought. "Todd's decided to stay for dinner tonight."

Hildago glanced over shoulder her at the young woman and shook her head in frustration at Jennie's nonchalant acceptance of neighboring rancher Todd Clarke's attentions. It was time Jennie came to realize just how Todd felt about her.

"Do you have a particular dress you'd like to wear?" she prompted.

"No. You go ahead and pick one out." Her answer was indifferent as she roused herself enough to begin to wash.

"How about your blue gown?" Hildago turned from her armoire with Jennie's best gown over her arm.

Jennie was surprised at her suggestion. "That's my best dress."

"Of course it is. That's why I think you should wear it." She spread it out on the bed and carefully smoothed out the wrinkles. "You'll look lovely for Todd."

"Todd? What's he got to do with anything?" Jennie was wide-eyed in her amazement. Todd was a friend of the family and she'd known him practically all of her life. Why should she dress up for him?

A certain maternal irritation was evident in Hildago's expression as she hinted. "Why do you suppose he's been visiting here so regularly? Surely he doesn't have that much business with your father."

Jennie frowned. "You think Todd has been coming over to see me?"

"Why else?" Hildago stood with her hands on her full hips watching the play of emotions that crossed Jennie's face as she considered the possibility. With an exaggerated sigh of impatience, she continued. "Sometimes, Jennie, I think your sister Carrie knows more about men than you do."

"That's ridiculous." Jennie scoffed at the mention of her younger sibling. "She's only a child."

"Your sister is sixteen now and more than a little interested in men. She's already told me that she wants to get married as soon as possible. When are you going to start thinking about it?"

"Getting married?" Jennie squeaked, sitting upright to glare at the other woman. Though she was eighteen she had never given the holy state of wedlock more than a passing thought. She was completely and totally happy living here on the M Circle C with her widowed father. She loved the wildness of the land and the freedom of her lifestyle. She was in control of her destiny and had yet to meet a man who'd given her a reason to change. Be a wife? Have children? Maybe later, but definitely not yet. "I don't want to get married. I like things just the way they are." Agitated, she picked up the bar of scented soap and started to wash again, hoping that by ignoring Hildago, she would go away. It didn't work.

"All right. Have it your way for now, but don't forget what I said. You're no longer a child. Look at yourself. You're a woman and a beautiful one at that." She paused to let her words sink in. "Maybe it's time you started thinking like one, eh? You could do far worse than Todd Clarke." Before Jennie could answer, Hildago hurried out of the room, leaving her alone with her thoughts.

It was almost an hour later when Jennie smoothed a soft, unruly curl back into place and took one last appraising glance in her mirror. Using decorative combs, she had fashioned her lustrous, dark mane up and away from her face, in a style that emphasized the perfection of her features. She studied her reflection for a moment, taking in the dark, expressive eyes with their softly rounded brows, the high classic beauty of the cheekbones, and the full, somewhat pouting mouth. It disturbed her to think that Hildago had been right, yet the evidence was there, staring back at her. She was startled as the realization dawned: She really was a woman now. Jennie found the thought oddly unsettling and was turning away from her reflection when she casually glanced down at the decolletage of her gown. Had she really changed so much and been unaware of it? Evidently she had, for where the bodice had fit comfortably and revealed little before, now, it was snug, forcing her full young breasts to swell above the lace-trimmed edge of the square-cut bodice.

Jennie tugged at the offending material, hoping to pull it higher, but she finally gave up the effort for fear of ruining the dress completely. And, though it did display a goodly amount of cleavage, she had to admit that the gown was far less revealing than many of those of European styling that Carrie had brought with her from her trip back East.

Suddenly aware of the direction her thoughts had taken, Jennie was amazed. Until now, she had never cared one bit about how she looked and now, just because Hildago had challenged her womanhood, she was suddenly concerned about her appearance. An embarrassed anger grew within her. Pa liked her just the way she was, she argued with herself. She was happy, so why worry? Lifting her chin in defiance of her feminine confusion, Jennie swept from the bedroom, her natural grace adding a certain elegance to her movements.

Mac and Todd were deep in conversation when Jennie ventured forth from the back of the house to join them in the study.

"Jennie, darling," Mac greeted her expansively. "You look beautiful."

"Thank you, Pa." She smiled in delight as his compliment reassured her of his affections. "Good evening, Todd."

"You do look lovely," Todd said wholeheartedly as she turned to face him and, when his gaze dropped to her breasts, so enticingly yet innocently revealed, his breath caught in his throat. My God, he'd had no idea that she was so amply endowed. It was an effort for him to look up.

"And thank you, Todd." She smiled at him easily, unaware of his excited turmoil. Glancing about the room, she asked, "Carrie hasn't come down yet?"

"Not yet, I don't know what takes that girl so long to just change dresses," Mac grumbled. "It wasn't like she'd been out on the range with us today like you were."

"Now, Pa," Jennie soothed, hoping to avoid another confrontation between her father and younger sister. "You

16

know how Carrie feels about such things."

"I know only too well!" Mac scowled, wondering how a child sprung from his loins could be so indifferent to the workings of the M Circle C. He was thoroughly disgusted with his younger daughter who, it seemed to him, had been a continual source of disappointment to him since her birth sixteen years ago. Why—it was her fault that Eve was gone—Eve, his wife—the woman he'd loved more than life itself. A cold impotent fury possessed him as he thought of the cruel tricks life could play.

"Carrie's a lovely young lady, Mac," Todd was saying. He had known both the McCaine girls for a long time now and, though Jennie with dark beauty and passion for ranch life was the one who had stolen his heart, he also found Carrie's delicate blond beauty very appealing indeed.

Mac fell silent, drinking long and deep from his tumbler of whiskey. There was no way he was going to get drawn into a discussion of Carrie's finer points, whatever they were.

"Good evening." Carrie swept into the room on a cloud of expensive French perfume and kissed her father dutifully on the cheek, not noticing that his expression turned thunderous as he took note of the gown she was wearing.

"Carrie you look more ravishing every time I see you," Todd told her quickly, wanting to blunt Mac's critical agitation. And indeed, Carrie did look enticing in her low-cut off-the-shoulder gown of pale yellow silk.

"Why, thank you, Todd," Carrie responded preeningly, pleased that she'd attracted his attention. She had worn her most expensive gown knowing that the color set off her fair good looks and that the revealing bodice emphasized the feminine beauty of her breasts. "You look handsome yourself."

Being tall and heavily built with features more rough-hewn than handsome, Todd was left speechless for a moment by her unexpected compliment.

"Let's eat, shall we?" Mac suggested, his tone tightly

controlled. His long suppressed anger grew within him as he'd watched Carrie's flirtatious and, in his mind, whoring ways. He wanted to drag Carrie back to her room, thrash her within an inch of her life and lock her in! Damn her! He seethed to himself. Why did life's past mistakes always have to come full circle?

Sensing that for some unknown reason her father was very upset, Jennie quickly took his arm and allowed him to escort her into the dining room while Todd gallantly assisted Carrie.

Jennie had never understood her father's attitude toward her younger sister. He always seemed to find fault with everything Carrie did. She had never been able to please him, not even as a child. It seemed that he was always waiting for her to make a mistake so he could berate her for whatever she did.

In their younger years, Jennie had defended Carrie, but Carrie had come to resent her interference. Now after having been caught in the middle of so many disputes, Jennie wisely held her tongue whenever things grew tense between her father and sister.

Often Jennie wished that their mother Eve was still alive for perhaps she would have known how to handle the tension between Mac and Carrie. Sighing inwardly, she realized that that was useless dreaming on her part for her mother, the beautiful Eve, had died soon after Carrie was born, when Jennie was two.

Relieved that Todd was here tonight and that his presence would help to ease the strain, Jennie instructed the servants to begin serving dinner. The meal progressed smoothly enough, although Mac was oddly quiet and gave only monosyllabic answers to any and all questions directed his way.

It was only when they had finished dining that Hildago's words of earlier that evening returned to haunt Jennie.

"Jennie," Todd said, "I was wondering if I could speak

with you alone for a moment?"

Surprised by his question, Jennie didn't notice when Carrie stiffened perceptively. "Certainly."

"Mac—Carrie—If you'll excuse us?" He rose from the table and moved to help Jennie with her chair.

"Of course, Todd," came Mac's hearty answer.

"Shall we go out on the veranda?" Jennie suggested as she stood.

"That would be fine." He guided her toward the door with a gentle hand at her waist.

Having become a master at disguising her emotions, Carrie watched, expressionlessly, as Todd left the room with Jennie. Throughout the entire meal, she had encouraged his interest in hopes that he'd finally come to realize she was a fullgrown woman, but it had all been for naught. He cared for Jennie and Jennie only—the same as everyone else! A barely controlled fury raged within her. Someday, she seethed, someday, she'd get even with Jennie if it was the last thing she ever did!

A sliver of moon hung low on the distant horizon adding little brightness to the star-spangled, fathomless canopy of the night. The breath of a soft spring zephyr caressed the now blooming land, gentling it for a moment in time before dancing lightly away in search of a more deserving lover— one more sweet and pure than this rock-rimmed, sun-abused expanse of nothingness that for a few weeks of every year pretended to become something it was not—something fresh and innocent.

Standing at the railing on the veranda of the sprawling white adobe ranch house, Jennie stared off into the peaceful darkness, savoring the heavenly scent of the blossoming countryside.

"It's beautiful this time of year," she murmured, glancing back over her shoulder to where Todd stood in the doorway silhouetted against the brightness inside.

"Yes. It is," he answered, suddenly tongue-tied and a bit nervous about what he wanted to say. Squaring his shoulders in an unconscious gesture, Todd stepped away from the harsh light and joined her at the rail. "You love this land, don't you Jennie?"

Facing him, her smile one of serene contentment, she spoke softly. "It's magical, Todd. Always changing—always restless and new. I don't think I could ever be happy anywhere else."

"I know what you mean. I felt the same thing when I first came here six years ago and I still feel that way today." In a bold move, he took her hand and lifted it to his lips. "Jennie—I feel that way about you, too."

Having been forewarned by Hildago that Todd did care for her, Jennie was not surprised by his declaration, but she was a bit unsure as to how to handle the whole situation. How did one tell a good, dear friend that that was all he'd ever be—just a friend.

"Todd—I think we need to talk," she said, wanting to pull her hand free of his ardent grip, yet fearful of offending him.

"I've been wanting to say these things to you for months now, but something always managed to interfere." He shook his head disparagingly. "But now that we're finally alone and you know how much I care for you—Jennie, will you marry me?"

He was so earnest and so sweetly humble that Jennie felt for just a moment like saying yes. As Hildago had said, she could do far worse than Todd Clarke for a husband. But her common sense finally won out. She knew in her heart that she wasn't ready for marriage. As much as she liked Todd and enjoyed his company, he did not inspire any of the emotions that Jennie had been told went with true love. She felt no passion or desire when she thought of him, only a warmth and a sisterly kind of affection, much like what she felt for her own brother Jake.

"Todd—" Jennie began, totally at a loss as to how to begin. "Todd, I care for you a great deal, but I just don't know if I'm ready for marriage yet."

"I can wait, Jennie," he replied ignoring the hesitancy in her tone. "After all, I've waited this long already."

Todd's smile was tender and, with a gentleness surprising for a man his size, he turned her toward him. Then, in what seemed like almost slow motion, he bent and kissed her. His lips were soft and warm and she found their caress not unpleasant. When he broke off the almost chaste embrace, his eyes were dark with his unspoken plea.

"I can wait," he murmured again, stroking the curve of her cheek with hesitant fingers.

His sensitivity struck a chord in Jennie's heart. Todd was such a dear man. She couldn't bear to hurt him. Maybe, in time, she would come to love him.

"Good night, Todd." Jennie answered, her nervousness clearly evident in her voice. "I'll see you in the morning."

Todd sighed in frustration as he watched her hurry back inside. The night hadn't been a total waste, he decided. At least she hadn't said no. That in itself was encouraging, for he imagined, and rightly so, that it was the first proposal of marriage Jennie had ever received. Stepping off the protective covering of the veranda, Todd stood silently in the comforting darkness of the Arizona night. Enveloped in its ebony cloak, he stared out across the range, pondering the best way to win Jennie's heart and make her his own.

As soon as Jennie and Todd had gone outdoors, Carrie had excused herself from her father's glowering, condemning presence and hurried off to the privacy of her own room. Consumed by a hatred she little understood, she stormed about her haven. Viciously she kicked off her shoes and then stripped off her gown, tossing it in a rumpled heap in the center of the floor. Pausing only long enough to untie the ribbons of her delicately made chemise, Carrie took it off, too, throwing it aside with the discarded dress.

Turning up the lamp, Carrie strode naked to her cheval mirror. Staring at herself with critical detachment, she had absolutely no doubt that she was prettier than Jennie. Her hair was a glorious mass of golden curls; her body was trim and shapely; her legs were slender and graceful. Why then, she seethed, wasn't Todd attracted to her? She had done everything but climb onto his lap at dinner tonight and yet, when all was said and done, it had been Jennie he'd wanted.

Twisting sideways, Carrie surveyed her profile and found no defects there. Her breasts, though not as full as Jennie's were high and round and, she knew from experience, very sensitive; her buttocks were tight, sensuously curved, and very enticing to a man's hand.

Muttering a curse under her breath, Carrie stalked across the room to the window. Staring out, she was little mindful of the fact that she was clearly illuminated by the lamplight. Damn! Her body was aching with a need that she knew full well needed to be assuaged. She had learned of physical intimacy during her year back East and now, forced into celibacy here on the ranch, she was becoming too frustrated to worry about being discreet. She needed release from the prison of her desires and she needed it now!

Thwarted in her effort to attract Todd's attentions, Carrie was left with only one opportunity. Her movements were rushed as she pulled on a dark-colored dress over her nude, sensitive body and slipped into low-heeled shoes. Knowing that no one would come looking for her for the rest of the night, she extinguished her lamp and then climbed nimbly out her bedroom window. Tonight, she was going to enjoy herself. Tomorrow would take care of itself!

Taking care not to be seen, Carrie skirted the main house and headed straight for the foreman Steve Douglas's private cabin. Approaching cautiously from the rear, she was delighted to find that Steve had not yet returned from his usual nightly inspection of the stables. Boldly, Carrie let herself in and, without lighting any lamps, she shed her clothes and slid beneath the covers of his bunk. Stretching languidly against the rough, scratchiness of the cotton sheets, she waited in breathless anticipation for his coming. She had never been with Steve before but knew anough about manipulating men to know that he would not be able to refuse her—boss's daughter or not. A small smile of lusty excitement lit her face as she relaxed in the bed.

It seemed to Carrie that an eternity had passed before she heard the jingle of Steve's spurs as he crossed the dusty grounds on his way back to his home. Artfully arranging the topsheet to enhance the view he would have when he entered the bedroom for the first time, she lay still.

Bone-tired and weary from a long day in the saddle, Steve Douglas strode slowly toward his cabin. Pausing by the watering trough, he set his hat aside and unbuttoned his dirty, sweat-stained shirt. Taking it off, he tossed it carelessly over the nearby hitching rail. It took only a second to prime the pump and, once the clean, cool water gurgled forth, he began to wash the day's grime from his torso.

Carrie wondered at his delay in entering the cabin and she peeked out the small window next to the bed. The night was dark, but the flickering lamplight from the main house helped to partially illuminte the yard, and she could make out Steve's very masculine form as he stripped down to the waist. Her eyes roamed hungrily over the taut, sinewy muscles of his back as he leaned forward under the pump to let the refreshing fluid wash over him. A sensual heat began to build within her as she imagined running her hands over the broad, now glistening smoothness of his shoulders. If only he'd hurry.

Straightening up, Steve shook the water from his head and then tried to brush some of the day's clinging dust from his pants. Gathering his things, he headed inside, anxious to get a good night's rest. Tossing his hat and shirt on the

23

nearby table, he lit one lamp and then began to unbuckle his gunbelt as he headed to his bedroom.

"Good evening, Steve." Carrie's purr froze him in his tracks, and his eyes narrowed in stunned confusion as he spotted her in his bed.

"What the hell are you doing here?" Steve demanded as, mechanically, he finished taking off his gunbelt and placed it on top of the small chest of drawers. He was unable to take his eyes off her so blatantly offered body for the sheet seemed to hug her every lush curve.

"Waiting for you." Her voice was throaty as she lifted her arms to him and smiled seductively. "Don't make me wait any longer, Steve."

"Get out!" Steve ordered, his tone quiet but his emphasis unmistakably clear.

"I don't think so." Carrie sighed dramatically, settling back more comfortably against his pillow.

"What do you mean, 'you don't think so'? What kind of game are you playing, little girl?" He was furious. This was the boss's daughter, not some whore from the cantina in town. What the devil was she up to?

Carrie understood far more of what he was thinking than Steve gave her credit for, and in a move designed to drive him over the edge, she sat up, letting the covers fall about her waist. "I'm not playing, Steve." Arching her back, she lifted the heavy mane of her hair in a sensuous motion and let the golden curls fall forward to partially curtain the seductive upthrust of her breasts. "I want you."

Steve's mouth went dry as he watched her, but being a very practical man, he still held back. "Carrie. You shouldn't be here. You don't know what you're asking for. For God's sake, you're little more than a child!"

"I'm a woman, Steve. All the woman you'll ever need." Swinging her lithe legs over the side of the bed, she tossed off the sheet and strode sinuously toward him. "Ever."

His gaze seared her, and when she stopped in front of him,

Steve could no longer deny himself. With a groan of mixed pleasure and pain, he clasped her to him and was rewarded by her throaty victorious growl as his mouth descended to hers in a burning passionate caress.

Eagerly, Carrie caressed the bare width of his chest. Driven by her insatiable hunger for satisfaction, she rubbed against Steve, taunting him and arousing him to a fevered pitch. Greedily, her hands moved to loosen his pants, and it was then that his control completely deserted him.

Pulling away from Carrie long enough to shed his boots and pants, Steve gave little thought to the aftermath of his actions. All that mattered was that she was there and more than willing. Lifting her into his arms, he moved quickly to the bed. Neither spoke, for this joining of their bodies was too elemental for words. There was no need for the usual simplistic promises of love and devotion. They both knew what they wanted and they both knew exactly how to get it.

There was no tenderness as Steve took her because his urgency to be within her was too great. And Carrie, her need spiraling with his each ardent caress, encouraged him, using all she had ever learned to heighten his excitement until they were both mindless with forbidden desire.

Reveling in his hard-driving possession, Carrie held nothing back as her body sought peak after peak of carnal rapture. Carrie cried out loudly as the throbbing release of her climax claimed her, and she bucked wildly against Steve until he joined her in that pinnacle of pleasure.

Momentarily sated, she rested in his arms as a small triumphant smile curved her lips.

Some time later, when Todd reentered the ranch house, Mac hurried out of the study to greet him. Without saying a word, he directed the younger man inside the privacy of his office and closed the door behind them.

"How did it go?" he asked as he poured them both a drink.

25

He was more than eager to find out how his favorite daughter had responded to Todd's proposal.

Todd shrugged his broad shoulders as he took the tumbler of bourbon from Mac. "I get the feeling that Jennie thinks of me as another big brother."

"Well, change her mind!" Mac ordered brusquely. "That shouldn't be too hard for you. She trusts you."

"Of course she does and I won't break that trust. I love Jennie, but there's no way I can force her to love me." Todd's jaw was set with determination when Mac glanced up at him. "I'll just have to be patient with her and hope that she'll come to return my feelings."

"Oh, all right. Have it your way." He acquiesced without his usual grace. "But I want you in the family—and soon."

"I'm honored by your sentiments." Todd grinned at the older man who was his close friend and confidant.

"Ha!" His response was tempered with good humor now that they'd cleared the air about Jennie. "And speaking of relations, when is that errant son of mine, Jake, coming home? You did see him in Santa Lucia yesterday, didn't you?"

"We had a drink together at Dolly's bar. Jake mentioned that he had another meeting with Robertson today and if everything went well, he'd probably be heading back tomorrow."

"Good." Mac stood up and moved to the bar to refill his glass with his favorite whiskey. "Do you want some more?" He held out the decanter to Todd when he'd finished pouring himself a generous libation.

"No. I'm done for the night. I've got to be on my way home first thing in the morning." Todd got up and started out of the room.

"We'll have an early breakfast then."

"Sounds good. Good night, Mac." And with that, Todd retired for the evening.

Mac was standing at the study window, staring out across

the night-shrouded land that he loved when the soft knock at the door drew his attention. "Come in."

"Mac—" Hildago entered, shutting the door behind her. Without pause, she hurried across the room and into Mac's waiting arms. Their embrace was not a torrid one; instead, it was the shared affection of lovers well known to one another. "How did it go?"

"Jennie surprised me again," he began after kissing her softly. "I was sure that she'd jump at the chance to marry Todd. I mean, she's known him for most of her life. Why not marry him? He's a good man."

"She said no?"

"Well, not exactly. She told Todd that she wasn't ready to get married yet." Mac released Hildago and picked up his tumbler of whiskey, taking a hefty swallow.

"At least she was being honest with him." Hildago was pleased by Jennie's answer. "And that doesn't mean that she won't marry him. It just means that she wants more time to think about it."

Turning to her, his solemn features brightened. "I'm glad you understand her so well."

She smiled at his compliment. "Sometimes I think I know her better than she knows herself."

"Then convince her to marry Todd. They'd be perfect together, and with the ranches adjoining each other—"

Hildago shook her head as Mac's thoughts turned invariably to the business side of the arrangement. "If there's one thing I do know about Jennie, it's that she won't be pushed. She's just like you that way, Mac."

Mac looked disgruntled but didn't respond.

"You shouldn't worry so much about it. When she's ready to get married, I'm sure we'll be among the first to know."

"But I want her to marry Todd," he persisted stubbornly.

"She may very well still marry him. We just have to let her decide."

"What's to decide?" He started to protest again.

"If she loves him. Mac—" Hildago's dark eyes caught, held and challenged Mac's gray ones. "What is a marriage without love?"

He tensed. "You're right." Taking her into his arms once more, he hugged her to his heart. "A marriage without love is pure hell on earth."

Hildago knew his pain and didn't speak for long moments. "You'll be understanding then? You won't try to influence her one way or the other?"

Mac sighed heavily and then stepped back to look down at her. "You win. Jennie can pick her own husband. I won't push her. But, damn it Hildago—I like Todd!"

Hildago smiled tenderly as she moved back into the circle of his protective embrace, an embrace she had shared for many years now. "I knew you'd listen to reason. And who knows? Todd may end up in the family yet, anyway."

Chapter Two

The patrons of Dolly's bar in Mesa Roja were a rowdy bunch, and Jake McCaine was no exception as he unceremoniously hauled the dance hall girl across his lap and zestfully kissed her inviting mouth. "Thanks for the drink, Mimi!"

"You're welcome, Jake," Mimi cooed, linking her arms around his neck and returning his embrace with equal fervor. "When you finish your drink we could go upstairs." She rubbed sensuously against his chest, enjoying just being close to him. Mimi found Jake's tall blond good looks irresistible, and she prided herself on the fact that she was the only girl in the saloon he'd bed.

"Maybe we will," he agreed, holding the scantily clad Mimi a willing captive.

With gusto Jake picked up his beer and took a hefty swig. Relaxing back in the chair, he let his gaze drift lazily around the crowded bar while he openly fondled Mimi's ample charms. He was feeling good this night and a celebration was definitely in order. His meeting with neighboring rancher Fred Robertson had gone well, and he was confident that the agreement they'd reached concerning the water rights would satisfy his father.

Jake was about to take Mimi up on her very attractive

offer, when the tall, dark-haired stranger entered the saloon. Though it had been a few years since they'd ridden together, Jake immediately recognized his old companion Rick Peralta, and he was eager to renew their friendship. Releasing his hold on Mimi, he stood up.

"Mimi, honey. Don't go anywhere." He nuzzled her neck affectionately. "I'll be right back."

Mimi started to pout, but when she recognized the promise in Jake's eyes she smiled. "I'd wait all night for you Jake." She pressed his solidly muscled arm to her breasts.

"Good. Stay here. I won't be long." Setting her from him, he made his way toward Rick.

Rick Peralta was uneasy as he glanced around the smoke-filled saloon because his sharply honed instincts were warning him of potential danger. But when he noted nothing out of the ordinary, he approached the bar with a casualness of manner that belied the tension in his lean body.

"What'll it be?" the barkeep asked, eyeing the dark-clad stranger suspiciously as he sensed the aura of barely leashed danger about him.

"Whiskey," Rick ordered abruptly, his gaze meeting the other man's impassively.

Scurrying to serve him, the bartender hurried to pour his drink.

"Leave the bottle."

"Right." And he moved quickly away.

Rick drained his glass and was lifting the bottle to pour another, when he saw Jake coming across the room. Muttering a violent curse under his breath, he pulled the brim of his black hat low over his face and shifted positions to better shield himself from Jake's curious gaze. The last thing he needed was to be recognized by an old friend—especially now, but it was too late.

"Rick?" Jake's question was barely out of his mouth when Rick moved.

It was a lightning blow, totally unexpected and completely

effective, and Rick stood over Jake's prone, unconscious body like a conquering warrior, his hand resting easily on the butt of his holstered gun. His chiseled features were fierce as he stared down the stunned crowd that remained motionless around him. When no one else made a move, Rick turned back to the bar.

"Get him out of here." He gestured toward Jake. "He bothers me."

"Yes, sir." The bartender's eyes were wide with frightened respect as he hurried to do his bidding. "Harry—John—take him upstairs to Mimi's room. Now!"

Rick paid little attention as the two men carried Jake's limp form from the room with Mimi following worriedly behind.

"Can I get you anything else, sir?" The barkeep was almost timid in his approach.

"The name's Cazador. Remember it," Rick said, sliding a coin across the wet slickness of the bar.

The man's eyes widened as he recognized the name. "Yes, sir."

"What's your name?"

"Ed."

"Well, Ed," Rick drawled, seemingly amused by the man's reaction to learning his identity, "I'll need a room for the night."

"Seventy-five cents and you can take your pick at the top of the stairs. A dollar more if you want a woman," he nodded helpfully.

"Just a room." His lips twisted into a semblance of a smile. "Thanks anyway."

"Yes, sir."

"If anybody comes looking for me, I want to know about it. All right?"

"Yes, sir," he hastily assured him.

"Good. Give me another bottle, then."

Ed pulled a full bottle of whiskey from under the counter.

"That'll be two dollars."

"Here." Rick tossed him a gold piece as he headed toward the stairs. "Keep the change."

"Thank you!"

"Just remember what I told you."

"I will." Ed watched until Rick had disappeared up the steep steps before turning to the other men at the bar. "Do you know who that was? That was El Cazador." An excited murmur stirred through the group of men who'd gathered nearby because they had all heard the tales of the infamous gunfighter El Cazador.

With softly measured tread, Rick made his way down the narrow, darkened hallway, listening carefully at each closed door. When he finally heard Jake's groaning voice behind one, he noted the number and then quickly chose a room of his own nearby. Letting himself in, he was unimpressed by his surroundings: a single bed, a washstand, a chair. All rented rooms were depressingly alike as far as he was concerned, but as long as the bed linens were clean he wouldn't complain.

Extinguishing the lamp that had been left burning, he pulled the chair to the window overlooking the main street below and sat down. Drawing his gun and resting it easily across his lap, he propped his feet up on the sill. Rick stirred uneasily as he wondered what else could possibly go wrong. Totally disgusted and more than a little edgy, he settled back to wait.

Rick knew that he had to get to Jake as soon as possible to explain his actions, but he couldn't make the attempt until he was certain that his friend was alone. What he had to tell him was a matter of life and death, and Rick knew he couldn't take any chances.

Thank God, Jake hadn't used his last name. He couldn't let his real identity become known. He was El Cazador again now for, despite his earlier vow to give up this way of life, there was no other way for him to handle his current

32

situation. To deal with killers, you had to act like a killer, and shortly he would have to deal with Miguel Malo, the most bloodthirsty outlaw in all the Southwest.

Rick cursed and tightened his grip on his revolver as he thought of Malo and how the lowlife bastard had raided the Peralta ranch, El Rancho Grande, two weeks before killing six ranchhands and kidnapping his elderly grandfather, Juan. Rick had been out on the range working the stock when he received the news of the attack and from the moment he'd found out, he'd known what he had to do. There was only one possible way to free Juan and that was by working within Malo's gang itself, and as El Cazador he could do that.

Rick realized how lucky it was that only a few people knew that Ricardo Peralta and El Cazador the gunfighter were one and the same, and he was determined to keep it that way. Secrecy was of the utmost importance to him now, for tonight he was to meet with some of Malo's men and begin the short journey to his camp.

Being accepted into their ranks was only the first step in Rick's plan to rescue his grandfather. No matter what he did, Rick knew it wasn't going to be easy to free Juan from their fiendish clutches.

The sound of Mimi's low, throaty voice in the hallway brought him back to the present, and he listened intently as she finally left her room.

"I'll be back in a few minutes, Jake. You just rest for a while, darlin'."

Once he was certain that Mimi had gone, Rick crossed the hall swiftly and silently let himself into her room.

"I was wondering when you were going to show up." Jake's voice was cool and his hand steady as he aimed his gun straight at Rick's chest, but Rick only grinned and sauntered across the room to where his old friend lay in bed.

"I would have come sooner, but I didn't want to interrupt anything." He sat down easily in the overstuffed chair by the bed and then leaned forward to push the barrel of the firearm aside. "Be careful with that thing—somebody might get hurt."

Staring at Rick assessingly, Jake let up on the hammer and placed the gun on the nightstand. Relaxing against the headboard as he gathered the sheets more strategically about him, he rubbed his bruised jaw and glared at Rick indignantly. "I already have been! Aren't you going to ask me how my jaw is?"

"I thought Mimi would have taken care of that by now." Rick chuckled at Jake's discomfort.

"She took care of some parts of me that were aching, but my jaw wasn't one of them." Jake gestured at his own barely concealed nudity and tried to smile, but the effort cost him a small groan. Swinging his long legs over the side of the bed, he stood up and started to pull on his pants. "Why the hell did you hit me?"

Rick's expression immediately hardened. "It's a long story, but the bottom line is no one knows I'm Rick Peralta and I have to keep it that way. I'm El Cazador again."

"What?" Jake was confused. "I thought you'd decided to give it all up and go home." He well remembered how Rick had grown tired of the suicidal life he'd been leading as a hired gun and how he had wanted to return home to his grandfather's ranch.

"I did. I've been back working at El Rancho Grande for almost two years. But that's all changed now."

"Why?"

"You've heard of Miguel Malo, haven't you?"

"Who hasn't? The man's scum." Jake's words were bitter as he remembered the stories of the carnage the bandit had wreaked across the Southwest. He was a cold-blooded murderer who killed for the joy of it.

"He's kidnapped my grandfather." Rick spoke softly, almost despairingly.

"Juan—why?" He turned quickly to face his friend.

34

"The gold mine. Evidently, he thinks Juan is the only one who knows the exact location. The housekeeper overheard them arguing about it. At first, Malo thought there was a map to the mine and when he found out there wasn't, he took Juan captive and is forcing him to guide them to it."

"Let's go get him out. All I have to do is send word back home that I'm leaving for a few weeks—"

"It's not that simple, Jake. We just can't go riding into their camp like vigilantes. Grandfather would be dead as soon as the first shot was fired." Rick's calm, controlled manner tempered Jake's impulsiveness, just as it had all those years before when they rode together. "I have a plan."

"I'll help."

"Thanks, but I'll handle it. I'm riding as El Cazador again." Rick watched the expression on his friend's face. "That's why I couldn't let you say my name downstairs."

"I'm sorry." He was contrite. "I could have ruined everything for you."

"Don't worry, The men I'm here to meet haven't shown up yet."

"So, what's your plan?"

"As El Cazador, they'll know me by my reputation. No one will doubt who I am."

"But how are you going to get your grandfather out of there without getting both of you killed?"

"Time is on my side. They're not going to do anything to Juan until they've reached the mine."

"Let me help you. We rode together once." Jake's offer was sincere for he knew of Rick's earlier traumatic experience in the Superstitions, and he knew how difficult it would be for him to go back.

"I know and I appreciate your offer, But not this time, Jake. I have to go alone. Any other way would only complicate things further." Rick paused and then smiled grimly. "Besides, I may have help getting rid of Malo."

"The Apache?"

"Exactly."

Jake fell silent as he contemplated the danger Rick was about to face. "Is there anything I can do?"

Rick stood up and turned away from him, walking slowly to the window. His answer when it came was simple, yet heartfelt. "Pray."

Chapter Three

The morning sun streaked the eastern horizon with streamers of pink and gold as it celebrated its escape from night's clinging embrace. Birds joined in a raucous chorus to add nature's music to the glory of the new day's dawning.

Hustling about her bedroom, Jennie finished buttoning her blouse and tucked the soft white material into the waistband of her fitted riding skirt. Plopping down on her bed in a most unladylike fashion, she made quick business of tugging on her riding boots. After taking only a moment to tie her hair back with a ribbon, she raced from her room, intent only on enjoying the pleasure of her morning ride.

Regardless of the weather, Jennie rode daily at dawn. The solitary hour she spent roaming the endless miles of the rugged McCaine ranch was a peace-filled sabbatical for her, continually renewing her respect and love for the land.

This particular morning, though, fate conspired against her, and her life would never be the same again. Striding purposefully into the stable, she came face to face with Todd who was busy saddling his stallion.

"Jennie—Good morning." His greeting was spontaneous and enthusiastic, and his broad, almost homely features lit up at the sight of her. "You look lovely this morning."

"Thank you, Todd." She was a bit self-conscious now that

37

she knew his true feelings. Noting his saddlebags, she inquired, "You're leaving?"

"I've got to get back. I've been away too long already." he admitted, reluctantly turning back to his mount.

"Why don't I ride part of the way with you?" she offered, not wanting the events of the past evening to have any effect on their friendship.

"I'd like that," he answered easily refusing to allow his sudden flare of hope that she'd changed her mind about his proposal to reflect in his tone.

"Just give me a minute to get Star ready." With the expertise of a practiced horsewoman, Jennie quickly saddled her mare and mounted up.

Although their horses were frisky and ready for a good run, Jennie and Todd rode slowly away from the ranch house, taking the time to savor the newness of the day.

"Have you given any further thought to what we talked about last night?" Todd inquired, unable to restrain himself any longer from asking.

"I've thought of nothing else since I left you," Jennie answered honestly, meeting his questioning gaze.

"And?" A glimmer of unspoken emotion lit his dark gaze.

"And my feelings are still the same. I'm just not ready to get married." She faced him squarely, knowing that he would respect her more for telling him the truth.

"Well, when you decide you are," he said good-naturedly, with a half smile, "I'll be waiting in line."

"That sounds good to me." Jennie smiled widely, pleased that he understood and would not pressure her. "Race you to Angel Spring!"

Giving Todd no time to reply, she put her heels to her mount. Playfully charging ahead, her delighted laughter floated back to him spurring him to action. Within seconds, Todd's massive stallion was at full gallop, narrowing the distance between them with long, powerful strides.

Jennie felt vibrant and alive as she and Star raced as one

across the land. The wind tore at her hair, whipping the loosely bound tresses about her face, but she paid no attention, concentrating instead on staying as far ahead of Todd as she could until they reached the rockier area near the creek. She knew the only way she could win was to outmaneuver him in that trickier terrain where Star's surefootedness would provide the edge over his bigger, less agile mount. Topping the final rise, Jennie veered sharply to the left and took the shorter more rock-strewn path to Angel Creek, while Todd rode straight ahead on the longer, less hazardous route past Tracker's Boulder.

As Todd rounded the massive boulder that served as a landmark and rendezvous point, the possibility of an ambush never crossed his mind. His thoughts were only of Jennie. The bullet caught him unawares as it exploded viciously into his shoulder, and the force of the impact knocked him from the saddle. He fell heavily and lay unmoving on the dusty ground as his assailants emerged from their hiding places.

"Why the hell did you do that?" Rick demanded angrily of his companion Luis Degas as he dismounted to go to Todd's aid.

"He surprised me and I don't like surprises, amigo." Luis glanced sharply at Rick and then shrugged indifferently, casually holstering his gun. "Is he dead?"

Bending over the big man's prone body, Rick carefully checked to see if the man was still breathing. "Yes," he answered, his flat tone revealing none of the emotion he felt at the senseless shooting. "You know, Degas, if they weren't looking for us before, they will be now."

"Are you afraid?" he asked mockingly.

"Hardly," Rick said, his steely gaze meeting Luis's shifty one. "I just don't think Malo will want us riding into camp with a posse on our tails."

"He's right, Luis. We'd better get out of here," Ray Pearce said nervously as he glanced around. "They might be after us already since we robbed that cantina. And someone might have heard the shot."

"All right. We'll ride," Luis ordered imperiously. "Cazador, let's go."

Rick stood up slowly, praying that the wounded, unconscious man would make no sudden moves and alert the bandits to his true condition. "Degas, I think there's something you'd better understand right now." Though he sounded conversational, there was a barely concealed threat in his words, and his hand caressed the butt of his still holstered gun. "I don't take orders from anyone—not Malo—and definitely not you."

Luis stiffened, about to respond to Rick's unspoken challenge, when they heard the sound of another approaching horse. Luis and Ray had time to wheel their horses out of sight, but Rick could only dive for cover behind the craggy monolith.

Jennie hadn't gone far when she heard the gunshot nearby, breaking the tranquil silence and making her blood run cold. Reining in, she twisted searchingly in the saddle as she tried to determine from which direction the sound of the shot had come.

"Todd!" She called out, hoping that he was still within earshot, but there was no response to her query.

Worried, Jennie kneed Star into motion again and slowly retraced her tracks to the point where Todd had crossed her trail. Unable to sight him from the rise, she followed the path he'd taken. As she rode forth, Jennie sensed an unearthly stillness about the morning and instinctively pulled her rifle from its scabbard, resting it comfortably across her forearm. Her father had taught her many practical lessons in her lifetime, and one of them was never to face the unknown unarmed.

Jennie didn't see the man who had climbed on top of Tracker's Boulder until it was too late. As he launched himself in her direction, she turned and tried to fire, but he tackled her full force; the impetus of his assault tumbling her to the ground and knocking her rifle from her hand. As the firearm flew from her grasp, it discharged, the unexpected gunshot frightening both her mount and Todd's and they galloped from the scene at breakneck speed. Jennie tried to roll away from her assailant and retrieve her weapon, but the man grabbed her by her hair, his action tearing the ribbon loose, and then yanked her viciously back beneath him.

"Oooeee, Luis. Look what you got!" Ray was almost drooling at the sight of Jennie held so helplessly in Luis's painful, dominant grasp.

"Sweet." Luis smiled showing black, uneven teeth.

"Get your hands off of me!" she ordered as she struggled to free herself. Trying not to let them see how terrified she really was, she demanded, "Who are you? What are you doing on McCaine land?"

"Why, we were just passin' through." Luis licked his lips as his eyes wandered over her twisting body. "But I think we may stay a while—now."

"Let me go! You won't get away with this!" She couldn't help but cringe as his hands boldly explored her.

"Hey, Ray. She says I'm not going to get away with this." He laughed evilly.

Ray jumped down from his horse and stalked toward them, his eyes alight with lust-filled appreciation as he began to unbuckle his gunbelt. "She sure is stupid for one so pretty. You want to stay pretty, little girl?"

"What do you mean?" Jennie felt almost nauseated by their presence, and she paled, grimacing, when Luis thrust his hips suggestively against her helpless form. The foreign hardness of him which pressed intimately against her thighs sent a shiver of revulsion through her, and she tossed wildly, trying to get away from him.

Ray's lewd gaze seared her, dwelling on the way her full, round breasts strained against the whiteness of her blouse and the way her leather riding skirt had ridden up, revealing

41

an attractive display of shapely leg.

"We mean you stop fighting and we won't mess up that pretty face of yours," Luis explained as he trapped her flailing limbs, pinning her arms above her head with one hand and ripping her blouse open with his other, exposing her breasts to their lascivious gaze.

"Hold it, Luis." The deep voice that rang out in the early morning quiet was cold and deadly.

Jennie turned her head to stare at the tall, dark-haired man who had stepped out from behind the boulder. Her eyes widened as he moved slowly toward them, his gun drawn and pointed straight at Luis's back.

"What?—" Luis glanced away from Jennie and in that instant she acted, grabbing a handful of sandy soil and throwing it in his eyes. "Ah!!!!" He screamed in agony as he released her.

Knowing that this would be her only chance to escape, she staggered to her feet and started to run away from them, but the sight of Todd's inert body halted her progress.

"Todd!" Her cry was anguished.

It was that one moment of shocked hesitation that provided Ray with the opportunity to catch her again.

"If you like to play rough, we can oblige. Luis already took care of your boyfriend there." Ray captured her wrists as she struck out at him in blind fury.

"Let me go! I've got to help Todd."

With full force, Ray slapped her, the blow driving her to her knees. Releasing her, she slumped weakly at his feet; her head bowed in defeat, her bare bosom rising and falling with each ragged breath she drew.

Recovered from her attack, Luis started toward them, wanting to teach the little bitch a lesson.

"Luis—Get a rope. Maybe if we tie her up."

"Both of you—get away from her." Rick spoke quietly, but immediately all action stopped.

Luis and Ray both looked up, their angry expressions

turning incredulous as they saw that Rick was still holding his gun on them.

"She's ours," Ray said heatedly, grabbing Jennie's arm and jerking her to her feet.

"I'm making her mine," he answered conversationally. "Now, take your hands off of her and move away." Gesturing with his revolver, Rick indicated where he wanted them to stand.

"We'll let you have a turn," Ray offered, unwilling to give up such a prize so easily.

"I don't want *a turn*," Rick said smoothly as Luis and Ray backed away from Jennie.

"What's the matter, Cazador. Don't you like women?" Luis taunted. His loins were still aching with the need to have the young she-cat standing before him and his frustrated fury with Cazador grew unbounded.

Rick smiled easily, ignoring the insult that was meant to provoke him to anger. "I like *willing* women very much."

"Then what are you going to do with her?" Ray pushed. "You know she'll tell everybody what happened, so you can't let her go. Why don't we share her and then kill her?"

"We won't be sharing her," Rick said with finality. "Like I said before, she's mine and I don't share what's mine." By casually cocking the hammer of his gun, he stopped their protests before they were spoken. "You know, Malo would want me to be happy. And she'll—" Rick glanced briefly at Jennie. "Make me happy," he concluded.

Luis and Ray knew they'd lost and it didn't sit well with them.

"Take her," Luis said seethingly and he turned away to get his horse, vowing to someday have his revenge against this arrogant gunslinger.

Ray followed suit, mumbling under his breath. He knew he was no match for El Cazador in a fair fight, but maybe he could find another way to even the score. Quickly retrieving Jennie's rifle, he swung up into the saddle, his hate-filled gaze searing Rick.

Rick waited until Luis and Ray had mounted up to holster his revolver. He knew he would have to be more careful from now on, for they would both be waiting for the opportunity to pay him back.

Turning to take his first good look at the woman he'd just claimed for his own, Rick immediately understood why the other two men had been so reluctant to let her go because even in her present state of disarray, she was lovely. His gaze swept over her assessingly, taking in her tall, slim figure and the way her mass of dark curls cascaded down her back, giving her a wild, almost untamed look. Her pale breasts were all but bared to him, despite her efforts to keep herself covered, and the sight of their rounded sweetness, so meagerly clad, sent a flare of heat through him. Irritated with himself for responding to her charms, he strode purposefully toward her.

It took all of Jennie's courage to face this stranger and his appraising regard. Clutching what was left of her blouse over her full breasts, Jennie lifted her chin in a small act of proud defiance as he came forward to claim her. The thought sent a shiver of apprehension down her spine, and she wondered what kind of man he was. Was he as ruthless as the other two or hopefully more civilized and more willing to listen to reason?

Jennie studied him openly, her eyes tracing his hard chiseled features, the straight slash of black brows over his piercing green eyes, the unyielding set of his jaw. Had the circumstances been different she would have thought him handsome, but her concern for Todd and her fear of the other men smothered the attraction.

When he stopped before her and she forced herself to look up at him, her dark eyes met his unflinchingly.

"I don't know who you are or why you're on McCaine land, but thank you for helping me. My name's Jennie Mc-Caine and—" she began bravely.

"McCaine?" Rick asked quickly.

"That's right." She wondered at his change of expression and she grew suddenly hopeful. "Mac McCaine's my father, and he'll see you well rewarded if you return me unharmed."

Rick's mind was racing. She was Jake's sister! Now what was he going to do? He couldn't just let her go—Luis and Ray had seen to that. There was only one way for him to salvage the situation, he realized, and that was to take her along—as his woman. Lord knows, he didn't want to; he had enough problems to deal with already, but there was no alternative. Under his protection, she would be safe and then, after he freed Juan from Malo's camp, he would see her returned to her family.

Turning so his back was to Luis and Ray, he spoke in low tones. "Is Jake McCaine related to you?"

"He's my brother—why?" She was suddenly cautious.

"I know Jake. He's a friend of mine."

"Jake's your friend?"

"Listen, there's no time to explain. You'll just have to trust me. For reasons I can't go into right now, I can't let you go."

Jennie was startled. "What?"

"Not while those two are around," he growled. "They think I want you for myself, so I'm going to have to take you along with me."

Jennie started to protest but before she could say anything further he dragged her into his arms and kissed her, his firm, demanding lips slanting across her softer ones in a sensuous assault meant to brand her as his own in front of the other men.

Jennie held herself rigid in his arms, refusing to give in to him but, when his kiss gentled to a tender, teasing caress, a spark of warmth that threatened to kindle into a blaze of unbidden desire was born deep in the cold recesses of her fearful heart.

When Rick abruptly ended the embrace, Jennie stood silently, stunned by her unexpected reaction to his touch.

She sensed that there was something very dangerous about this man they had called Cazador and, though he had asked her to trust him, her instincts told her to run—to try to escape before it was too late—before she was lost. Without further thought, Jennie bolted, running as hard and as fast as she could to get away.

Jennie's flight surprised Rick, but he caught up with her easily. Grasping her from behind, he hauled her tightly back against him, pinning her arms to her sides.

Jennie struggled to free herself from what she was sure was certain ravishment and death. Fighting on, she twisted violently in his arms and kicked out at him as best she could, but her futile battling only loosened her blouse, allowing it to fall completely open.

When Rick heard Luis's and Ray's muttered lewd comments about her state of undress, he gave her a violent shake and mercilessly tightened his grip on her.

"Hold still, you little idiot!" he seethed in her ear. "If I have to kill them over you it's going to ruin all my plans!" Roughly, he turned Jennie to face him, crushing her to his chest to shield her breasts from the others' view.

Sobbing in frustration at having failed to escape, Jennie tried to pull away, but his arms were steel bands, shackling her to him.

"If you're really a friend of my brother's why don't you just let me go?"

"Think about it! Do you really believe that Luis and Ray would let you go, even if I did?" he asked derisively. "Now, just shut up or we're both going to end up dead!" Rick knew she was afraid, but there was nothing he could do right now to reassure her. He had to play his part convincingly.

Satisfied that she'd temporarily stopped fighting him, Rick was relieved. "Good. Now, let's go."

"No!" Jennie gasped, casting a frightened glance in the other men's direction.

"Listen to me!" His patience was at an end. "If there was

any way I could possibly avoid taking you with me, I would, but right now it looks like we're stuck with each other. Just play along with me and I promise I'll take you home as soon as I can. All right?"

"What about Todd?" She balked.

"There's no time to worry about him, they think he's dead," he told her dismissingly. "Now, are you going to come along without a fight or do I have to throw you over my shoulder and carry you?"

Realizing that she had no alternative, Jennie finally nodded in agreement. "All right. I won't fight you."

"Good. Wait here while I get my horse." Rick then strode off behind the boulder.

As soon as Rick released her, Jennie wrapped her arms about her bosom trying to shield herself from the other men's hungry looks, but her actions only drew lecherous chuckles from them.

And when Rick had moved out of sight, Luis took the opportunity to ride over to her. "You may think you're safe, but Cazador won't be able to protect you all the time—I'll have you yet!" he promised. "And Ray, here, will hold you down while I—" He cut off his words as Rick rode out from behind the boulder.

"Let's ride, Luis" He spoke sharply as he stopped close by Jennie's side. "Lead out."

As Luis and Ray headed off in the direction of Malo's camp, Rick opened his saddlebag and pulled out one of his own shirts. Handing it to her, he said, "Here. Put this on."

"Thank you." Jennie took it from him gratefully.

Quickly pulling on the man-size shirt over her own ruined blouse, she buttoned it and rolled the long sleeves up off of her hands. Jennie was trying to tie the shirt tails in a knot at her waist when Rick reached down to scoop her up. Settling her on the saddle in front of him, he pulled her back so that she was resting against him. Then, keeping one arm round her waist, he kneed his horse and they started off after Luis

47

and Ray.

Jennie stiffened as his arm came around her in firm familiarity, and she leaned forward in silent mutiny, breaking that close contact between them.

At any other time, Rick might have found Jennie's aversion to being held against him amusing, but with Luis and Ray close by watching, he knew he had to appear to be dominant over her. If she wanted to stay alive, she was going to have to learn to follow his orders.

Pulling her recalcitrant body back tightly to him once more, he growled in her ear, "Stay close, Jennie. Don't move away from me. We have to make this look good."

"But why?"

"It's strictly for their benefit. Just trust me. I'll make sure nothing happens to you."

Jennie nodded and forced herself to relax, leaning once more into the hard strength of him. Sighing, she temporarily resigned herself to her fate and silently prayed that her father and brother would soon come to her rescue.

Chapter Four

No one on the M Circle C noticed when Jennie was late in returning from her morning excursion. It was not unusual for the young woman to lose track of time when she was enjoying herself and, it wasn't until the riderless Star returned to the stable at mid-morning that anyone became truly concerned.

Steve spotted the mare first as she made her final mad dash for the stable and the security of her home. Lathered and wheezing, Star slowed, and he ran out to intercept her.

"Whoa, Star." He spoke to the agitated mare in an easy tone. "What's the matter, girl? Where's your Jennie?" Snatching up the reins at the first opportunity, he ran his hand along her sweaty neck searching for possible injury. When he found none, he inspected the saddle and was startled to find Jennie's rifle missing from the scabbard. "Dusty—rub her down. I'd better tell Mac."

Mac was finishing his breakfast with Hildago in the dining room when he heard Steve burst into the house without knocking.

"Steve? What's wrong?" he asked as he hurried out to meet him in the entry hall.

"It's Jennie—" he began worriedly. "Star just came back

49

without her."

Mac was instantly concerned because Jennie was an excellent rider. "Is the mare hurt? Does she look like she might have taken a fall?"

"No. She's just lathered from the run."

"What time did Jennie ride out this morning?"

"One of the men told me earlier that he'd seen her start out at dawn with Todd Clarke. It looked like they were heading toward his place," Steve informed him. "But Mac—there's something else."

"For God's sake, Steve, what is it?" he demanded anxiously.

"Her rifle's not in its scabbard."

Mac's expression darkened. "Get my horse ready. I'll meet you at the stable in five minutes."

"Right." He started from the house.

"And Steve?"

Steve looked back questioningly. "Yes sir?"

"Have Jerry and Sandy saddle up, too. We don't know what we're up against. It could be nothing. But let's not take any chances."

Nodding his understanding, Steve hurried off to do his boss's bidding.

"What's wrong?" Hildago asked as she came to Mac's side.

"It's Jennie. Her horse came back without her." Mac's words were terse. "We're going out to look for her."

"Is there anything I can do?" she offered, understanding his worry.

"Not right now. With any luck this won't take too long." He strode to his gun case and unlocked it. "She was riding with Todd, so hopefully, they're together."

Hildago followed him, watching with ill-concealed anxiety as he took out his rifle and a generous supply of cartridges. "You'll be careful, Mac?"

"Of course. I really don't expect any trouble, but it never hurts to be prepared." He started toward the door.

"Mac?" She called his name softly and he turned to look at

50

her. "Find her."

"I will." Mac spoke without hesitation, knowing that he wouldn't rest until he knew she was safe. Going back to Hildago, he hugged her reassuringly and then, together, they went outside.

Hildago accompanied him to the stable where Steve and the other ranch hands had already mounted and were awaiting his arrival.

Mac secured his rifle in the scabbard and, after storing the extra ammunition in the appropriate pouches, he swung up into the saddle.

"Steve, did you pack some medical supplies?"

"I've got 'em right here." He indicated his own saddlebags.

"Good." Turning to Hildago, he told her, "If Jake gets back, have him wait here for me."

"All right," she answered and then called, *"Vaya con Dios."*

Mac raised one arm in farewell as they galloped off in the direction of Todd's ranch.

Hildago watched until they had disappeared from sight and then walked slowly back to the house.

Carrie, clad only in a flowing frothy dressing gown, had heard Steve's voice earlier and had come out of her room to find out what was going on.

"What was all the excitement about?" Carrie asked as she met Hildago in the hall.

"Your sister's horse came back without her, so your father and Steve have taken some of the men out to look for her." Hildago couldn't prevent the disapproving frown that marred her features as she surveyed Carrie's scanty attire. Perhaps it was a good thing Mac was gone, for he would never condone Carrie's wearing such a revealing garment outside of her bedroom.

"I'm sure she's all right." Carrie shrugged her indifference to both Jennie's absence and Hildago's very obvious dislike of her dressing gown.

"It's not like Jennie to be so careless," Hildago continued.

"I wouldn't worry if I were you. She's tougher than half those men out there," she answered spitefully.

"Carrie!" Hildago was shocked by the venom she heard in her voice. "What a hateful thing to say about your sister!"

"You know it's true." Carrie gave her a bored look as she turned and went into the dining room.

"You would do well to learn from her!" Hildago said as she followed her into the room. "She's a very sweet, kind person."

Having no desire to listen to another lecture on Jennie's virtues, Carrie poured herself a cup of coffee from the silver service on the sideboard and sat down at the table. "I know, I know, I've heard it all before. From both Father and you. She's a virtual paragon, I'm sure," she remarked sarcastically. "Now, may I have my breakfast?"

Outraged by Carrie's attitude, Hildago left the room muttering under her breath.

When she had gone, Carrie smiled to herself and stretched sensuously. For the first time in ages, she felt satisfied. Steve had been all the lover she'd hoped he would be and more! She might just go to him again sometime if her plan to seduce Todd fell through. Why, she hadn't made it back to her own bed until just before sunup!

Carrie stifled a giggle as she imagined what Jennie would have said had they run into each other this morning—Jennie on her way to the stables and she on her way back from a passionate night in her lover's arms. The thought was positively amusing.

The sound of Hildago's bustling return with her meal banished her titillating thoughts temporarily, and Carrie turned her attention to her food.

"Will they be gone long?" Carrie asked.

Hildago, thinking that the girl had had a change of heart, smiled. "I don't think so. She was riding with Todd and the horse probably just got away from her."

52

A black rage swept through Carrie at the news. Jennie had gone riding with Todd! Damn! Last night she'd monopolized him after dinner and now she'd gone riding with him! Carrie was furious. She had had great hopes for this morning. After her night with Steve, she was confident once more of her desirability, and she had planned to use all of her more seductive wiles on Todd today.

Jennie's horse had gotten away from her, had it? She almost laughed out loud. She could just imagine what they had been doing when her horse had so conveniently run away! The thought of Jennie in Todd's arms infuriated Carrie even more. And the possibility of her sister's returning to the ranch, riding double with Todd, just increased her frustration.

With an effort she forced a smile. "If she's with Todd I'm sure she's safe."

"Todd's a good man," Hildago said. "He'll take care of her."

Carrie could say nothing more. Her hopes for a glorious morning of flirting with Todd had been dashed and it was all Jennie's fault. Viciously, Carrie hoped they wouldn't find her. It would not upset her in the least if she never saw her sister again as long as she lived!

The silence of the late morning was disturbed only by the rhythmic drumming of horses' hooves as they galloped across the cactus-studded terrain heading for the mountains to the north. As the riders neared a low-rising, rock-encrusted ridge, the lead man reined in his mount and turned to the others.

"Since it rained just a few days ago, there should still be water at the top." He indicated the rocky summit. "The going's rough, so ride single file."

Turning his horse, he led the way along the stony path

leaving the others to follow behind.

"Cazador—" Ray motioned for Rick to ride ahead of him.

"After you." He smiled easily, knowing better than to present his back to this man.

Growling at his response, Ray kneed his horse to action and hurried to catch up with Luis.

"What was that all about?" Jennie glanced over her shoulder at Rick because she had felt him grow tense during the curt exchange.

"I've learned it's not always wise to turn your back on men like Ray and Luis." He tightened the arm he had around her waist, bringing her more securely against him as they started up the incline.

Jennie frowned at his reply. If Cazador was riding with these men, why would they want to shoot him in the back?

"But you're partners, aren't you?"

"Of sorts—but I'm sure they didn't take kindly to my taking you away from them."

"If you knew it was going to cause trouble for you, why did you do it? You didn't know me. Why take the chance?"

"Do you understand what would have happened to you by now if I hadn't stopped them?" There was a thread of steel in Rick's tone as he made his point.

"Yes," Jennie whispered and her doubts about trusting him vanished before the realization that, had his intent been rape or murder, he could have accomplished both this morning. There had been no reason for him to step in and rescue her from Luis and Ray, but he had, and in the process, she realized with painful clarity, he had saved her life. That revelation soothed her and she knew then that he was not like the others. But why, she wondered, was he riding with them? Her thoughts were interrupted as they came to a clearing at the end of the trail.

The watering hole was a small protected pool, its presence neatly hidden from view by a surrounding jumble of good-sized boulders. Guiding his stallion to the water's edge a short distance away from where Luis and Ray had tethered their horses, Rick dismounted and then waited as Jennie jumped easily to the ground.

"Stay here," he told her as he pulled his rifle from the scabbard.

"Where are you going?" Jennie almost panicked as he started to leave her alone, for there was no sign of the other two men anywhere.

Rick lifted one dark brow at her mickingly as he drawled, "To find Luis and Ray."

"You trust me here alone?"

"You answer that for me."

After quickly considering her chances for escape—one unarmed woman against three heavily armed men—Jennie nodded. Rick noticed then for the first time the bruise on her cheek from where Ray had hit her, and he couldn't stop himself from lifting his hand to gently caress the discolored flesh.

"I'll be back as soon as I can." Rick started to walk away but then hesitated and turned back to her. "There was one thing I did want you to know."

"What?"

"Your friend—Todd—was that his name?"

"Todd—yes." Her expression saddened and she felt again the despair of that morning.

"He wasn't dead. I just told Luis he was. Luis had only winged him in the shoulder."

"Todd's all right?" She was incredulous and wanted the good news reaffirmed.

Rick would always remember the joy that showed in her face at that moment. "He should be," he answered, feeling a flare of irritation at her obvious affection for the other man.

Jennie was so happy that she wanted to throw herself into his arms, but she held back. "Thank you for telling me."

Lifting her eyes to his, she met his gaze evenly and was

surprised when he suddenly frowned and turned abruptly, stalking off in search of the other men.

Jennie watched him move away, his easy male grace evident in his long, self-confident strides. She admitted to herself, almost reluctantly then, that he was a very attractive man. And now that she was no longer terrified of him, she could appreciate his dark good looks and the powerful strength of his tall, muscular body.

Still, she wondered why Cazador was riding with these desperadoes. The man was an enigma, and Jennie knew that she would only learn the answers when he was ready to give them. Feeling almost content, Jennie sat down on the bank to await his return.

Rick joined Luis and Ray at their vantage point on top of the rocks.

"Any sign of a posse?"

"No, not yet. And as long as we can hold this pace, we'll be all right."

"Good." Rick was relieved. He was too close to success to let anything interfere now.

"Are you going to be able to keep up?" Ray questioned. "It's going to be hard riding from here on out."

"Don't worry about me." Rick brusquely cut him off. "I'll manage."

"If you can't—" Luis added, "we aren't going to wait for you."

Rick stared coldly at the outlaw. "I said I'd manage."

The hostility between Luis and Rick hung heavily in the air as they measured each other's worth.

"How soon are we leaving?" Ray finally said to break the tension of the moment.

Glancing at his friend, Luis replied. "In about an hour, after the horses have rested."

"I'll be ready," Rick told them and he headed back down to where Jennie waited.

Luis watched him go, his fury barely contained. "Someday, I'm going to kill him."

"Let's do it now," Ray encouraged. "Then we can have the woman."

Luis smiled at the thought. "If I hadn't already sent word on to Malo that he'd be riding in with us, I would."

"Damn."

"Don't worry, there'll be another time and another place."

Moving easily, Rick climbed down from the rocky precipice. Jennie didn't notice his approach, so he took the opportunity to observe her, unawares. A rush of desire burned through him as he let his gaze sweep hungrily over her. She appeared serene as she leaned back, surrendering to the sun's heated possession, and her body arched to that warmth with an innocent sensuality. He had sensed the awakening of her passion earlier when he'd kissed her, and he wanted to explore it to the fullest. Rick longed to take her in his arms and press sweet kisses along the slender column of her throat, and he wondered idly how the heavy silken strands of her hair would feel beneath his caress. He wanted her.

Irritated by the direction his thoughts had taken, he jerked himself back to reality. He had brought her along to protect her, not seduce her. She was Jake's sister.

"Jennie?" His tone was harsher than he'd intended and she looked up at him in surprise.

"Cazador! I didn't hear you come back. Where are the others?"

"They're still keeping lookout." He noticed her suddenly hopeful expression and told her plainly, "But there's no sign of a posse."

"Oh."

"We won't be riding out for at least an hour, so if you're hungry you'd better eat now. You probably won't get another chance until late tonight."

"Thank you. I am hungry." She stood up and followed him back to his horse.

Rick opened his saddlebag and took out some jerky, handing her a share. Then together, they went to sit in the shade of one of the massive boulders. The silence between them was almost companionable as they ate their meager meal, and it wasn't until Jennie spoke that the peace was broken.

"Cazador?"

Rick looked over at her questioningly, his eyes startling green in the tanned darkness of his face.

"You know that Jake and my father will come looking for me, don't you?"

He nodded and glanced away. "They may try, but we're moving too fast for them. They won't catch up."

"Well, isn't there some way you can leave me behind? I know it would only be a matter of time before they'd find me—"

"No." His answer was curt.

"Well, why not? And just when are you planning to take me home?" Jennie pushed for a direct answer and Rick glared at her, his temper flaring.

"There is nothing I'd like to do more than take you home, little girl, but right now I'm afraid it's impossible."

Little Girl! How dare he? Jennie seethed.

"But why?"

"That, my dear, is none of your business." He cut her off coldly as he stood up abruptly and strode away.

Jennie was furious as she watched him walk calmly away. She had never been treated this way before in her life! She was Jennie McCaine! She was always the one in control. She gave the orders; she didn't take them.

Frustrated by his refusal to free her and his unwillingness to answer to her questions, Jennie stomped off in the opposite direction. Skirting the edge of the water hole, she reached the far side and started to climb up the rocks in hopes that she could spot her father coming after her. Driven on by her anger, she scrambled upward, unmindful of the dangers she might encounter near the top.

Rick was filling his canteen when he caught sight of Jennie climbing the rocky rise at the far side of the clearing. He knew she was angry, but he hoped that she was smart enough not to do anything foolish—like try to escape.

Rick could well understand her frustration at the predicament she found herself in, but it couldn't be helped. He was not about to reveal anything to her that might ruin his plans. Not that he thought she would deliberately give him away to Luis and Ray; on the contrary, he knew that she wouldn't. It was just that he didn't want to take any chances. Only his continued anonymity could guarantee the success of his rescue attempt.

A flicker of movement on the next small ledge above her head caught Rick's eye and he paused, trying to make out exactly what it was he had seen. When it moved again, he knew.

"Jennie! Come down!" he shouted as she started to reach for the handhold without looking.

"Leave me alone!" she called back to him without stopping her climb.

"Wait!" he yelled, drawing and firing just as the rattler launched itself to strike.

Her scream of terror echoed across the clearing as she lost her balance and tumbled backward, down the rocky incline.

Rick was running toward her even before he'd holstered his gun. A cold fear embraced him and terror clawed at his chest with painful menace. Jennie! Oh, God, Jennie! He wasn't sure if his bullet had hit her or if the snake had managed to make its strike, but he was filled with dread.

Racing to her side, he knelt down and gently rolled her over.

"Jennie?" His voice was choked with emotion as he took her in his arms and smoothed her hair back away from her face.

Jennie heard someone saying her name, but it seemed that

they were miles and miles away. She wanted to see who it was who sounded so worried about her, but her eyes were heavy and they wouldn't open. Gentle hands were touching her, caressing her, and she sighed under their tender ministrations.

"Jennie! Open your eyes."

The voice seemed closer now and more demanding, and she frowned as she tried to remember exactly who the man was who was caring for her. Her blissful state of uncertainty lasted only a moment longer until painful reality intruded, and her eyes flew open.

"You tried to shoot me!" she cried, staring at Rick in abject horror as she scrambled away from him.

But Rick quickly pursued Jennie and grabbed her by the shoulders, turning her to face him. His hold on her was firm and he refused to let her go. "You're crazy. That's what I was shooting at!" He indicated the gory remains of the snake where it lay lifelessly in the dust, half of its body blown away by his accurate shot. "The damned snake! If I'd been aiming at you, you'd be dead."

"A snake?" Jennie glanced over at the bloody reptile and shuddered.

"It was on that next ledge—the one you were about to grab."

"Oh, God! Thank you." She went into his arms spontaneously, suddenly needing the protection of his strong embrace.

"Jennie—" Rick's eyes met hers searchingly, as he assured himself that she was all right. He had intended to release her, but his determintion not to touch her weakened before her guilelessness, and with infinite care, he bent to kiss her.

As his lips played sweetly across hers, Jennie's mind reeled at his intoxicating nearness.

"Jennie." He growled her name as he pulled away for a moment to look down at her, wonderingly, and then his mouth claimed hers again, parting her lips to deepen the exchange.

She gasped as he slipped his hands down her back to her hips, pulling her closer so he could fit himself more intimately to the softness of her womanly curves. The hard heat of his desire was pressed searingly against her, but instead of feeling threatened by it, Jennie was thrilled.

A low moan escaped her as he moved to caress her breast, and she arched more closely to him, her body instinctively telling her that there was something more she needed from him—something that would fill the burning, aching emptiness deep within her.

Rick sensed the change in Jennie's response to him, and he thrilled to know that she wanted his touch. He wanted to go on, exploring the wild sweetness of her, but the sound of Luis and Ray rushing down from their vantage point froze his desire. Breaking off the kiss, he released her and moved quickly away.

"Cazador?" Lost in the realm of her first real sensuous awakening, Jennie was stunned by his unexpected actions.

"We've got company," he said gruffly.

"Hey, Cazador! What were you shootin' at? She looks plenty willing to me!" Ray shouted.

Luis, who had been avidly watching their lovemaking, called out: "Why'd you stop? She was ready. Weren't you man enough for her?" He started to drink from the bottle of tequila he'd just taken out of his saddlebag when the shot rang out and the bottle shattered in his hand. "What the hell!"

Unnerved, he glanced up to see Rick standing on the opposite bank, his gun in hand. "You got anything else you want to say to me, Luis? You know, that could have been your head."

Cursing viciously, Luis mounted his horse and rode off, leaving Ray to follow behind him.

Jennie was mortified—not only by her own passionate reaction to Rick's advances but also by the knowledge that

Luis and Ray had seen the whole thing.

Rick was annoyed with himself. He had no time for romantic involvements, no matter how attractive he found her. He had to focus all of his attention on the real reason he was here—his grandfather. He couldn't risk losing control this way, not with Jennie and definitely not with Luis and Ray. He needed them to reach Malo.

Determined to keep his distance from Jennie from now on, he refused to dwell on what had just passed between them. Holding himself deliberately aloof, he turned to her.

"Let's go." Rick barked the order as he holstered his gun.

Jennie hesitated. A moment before he'd been kissing and caressing her and, now, he was ordering her about like a servant, or worse yet, a child. What had she done to make him so angry with her?

Worried that Luis and Ray might get too far ahead of them, Rick hurried to mount up. When Jennie caught up with him, he lifted her in front of him again, settling her as comfortably as possible.

More aware than ever of his masculinity, Jennie found her seat most disturbing. She was pressed intimately to the hard strength of his hips and thighs, and his very closeness fed the fires of the desire he had stoked to life within her. The fact that Rick seemed totally indifferent to her now left Jennie feeling frustrated and resentful, and she hung on tightly to the pommel for support as he kneed his sturdy stallion to action, heading down the path in search of the other two men.

Chapter Five

It was near noon when Mac and his men topped the final rise near Tracker's Boulder. The going had been tedious, and he was beginning to despair of finding Jennie and Todd safe and unharmed. As they paused, Steve dismounted and surveyed the area with the careful expertise of a man long used to tracking.

"It looks like they must have split up here for some reason," Steve said as he hunkered down to inspect the hoofprints. "And then Jennie evidently doubled-back and followed Todd off in that direction." He indicated the path past Tracker's Boulder.

"Let's ride," Mac commanded.

Steve remounted and followed his lead down the trail toward the massive rock. They hadn't gone far when they heard a shout for help.

"Steve—take one of the men and circle behind. We'll go in this way," he ordered and his foreman was quick to obey.

Mac cautiously urged his horse forward in the direction of the call. Rounding the boulder, he reined in sharply as he found Todd staggering up the path, clutching his bloodied shoulder.

"Mac! Thank God!" he said.

"Todd! What happened to you? Where's Jennie?" Mac

quickly dismounted and went to his aid.

"Jennie?" Todd looked confused. "She's not with you?"

"No. She never came back from your morning ride. You rode out together, didn't you?"

"Yes, but she took the other path." He frowned, trying to concentrate.

"She started down the other trail and then doubled-back to follow you. What were you two doing?" Mac demanded, unconcerned momentarily with Todd's injury. Right now, he only wanted to know what had happened to his daughter.

"She wanted to race to the creek. But if she doubled-back, they must have gotten her, too."

"They? Who got her, Todd?" Mac insisted.

"Whoever ambushed me. She must have heard the shot and thought that I was signaling for her."

"Did you see anything? Hear anything? he demanded.

"Nothing." Todd admitted, dejectedly. "They got me as soon as I rounded the curve. By the time I came to, everyone had gone."

Todd was interrupted as Steve, having circled the landmark, joined them from the other direction.

"Any sign of her?" Mac asked hopefully.

"No. Only a burned-out campfire and a spent shell, but I did pick up tracks heading due north. It looks like there were three of them." His words jolted Mac painfully.

"Have the men search the area," Mac instructed.

Quickly fanning out, his hired hands began to scour the surrounding land looking for clues to her disappearance as Mac turned his attention to Todd's wound.

"I'll need the bandages, Steve." Putting his arm around Todd's waist, Mac helped him into the shade of a rocky outcropping, while Steve retrieved the medical supplies.

"How bad is it, Todd?" Mac asked.

"The bullet passed through." Todd groaned as he settled himself on the hard ground.

After helping him take off his shirt, Mac took a better look at the injury. "You're lucky. It looks pretty clean and the bleeding's stopped."

"Good." He gritted his teeth as Mac doctored his shoulder.

Mac had just finished applying the bandage, when a shout brought him to his feet. He watched anxiously as one of his men rode quickly toward him carrying a hair ribbon and a scrap of cloth.

"I think this may be your daughter's." He handed the ribbon to him. "And I found this piece of material nearby."

"It's Jennie's ribbon, all right, I bought it for her last year," he said gravely, holding it tightly in his clenched fist. "And this might have been part of her shirt, but I can't be sure."

"What do you want to do, Mac?"

"We'll have to take Todd back to the ranch and then get the provisions we'll need and fresh horses. With any luck, we can be back on the trail by mid-afternoon."

"Don't even think about leaving me at the ranch. I'm going with you," Todd argued, getting slowly, painfully to his feet.

"You're in no condition—" Mac started to protest, but Todd cut him off sharply.

"Don't tell me what to do, Mac. Jennie's in trouble and I intend to help her. Get me a horse and I'll be as ready to ride as the next man," he told them, drawing himself to his full, impressive height.

"All right, all right." His agreement eased Todd's agitation. "Mount up with one of the men and let's get out of here."

"How long ago did they leave, Hildago?" Jake asked as he settled himself at the table to eat lunch.

"It was early this morning," she told him. "I guess about eight-thirty or nine."

Jake nodded, not overly concerned with Jennie's purported disappearance for she was renowned for her adventurousness. "And he didn't leave any other message for me?"

"No," Hildago answered. "So I guess you'd better just wait here until we hear from him." She paused as she heard horses coming toward the house. "They must be back."

Pushing away from the table, Jake followed Hildago to the front of the house, intent on greeting his vixen of a sister. He was smiling at the prospect of hearing her excuse for losing control of her horse. But when he stepped out onto the veranda and caught sight of Todd, his expression froze.

"What the hell happened?" he demanded, hurrying to help his friend down.

"Todd was ambushed and evidently whoever did it has taken Jennie captive," Mac explained.

"What?" Jake was totally stunned by the news.

"We just came back to get provisions and fresh horses," he said impatiently. "Hildago, there will be eight of us riding out, and we'll need enough food for at least three days."

Without pause, she hurried to prepare the necessary foodstuffs.

"Steve—I want three more men with us, fully armed, and have them bring plenty of extra ammunition. Also, saddle up fresh horses for all of us and fill two canteens apiece. Bring an extra horse for Jennie, too."

"Right away." Steve and the two hands who'd ridden with them headed quickly for the stable.

Carrie had been eagerly awaiting their return, for she was anxious to see Todd and to gloat over Jennie's misfortune. Venturing forth wearing her very best pale blue daygown, she had expected to find a very contrite Jennie, but instead, she came face to face with Todd, his shirt covered with blood, his face, pale and clearly showing the strain of the past few hours.

"Todd! What happened to you?" She went to him immediately, slipping her arm around him, unmindful of the

66

damage the gore would do to her new dress.

"I was ambushed," he explained curtly.

"Jennie—?" she whispered, wondering in morbid fascination if her wish had come true.

"She's disappeared. We think she's been taken captive by the same men who shot me." Todd mistakenly thought that Carrie was concerned about her sister, and he hastened to reassure her. "We're going after them as soon as the provisions are ready."

"But how can you ride in your condition?" she protested but before he could answer, her brother came inside.

"Carrie—" Jake instructed. "Take him back to my room and see what you can do for him."

"Jake," Todd asked quickly, "do you think you can find a shirt around here that will fit me?"

"I'll find you something. Just rest until I get back."

"All right." He grumbled, aggravated by the inconvenience of his injury.

Carrie accompanied Todd down the hall to Jake's bedroom and then helped him to lie down.

"Thanks, Carrie." Todd's tone was a muffled moan and she knew he was in pain.

The thought of caring for Todd thrilled her but she couldn't bear to see him suffer. Hurrying from the room, she went to her father's study to fix him a glass of bourbon, hoping the liquor would dull his discomfort. Returning to his side, she handed him the half-filled tumbler. "Here. This should help a little."

"It'll help a lot." Taking the proffered glass gratefully, he drank deeply of the potent amber liquid, eagerly anticipating its numbing effect. "Thanks."

"If you can lift yourself up a bit, I'll get this shirt off and check your shoulder," Carrie said, taking the now empty glass from him.

"Sure," Todd said and, using his uninjured arm, he maneuvered himself up to a sitting position. "How's that?"

"Fine. Now just hold still." As gently as she could, Carrie stripped the torn, stained garment from his broad, muscular shoulders, taking great care not to hurt him. Once she had it off, she tossed it carelessly across the room and began to remove the bandage her father had applied earlier. "There," she said a bit breathlessly as she pried the last of the wrappings from the open wound. "Now, lie back down while I get some warm water."

"Hurry. I don't want them to leave without me." Todd stretched out on Jake's bed and allowed himself the luxury of closing his eyes for a moment, missing the expression of jealous rage that crossed Carrie's delicate features as she hurried from the room.

Stalking silently down the hall, Carrie could barely contain the anger that flushed through her. Here she was, doing her very best to care for him, and all he could think about was Jennie! Her feelings for Todd were strong; he meant a lot to her, and the thought that he might have been killed this morning had frightened her. A firm resolve overtook her. She wanted Todd Clarke and she was going to get him, no matter what.

Her new determination calming her, Carrie entered the kitchen and quickly set about pouring out a pan of warm water. After getting a washcloth and the medicine and bandages she needed to rewrap his shoulder, she hurried back to Jake's bedroom. Todd was resting easily as she returned to his side and she spoke softly, not wanting to surprise him with her touch.

"Todd—" His name was a caress on her lips, and his eyes flew open at the sound.

"Oh—Carrie—I'm sorry, I didn't hear you come back." He shook his head as if to clear it.

"I know. I didn't want to disturb you, but I've got to clean your shoulder. I'll try to be gentle."

"Don't worry. I'll hold real still for you," he assured her. Placing the dish of water and her other supplies on the nearby table, Carrie soaked the cloth and tenderly began to wash the dried blood from his damaged flesh. She could tell that it was painful for him because his jaw tensed even at her lightest touch.

"How does it look?"

"Not bad," Carrie told him confidently as she put the cloth aside and got ready to administer the antiseptic. "I've got to use this now. Would you like another glass of whiskey?"

"No. Go ahead. I'll be fine," he told her, eyeing the brown bottle of medicine skeptically.

Without further delay, she proceeded with the most painful part of her ministrations, and Todd bit back the cry of agony that threatened as the medicine seared into his shoulder.

"I'm sorry." Carrie truly felt his pain and wanted to comfort him, but she knew it was important to get him bandaged up as soon as possible.

"It's all right." He drew a long, ragged breath and then relaxed as the burning eased.

With more efficiency than she thought herself capable, Carrie soon had his wound bound tightly with fresh, clean wrappings.

"There. I think you're all set." She helped him sit up and watched as he flexed his massive arms, his face reflecting only a minimum of discomfort.

"Thank you. It feels much better." He smiled at her.

Carrie was pleased with her handiwork and had enjoyed immensely the intimacy of tending him. How she wished she could go with them when they left. It would be perfect to be with Todd out on the range. She wasn't overly fond of riding horseback, but it would be worth it just to be with him on some dark, moonless night.

Maybe there was a way. A glimmer of an idea flared to life, and Carrie smiled as she considered the possibility. It would require a lot of acting on her part, but she was sure she could pull it off.

"Todd?" Jake's call preceded him into the room. "I found this shirt. It looks like it should fit." He handed the muted plaid, soft cotton garment to him.

"Thanks."

"Did Carrie take care of you?"

"She did just fine. Is Mac ready to go yet?" He stood up, anxious to be on his way.

"They're waiting for us now."

"Do you want to take these extra bandages along?" Carrie suggested helpfully.

"It can't hurt." Jake took them from his sister and left the room.

"Do you need any help with the shirt?" she offered, going to stand by Todd after her brother had gone.

"Yes, please." He handed her the garment and then slipped his arms into the sleeves as Carrie held it for him.

Now that Carrie knew he was out of pain, she longed to run her hands across the width of hard-muscled back, to smooth the shirt over his massive shoulder. But her common sense restrained her. She knew any such overtures on her part would startle and possibly distract him. No, she would have to wait until the time was right and Jennie wasn't on his mind.

"Are you sure you feel up to this?" she questioned, wanting to reassure herself that he was strong enough.

"I have to go, Carrie. Jennie's in very real danger."

"You'll be careful?" She couldn't stop the note of true concern that crept into her voice.

Todd paused and looked at her, slightly puzzled by her manner. "Of course. *This time*." His words were bitter and he strode from the room, without looking back.

Carrie joined Hildago on the veranda just as Mac rode up. She longed to ask his permission to go along, but she knew what his answer would be. Managing to look very worried, she went to meet him.

"Is there anything else we can do to help?" she asked.

70

Mac, surprised by her show of concern, replied gruffly, "No, but if by some chance Jennie should turn up back here, send one of the men after us. We'll be heading due north from Tracker's Boulder.

Carrie nodded her understanding, inwardly gloating over the information he'd just given her.

"Good luck!" she and Hildago told him and, with that, he returned to the head of the group.

After her father had rejoined the men, Carrie turned her attention to Todd. He had mounted up and was sitting on the saddle easily as he listened intently to Mac's instructions, his relaxed manner giving no indication of the trauma he had so recently suffered. Her eyes traced over him lovingly as she quietly admired his strength and goodness. With any luck, she thought delightedly, she'd be riding by his side tonight.

Carrie was so completely enamored with Todd and her plot to join him that she hadn't even noticed Steve or seen the hungry, knowing look on his face when he'd glanced in her direction before riding off.

When they had disappeared from view, she followed Hildago inside.

"Would you like some lunch?" the older woman offered.

"No. No thanks," Carrie said distractedly as she headed back to her bedroom. "I think I'll just go rest for a while."

Closing the door behind her, Carrie locked it securely, not wanting any interruptions while she finalized her plans. Going to her window, she stared out in the direction of Tracker's Boulder. Getting there would be the easy part. What was going to be difficult, she realized, was staying on their trail past that point. Never before had Carrie ever regretted not taking a more active interest in the ranch, but at this moment she did. She determined that she wouldn't get lost while trying to follow them. She couldn't afford to catch up with the men much before sundown for there was no doubt in her mind that if there was enough daylight left, her father would send her directly back home.

With no further hesitation, she pulled her riding clothes out of her armoire. And it took her only a few minutes to change, shedding her sedate daygown in favor of a pale yellow shirt and a pair of breeches, not unlike those the men wore. Though her father thought the snug-fitting pants she'd had designed for herself back East were scandalous and had forbidden her to wear them, today she didn't care. She was going to do everything in her power to attract Todd. Pulling on her boots, she donned her low-brimmed white hat and, picking up her leather riding gloves, she left her room.

Easily avoiding Hildago, she made her way to the stable. "Dusty?"

The young stableboy quickly answered her. "Yes, ma'am?"

"I need a horse," she told him.

"Any one in particular?" Dusty asked, his eyes widening at the sight of her in men's breeches. He had never seen a woman in pants before.

"No. Just make sure it's one that's not too spirited."

"Yes, ma'am. I'll get Poker for you."

"Fine. And I'll need a bedroll, a rifle, and a canteen of water, too," Carrie ordered, thoroughly enjoying his discomfort over her unorthodox attire.

Dusty nodded and hurried to do her bidding. It took him only a short time to saddle the horse and he led it out and handed her the reins. "Here you go."

"Thanks. I'll need a hand up."

He was unable to stop the sudden flush that stained his cheeks at the thought of touching her. "Um—yes, ma'am, Miss Carrie. Just grab the pommel and I'll help you."

In one smooth move, she was in the saddle and ready to ride.

"You be careful," he said automatically and then wondered where she was going.

"If anyone asks, tell them I've gone to join the men. Otherwise, don't say a word." Her tone was imperious.

"But won't you have trouble finding them? They've been

gone for over an hour!" he said.

"That is none of your business," she said sharply.

"Yes, ma'am," he replied and then watched as she rode slowly off in the same direction the others had gone.

As the encroaching darkness threatened to make tracking impossible, Mac regrettably instructed the men to set up camp. The afternoon had been a long, tense one for him for he had passed each mile fearful of finding Jennie dead along the side of the trail. But, as the hours and miles had passed with no sign of her, he began to feel more confident that there was a chance for them to rescue her. Now, as they tethered the horses and settled in for the night, he sat down with Todd to plan their strategy for the next day.

"We made some progress today, but not enough. I want to be riding out of here at sun-up"

Todd nodded and was about to respond when Steve shouted, "There's a rider coming!"

"Which direction?" Mac stood up, grabbing his rifle, and rushed to his foreman's side.

"From the ranch, Mac," Steve answered, and Mac's hopes grew as he imagined it to be a messenger informing them of Jennie's safe return.

"Is he armed?"

"I don't think so."

"Maybe he's got some good news," Todd said as he joined them, his thoughts the same as his friend's.

"Lord, I hope so, but I wonder who it is. He doesn't look familiar." At first, in the dim light of the early evening, he could not identify the man making directly for their camp. Then, suddenly, he recognized his daughter. "What the hell!"

Mac's sudden comment surprised Todd and Steve and they looked at each other in bewilderment as he raced off in the rider's direction, leaving them to follow.

Carrie saw her father coming and girded herself for the upcoming confrontation.

"Carrie! I'd expected one of the men to bring the news, not you."

"News?—" She was startled by his manner.

"Of Jennie—she is back, isn't she?" Mac asked, eager to have word of her safety.

"No, Pa, I'm sorry. There's been no word."

"Then why are you here?" He was confused as he stared up at her.

"I had to come." She managed just the right amount of desperation in her voice. "I was so worried about Jennie and I couldn't bear to just stay at the ranch and wait."

Mac's gaze turned icy as he stared at her in disbelief. "You came to ride with us?"

"I want to help, Pa."

"You could best have helped us by staying home where you belong!" he snarled. "You've been nothing but a tribulation to me since the day you were born!" The emotional strain of the day caught up with him and he lost control.

Todd and Steve joined them just as Mac finished his tirade.

"I'll ride back first thing in the morning, Pa. I just thought maybe I could do something to help." She spoke softly as if she were contrite, and Todd immediately jumped to her defense.

"Mac, she can't go back alone. It's a miracle that she caught up with us without running into trouble."

Mac snorted derisively. "Well, missy, since I can't spare any men to escort you back home, it looks like you got your wish. You can ride along, but I don't want to see you or hear you. If I get wind of any complaints on your part, I'll leave you behind, no matter where we are. Do you understand me?"

"Yes, sir." She affected the perfect amount of humility in

her answer.

"Don't worry, Mac. I'll keep an eye on her." Todd said, wanting suddenly to protect her from Mac's irrational anger. She seemed so fragile and helpless before his onslaught.

"You do that," he said with finality and stalked away, gesturing for Steve to follow him.

Steve was sure that Carrie had staged the entire scene just to be with him, but he had no time to compliment her on a job well done. Mac was the boss and his every command had to be obeyed. Giving her a quick knowing glance, he followed Mac to the other side of the camp.

Carrie shivered as she read the message in Steve's eyes. In her haste to be with Todd, she hadn't even considered his presence, and now the prospect of being in camp with both of them really excited her.

Smiling tremulously up at Todd, she feigned a very believable, helpless little sigh. "Thank you for defending me."

Chapter Six

It was twilight and the strength of the sun was failing before the night's unrelenting siege. The breeze had quieted and the Earth seemed to pause in tired contemplation of the death of yet another day.

The long hours of riding had left Jennie exhausted and she remembered, with no little irony, the previous night when she'd complained of being tired to Hildago. Had it not required such effort, she would have smiled at the thought for, until today, she hadn't known the meaning of tired. Shifting awkwardly, she sought to relieve her aching muscles by seeking a different position, but Cazador's quickly voiced protest stopped her squirming and forced her to sit still once again.

How was it possible for her life to change so drastically in less than twenty-four hours? This morning, she had been the protected daughter of one of the territory's richest men, and tonight she was the captive of a mysterious gunfighter who was dragging her off across the country against her will.

Jennis was confident that Star's return to the ranch had alerted her family to her disappearance and that even now they were searching for her. She knew Steve was an expert tracker and would have no problem following the trail because no effort had been made to cover their tracks. It was just a matter of time before they caught up with them and then—Jennie frowned as she wondered what would happen.

While it was true that Cazador had taken her hostage, she realized that he had done it primarily to protect her from Luis and Ray and, though he had kissed her when they were at the watering hole, he had been cool and indifferent to her ever since: an attitude on his part that had left Jennie both relieved and bewildered. She was glad that she didn't have to fight him off, but she wondered why he didn't find her desirable. Certainly the other men did. Dismissing her thoughts as too confusing, Jennie rode silently on, ever conscious of Cazador's disquieting nearness.

As they continued ever onward, the night finally claimed the land for its own, but the only concession the men made to the victorious darkness was a slowdown of the steady ground-eating pace they'd maintained since morning.

When there had been light, Rick had been content to follow a short distance behind the other men's lead, but, now, with the advent of the night, he'd closed the gap between them.

"Here." Luis's command was sudden and unexpected as he swung his horse abruptly through a well-camouflaged opening in the massive jumble of rocks they had been skirting for the past few hours.

The heavy cloak of the moonless night made the going slow up the narrow rutted trail, and they were forced to guide the horses with great care, lest they injure themselves on the tricky footing. They followed the twisting path a short distance to where it opened into a natural campsite that was protected on three sides by boulders and offered an unobstructed view of the cactus-studded flatlands they'd just crossed.

Rick was exhausted as he reined in near Luis and Ray. He had gone without sleep for almost forty-eight hours and tonight he needed to rest. Swinging slowly down out of the saddle, he paused to stretch his cramped muscles before reaching up to help Jennie dismount.

Jennie felt awkward as he lifted her from the saddle. "I'm not sure I still know how to walk." She groaned, gingerly testing her legs.

"I'm sure it'll come back to you with a little practice," he remarked offhandedly as he unfastened his bedroll and handed it to her. "Find a spot and bed-down while I talk to them."

"Where are you going to sleep? You've only got one blanket here." Her question was innocently put and she was totally unprepared for his answer.

"Jennie," he began with exaggerated patience. "I'll be sleeping with you . . ."

"But—"

"Be quiet." His tone was cold. "If you think for one minute I'm going to give up my bedroll, you're mistaken. We'll share it. Besides, it'll be safer that way."

"Safer?" she asked nervously.

"They won't think of coming near you as long as you're with me." Rick nodded toward Luis and Ray, who were busy bedding their horses down for the night.

"But how safe am I going to be from you?" she asked in a heated whisper. "You practically mauled me this morning and—"

"Mauled you?" He sounded incredulous and angry at the same time. "As I remember it, what we shared has hardly a mauling. You were quite the willing participant—" Rick paused when she gasped in dismay. "But you don't have to worry. It was only a momentary lapse on my part. It won't happen again. I find experienced woman more to my liking, not naive young virgins. Now, get busy while I find out where we go from here."

Jennie glared at him as he moved easily away to speak with the other two men and then set about her task, her upset reflected in her every move.

Naive! Young! She fumed to herself as she spread out the

78

blanket on the rocky ground.

His words reminded her of Hildago's comments the night before, and a seed of self-doubt was born within her. Was that why he'd been so uninterested in her? Was she really so ignorant of men and their ways? What more had he expected of her?

At the sound of his return, she jumped up nervously to face him.

"Roll that back up," Rick directed without explanation.

"But why?" she asked automatically.

Rick was growing tired of her constant questioning of his orders but tonight he was too worn out to call her on it.

"Because," he drawled. "I'm taking first watch tonight and I want you to stay with me."

A quick glance at Luis and Ray convinced Jennie of the wisdom of his plan. Hurriedly scooping up the blanket, she followed him past the other two men and up a steep incline to the top of one of the encircling boulders. As they reached the pinnacle, Rick quickly began his search for the best vantage point from which to maintain his watch, leaving Jennie by herself.

Fascinated by the glory of the diamond-dusted night sky, Jennie stared out across the pale image of the unending expanse of flatlands below. Without the other men's threatening presence, the night seemed suddenly peaceful to her, and she enjoyed the quiet moment of solitude. Gazing up at the myriad of twinkling stars above, she sighed. "It's beautiful tonight."

Having found the best spot from which to keep watch, Rick was intent on scanning the darkness and paid little attention to her. When he found no trace of a campfire on the distant horizon, he allowed himself to relax a little.

"Did you say something?" he inquired indifferently, turning briefly away from his vigil.

"No. Nothing important." Jennie suddenly felt very alone and very vulnerable, and she wondered why his detached

79

attitude bothered her so much.

"You might as well find a place and lie down." he said casually. "I'll wake you when it's time to go back."

"All right."

Curling up in a sheltered spot, she pulled the blanket close around her to ward off the chill of the night. Her eyes were upon him as he sat some distance away, staring out across the night-blackened terrain, and once again she admired the lean lines of his body.

"Cazador?" she said softly.

"What?"

"Thank you for not letting them take me this morning." Her words sounded heartfelt.

"Go to sleep, Jennie," he said brusquely. "You're going to need your rest tomorrow."

"All right." There was a pause while she sought comfort on her hard bed. "Well, good night."

"Night."

Where moments before, Rick had been worried about falling asleep during his watch, now he was worried about not being able to keep his hands off Jennie. Glancing over at her, he swore under his breath at the lovely sight she made. Even after a day of arduous riding that would have been hard on the best of men, she still looked beautiful. In repose the wary, headstrong girl had disappeared and only an innocent-looking beauty remained.

It irritated Rick that he felt an overwhelming desire to sweep her into his arms, to protect her and keep her safe from all of life's ugliness. He had never cared about a woman in this way before. These emotions were all new to him, and he found them most distracting at a time when he could scarcely afford the distraction. He had vowed not to become involved with her, and he was going to hold himself to that pledge. Right now his grandfather's rescue took priority over everything, even his own feelings.

As she drifted off to sleep, Jennie's dreams were jumbled and frightening, and she tossed restlessly on the hard ground. Her mind was playing out scenes before her: scenes of Hildago lecturing her on being more of a woman; of Luis and Ray attacking her and of Cazador saving her, touching her so gently and then coldly ignoring her. In the dream, she saw herself chasing after him as the other men followed leeringly behind her. She called out to him over and over to stop, to wait for her. But he walked away without looking back, and the pain of his leaving seared her heart. The memories and the fantasies all swirled together in a whirlwind of fearful denial and she awoke abruptly, startled from her much needed rest.

"Wait! Don't leave me!" Jennie jerked awake, sitting up quickly. She stared about her in confusion, shivering at the intensity of emotion the dream had aroused. What had it all meant? Was he going to go away and leave her here?

"Jennie? Are you all right?" Cazador asked, climbing down from his lookout perch.

"Yes. Yes I think so." She sounded more confident than she felt. "It was just a bad dream."

"You're sure?"

"Positive," she stated firmly, not wanting him near; not wanting him to find out how big a part he had played in her nightmare. "Is your watch almost over?"

"No. I've still got a couple of hours to go. Why don't you try to go back to sleep? I'll be right here."

"All right." Jennie reluctantly lay back down and this time, when she drifted off, she slept deeply and dreamlessly.

Rick's hours on guard seemed to drag on into eternity. Alone and past the point of exhaustion, he could no longer fight off the memories he had held at bay for so long. They returned full force, etched in blood in his mind: the mountains, the Indians, the useless slaughter, and the gold.

Until now, Rick had thought that he had come to accept

the horror of the massacre all those years ago, but now he knew that he hadn't. It haunted him again this night, returning to fill him with an overwhelming sense of dread, and he girded himself against it. There was no way to avoid it; he was going back. Back to the Superstitions; back to face the Apache if fate so decreed; back to relive the most painful, agonizing time of his life. But this time, he swore viciously, he would come out the victor, not the vanquished.

He was thankful when the end of his watch neared for he needed distraction from the torment of his memories. Approaching Jennie silently, he stood above her, letting her loveliness soothe the burning emotions inside of him. When he bent down to lift her into his arms, she stirred and looked up at him sleepily.

"Hello." Her smile was soft and inviting.

"It's time to go back," Rick said quietly.

"Oh." She blinked sleepily and then her open expression suddenly became guarded. Shrugging away from him, she answered quickly, "All right, but there's no need for you to carry me. I can walk." She struggled to her feet and stepped away from him as he, too, stood up. "I'll follow you down."

Rick picked up the bedroll and led her back down to the camp. He stopped long enough to wake Ray and then directed Jennie to the far side of the clearing where he quickly arranged the blanket into their makeshift bed.

"Come here," he ordered after he'd made himself as comfortable as possible.

With Luis and Ray so close by, Jennie obeyed unquestioningly but she was nervous and on edge. Tensely she lay beside him, taking care not to let their bodies touch in any way.

Rick could feel the tension in her and wondered at it, for she was, after all, no stranger to his touch.

"Jennie, try to relax."

"I am relaxed," she lied and then hastened, nervously, to convince him. "I'll be asleep in just a minute."

When Rick shifted position and accidentally brushed against her, Jennie jerked away from him.

"What the hell's the matter with you?" he demanded irritably. "I held you all day while we were riding and you weren't this jumpy then."

"I'm sorry. It's just that I've never slept with a man before." She hated making the admission after his caustic statement about naive young virgins.

Her statement jarred him, but he managed to maintain his composure and said, "Believe me, you don't have a thing to worry about, because that's all we're going to do—sleep. Now, lie still. I need some rest." And without another word, he turned on his side and slipped an arm possessively about her waist. Pulling her against him he rearranged the blanket over both of them.

The heat of his lean male body sent a shiver of expectancy through her.

Rick, thinking her chilled, drew her even closer and said, "You'll be warmer in a minute."

And indeed she was warmer, but not in the way Rick thought. A flare of sensual heat flushed through her as his hand rested innocently just below the tempting swell of her breast. She wasn't sure whether she wanted him to stroke that sensitive flesh or release her and leave her in peace.

Part of her longed for that intimate caress she had experienced only briefly this morning, and she remembered with pleasure his kiss. But the memory of his deliberate coldness afterward and his stated dislike of virgins stifled any attempt she might have made to recapture that moment. Forcing herself to endure Rick's unintentionally arousing touch, she stirred fitfully against him, seeking comfort. Finally, nestled in his arms, she drifted off.

Rick, however, found sleep more difficult to come by. Her guileless snuggling against him was more sexually exciting than anything he'd ever experienced before, and he had to fight down the fires of his desire. Rick wondered wearily how he was going to refrain from making love to her over the next long weeks when she was so desirable and so attractive.

Dragging his thoughts away from her, he cast one last glance in Luis's direction to make sure everything was quiet. Closing his eyes, Rick sought relief from Jennie's naive, erotic torture in the restful oblivion of sleep.

Chapter Seven

The campfire was burning low, its faltering flames sputtering forth in desperate final flares of golden light until its strength ebbed and it retreated in surrender to its final destiny: the fading warmth of the glowing embers.

Gathered around the dying blaze, the men of the M Circle C were quiet as their thoughts dwelled on Jennie and what they would find when they continued their search for her the next day. Mac, Jake, Todd, and Steve were sitting slightly apart from the others, the tone of their conversation intense as they plotted their strategy for catching the desperadoes.

"She can't be dead!" Mac was barely able to control his anguish.

"I don't think she is. If they were going to kill her, Pa, they would have done it this morning when they shot Todd." Jake tried to rationalize the outlaws' actions.

"Do you think they're planning to make a ransom demand?" Todd asked.

"We'd have heard something by now," Mac concluded defeatedly. "No, they wanted to take her along. And we all know why."

"Then we have to hurry."

"If we ride out at sunup, we stand a good chance of catching up with them by late tomorrow," Steve told them hopefully. "They can't possibly keep up the pace they set today."

"Why not?"

"There's four of them on three horses."

"You mean whoever's got Jennie is riding double with her?"

"Yeah." Steve was quiet for a moment, debating whether to tell them the bad news. "But there's one other thing and it might prove a problem for us."

"Well, what is it?" Mac demanded, wanting to know all the possibilities.

"They're heading due north—toward the Superstitions. If they should get to the mountains before we can catch up, it'll be virtually impossible to find them."

"Then we'll ride our damn horses into the ground tomorrow if we have to, but we're going to catch those bastards and get my daughter back!" he said savagely.

Steve stood. "We'd better turn in soon then. Jake, you want to take first watch?"

"Sure." Jake got up to follow Steve. "I'll see you in the morning, Pa."

"Fine," Mac answered curtly.

"Good night."

After Steve and Jake had gone, Mac turned to Todd, despair written plainly on his features. "If they've harmed Jennie in any way, I'll personally see them all dead! She's all I've got."

Todd glanced up at him quickly, glad that Carrie had already retired and had not heard his comments. He couldn't understand why Mac continually chose to ignore Carrie. Here the poor girl had risked life and limb just to join the search for her sister, and Mac had treated her as if she'd committed a crime.

"What about Carrie, Mac?" Todd ventured, keeping his voice low. "She's your daughter, too."

"Carrie?" He snorted derisively. "That girl has caused me

nothing but trouble since the day she was born."

"Surely you don't mean that—"

"I do mean it."

"But she's a lovely young woman—beautiful and intelligent—"

"Todd, I don't want to hear it. Of course, she's beautiful. She looks just like her mother and—" Mac suddenly cut himself off. "Never mind. It's not important. I'm just tired. I'm going to get some rest, and I'd advise you to do the same." Getting up, he walked away without another word, his shoulders slumping under the weight of his worry.

Puzzling over his harsh judgement of Carrie, Todd painfully got to his feet and headed to where he'd placed his bedroll near hers. His shoulder was throbbing and his whole body ached from the long hours in the saddle. Pausing to stretch, he unconsciously favored his injured side.

"Todd?"

"Carrie?" He was surprised to find that she was still awake. "I thought you'd gone to sleep."

"I couldn't. I was too worried," she told him, trying to sound earnest. "Your shoulder—is it bothering you a great deal?"

"Just a tinge now and then." Todd tried to dismiss his discomfort.

"Why don't you let me take a look at it? It probably needs to have the bandage changed anyway." She brushed back her blanket and went to Todd. "Sit down and I'll try to be as fast and painless as possible."

"Thanks," Todd said gratefully as he lowered himself to sit on his covers. Quickly unbuttoning his shirt, he stripped it off, taking care not to disturb the wrapping. "Is there enough light?"

"I should be able to see," Carrie murmured as she knelt in front of him. She wanted to caress that broad expanse of his lightly furred chest but she held herself in check, knowing that this was not the right time or place. With gentle fingers, she concentrated on the task at hand and tenderly began to pry the soiled bandage from his wound. "There." She breathed an audible sigh of relief when it came loose. "Now, let's take a look."

The injury was ugly but beginning to heal. Carrie cleaned it thoroughly and reapplied the antiseptic she'd used earlier that day. Then, using the fresh bandages that they'd brought along, she rewrapped his shoulder and helped him with his shirt.

"Feel any better now?"

Todd finished buttoning his shirt and flexed his arm to test its mobility. "It is easing up a little."

"Good. If you need anything else, just let me know." She hesitated in front of him, wanting to throw herself into his arms but knowing that it was too soon.

"I will. You go on to bed now. We're going to be riding out of here early in the morning, so try to get as much sleep as you can."

"All right. Good night, Todd."

"Good night, Carrie. And Carrie?"

"Yes?" She turned to him, hopefully.

"Don't worry too much about Jennie. We're going to find her and bring her back." Todd thought he was reassuring her.

"I know," Carrie responded, forcing herself to hide the bitterness she felt at his remark. Was Jennie all he ever thought about?

Resentfully, she lay down, pulling the blanket tightly about her. What did she have to do to make him notice her? A burning restlessness seized her as she watched Todd bed down nearby. She wanted to be lying with him. She wanted him to hold her in his arms and make love to her.

Annoyed at the effect her imagination was having on her body, Carrie rolled over and closed her eyes, hoping that sleep would release her from her sudden desires.

It was well after midnight when the sound of voices woke

her from her unsettled sleep. Listening intently, she recognized Steve's and Jake's voices, and she watched from beneath lowered lashes as Jake went on to bed and Steve began his turn at guard.

The heat that her thoughts of Todd had created had not abated, and the chance to be alone with Steve excited her. Carrie bided her time until she was certain Jake was asleep and then quietly left her bed in search of Steve.

"Steve?" Carrie's voice was hushed as she left the circle of sleeping men and ventured out past the boulders that encircled the camp.

Steve was stunned when he heard her soft call. He had been wanting some time alone with her, but he had not expected her to come to him so brazenly and so soon. Smiling to himself with confident male pride, he called out to her. "Here."

Carrie didn't care that at any moment they might be discovered; if anything she found the prospect stimulating and wondered how Todd would react to finding her in Steve's arms. Would he think of her as a woman *then*?

"Carrie, what are you doing up at this time of night?"

"Looking for you," she replied in sultry tones, moving toward him with sinuous grace.

At that moment, Carrie was the ultimate female predator, and Steve was her more than willing prey. Watching her approach, he was fascinated. She was gorgeous. Her long blond hair was loose and flowing about her as she walked, and those tight-fitting pants—His body responded to just the sight of her.

"I thought we could use a little time alone." She stopped tantalizingly close before him.

Steve smiled easily, confident of his ability to please her. "We could use a lot of time alone, but right now we'll have to settle for what we can get."

Snaring her, he drew her back with him behind the dark protection of the surrounding rocks. Pulling her into his arms, he kissed her, the rawness of his need obvious in his devouring embrace.

Carrie responded physically to Steve's passion, but her thoughts were of Todd: Todd loving her, caressing her, entering her. She moaned as Steve's hands slid appreciatively downward over her snug pants to cup her buttocks and hold her fully to his throbbing hardness.

"A lot of time," Steve murmured, grinding his hips against hers suggestively.

Carrie went wild with the sensations his arousal inspired, and she tried to put all thoughts of the other man from her mind as she matched his movements.

"Please—" Her words were low and seductive in his ear as she moved hungrily against him, wanting to ease the ache inside her.

Unbuttoning her blouse, he bared her hard-tipped breasts and covered them with heated kisses. As his tongue teased the taut sensitive peaks, a raging fire of desire surged through her entire body, and she arched to him, begging for more.

As his mouth sought hers again, his hands worked diligently to free her from her pants. Carrie kicked off her boots and then, ending the kiss, she stepped slightly away to slide the offending garment over her slim hips. Moving provocatively back into his arms, she reveled in the feel of his body against her.

With little hesitation, Steve backed Carrie against one of the boulders. After removing his breeches, he lifted her, guiding her legs about his waist and plunging into her pulsating depths.

Carrie wrapped herself tightly around him and clung to his shoulders as the spiral of her passion began to grow taut, coiling with ever-tightening pleasure within her.

She could surrender her body to the burning heat of Steve's ardor, but she couldn't completely yield her thoughts. As her climax neared, in her mind it was Todd who was holding her and as she attained that peak of sensuous release, she had to bite her lip to keep from crying out his name.

When Steve felt the throbbing thrill of her sated splendor, he drove deeply into her in a lustful frenzy. Losing himself in the ecstasy of his own need, he shuddered as the excitement pulsed through him, leaving him spent but satisfied.

As his motions ceased and he rested, Carrie slid down his body and leaned against him. Though her body was sated, she felt strangely empty. Frowning to herself, she moved away from him and began to dress.

Steve quickly adjusted his clothing and then leaned against the rock to watch her. When she began to button her blouse, he came to her. "We'll have to make sure we can find time for each other."

Carrie's tight smile was the only sign of her feelings of unease. "I've got to get back. I took a big enough chance as it was."

"We can work something out," Steve intimated boldly and then kissed her, not noticing how stiffly she held herself in his arms.

When he released her, Carrie hurried away from him and quietly slipped back into the safe folds of her bedroll. She lay slumberless the rest of the night as she tried to understand what had happened to her. The night before she had enjoyed Steve's lovemaking and had actually encouraged it. But tonight, her thoughts had been only of Todd, and his unseen presence had subtly altered her feelings.

It was a few hours before dawn when Carrie heard Steve return to camp, and she was careful to keep her eyes closed so he would think she was asleep.

Chapter Eight

"We should reach the rendezvous point late tonight if we ride steadily," Luis said, giving Rick a cursory glance. "But I meant what I said about your keeping up. Malo expects us tonight and I intend to be there."

Rick returned his regard with a cool passivity. "I'll have no trouble keeping up with you, Luis. Where are we meeting him?"

Luis and Ray exchanged looks before he answered. "Willow Canyon."

Though outwardly he remained stoic, inwardly he flinched. Willow Canyon—"I know where it is," he remarked with composed precision. "So, even if we do get separated, for whatever reason, I'll be able to find the camp."

"Then let's ride. I'm ready to get my hands on some of that gold!" Ray laughed loudly.

The sound of his raucous laughter roused Jennie from sleep, and she frowned as she opened her eyes. It hadn't been a bad dream—it really had happened.

Struggling to a sitting position, she smoothed the tangle of unruly dark curls back from her face and looked over to where the three men stood in conversation.

"Me, too!" Luis was agreeing to something Ray had said. "Why, thanks to Malo, with the gold I bring out of those mountains, I'll be able to buy anything I want! What about you, Cazador?" he asked expansively. "What are you going to do with your share?"

"I'm going to save what I bring back," he answered easily.

"Money's no good if you only save it," Ray protested. "It only gives pleasure when it's spent. And I can think of a lot of pleasure I'd like to buy right now!"

"Enough." Luis cut him off. "Let's get going. It'll be dawn soon and I want to make the next water hole before noon."

Wide-eyed, Jennie watched as Rick headed toward her. They were on their way to meet up with Malo? Terror struck. She'd heard of Miguel Malo and she knew what a bloodthirsty killer he was. Surely Cazador couldn't be involved with him!

"Jennie—you heard?" he asked in low tones as he crouched down beside her.

"I heard," she whispered in a strangled voice. "Are you one of Malo's men?"

"When it suits my purposes," he answered cryptically, shrugging. "Now, get up. We're riding out now."

Nodding nervously, Jennie stood and began to roll up the blanket.

"You're very submissive early in the morning." He was surprised by her lack of resistance to his orders.

She glared at him but restrained her sudden irritation at his mocking tone. "I did a lot of thinking last night."

"And?"

"And I realized that there was no point in fighting you anymore." Jennie thought briefly of the strong feelings her dream had aroused.

"Oh, really?" He wasn't sure whether to believe her or not.

She sounded most logical as she explained: "You haven't harmed me though you've had plenty of opportunity; you've kept me safe from Luis and Ray; and, you've promised to take me home as soon as possible. I've decided to cooperate with you," she finished magnanimously.

93

Rick grunted dismissingly and took the bedroll from her. "Good. Now get ready to go."

His blasé acceptance of her willing capitulation left Jennie irrationally angry, but she bit back a heated response to his aloofness and stomped away to take care of her morning needs. Returning to the clearing moments later, she knelt beside the small pool of water to hurriedly wash as best she could.

As Rick went to tie the sleeping gear to his saddle, he protectively watched her every move. Damn, but she was unpredictable! He wasn't sure whether her sudden agreement to go along with him was good news or bad. When she was nervous and arguing with him, he could control his desire for her, but if she suddenly became compliant—His expression grew thunderous as she finished washing and came toward him.

"I'm ready." Jennie smiled, hoping to improve his obviously black mood, but his reply was brusque.

"It's about time. Get on."

Jennie quickly climbed into the saddle and Rick swung up behind her. Pulling her back against him, he kneed the horse into action, and they resumed their position of yesterday as they followed the path from the campsite that the others had taken a few minutes before.

Rick was tense. At that moment, there was nothing he wanted to do more than to kiss her but, though Luis and Ray were out of sight, he restrained himself with an effort. Jennie had just agreed to cooperate with him and he wasn't about to challenge her. She believed that he would treat her fairly and he refused to abuse that faith.

Jennie leaned back, enjoying the support of Cazador's broad chest. She was practically sitting on his lap, and the sensation of being fitted so snugly to his masculine strength was both frightening and exciting. The emotions her dream had awakened within her stirred anew with the intimacy of her seat, and she wondered if he would ever kiss her again.

As Rick and Jennie rode out of their rocky shelter, the red-gold morning sun was just edging over the eastern horizon. In the distance, he could see the other two men riding on ahead and, putting his heels to his horse, he galloped after them.

Jennie—Jennie—Jennie! If Carrie heard her name again, she was going to scream! Since the moment everyone got up this morning, all conversation had been about her sister. Would they find her? Where were the outlaws taking her? Would they have to fight for her or would they let her go without a showdown?

Who cared! Carrie thought with a vengeance as she shifted miserably in the saddle. She was beginning to think that her plan to attract Todd had been a bad idea, for he had shown no inclination to be with her at all today. Though it was already mid-morning, he had only spoken to her once and then it had been only to reassure her about Jennie. After that, he'd ridden off to join Mac, Jake, and Steve at the head of the posse. Carrie knew better than to follow him for Mac had made it perfectly clear how he felt about having her along. So, she'd remained, riding in the rear and suffering through the wretched trek across the desert.

A sudden wave of concern washed over her at the thought of Todd's riding with Steve. What if Steve bragged to him about their involvement? Carrie paled as she considered the possibility. She knew how men talked, but it had never mattered to her before what anyone thought. Now, she realized painfully, it did. Todd's opinion of her was very important, and she decided then and there not to go to Steve again. She would save herself for Todd and Todd alone.

Glancing up ahead, she was relieved to see that Steve had ridden on ahead with Mac and Jake for some reason and that Todd was by himself. Spurring her horse to a quicker pace, she cantered to his side.

"How's you're shoulder holding up?" she asked, her concern real.

"It's just fine this morning, thanks to you." He smiled warmly at her.

Carrie's heart tightened joyfully as she savored his smile and she could breathe easier now that she knew Steve hadn't told him of their tryst.

"Good. I'm glad," she answered brightly.

Todd stared at Carrie for a long moment, distracted by her loveliness. She seemed to be such a delicate young woman and yet here she was, withstanding the ruggedness of this journey without complaint. A new respect for her grew within him.

"How are you making it?" Mac had always told him that Carrie had no affinity for the ranch, but she seemed quite knowledgeable in her handling of her horse.

"I'm doing all right. I just wish this was all over with."

"We all do, honey. We all do," Todd answered, the endearment slipping out unnoticed.

"Where did the others go?" Carrie asked, wanting to keep him engaged in conversation.

"See those rocks up ahead?" He pointed toward a boulder-strewn rise.

"Yes."

"Steve's gone to scout them. Your father and brother went along to back him up."

"Do you think the desperadoes might be hiding out there with Jennie?"

"You never know. It's the perfect place for an ambush. It's high and protected and they'd be able to see us coming for miles. Carrie—" He spoke with such intensity that she quickly looked over at him.

"What?" she asked as she read sudden concern on his rugged beloved features.

"If any shooting starts, I want you to get out of here as fast as you can," Todd instructed.

"But why? I know how to shoot. Father saw to that. I'll be able to help you."

"You might be a good shot at target practice but when it comes to killing a man, I don't want you involved," he said sternly. "I don't want to have to worry about you if bullets start flying."

A thrill surged through her at his revelation. He would worry! He did care! There was a chance for her!

"I won't give you anything to worry about, Todd. Ever," she told him huskily.

He nodded and then glanced up. "Look! Steve's signaling from the top of the boulder!"

Kneeing his mount, he galloped forward with Carrie following closely behind.

By the time they'd reached the rocks, Steve, Mac, and Jake had already ridden down from the abandoned campsite.

"Did you find anything?" Todd demanded anxiously.

"This. It's a piece of Jennie's blouse." Jake handed Todd the piece of soft material.

"They were there last night," Mac told him hurriedly, anxious to be on their trail. "So that means they've got at least a four hour head start on us today."

"What about water?" Todd asked. "Is there any up there?"

"There is a small collecting basin, so you men might as well go on up and water the horses while we're here.

"Right." And they filed away up the narrow path toward the clearing at the top of the rise.

"Did it look like it had been ripped off of her or did she deliberately leave it for us?" Todd asked.

"She left it. There was no sign of a struggle."

"Good." He breathed a sigh of relief.

Carrie, who had stayed back so as not to irritate her father, sneered inwardly at his obvious concern.

"We've got a lot of time to make up," Steve said. "So, as soon as all the horses have been watered, we'd better ride."

Todd noticed how discreetly Carrie was remaining in the background and he spoke to her, drawing her into their conversation. "Carrie, let's go up and take care of our horses now."

"Fine." And she started up the track with Todd behind her.

Mac watched her go, his eyes narrowed in contemplation of her quiet endurance. "I never would have thought—"

"Thought what, Pa?" Jake asked.

"Nothing." He dismissed the idea that he might have misjudged Carrie. He knew her too well to be fooled by this current docile display she was putting on. She was up to something, but he didn't have the time or inclination to worry about it right now. Jennie was all that mattered. Only Jennie.

His mind returned to those years of happiness so long ago, when Jennie had been a baby. Things had been so different then. He'd had a fine, strong son, a beautiful daughter and wife he adored.

Eve. The memory of her seared across his thoughts, making him almost recoil with the intensity of anger and hatred that suddenly filled him. All those years he'd loved her so and then—she'd betrayed him!

He wondered briefly if his telling the children that she'd died had been a mistake, but he put the self-doubt aside without giving it serious consideration. It was better that they thought their mother dead and revered her memory as something precious than to know the truth about her: that she was a slut who'd run off from her family, deserting those who loved her most in the world.

She had left only a note behind, saying that she couldn't take any more: that she was too young to be tied down to another screaming baby; that she was tired of being poor and that she needed to get away. Eve had gone right after Carrie had been born and from that time on he had not been able to deny the resentment he'd felt toward his youngest child. It was her fault that Eve had left.

As the years had passed, he had worked day and night to make the ranch a success in hopes that one day she would return to him. But he had never heard from her again, and as Carrie had grown to look more and more like Eve, his feelings toward her had become ever more hostile and his bitterness almost too painful to bear.

He thanked heaven for Hildago, for without her gentle, supportive help he would never have managed to raise the children and establish the M Circle C. She had always been there for him, and he regretted that he wasn't legally free to marry her, but a divorce was impossible for it would reveal to one and all that Eve was in reality alive.

Suddenly angry that he'd allowed Eve to creep into his thoughts, Mac forced his attention back to the present, waiting nervously for the others to return from their trip to get water. Soon, he decided, this would be over and Jennie would be safely back home. He couldn't lose her. She was too important to him. It couldn't happen twice in his life.

It was late in the afternoon when Rick and Jennie neared the entrance to Willow Canyon. Since his first sighting of the all too well remembered landscape, he had been lost deep in thought. The Superstition Mountains' looming, menacing presence had not changed in the eleven years since the massacre, and Rick felt as if he'd been thrust back through time; as if the horror of his loss was happening again, now. Struggling, he sought to contain his emotions, and in doing so he grew tense and silent.

Jennie could feel the tightness in him and wondered at the cause. "Cazador? Is something wrong?"

Interrupted from the morbid contemplation of his last desperate flight from this valley, Rick was suddenly glad for her company. Somehow her gentle presence made his past seem less alive.

"No. Nothing's wrong." His answer was softly spoken.

Jennie was baffled by his quiet response, for she had expected a curt, gruff reply.

"Where did Luis and Ray go?"

"They're about a half mile ahead, but I doubt we'll be able to see them. This is rugged terrain."

Jennie nodded but didn't speak as she let her gaze wander over the jagged spires. She had heard of these mountains, but she had never before been witness to their cruel beauty.

"How far in do we have to go?"

"I don't know for sure. Malo's camped up there somewhere. If we don't find him, I'm sure his men will spot us," Rick said slowly as he kneed his horse in the direction of the other mens' tracks.

Jennie wanted to ask what was going to happen once they reached the camp, but she knew that he would only grow angry at her inquiry and that it would ruin the small peace that had been established between them. Settling back as they began their uphill climb, she fell silent as Rick expertly maneuvered the horse around the prickly cacti and the scrub brush that grew with a desperate vengeance in the shallow, arid soil.

As they rounded the curve of a mountainside, the panorama of the entire canyon opened before them in an awesome display of stark natural beauty. But above the tops of the craggy, towering peaks the sky was black and threatening.

"I don't like the look of those clouds," Rick said as they headed ever deeper into the bowels of the Superstitions.

Looking ahead, Jennie, too, spotted the ominous, dark clouds that hovered over their destination, and a shiver of frightened expectation went through her. She knew how dangerous a cloudburst could be in this type of environment, and she was glad when he headed for even higher ground.

The mountains were presiding over the storm's birth with hideous glee. The winds, swirling through the canyons,

100

gained force and swept the rain-heavy clouds along the rock-studded cliffs with powerful surges of invisible violence.

The menacing blackness of the storm's roiling depths enshrouded the land, kicking up dust and sand and stripping away all vestiges of tranquility. Jagged blades of lightning stabbed viciously through the seams of the darkened sky, illuminating the canyon in stark, startling relief. Thunder rumbled forth, echoing eerily and threatening, in its deep-voiced warning, all in the tempest's path.

Anxious to be away from the steep ravine that would in moments become a deadly, gushing river of destruction, Rick directed their mount up a steeper path.

"Hold on tight," he said as the horse clamored to gain better footing in the loose, rocky soil.

The wind was whipping at them now, punishing them with stinging blasts of sand and grit as they struggled to reach the haven that the higher ground would afford them. The rain, when it started, was forceful and cold, soaking them to the skin in seconds. Closing her eyes and ducking her head, Jennie huddled as best she could against Rick as the fury of the freshly brewed storm vented itself upon them.

Rick tried to protect her, but the rampant waters were suddenly upon them, crashing against the steed's straining haunches in a gushing, rushing torrent. In the jolt of the impact their mount momentarily lost its footing and slipped perilously backward.

Jennie hung onto the slippery pommel for dear life as the horse rallied for another try at breaking away from the surging waters. But when the stallion's precarious footing gave way again, Jennie found herself thrown sideways from his back; luckily landing clear of his thrashing hooves and the threat of the coursing flashflood. Stunned, she was knocked momentarily breathless and she watched helplessly as the horse lunged forth riderless, dragging itself up beside her, away from the turbulence.

"Cazador!" Jennie screamed as she grabbed the terrified

horse's reins and scrambled back to the edge of the gully.

"Here! Jennie!"

The sight of him as he clung to a bush that was rapidly weakening under the onslaught of the racing water spurred her to action. Moving with the seasoned knowledge of an experienced ranch hand, she retrieved the rope and tied it securely to the saddle horn before tossing the lifesaving length of it down to him.

"Grab this and we'll pull you up!" As the wind and rain buffetted them with increasing ferocity, Jennie used the horse to drag him to the top. "Oh, thank God!" she exclaimed as he pulled himself onto the level ground next to her and, without conscious thought, she threw herself into his arms.

Soaked, muddied and more than a little grateful for his rescue, Rick embraced her warmly. He had no intention of anything more happening as they stood there wrapped in each other's arms in the pouring rain, but when she looked up, her expresssion was so joyous that a thrill soared through him, and it seemed perfectly natural and right that he should kiss her. Bending down, he drew her near, his mouth seeking hers in the most tender of exchanges.

Jennie's response was tentative, at first. She had longed for his touch all day and when she'd thought he'd been injured, her fear had been great. But now, Cazador was here, and he was fine and kissing her! Sighing, she relaxed against him, savoring the gentle caress of his lips on hers. Some part of her mind told her that this embrace was different from the one they had shared yesterday, but she didn't really realize how different until Rick deepened this kiss.

He had wanted to hold her—to let her know how much her help had meant to him, but at some point during their interplay, the rigid control he'd maintained over his emotions had broken down, freeing the long-denied passion he felt for her. Framing her face with the warmth of his hands, he pulled away for a moment to stare at her. She was

102

lovely—so lovely that his heart ached for the feel of her against him. He remembered well the beauty of her breasts, and he longed to touch the ivory smoothness of them.

The rain forgotten, he dipped his head again and his mouth slanted across hers in a blaze of desire. Parting her lips in breathless victory, his tongue thrust within, tasting of her sweetness. At the knowing exploration of his mouth, Jennie arched to him, wanting to be nearer.

A brilliant crack of lightning broke them apart and Rick quickly looked around, hoping to sight some kind of shelter for he knew it was far too dangerous for them to remain standing out in the open. With the help of another illuminating bolt of nature's stormy brightness, he spotted what looked to be an opening in the rain-slick, treacherous face of the hillside.

"There!" He pointed slightly above them. "Let's go!"

Grabbing the horse's reins and then grasping her securely by the arm, Rick led the way up the perilous mountainside. Forging his way carefully through the stands of jumping cholla and underbrush, he made slow but steady progress, until at last they reached the protection of the deserted diggings.

"Wait for me here. I'll take care of the horse and be right back." He directed her inside as he spotted a broken-down lean-to some distance back from the mine.

Jennie stepped into the chilly confines of their secluded haven. The darkness surrounded her totally as she moved a bit further into the cavernous shaft, and she hurried back to stand by the main opening. Within minutes, Cazador was back, dripping wet, bringing the bedroll, rifle, saddlebags, and canteen with him.

Where just a short while before she'd been surrendering to his embrace, now she suddenly felt tongue-tied and more than a bit bashful in his presence.

"I brought the blanket. It's got to be drier than we are." He smiled as he set aside the items he'd brought with him.

Facing her then, his gaze traveled over her with slow enjoyment, lingering on the impudent thrust of her hard-tipped breasts against the wet cloth of the shirt she wore. "Is there anything in here to start a fire with?"

"I don't know—I couldn't see much past the entrance," she stammered, both from the cold and her nervousness at his nearness.

Cazador looked so virile standing before her that she couldn't take her eyes off of him. His shirt was plastered to him, outlining the powerful width of his chest and shoulders, and his trousers, which, in their wetness, clung to him like a second skin, did little to disguise his manhood. As her eyes met his in the semidarkness an ageless understanding passed between them and it was a message that needed no words.

"Let me take a look around," Rick said quickly, ending the delicate imtimacy between them. And, as once again lightning split the sky, he began to search their surroundings for dry, usable wood. "See if the matches in my saddlebags got wet."

Jennie hastened to do his bidding.

"They're dry," she announced, taking them from the protective pouch.

"Good." Rick knelt beside her and began arranging the pieces of wood he'd found. "I'll have a fire going in no time." Taking the matches from her shaking hand, he efficiently started the blaze. "There," he said proudly. "In a few minutes, we'll start to dry out."

Glancing over at Jennie in the flickering golden light, he felt once more the poignant pull at his heart. How many women could have survived what he'd just put her through? And why did she bother to save him, when, had he been injured or killed, she could have gone free?

When he noticed how badly she was shivering, Rick got up quickly. "Let me get something to warm you."

His thoughtfulness surprised Jennie for she hadn't been sure what to expect from him. The last time they'd kissed he'd been cold and aloof afterward, but now he seemed so—so nice. She watched as he unrolled the bedroll and then as he strode purposefully back to her to wrap it about her trembling body.

"Thank you," Jennie murmured, grateful for the protection not only from the cold but also his searing regard, for the touch of his eyes upon her had been as arousing as any physical caress. When his arms didn't release her, she looked up at him expectantly.

"You're welcome." His words were a growl as he nestled her close.

With slow precision, his mouth took hers in a devouring, passionate kiss that swept away all her inhibitions. Responding with the fullness of a woman, Jennie slipped her arms about his neck and hugged him nearer, forgetting about the storm and the mine and the blanket, which slipped unheeded from her shoulders. As the heavy barrier fell away, leaving them separated by only the dampness of their clothes, Rick began to move restlessly against her welcoming softness. The taut peaks of her bosom wreaked havoc on his already inflamed senses, and his desire was stretched to the limits as she moaned low in her throat.

Tenderly, he drew away and with gentle fingers he unbuttoned the front of her shirt, parting the clinging fabric just enough to reveal the swells of her breasts.

"You're so lovely," he said almost reverently as he traced an erotic pattern on the exposed flesh.

Desire coursed through her at his deliberately teasing touch, and she moved closer to him, wanting more. Slipping his hands within the cold, clamminess of the garment, he massaged the softness of her breasts. The play of his warm knowing hands on her chilled body lit fires of need within her, and when he bent to suckle at her aching nipples, she gasped at the sensation he aroused.

Never before had she been touched so intimately by a man and yet she felt no shyness as she surrendered to his excitement. It thrilled her to know that he found her desirable, and she wanted his embrace to go on and on.

When Rick abruptly pulled away Jennie was afraid that he was going to leave her. "Wait," she protested huskily.

Rick read the worried invitation in her tone and kissed her gently once more before moving to spread the blanket out. Going back into her arms he held her close for a long minute and then drew her down with him onto the improvised bed.

Slipping the shirt from her slim shoulders, he carelessly tossed it aside and gathered her in his arms. Though he knew he should not take her, he could no longer deny himself. The fire that had been smouldering within him burst into flame as he moved over her, and his mouth found hers in a breath-stealing exchange.

At the thrust of his hard thighs against her pliant flesh, Jennie surged upward wanting—no, needing more. She had never known that a man's touch could be so exciting and she writhed feverishly beneath him.

"Easy, love," Rick murmured softly as he lowered his head to her breasts and pressed heated kisses to the taut, pink crests.

Starbursts of passion soared through her as he teased each one in turn, and she held his head to her, savoring the joy of his caress. She could feel the hard strength of him pressed to her thigh, and with a tentative hand she reached out to touch him, wanting to give him the same pleasure he was giving her.

Rick was surprised by her innocent boldness, and he pressed his hand over hers and rotated his hips against her. Jennie nervously started to pull away, but he hastened to reassure her.

"That feels wonderful, darling." He kissed her gently. "I want you, Jennie. More than I've ever wanted any woman."

His admission made her spirits soar! He wanted her and he'd called her a woman!

"I want you, too." She spoke the words for the first time, hesitantly.

Her sweet confession was all the encouragement he needed. Moving quickly, he stripped off his own shirt and then turned back to her. With patient hands, he unfastened her riding skirt and with Jennie's help, slid it from her, along with the rest of her clothes.

"You're perfect," he whispered, his eyes sweeping over her appreciatively, taking in her silken breasts, the smallness of her waist and the slender length of her legs.

While Jennie watched him in wide-eyed anticipation, he bent slowly to kiss her. At the touch of his lips on hers, she sighed in total abandon and looped her arms about his neck, pulling him down. The hair on his chest felt crisp against her bared bosom, and she rubbed sinuously against him. But when his hand sought the satin smoothness of her stomach, Jennie jerked in surprise.

"It's all right. I'm not going to hurt you," he said soothingly and was relieved to feel the tenseness ebb from her. "I want to touch you, Jennie. To know you as only a man can know a woman."

"I know," she whispered as his lips claimed hers again and his hand dipped even lower.

Jennie arched in passionate response as he explored the tight center of her womanhood, and when he began his skillful caresses, creating within her body sensations she hadn't known existed, she writhed in ecstasy. His magical, stimulating touch brought her to the peak again and again until she was begging for release from his sensual torment.

"Cazador." She panted, her eyes glazed with passion. "Please—I need—"

Rick knew that she was ready for him but he fought against taking her just yet. She was an innocent—a virgin— and he wanted more for her than a quick coupling. He wanted to please her and to teach her about the ways of love.

With gentle pressure, he increased the tempo of his stroking as he captured her lips in a quick, devastating kiss. "Now, sweetheart. I'll please you now." Trailing kisses down her throat, he paused briefly to savor the pulse beating wildly there and then moved lower to continue his erotic foray at the tempting pale mounds of her breasts.

"Oh, yes. Yes," Jennie cried.

Grasping his shoulders, she clung to him as his lips and tongue worked their wonders on her willing flesh. The feelings he'd aroused were spiraling out of control, and she bucked wildly beneath his knowing hand, seeking and finally finding the ultimate pleasure in a burst of rainbow glory that left her weak and sated in his arms. Eyes closed, she rested languidly against him, savoring the beauty of the joy he'd just given her.

Rick knew he'd satisfied her, but he wanted now to introduce her to real love. "Now, you're ready for me."

Jennie's eyes flew open and she regarded him in stunned surprise. "You mean there's more? How could anything be more wonderful?"

"We've only just started, love," Rick growled as he turned her gently to him and began to caress her again, this time with more daring.

She had thought the passion he'd aroused within her had been satisfied, but his bold, agressive touch awoke new more exciting feelings. Reveling in his lovemaking, she gave herself up to him without question, parting her legs for his questing caresses. Raking her hands through the black silkiness of his hair, she pulled him to her, but this time she was the aggressor as she kissed him provocatively, breaking his determination to go slowly with her.

As she eagerly came to him, Rick could no longer hold back. Rolling slightly away from her, he shed the rest of his clothes and quickly returned to her waiting embrace. Moving over her, he covered her body with his in that most sensuously intimate of positions.

Jennie could feel the hardness of his manhood probing at her sensitive flesh and she wriggled invitingly beneath him. She was feverish with desire for him and she wanted to know the fullness of his love. Boldly Jennie reached out to touch him.

She was velvet and fire, and Rick was lost when she reached out to guide him to her. Slipping his hands beneath her buttocks, he lifted her hips and pressed his entry, moving easily so as not to frighten her. Jennie gasped at the pain of accepting him and, though she wanted to please him, she couldn't help but tense against this alien intrusion.

Rick groaned his intense pleasure as he slid deeply within her tight, silken sheath, but he soon realized that she was not sharing his ecstasy.

"Jennie—I'm sorry if I hurt you, love." Rick pressed heated kisses against her throat, hoping to rekindle the desire she'd been experiencing before he'd entered her. "Try to relax, darling. It'll get better, I promise," he said soothingly, caressing her gently. He was aching with the need to take her, but he knew he had to wait until she was ready or risk destroying the joy between them for all time. With great effort, he held himself in check and continued to stroke her with tender yet provocative intent.

"I'll be fine," she told him throatily, making an effort to physically relax. "It's just all so new to me and you're so big." Jennie blushed as she realized what she'd just blurted out.

Rick chuckled at her naive observation. "Thank you, sweet." And he bent to kiss her softly. "I hope I please you."

"You do, you do." She hugged her arms about his neck and passionately lifted her lips to his. Rotating her hips experimentally, she was surprised to find that the discomfort had passed and was replaced by only a tingling sense of fullness.

Her small movement was all the invitation Rick needed and, at last, he gave his passion full rein.

"Move with me, sweet," he said and, pacing himself, he thrust into her, delving into the molten silken core of her womanly depths.

Offering him the very essence of her love, Jennie met him tentatively at first and then eagerly as his driving hips branded her as his own for all time. Enraptured, Rick was swept along by the tide of her uninhibited response and they were soon lost in the ecstasy of the moment, achieving together passion's ultimate release. Shuddering in the bliss of their joining, he held her close.

Jennie felt a wonderful sense of womanly power as she lay with him in her arms. Cazador had been hers, if only for a short while. Sighing in peaceful contentment, she caressed his whisker-roughened cheek and was surprised when he took her hand and pressed a heated kiss on her palm.

As Rick shifted positions to rest on his forearms above Jennie, he looked up at her and marveled once again at her natural beauty. Her dark, expressive eyes were sparkling now with new and wonderful woman knowledge and he couldn't prevent the smile that curved his chiseled lips.

"You're beautiful, Jennie," he told her huskily as he bent to kiss her one more time.

"You make me feel beautiful," she said, moving languidly beneath the pleasant weight of his hard-muscled body. An unspoken worrisome thought was haunting her: He had said he liked experienced women and she was far from that, and she knew she had to ask. "Did I please you, Cazador?"

"Couldn't you tell?" he answered, seeking her lips for another sweet soft kiss.

"Well," she began hesitantly, "I think I did, but—"

"You pleased me, love," he growled just before his mouth claimed hers possessively. "Very much."

When the heartrending embrace ended, Rick shifted away from her briefly to get the canteen and the shredded remains of her blouse. With tender consideration, he wet the torn material and gently bathed her. Jennie gasped as the cool cloth skimmed over her most sensitive flesh, and her eyes widened when she saw the evidence of her virginity on the damp material just before he tossed it aside. Rick had seen the stain, too, and in that tender moment, he lost his heart to her forever.

Rick briefly considered telling Jennie everything. He knew it would certainly help to ease the mistrust between them if he could explain to her all his actions and his plans, but cold reality intruded as lightning flashed brilliantly in the canyon beyond and he knew, for her own well-being, he could not reveal his true identity to her. Later, after he had Juan safely away from Malo's clutches, there would be time for total honesty between them, but not yet.

"I guess, we'd better see to our clothes." His words cut as viciously across the intimacy of their haven as the lightning had.

Jennie sensed his emotional withdrawal from her and, though she wondered at his sudden change in mood, she knew better than to ask. She didn't want to endanger the precious, almost friendly peace that existed now between them.

"All right," she said quietly and watched appreciatively as he stood above her like some great and powerful man-beast of old. When he extended a hand to her to help her up, she took it gratefully. "Does it seem like the storm's letting up?"

"A little, but not enough that it'd be safe for us to try to travel yet," he told her, hugging her near for a brief moment, before releasing her. Retrieving his pants he pulled them on and then handed Jennie his shirt. "Put this on."

She took the proffered garment and slipped it on, buttoning it quickly against the chill. Rick smiled ruefully as he noticed how his shirttails covered all the more delectable parts of her.

"I'll have to start buying small shirts," he remarked, grinning at her lustfully, and Jennie smiled to herself. "We'll eat now while there's time," he continued and, as Jennie set about spreading out the rest of their damp clothing before his small but warm fire, he rummaged through his saddlebags to see what they had to share.

Two pieces of jerky and a small quantity of coffee limited their choices, but neither complained as they consumed the

111

sparse fare.

"Cazador?" Jennie finally asked as they sat quietly near the fire, wrapped in the blanket.

Rick longed for the day when she'd learn his true name. "What, Jennie?"

"Do you have to go on and join Malo? Couldn't we both just turn back, now that Luis and Ray are gone? You said you were a friend of Jake's. We could tell my father that you rescued me and let it go at that."

"You'd lie to your family for me?" he asked quickly.

"It wouldn't really be a lie," she said.

Rick fell silent again as he debated again how much he could afford to tell her. "At this moment, there is nothing I'd like to do more than take you back. But I can't, not yet."

"And you can't tell me why?"

"No. I'm sorry. I have my reasons. You'll just have to believe in me, Jennie. Can you do that? Can you trust me implicitly?" His eyes caught and held hers challengingly.

She met his gaze for long thoughtful minutes before answering him truthfully. "Yes, Cazador. I know I can trust you."

"Remember that always, Jennie, no matter what happens." His expression hardened as he thought of the dangerous days to come, and he prayed silently that she would not forget.

Chapter Nine

Having vented some of its fury on the hapless canyon, the storm swept forth from the Superstitions' protective embrace and launched its assault on the unsuspecting desert beyond. Vicious in its rampage, it convulsed with lightning and threw up a barrage of dust and sand in advance of its attack.

The posse had been watching the storm's rapid approach with considerable trepidation.

"We'd better get to higher ground and fast," Mac said as he accurately gauged its speed.

"I'll take care of Carrie," Todd offered, wheeling his horse around to search her out in the crowd of riders.

With Mac in the lead, they raced across the rugged terrain, heading for higher ground to seek refuge among the scattering of massive boulders. But a short distance from their goal, Carrie's horse stumbled and she was thrown.

"Carrie!" Todd was instantly at her side, his heart twisting at the thought that she might have been injured. There was a trickle of blood on her forehead and he wiped it carefully away with his handkerchief to reveal a small cut at her hairline. Cradling her in his arms, he glanced up worriedly in the direction of the racing black, ominous clouds.

Steve, followed by Mac and Jake, started toward them to

help, but Todd waved them back, knowing that there was little sense in all five of them being caught in the coming duststorm.

"Go on! I've got her!" he called.

Carrie blinked in confusion as she opened her eyes and saw Todd peering down at her, his expression worried. "What—what happened?"

"Your horse stumbled and you lost your seat. Are you all right?" His concern was very real.

"I think so," she said softly, not trying to sit up yet. She had wanted to be held by him for so long that she wasn't about to waste this moment by reacting too quickly. "My head hurts." She lifted a shaky hand to her brow and gasped when her fingers came away with blood.

"Here, hold my handkerchief on it. That should help to stop the flow." He handed her the already bloodied cloth.

"Thank you," she said as she pressed it to her forehead.

"We've got to move or we're going to get caught out here. Can you walk?"

"I don't know. Help me up and I'll try." Carrie regretted moving away from him, but she knew he was right. They had to find some shelter and fast.

As Todd set her on her feet, the first blast of the punishing wind hit them and she swayed against his massive chest.

"Can you make it?"

"Yes. I'll follow you."

Todd hurried to grab their horses' reins and then ran toward the higher ground. They made it as far as the first boulder before the billowing dust reached them, its painful onslaught blinding them temporarily. Skirting around the rock, they finally located a small, low overhang.

"Crawl in there!" Todd shouted over the force of the wind.

"But what about you?" she cried, wanting to stay with him.

"I've got to take care of the horses." He watched as she disappeared beneath the ledge and then quickly blindfolded

114

their mounts with garments from their saddlebags. Tying them nearby, he grabbed their bedrolls and followed Carrie into the refuge.

The sanctuary was neither deep nor high but at least it afforded them some protection from the elements.

"How is your forehead?" he asked as he slid in next to her, stretching out full length facing her.

"I think the bleeding's stopped. Could you take a look?" She rolled to her back and held the cloth away from the cut so that he could see.

"It's stopped bleeding, but you're going to have a bad bruise." Bending over her, he took the handkerchief from her and wiped gently at the wound to remove the last of the dried blood. "There," he said smiling down at her. A sudden realization hit him as he stared into her delicately molded features. She was so lovely—and when he'd thought her injured—Shaking himself mentally, he leaned back, breaking the unexpected intimacy of the moment. What was wrong with him? This was Carrie, not Jennie! It was Jennie he loved—or was it?

Carrie had sensed a tension growing within him, but she wasn't sure how far she could push him. Her ponderings were interrupted as a blast of viciously stinging windblown sand exploded into their shelter, and Todd quickly leaned over her to protect her from its painful bite. Huddling together quietly, they waited until it had died down again before moving apart.

"Has it started to rain yet?"

"Not yet, but it won't be long."

"Can we block the opening somehow with our blankets?" Carrie suggested. "If we don't, you're going to be awfully uncomfortable once the rain begins."

"There's no way to shut off the entrance, but we can wrap them around us," he told her as he unrolled the blankets.

Shifting back up on his elbow, he lay facing her with his back to the opening. Spreading one cover over their legs, he

115

tucked the other beneath his shoulder and drew it over their upper bodies.

"That should help some," Todd remarked out loud, but as he spoke the wind gusted into their haven again, and he quickly pulled the blanket over their heads, encasing them in a warm, intimate cocoon.

Carrie was thrilled! Here she was wrapped in a warm blanket with Todd, pressed full-length to his massive body and totally isolated from the rest of the world. The temptation to reach out and touch him was too great to resist, and she reached out to the hardness of his broad chest.

"Todd. Is your shoulder all right?" She kept her voice deliberately soft and feminine.

"Just fine," he replied tersely, suddenly feeling the need to shift slightly away from her. He was finding that being in such close quarters with a woman as attractive as Carrie could be very stimulating, and the seductive way she'd said his name hadn't helped matters any. Didn't she realize he was a man, with a man's desires? Just because he was in love with Jennie didn't mean that he couldn't find another woman attractive.

"Good. I was worried about you. That was one of the reasons why I came along on this trip." She rested her hand over his heart and was pleased to feel its powerful erratic thudding beneath her palm.

"You were worried about me? Why?"

"That was an ugly wound and—" She hesitated for a moment and then rushed on. "And I care about you. I always have."

Todd was startled by her statement. "I care about you, too, but it was foolish of you to risk your life following us."

"It wasn't foolish. I wanted to be with you." Carrie awaited his response breathlessly.

"You did?" He was totally taken by surprise. He had always thought highly of her, but he had spent so much time with Jennie that he'd never given her serious thought.

116

"Yes," she told him throatily, and he suddenly had a flash of the woman beneath her cool exterior. "Do you like being with me?"

"Well, of course."

"How much?" she asked as she encircled his neck with her arm and drew his head down to hers.

Todd was startled by her flagrantly seductive move, and he knew he should pull away, but he was mesmerized by her metamorphosis. And when her lips touched his in a featherlight caress, he felt the stirrings of desire deep within his loins.

It seemed perfect to Carrie that lightning cracked overhead just as they shared their first kiss. Her love for him was as powerful as the unleashed storm that surrounded them. Suddenly weary of waiting, she wanted Todd to know the depths of her feelings for him. With practiced finesse she pressed closer to him as her mouth found his in a rapturous exhange.

"Oh, Todd," she sighed against his mouth as she felt the strength of his manhood against her. Carrie wanted to caress him, to bring him to the peak of passion, but common sense ruled her actions.

Todd's senses were reeling. This was Carrie who was kissing him—Carrie who was lying next to him. And the kiss they'd just shared had been more potent that the most heady brew. She was bewitching him, enchanting him. Suddenly the feel of her small womanly body so close to his was too exciting. With gentle yet restrictive hands, he gripped her forearms.

"Carrie." Her name was almost a groan.

"What?"

"We've got to stop."

"But why? You make me feel so good—so safe and protected." She tried to move closer to him, but he held her at bay.

"Believe me, if we don't stop now, there's no way I'll be

able to protect you from me. I'm sorry, but I can't hold you like this."

"Why?" she asked with seeming innocence.

"Because you're a very beautiful woman, Carrie, and I don't want to do anything we might both regret."

"What is there to regret? If you find me attractive, why is it wrong to kiss me?"

"Because I've proposed to Jennie." He said it quickly, and the silence that stretched between them was painful.

"Oh—I didn't know. She hadn't told me." Carrie fought to keep the hurt out of her voice. *Damn Jennie, anyway!* She seethed.

"It isn't official. She wasn't sure that she was ready to get married yet, so we agreed to wait a while."

"Oh." Carrie's mind was racing. Todd might have proposed to Jennie, but she hadn't said yes. Carrie could see absolutely no reason why she should stop her pursuit of him. She would just have to be more subtle, more helpless. Todd reacted well to those feminine wiles that she had so artfully polished. A smile lifted the curve of her lips as she plotted further strategy, for she knew after the embrace they'd just shared that there was no way she'd ever give him up. "Well, I'm sorry. I hope I haven't made things uncomfortable for you. I hadn't meant to."

"No. Nothing's changed between us," he told her, but in his heart, as he remembered the ecstasy of their kiss, he knew he was lying. His cool, detached feelings for Carrie were gone. He knew her as a full-blooded woman now, and he liked what he'd discovered.

"Good." She smiled openly in their darkened hideaway.

They fell silent for a moment, listening to the sounds of the tempest as it roared overhead, angrily lashing out at the barren land.

"Will we be able to find their tracks after this rain?" Carrie asked the question that Todd had been avoiding in his own thoughts.

"No. Not unless Steve is a miracle worker." He voiced his disgust with the weather.

"What are we going to do?"

"We were pretty sure that they were heading up Willow Canyon; so, I guess we'll start looking there and hope we can pick up their trail again."

"Surely the storm slowed them down, too."

"I'm certain it did," he answered. "But even so, they had quite a head start."

Now it was Carrie's turn to play the supportive one and she touched his arm reassuringly as she told him, "I'm sure you'll find her, Todd."

"I hope so, Carrie." His tone was flat as his thoughts went to the stories he'd heard about the women who'd been taken captive and abused by desperadoes. From what he understood, the lucky ones died right away.

Jennie sat on the blanket near the fading fire; her dark-eyed gaze on Cazador as he stood at the opening staring out across the rain-drenched canyon. Her eyes lovingly traced his handsomely carved features, and she shivered in delight as she remembered the touch of his lips on hers. He was a magnificent specimen of a man, and she knew a quickening of her pulse as she savored the sight of his bare chest and powerful arms.

How had it happened so quickly? Yesterday he'd been a terrifying stranger and today—today he was the man she loved. The realization startled her for only a moment and then settled over her thoughts in a warm cloak of tenderness. Yes, she admitted honestly to herself, she did love him.

Jennie reflected with wonder on the joy they had just shared. It had been a mutually giving interlude—a time of discovery and ecstasy, and she never wanted it to end. There was so much about this man she didn't know: who he really was; where he'd come from; what the terrible secrets were that he kept locked so deeply inside of him. And caring for him the way she did, she wanted to learn everything about him, to know him as well as she knew herself.

Sighing quietly, Jennie got up and moved to stand with him at the entrance. Though she wanted to slip her arm about his waist, she stood slightly away from him unsure just how one behaved after having made love.

"Cazador? Is it still raining?"

"Yes, but it'll be over in a few minutes." He glanced down at her, distracted from his purpose by her nearness.

"I guess we'd better get our clothes ready, then." She started to turn back to the fire when his hand snaked out and grasped her by the arm.

"Not yet. There's time," he murmured as he pulled her tightly to him and then reached down beneath the shirttails to cup her buttocks.

Damn! But he couldn't keep his hands off of her. He had hoped that, having once made love to her, he would be able to put her from his mind. He had expected her virginal ways to leave him uninspired, but just the opposite had happened. Instead of being able to casually dismiss her from his thoughts as he had done with so many other women, Jennie had become like a fire in his blood, and the feelings she aroused seemed nearly unquenchable.

"Time? For what?" Her eyes were luminous as she stared up at his beloved face so serious above hers.

"For this." His head dipped to hers and their lips met softly, once, twice and then again with increasing ardor.

Ending the kiss, Rick swung her lightly up into his arms and strode back to the blanket. His eyes locked on hers searchingly, her earlier moment of nervousness giving him pause, but when she slipped her arms willingly around his neck he put aside his concern. Kneeling, he lay her gently on the bedroll's softness.

Jennie's color was high and her eyes were shining with the

promise of his kiss. Under his heated regard, her lips curved in a sensuous smile of invitation that sent his senses reeling. Her womanly instincts were directing her moves now and with lazy seductiveness, Jennie began to unbutton the shirt. As she finished the last button, she glanced up at him from beneath lowered lashes.

"Cazador? Will you help me slip this off?" Her voice was husky and grated provocatively on him.

Without speaking, Rick went to slip the garment from her, but her arms entrapped him, bringing him to her with surprising ardor. Their lips touched, their mouths blended; savoring, tasting, challenging.

Jennie's heart beat wildly as his hands separated the shirt and slipped within to caress the ivory-tinted loveliness of her bosom and then wander lower to the very heat of her. As Rick's stroking touch built her desire to a feverish pitch, Jennie rubbed restlessly against him, intertwining her legs with his and straining to get closer to him. Her boldness increased as her excitement grew and she ran her fingers through the matted hair on his chest before following its downward, narrowing line to the top of his breeches. With sensuous intent, she traced the waistband's edge with a single, teasing finger and at his sharp intake of breath she felt a surge of feminine pride.

"Love me, Cazador," she whispered as her lips sought his once more, and he answered her with a heart-stopping kiss.

All time seemed suspended in that moment. It was as if they had been transported to another world. A world consisting only of enchanted ecstasy where tomorrow didn't exist and yesterday had never happened. They were together. They were alone. They were one.

All thoughts of desperadoes and Malo and danger fled Jennie's mind as she gave herself up to the maelstrom of his love. Together they shed their clothing, each helping the other. Holding her arms out to him in welcome, she purred in contentment as he came to her, parting her sweet thighs and moving between them to press deep within her.

Rick shuddered violently as her hot, velvety softness surrounded him, enveloping him in liquid fire and drawing his very soul from his body. And for that fraction of time, Rick, too, was able to give up the demons that were haunting him and lose himself in the whirling wonder of her love.

"Oh, Cazador, it feels so right, so good," she whispered as he began his rhythm, moving to pierce her sweetness again and again.

"I know, love," he groaned, his desire building to a demanding crescendo with each slow, perfect thrust.

Suddenly, the steady, measured pleasure-giving pace was not enough for them. Impatient to renew the glory they'd found with one another, the power of their need great, they strained together, eager for a new draft of love's fulfillment.

Reveling in his potent possession, Jennie caressed his hard-muscled body with eager hands, moving easily with him, atuned to his every move, every nuance. Guiding and following, taking and giving, teasing and pleasing, they soared as one to the heights, their second mating even more glorious than their first. Bursting into flame at the pinnacle of ecstasy, they surrendered to love and were made willing captives of their spent dreamlike desire.

Sated and content, they lay clasped in each other's arms, unwilling as yet to face the reality that awaited them. And it was only when a shaft of bright sunlight broke through the rapidly dwindling clouds and shone harshly into the mine that their awareness slowly, and regrettably, returned.

"It's over," Rick murmured as he lifted his head to squint into the light.

"The rain?" Jennie found it hard to focus her drifting, mellow thoughts.

"Um," Rick growled. "The sun's back out in all its glory." He paused, his heart heavy as once again he had to focus on the grimness of their circumstances. "We have to go."

He didn't want to leave Jennie's embrace, but he knew it was time. The few luxurious moments he'd allowed himself to pretend that Malo didn't exist were over. Shifting his weight from her loving warmth, he began to dress, pulling on his pants and boots and then rising to get his shirt from where Jennie had spread it out by the dying fire. Shrugging into the still damp garment, he then brought her the rest of her things so that she, too, could get ready to leave.

Jennie had heard the thread of steel in his voice and knew there was no point in trying to dissuade him from continuing on in his quest to join Malo. Girding herself against the inevitable, she stood up and quickly pulled on her clothing.

Though his movements seemed casual enough as Rick moved a distance away from her, in reality, they were anything but casual. He found the very sight of her stimulating and he felt an overwhelming need to take her in his arms and hold her. A part of him wanted life to be as sane, tranquil, and easy as Jennie thought it was, but he knew better. Their time here was over, for her sake and his own.

"How does it look outside?" she asked as he went to stand in the opening. "Do you see anything?"

"No. It's pretty quiet." Rick's gaze swept the canyon, hoping to catch sight of Luis and Ray.

"I'm glad Luis and Ray were ahead of us when the storm broke." She shivered at the thought of being trapped in the mine with them as she slipped her arms into the shirt.

Rick regarded her silently, his eyes dwelling on her breasts, and he couldn't stop the desire that surged through him as he remembered their soft sweetness. As she buttoned the last button, he forced his heated gaze away.

"I'll see to the horse," he said abruptly, wanting to be away from the torture chamber the mine had suddenly become.

Jennie looked up questioningly, wondering at his hasty

exit. Realizing that he was probably just anxious to catch up with the others, she hurriedly put out the fire and rolled up the blanket.

As Jennie was putting his things back into the saddlebags, she found the remains of her torn blouse, bloodstained now with the proof of her lost innocence. For a long moment she stared at the cloth, her expression solemn as she considered the import of her actions. Hildago's lectures on remaining chaste until after marriage rang hollowly in her mind. Jennie knew she was no longer the naive maiden, but in her heart, it didn't matter. She loved Cazador and she had wanted to share that love with him. A smile lit her face as she remembered his tenderness and his passion, and she knew that he was the man she wanted to spend the rest of her life with. All other men paled in comparison.

At the sound of Rick who was returning with their mount, she gathered the bedroll and the saddlebags and went out to meet him.

"Thanks," he said as she handed them to him.

Glancing back in the direction from which they'd come, Jennie noted the storm's blustering path and felt a great sense of relief, knowing that the tempest would slow the progress of any posse that was following them. Where before she'd been hoping for rescue, now she knew she could not bear to be parted from Cazador, and she hoped that her father would not be able to find them.

Rick watched as she gazed back toward the desert. Thinking that she was still anxious to be rescued, he spoke his words harshly: "There's no one there, Jennie."

She was puzzled by his tone, but before she could question him about it, he strode back into the mine. Thinking his changing mood was due to his need to hurry, she mounted the stallion and awaited his return.

Picking up the last of their gear, Rick checked to make sure that the fire was dead before heading outside. Without speaking, his expression unreadable, he stowed the equipment and then swung up into the saddle behind her.

Jennie waited for his arm to come around her and pull her back against him in their usual riding style, but he didn't. And she was left feeling strangely bereft as he took up the reins impersonally on either side of her and kneed the horse to action, guiding it onward, ever deeper into the canyon.

Chapter Ten

Miguel Malo stood, rifle in hand, his attention directed down the canyon to where two riders were approaching. "Only two? I understood there were to be three of them!" he said angrily to Ramon, his lookout. "Can you make out who they are?"

"No. Not yet," Ramon told him nervously as he continued to stare at the men who were nearing their camp.

"We are expecting only Luis and Ray and Cazador. I don't want anyone else to get near this cave, do you understand?" He fixed him with a cold-eyed glare.

Shifting under Malo's penetrating look, he answered hurriedly, "Yes, Malo." Ramon knew better than to question his orders for Malo was the boss and he was renowned for dealing quickly and ruthlessly with anyone who dared cross him.

"I want to know who they are as soon as you can identify them," Malo said and then turned away, satisfied that Ramon would follow his instructions.

Working his way back down the rocky incline into the protection of the cave, Malo surveyed, with smug approval, the campsite he had personally chosen. Wide and deep, the cave was situated high in the bluffs at the end of Willow Canyon; its entrance was camouflaged by huge rocks and sparsely growing mesquite and creosote bushes. He knew that from below they were virtually invisible, while their view of the valley was unobstructed; that had been his main reason for selecting it, because it guaranteed no surprise attacks, either by Indians or whites.

Malo was pleased with how well things had gone so far in his plan to find the Peralta gold, and he smiled when he thought of how easy it had all been. It amazed him that no one had thought of doing this before, and he wondered why old man Peralta hadn't gone for it himself. Obviously, Malo concluded, Juan Peralta was a fool.

"Malo?" Ramon's voice from behind him startled Malo from his thoughts.

"What?"

"Luis and Ray are the two riders we saw, but there's no sign of Cazador."

Malo scowled. "I was counting on having him along. Send the other two to me as soon as they arrive."

"Right." And he disappeared back outside.

"Old man!" Malo called as he moved deeper into the cave to where Juan was being kept bound and under guard.

Juan Peralta looked up quietly as the bandit approached, taking care to keep his expression blank as his hatred for Malo welled up inside of him.

"It won't be long now," Malo bragged. "The rest of my men are almost here."

"Pity," Juan replied through swollen bloodied lips. "I had hoped that the storm might wash the filth from the mountains."

Malo chuckled evilly and leaned closer to leer in Juan's bruised and battered face. "If you value your life, you would do well to learn to hold your tongue."

"You will not kill me, Malo. Not yet." Juan showed no trace of fear as he calmly met his adversary's eyes.

Malo drew back and regarded him malevolently as he pulled his knife and toyed with the blade. "We shall see,

127

old man, we shall see." His thoughts were interrupted by Luis's and Ray's call.

"Malo!"

Turning from his torment of Juan, he headed to where the last two members of his gang were waiting for him. "Where the hell is Cazador?" he demanded without preamble as he came to stand before them.

"He's coming," Ray answered quickly.

"What do you mean, 'he's coming'?" Malo snarled. "I thought he was riding in with you."

"He is. We were separated by the storm," Luis lied. "He'll be along in another hour or so."

"And he's bringin' a woman with him," Ray added, hoping to cast his hated enemy in a bad light.

Malo shrugged his indifference, for women were of little concern to him. "No matter. I brought Chica and Lucia along. His woman can help them with the cooking."

"How close are we to the mine?" Luis asked eagerly, changing the subject.

"The old man is sly as a fox," Malo told them. "He gives us only one day's direction at a time."

"Can't you just get him to draw a map?" Ray asked, anxious to get his share of the gold.

"In these mountains I would not trust a map. No, he will lead us directly to the mine."

"What are you going to do with him after we get there?"

"I have not decided yet whether to leave him in the middle of the desert for the Apache or just to kill him outright." Malo smiled as he contemplated both alternatives.

Luis nodded his understanding. "Is there food? We were running short on the way in."

"Check with the women," he told them. "I'm going up to watch for Cazador." When he noted the lusty light in their eyes at the thought of being with the women, Malo said, "Lucia is mine."

"Right." They hurried to reassure him, respectful of his

place as their leader.

"Oh," Malo said, "was there any sign of any Apache?"

"No. Our only worry was a posse."

"A posse?" he asked. "Why would a posse be coming after you?"

"Cazador's woman." They hastened to explain, wanting to put Cazador in as bad a light as possible. "He took her captive even though we told him to just kill her. She's Mac McCaine's daughter."

Malo growled. "McCaine? The M Circle C?"

"The same."

"They'll never be able to find us in these mountains and, maybe when we're finished with the gold, we can ransom her back for a tidy sum." He smiled at the possibility as he turned away to rejoin Ramon.

Luis was pleased as he watched him walk away. "Hey, Ray."

"What?"

"What do you think Cazador will do when Malo decides to ransom the McCaine girl?"

Ray grinned. "I don't know, but I'm sure gonna enjoy watchin'."

And, after exchanging knowing glances, they headed toward the women to get something to eat.

Again, Malo waited at the lookout point, watching for some movement in the rock-strewn valley below. When at last he spotted their approach, he followed their progress avidly. Malo had heard many tales of the infamous El Cazador, and now he would finally get to see him for himself.

Cazador had been the fastest gun in the territory a few years back and then suddenly, he'd disappeared. He hadn't been heard from again until just recently. No one really knew where he'd gone or why, and Malo was curious. Why would a gunfighter with the best reputation around vanish for a long period of time, only to reappear years later? Before his association with Cazador was over, Malo was determined to have the answer.

With avid interest, Juan watched the interchange between Malo and his newly arrived men. He could tell by Malo's stance and actions that he was angry about something, but his words were lost to him in the echoing cavern.

Bound hand and foot, he awkwardly shifted positions, seeking some small amount of comfort where he sat on the cave floor, and he wondered how long it would be until they killed him. He had managed to maintain a certain bravado in spite of Malo's devious cruelties, but he didn't know how much longer he could hold out against the continual abuse.

Had there been some hope of rescue, Juan knew he could have lasted forever, but there was no ray of hope. According to the rumors he'd heard among Malo's followers, Ricardo had been killed in the attack on the ranch.

His heart grew heavy as he thought of his grandson's short and tragic life. So much had happened to Rick: first his mother's passing when he was still just a boy, and then the massacre and the years Rick spent riding as a gunslinger, trying to forget.

The ache inside Juan became almost unbearable as he remembered the sons he'd lost in that last, horrendous trip here to the Superstitions. After the deaths of Rodrigo and Antonio, Juan had vowed never to return to these cursed mountains. There was not enough gold in the world to make up for the loss of his two fine sons.

He had tried to cling to Rick, his only living heir, to bind him to him with love and family responsibility, but Rick had balked. Weighted down by his own unspoken misery, he had left El Rancho Grande and sought forgetfulness in the wild lifestyle of a hired gun. Juan knew it had taken him all those years to come to terms with the deaths of his beloved father and uncle. When Rick had finally made peace with himself, he'd returned home and Juan had welcomed him with open arms, for he loved his grandson beyond all else. But now, even Rick was gone, lost to him forever, and Juan cared little what the future held.

It had infuriated him to know that he had to lead them to the gold, but Malo had threatened to slay all of the women at the ranch house unless he cooperated; so he had gone with them, knowing that he would probably never see his home again.

At the sound of someone's approach, Juan looked up, and his expression softened as he saw Lucia coming toward him carrying his evening meal. Though she was Malo's woman, she had been the only one who had not mistreated him, and he was truly grateful for that.

"I have your dinner," Lucia told him as she squatted down beside him and untied his hands.

"Thank you, my dear," he told her as he briskly rubbed his wrists and then took the bowl of stew she offered.

"You're welcome." Lucia was continually surprised by the courtesy the old man had shown her. Never before in her life had a man treated her with such kind regard, and she found herself growing fond of Juan, despite her determination not to. "Do you need anything else?"

A great sadness filled him as their gazes met. "No, Lucia."

His haunting melancholy disturbed her and for a fleeting moment she wished that she could help him; that she could defy Malo and free him from his captivity so he could return to his home. But she knew it was impossible because Malo would find out; he always did when someone plotted against him. She had been with him long enough to know that she took her life in her hands if she dared to cross him.

"All right." Lucia stood up and looked nervously around for Malo, afraid that he might have been able to read her thoughts. She breathed an inward sigh of relief when she found that he'd left the cave. "I'll be back later, when you've finished."

131

"Lucia?"

"Yes?" She paused as she started to turn away.

"I saw those other two men ride in. Are all the men in camp now?"

"There's still one other man coming. He was supposed to ride in with Luis and Ray, but from what Luis says, Cazador got separated from them in the storm."

Juan was stunned at the mention of Cazador for there was only one man in all of the territory who used that name. Forcing himself not to respond outwardly, he asked with carefully tempered curiosity, "Isn't he that gunfighter?"

"Yes," Lucia told Juan as she glanced over toward the cave entrance. "And he should be here soon. I'm anxious to see him. It'll be interesting to find out if he's as good as they say he is."

"I'm sure he must be or he wouldn't still be alive," he said as excitement and hope began to grow within him. Ricardo was alive! But why had he resumed his identity as Cazador? Had he done it just to infiltrate Malo's gang? What was his plan? Worried lest he give himself away, he remained passive as she continued to talk.

"That's true," she said and then, deciding to join Malo outside so she could get a firsthand look at Cazador, she walked away. "I'll be back."

As Juan watched her go, he wondered what Ricardo had planned, and he worried about his safety. One man against all of these? But glancing around, measuring the desperadoes, his confidence returned. He knew his grandson well and if anyone could effect a rescue under these circumstances, Ricardo could.

A sense of peace overtook him and he began to eat, knowing that he would need his strength to help.

"We're almost there," Rick told Jennie as he guided the horse up a slipping incline. "They disappeared behind that boulder and that's the same place I saw the sun glint off that rifle barrel." He pointed toward a massive rock near the crest of the mountain.

"Are you sure it's safe to just ride in?" she asked in a worried voice.

"Believe me, Jennie. If they'd wanted us dead, we wouldn't have gotten this far." Rick was growing apprehensive about his upcoming meeting with Malo, and his words came out more tersely than he'd intended. "These men don't play games. Remember that."

"How could I forget after Luis and Ray?" she returned caustically.

"They're amateurs compared to Malo, Jennie. The man's an amoral animal who'd just as soon kill you as talk to you. Stay as far away from him as you can and try not to draw his notice."

"If he's so terrible, then why are you riding in there to join up with him? Is it the gold? I told you my father is rich. If it's money you need, all you have to do is ask." Jennie was growing nervous now that they were actually nearing the outlaws' camp.

"No, it's not the damn gold!" he exploded almost violently, though he kept his voice down. "That gold is the last thing I want or need! Now shut up or I swear, I'll gag you!"

Completely cowed by his unexpected outburst, she stiffened her back and fell silent.

The armed guard stepped out from behind the rocks, his rifle aimed directly at Rick. "Hold it right there," he ordered as he eyed them suspiciously.

"I'm Cazador," Rick said, maintaining a casual seat but moving slightly so that his hand rested near his sidearm. "I'm here to see Malo."

Jennie felt his body tense and she knew that this was their most dangerous moment.

"I've been waiting for you, *compadre*." Another

133

shorter, more wiry man appeared behind the guard and swaggered forward to greet him. "I am Malo. Come join us." He gestured expansively to the cave behind him.

"That's what I've been wanting to do ever since I heard about the gold," Rick replied easily, swinging down off the horse. "Did Luis and Ray get here?"

"Yes, they arrived a short while ago and told us that you were coming." He leered up at Jennie for a minute. "Your woman?"

"Yes." His answer was casual but firm.

"Nice." Malo moved to stand by Jennie, and he pawed her thigh appreciatively. "Very nice." Then abruptly he turned back to Rick. "Let's eat and drink. Then, we will talk. Have your woman go with the others, and Ramon will see to your horse."

Handing Ramon the stallion's reins, Rick glanced quickly up at Jennie as he threw his saddlebags over his shoulder and pulled his rifle from the scabbard. "Join the women in the cave and make yourself useful." Then, without a backward glance, he walked off with Malo.

Jennie was tense as she watched them go. Malo had exceeded all of her most terrible expectations. He was a hideous little man, and her flesh still crawled from his touch. Short and dark, with black obsidian eyes and a drooping mustache, she had sensed the evil in him, and it was no wonder just the mention of name could strike terror in the hearts of settlers. Shivering despite the heat of the day, she stared after them until the guard roused her with a curt order.

"Get down. You heard what Malo said. Go join the other women. I'm sure they can find work for you to do." He smiled lecherously at her. "If not, come back and I'll find something to keep you busy."

Jennie dismounted quickly and glared at the desperado as he ran a hand down her arm. "Keep your hands to yourself," she spat.

Ramon looked at her for a long moment and then, remembering Cazador's reputation, he shrugged and unhanded her. But even as Jennie strode calmly away from him into the protection of the cave, she could still feel his hungry gaze upon her.

Lucia stood off to the side, watching, as Malo entered the cavern with Cazador, and her eyes widened at the sight of the infamous gunman. It had been said that he was as successful with women as he was with guns and now Lucia understood why. He was the most handsome man she'd ever seen! Tall and dark, with broad shoulders and narrow hips. He moved easily at Malo's side and had the air about him of a man totally in control.

Lucia sighed, her heart fluttering as she stared at him unobserved, and she wondered what it would be like to make love to him. Her body roused at the thought for he was so magnificent a man that she was sure it would be heavenly. Suddenly tired of Malo's self-gratifying ways, Lucia determined then and there that she would be with Cazador, somehow, someway.

As soon as Rick's eyes adjusted to the semidarkness in the hideaway, he visually searched the cave's natural room for a sign of his grandfather, and joy shot through him as he spotted Juan sitting at the back of the cavern. Any previous worries he'd had about succeeding were dismissed from his mind. Nothing could go wrong now, nothing. He'd found Juan alive and apparently not in too bad shape. All he had to do was figure out a way to free him from the camp and then it would be over. Relief flooded through him for he knew exactly what he had to do.

Following Malo to his pallet, he sat down beside him. "You chose your hideout well."

Malo smiled, pleased at getting a compliment from him. "I wanted to be protected from everybody, Indians and whites."

Rick kept his expression carefully blank at the thought of

the cutthroat Apache. "Have you seen any Apache? They're usually pretty thick around here."

"No. None yet," Malo said as he handed Rick a bottle of tequila.

"We didn't either on our way in." He drank deeply of the fiery liquid and handed it back.

"So Luis told me," Malo responded and then changed the subject. "I had heard that you were familiar with this area. Is that true?"

"Yes, I know it."

"Good. I'm sure I'll need your help before we're through here." He swallowed deeply of the liquor and wiped his arm across his lips before bellowing, "Chica!"

The woman who'd been tending the fire hurried toward him.

"Chica, this is Cazador. He is one of us now. Treat him right." Malo chuckled suggestively.

"Yes, Malo."

"Now, bring us something to eat. We have much to discuss."

Chica didn't bother to answer but hurried to do his bidding.

"She is a good woman. She takes care of my men for me. If you want her, take her. I'm sure she'd be good to you," Malo said in an expansive tone.

"Had I not brought a woman of my own with me, I would take you up on your offer."

"Ah, yes. Your woman." He glanced over to where Jennie had just entered the cave and was standing hesitantly in the opening. "She's lovely. You must enjoy her."

"She's a woman, Malo." Rick did not want to attach too much importance to Jennie's presence. "Like all others."

"Luis tells me that she's Mac McCaine's daughter."

"That's what she says, but who knows? She could be lying."

"Perhaps. But maybe she is telling the truth and if she is,

136

she could be worth a lot of money.

"When I tire of her, we'll talk of ransom, but until then, Malo, she's mine." Rick's tone was steely.

"Fine," he replied indifferently. "Lucia!" He called as he spotted her entering the cave behind Jennie. "Bring the girl here."

Lucia heard Malo's call and pointed Jennie in their direction. "Malo wants to see you. Let's go," she said coldly, resenting her and feeling that her presence would interfere with her own plan to have Cazador.

Leading the way, Lucia didn't speak again as she kept her gaze fixed on Malo. She knew she could not afford to look at Cazador for she might not be able to disguise the surging sensual desire she was feeling for him.

"Cazador, this is Lucia, my woman."

Rick nodded to the young Mexican girl and wondered why a female as pretty as this one would be mixed up with Malo.

"Lucia," he continued, "take care of his woman. Put her to work, but keep an eye on her. We don't want anything to happen to her."

"Yes, Malo," she replied respectfully.

"You've chosen well again," Rick said selecting his words carefully.

"Yes, I found her a few months back working in a cantina in Mexico and I've had her with me ever since." He smiled leeringly, revealing blackened, snarled teeth.

"I can understand why you'd want to keep her."

"So," Malo said, drinking again from the tequila, "where have you been? There had been no news of you for so long that some rumors had it that you'd been ambushed and killed."

Rick smiled thinly. "No one ambushed me. I tried ranching for a while."

"Ranching?" He was astounded at Cazador's admission and he laughed heartily. "If I hadn't heard it from you, I

137

wouldn't have believed it. The fastest gun in the territory pushin' cows?"

Rick shrugged off Malo's amusement, answering with a reply that he knew the other man would believe. "You're right. It grew boring. I needed some action and that's when I heard what you were doing. It sounded pretty challenging, plus the money should be good." He let the sentence hang.

"When I heard from the men that you wanted to ride with us, I was surprised. From your reputation, I never pegged you as one who needed money."

"Before I tried ranching, I didn't. But I lost everything I had on that damned ranch," he growled, in a good imitation of a frustrated gambler. "I figured it was time to cut and run, so here I am."

"I'm glad." Malo sounded content with his explanation. "I think you'll find that we have a lot in common."

And they were exchanging measuring looks when Chica returned with plates of hot food for them. They ate the stew hungrily and then sat back to share the tequila once more.

"You had to bring Peralta with you?" Rick gestured toward Juan as he took the proffered liquor and lifted the bottle to his lips.

"It was the only way. There was no map," Malo assured him, taking back the tequila and drinking deeply.

"Did he give you a lot of trouble?"

"Only in the beginning. After a few days, he came around. I have very effective methods for dealing with stubborn people."

"So I've heard."

Malo lifted his shoulders in a gesture of helplessness. "A man does what he must do. Come, we will see just how cooperative he is tonight."

Rick was taut with anger, but he was careful to keep his outward appearance calm. What had Malo done to Juan during the past weeks? The thought of the anguish his grandfather had suffered made him want to kill Malo right now and put an end to the charade, but he knew the chances of freeing both Jennie and Juan safely in a shoot-out would be nonexistent. Controlling his desire for quick revenge, he got up and followed Malo across the camp.

Juan watched as Malo headed in his direction with Rick by his side, and he wondered what the outlaw had in store for him tonight. Schooling his features into a mask of indifference, he met Malo's eyes in unspoken challenge, taking care not to even give Rick a second glance.

"Am I to be the entertainment for your men again tonight?" he asked brittlely.

"There is no need. Tonight we are celebrating," Malo proclaimed most jovially. "With Cazador's arrival, all my men are in camp."

"So." Juan eyed Rick scathingly. "You're the famous gunfighter?"

"I am." Rick kept his tone cold.

He swung his gaze back to Malo, saying cuttingly, "One fast gun is not going to save you if the Apache decide to attack."

"Shut up, old man. We haven't seen any Indians and we're not going to."

"As you say." Juan shrugged his indifference to the man's foolish attitude.

"We will be heading out tomorrow. Be ready."

"Malo, I am at your constant disposal." His sarcasm was obvious as he gestured to his bound feet.

He snorted in irritation. "How many days until we reach the mine?"

"Two, maybe three. It depends." His answer was deliberately vague.

"Depends on what?"

"Landslides. If the terrain has been altered it may take me longer to find it. It's been a long time since I ventured here, Malo. A very long time." Juan's words were full of subdued grief.

"Cazador." Malo turned away from the old man's mental wanderings and beckoned for Rick to follow him. "Let's join the men. I'm sure they want to meet you."

"All right." Rick, who had remained stoically silent during their conversation, cast Juan a reassuring glance as Malo started to walk off.

Juan was only able to meet his beloved grandson's eyes for a brief moment, but it was long enough for Rick to see the tears of gratitude and love that shone there. Nodding slightly to comfort him, he followed Malo to where the men had gathered a distance away.

Chapter Eleven

"Here, have something to eat." Lucia handed a plate of the hot, steaming stew to Jennie as they sat by the cooking fire.

"Thank you." Jennie took the plate gratefully. "It looks good."

"Enjoy it. It may very well be the last hot meal you have for quite a while."

"Why?"

"Well, now that Cazador's finally here, we'll be heading out again and once we're in the open, it won't be safe to have any fires. We don't want to do anything that will draw anyone's attention, especially not the Indians," Lucia told her as she settled down next to her to eat.

"Where are we going?"

"Didn't Cazador tell you about the mine?"

"Mine? What mine?"

"The Peralta gold mine." Lucia sounded proud and excited. "Malo's plan is perfect. See that old man over there?"

Jennie noticed for the first time the gray-haired man who was bound and under guard at the far side of the campsite. "Yes."

"That's Juan Peralta. He's the only one who knows the exact location of the diggings."

"But why is he tied up?"

"Malo has had to force him to lead us to the treasure. Surely you've heard the stories of the Peralta gold?"

"The name sounds familiar, but I don't remember anything about a gold mine."

Lucia sighed in exasperation. "The mine belongs to the Peralta family, but they haven't worked it in years. It seems that both of his sons and some workers from his ranch in Sonora were massacred by the Apache during their last expedition, and Juan swore never to return to it or to reveal its location to anyone."

"Until Malo," Jennie put in.

"Until Malo." Lucia nodded her agreement. "Malo convinced him otherwise."

"You mean Malo beat it out of him."

"Convinced, beat." She shrugged. "It's all the same, because the important thing is we're all going to be rich just as soon as we find it."

"And what's going to happen to him once he leads us to the gold?" she asked, suddenly growing concerned about the helpless victim of Malo's lust for riches.

Lucia was about to answer when Chica joined them.

"Your Cazador is some man." Chica smiled in friendly appreciation. *"Que hombre!"*

Jennie couldn't help but smile at her enthusiasm, and she missed the quick flash of jealousy that flared on Lucia's pretty features. "That he is."

"You are one lucky woman," she continued as she fixed herself a plate of food.

And Jennie couldn't help but agree with her as she glanced over to where Cazador stood in conversation with Malo and the other men. Her heart beat faster as she watched him, admiring the wide set of his shoulders and the way his dark trousers clung to his hips and muscular thighs. It seemed almost as if Cazador had felt her gaze, for he suddenly looked up in her direction. Their eyes met for a long, heated moment across the width of the cave before he turned his attention back to the men around him.

His earlier harsh words were forgotten as the memory of his ardent embrace swept over her like a caress, and Jennie sighed inwardly, wishing that they were back in their haven, alone.

Lucia had seen the look they had exchanged, and she vowed silently to herself that one day, Cazador would look at her in the same way.

Though he appeared to be listening, Rick was actually paying little attention to the verbose bragging of the half-drunken outlaws. His thoughts were focused, instead, on finding the safest, fastest way to free Juan and make their escape. While they were camped in the cave, Rick knew there was no point in even trying to get away. His best opportunity would be later, when they were on the trail.

Sensing someone's eyes upon him, Rick glanced up and saw Jennie watching him. As their gazes locked, he was stunned by the power of the emotion that flowed through him. He had hoped to put her from his mind while he was in camp with Malo, but he was finding it an impossible task. God, how he wanted her!

Shaking himself mentally, he forced himself back to the present and took the bottle of whiskey that was thrust at him by Ramon.

"Your woman is some beauty. When you get tired of her, give her to me! I'd like to lose myself between her thighs." He clapped Rick on the back in a gesture of male camaraderie.

A violent rage surged through Rick as he thought of Ramon touching Jennie, and it took all of his control not to punch the man out. With a casualness he didn't feel, he smiled.

"When I get done with her, I'll let you know." Drinking from the bottle, he handed it back and the men all laughed.

Though the remark, in reality, had been a harmless one meant for men's ears only, Jennie had overheard it and terror seized her. Had Cazador really meant it? Would he really turn her over to those animals? But in the midst of her panic, she remembered their earlier conversation and his entreaty to trust him no matter what. Hanging on to that memory, she dismissed her fears.

Lucia was pleased and encouraged by what she'd just heard, and she gave Jennie a sidelong glance. "I guess Cazador plans to share you the same way Malo does Chica."

"Only after he tires of me," Jennie answered with calm confidence as she remembered their rapturous loving. "And I plan to make sure that that won't be for a very long time. Does Malo share you?"

"No. I am his woman alone," she boasted, needing to assert the importance of her position in camp. "He would not want others to have me," she asserted, wanting Jennie to know just how valuable Malo considered her to be.

"Lucia," Chica interrupted. "I found a small pool this afternoon, after the rain."

Lucia's eyes twinkled in excitement. "Is it close?"

"Just atop the rocks. We should be able to get away long enough to wash." She looked over at the drunken men. "I don't think they'll miss us. Do you want to come, Jennie?"

"You're going to bathe?" Jennie found the possibility delightful.

"Yes and wash a few things while we have the water. We may not get another chance while we're here in the mountains."

"I'd like that. I do need to wash these clothes." She looked ruefully down at her filthy skirt and Rick's stained shirt.

"I've got an extra blouse and skirt." Chica got up to rummage through her things. "They will be big on you, but you could wear them just until your things dry."

"Thank you," Jennie said gratefully, taking the change of clothing and soap she offered.

"Let's go quickly before the men remember we are here." Chica knew that once they started drinking they would be wanting her soon. As they left the cave, only one set of eyes followed their progress.

The sun was just setting, casting the world in a gold and black mist as the three women left the cave and climbed the short distance to the pool Chica had discovered. Close to the cavern, yet protected from the prying eyes of the lookout, the basin of rainwater was tranquil, its shining surface reflecting the fading light of the day. Chica and Lucia were like young animals at play. Quickly stripping down, they ran into the knee-deep waters and splashed each other thoroughly before beginning to wash.

Jennie watched them for a moment and then hurried to join them. Undressing, she took only enough time to wash her clothes and spread them out on nearby rocks before wading out into the water.

Chica looked up as Jennie came toward them and in that moment, she knew that her chances with Cazador were nonexistent. The girl was gorgeous. She felt no jealousy, only resigned acceptance. Why would he even look at her when he had a woman with the body of a goddess?

Lucia, too, watched Jennie as she stepped into the water. Tall and slender, her skin was like alabaster and her breasts were full and round. Lucia glanced down at her own slim body, quickly comparing herself to Jennie, and she knew that she came out the loser. She wasn't tall, her breasts weren't as full—Anger replaced envy. Jennie might be lovely to look at, but did she know how to keep a man satisfied? Lucia doubted it and her own sense of worth returned. If there was one thing she was proficient at, it was pleasing men.

Jennie found the thought of bathing so enticing that she took little notice of the other women's expressions. Splashing herself thoroughly, she remained standing and began to soap her body, scrubbing at her skin until it tingled. Finally, when she felt clean once more, she sat in the middle of the pool and arched back to soap and wash the heavy mane of her hair.

Rick had watched Jennie leave the cave with Lucia and Chica and didn't think too much of it, but when they did not immediately return, he grew worried. Slipping away undetected from the group of rowdy, now drunk desperadoes, he escaped outside and followed their tracks up a steep path to the top of the rocks.

Jennie had just begun to wash her hair when Rick located the pool. He paid scant attention to Lucia and Chica, choosing instead to stand quietly and enjoy the sight of Jennie, nude in the water. It was only when he discovered that the lookout had been lured there by the sound of their splashing that he grew angry.

"Gorgeous, aren't they?" Pablo the guard remarked to Rick as he leered at all three women lustfully from his hiding place. "Can't decide which one I like best, though. I think the new one, 'cause she's real pretty and she's not as fat as Chica or as skinny as Lucia."

"Sorry," he said easily, disguising his fury at finding the bandit ogling Jennie. "She's mine." Then with a coldness in his tone, he added, "Now, do you think I should tell Malo that you were not on guard when you were supposed to be?"

Pablo turned reluctantly away from the view of the naked women and grudgingly went back to his post.

At the sound of the men's voices, Jennie slid as low as she possibly could in the water and nervously crossed her arms across her breasts. Lucia and Chica, recognizing one of the voices as Cazador's, stood up and proudly displayed themselves, laughing at Jennie's modesty.

"What are you afraid of?" Lucia chided. "In another few weeks when Cazador is finished with you, all the men in camp will not only have seen you, they'll have had you."

Before Jennie could retort, Rick appeared at the side of the pool. "Get out, Jennie," he ordered curtly, torn between anger that the guard had seen her and relief that he hadn't attempted to take her.

Hurrying as best she could on the slippery rock, she climbed from the water and snatched up the white, peasant-style blouse Chica had loaned her and the full, brightly colored skirt. Pulling them on under Rick's dispassionate regard, she finally stood before him, clothed.

Rick's expression grew thunderous as he stared at her. The wide-necked blouse was too big and slipped seductively off one shoulder to reveal the beginning swell of her breast; the skirt billowed around her slim waist and beneath its mid-calf length, her slim ankles and feet were bare; her hair was wet and shining, hanging down her back in a silken cascade. To Rick, she looked the wanton, sexually aware and ready for a man, and his body instinctively hardened at the thought.

He had wanted her to go unnoticed in camp, but he knew now that it would be impossible. She was too beautiful for the men to ignore her. Fighting down the desire to pull her into his arms, he was suddenly irritated that she'd managed to distract him again from his main objective. His tone was gruff when he spoke. "Get your things. We're going back to camp."

Jennie blinked in surprise at his curt command and then quickly gathered her clean clothing, worrying all the while about what she had done to incur his wrath. She was unaware of the sensual aspect of her dress. To her, it was an aggravation to have to keep pulling the top back up, and she wondered why Cazador was scowling at her so fiercely.

Making her way ahead of him along the rocky path on the way to the cave's entrance, her heart contracted painfully when she heard Lucia call out in invitation.

"Cazador? Do you have to go with her?"

For the first time in her life, Jennie knew what it meant to be jealous. She was very much aware of just how much the other women really wanted him, and she was furious when he answered them easily. Had she been able she would have stomped on ahead of him, but being barefoot she had to be satisfied with gritting her teeth and picking up her pace.

"Malo will be looking for me." He gestured in friendly helplessness while Jennie seethed in silence behind him.

"Maybe later," Lucia responded, flirting with him brazenly, and she watched in disappointment as Cazador turned and once again began to follow Jennie up the path.

Chica looked at Lucia with open amusement.

"What's so funny?" Lucia demanded hotly.

"I've never known you to chase a man before." She smiled.

"I've never felt this way about a man before," Lucia admitted to her friend. "Cazador—he is special."

"He's very special," Chica answered, thinking of his strong physique and handsome features. "But he has eyes only for the gringo and while he has her he will have no need for us."

Chica waded from the pool and began to dress, leaving Lucia standing alone in the chilling waters.

"We will just have to see how long she can hold his interest," she remarked, feeling challenged rather than rejected by his refusal. And she walked slowly from the basin, contemplating the best ways to attract him.

Jennie turned angrily to face Cazador, once she was sure that they were out of sight. "Why did you do that? I've never been so humiliated in my life."

"Humiliated? Because I came to get you?"

"Came to get me? Is that what you call it? You embarrassed me!"

"I don't know why." He shrugged. "They will only think that I want you."

"But—" She sputtered furious at his indifference.

"But nothing." Rick grew suddenly impatient with her childishness. "I want you in my sight at all times."

"Me and Lucia and Chica, too!" Jennie responded heatedly. "You certainly had us in your sights tonight!"

She turned and started to walk away from him, but Rick reached out and grabbed her by her arm, pulling her viciously back against him.

"I wasn't the only one watching you, Jennie," he growled, giving her a little shake for emphasis.

"What?" Jennie was suddenly horrified.

"I said, I wasn't the only one watching you. Didn't you hear me talking to someone else before you saw me?"

"Yes, I did hear voices, but—"

"The other voice belonged to the guard who was so busy watching you that he forgot to do his job. Would you like to hear what he had to say?" Rick said, wanting to impress her with the other man's crudity. "He liked you best and—"

"No!" She gasped in disgust.

"You're very lucky that I came for you when I did. He might have decided to take you by force."

"But you told me to stay with the women," Jennie said miserably, hating to admit that he was right; hating to think that another man had seen her unclothed. "And when Chica suggested that we bathe and wash our clothes, I thought it was a good idea." The loose blouse slipped off her shoulder again and she wearily tugged it back up.

Rick felt his anger dissipate before her defeat. "You've got to remember where you are and who you're with," he lectured sternly.

"Who am I with?" She raised her dark searching eyes to his shuttered green ones. "What are you doing here? You said it wasn't the gold. Then why?"

"I don't owe you any explanations," he replied cuttingly, releasing her. "Be satisfied that I'm willing to protect you. Now, let's go inside and get to bed. It's been a very long day."

Effectively silenced by his dismissal of her questions, Jennie moved ahead of him and entered the cave.

The light from the fire's flickering flames projected eerie, distorted shadows on the damp, curving walls, giving an almost palpable air of unreality to the scene in camp. The revelry among the men had died down, and only a few hardy souls remained awake, still drinking their tequila.

"Found your woman, eh Cazador?" Malo leered, drinking greedily from his bottle as he staggered toward them.

"I hadn't lost her," he replied coolly, knowing how dangerous some men became when they were drunk. With an easy move, Rick slid his arm about Jennie's waist, pinning her to his side possessively, as his other hand, hovered imperceptively over his sidearm.

"She is pretty." Malo stopped before Jennie and reached out to stroke the long dampness of her hair as his black eyes visually stripped her. "You took a bath?"

"Yes," she answered, knowing that he would respect bravado more than cowardice. "With Lucia and Chica."

"Ah, my little Lucia is bathing now? Chica, too?" His face lit up at the thought. "I think I will go and try to find them."

Rick breathed easier as Malo headed weavingly from the cave in search of the other women, and Jennie shivered at the thought of what would have happened if Malo had been the one to discover them at the pool.

"I'm sorry, I didn't think there'd be any danger if I stayed with the others" she whispered to Rick as they walked together to his bedroll.

But rather than soothing her, Rick only grunted indifferently and began to spread out their blanket. When he'd arranged it as comfortably as possible, he started to go through his saddlebags.

"Here," he said, handing her a comb.

Appreciating his gesture, but knowing better than to remark on it, she sat down beside him on the blanket and began to work the tangles from her long tresses. Rick sat back, watching as she efficiently combed the snarls out of her hair. Mesmerized, he couldn't stop himself from reaching out and caressing its wet silken length when she'd finished.

"It's gorgeous," he murmured.

"Thank you." Jennie was pleased with his compliment.

"Do you think I should braid it? Lucia mentioned that we were going to be riding out tomorrow and—"

"What else did she tell you?" he asked, suddenly suspicious of what she might have heard.

Jennie frowned at his sharpness. "Not much, really, just about Malo's plan to make Juan Peralta lead them to the gold mine."

"Oh."

"They'll let him go once they find the mine, won't they?" She said, glancing over to where the old man lay, unmoving, on his blanket.

"Malo won't want anyone left alive who could possibly take the treasure away from him. He will kill him at the first opportunity," Rick told her bluntly, and he watched as her eyes widened in tortured acknowledgment. "Now, go ahead and braid your hair. You'll be cooler tomorrow with it off your neck."

He watched with interest as she parted the heavy mass and quickly began to plait it into a single length. Taking a rawhide strip from his saddlebags, he waited until she'd finished and then gestured for her to turn her back to him as he efficiently tied the braid.

"Thank you." She smiled over her shoulder at him as the blouse once more slipped low.

Rick swallowed with some difficulty and stifled a groan at the innocently seductive look she gave him.

"I want you to sleep between me and the wall," he said, shifting positions to let her climb to the other side.

As Jennie stepped over him, he caught a glimpse of her long, slender legs and had to resist the urge to pull her down to him. When she had settled in beside him, he drew his revolver and checked the chamber to make sure it was loaded before reholstering it.

"Good night," she whispered as he stretched out on the hard ground beside her and drew the blanket over them.

"Good night, Jennie," he responded distractedly as he

glanced one last time in Juan's direction. Then, tilting his hat over his face, he crossed his arms behind his head and sighed heavily.

Curling on her side, she lay a hair's breadth away from him, longing to be in the security of his arms yet afraid of what he'd say if she reached out to touch him. Filled with thoughts of their afternoon of love in the abandoned mine, Jennie closed her eyes and was soon fast asleep.

"Are you ready to go back now?" Lucia asked Chica as they finished washing the last of their clothing.

"Yes. I just hope the men are all asleep when we get there."

"Ah, but I heard them talking earlier. They were all hot for you tonight."

"Too much tequila has put out many a fire," Chica retorted, laughing. "What about you? Malo has been drinking all day."

"You doubt my abilities, Chica? You, of all women, should remember how good I am—" His voice boomed from the top of the rise, and both women turned in surprise to find Malo watching them, his gaze on Chica contemptuously.

"I wasn't doubting you." She hurried to correct her mistake, but it was too late.

Malo strode toward her, his eyes glistening with a frightening mixture of anger and lust. "I think I will prove to you just how capable I am." Savagely grabbing Chica by her hair, he jerked her to him and stared down at her wide-eyed terror scornfully. "You do well to fear me and when I am done with you, you will never forget again."

His mouth descended to hers in a brutal kiss, his tongue raping her mouth. Chica instinctively fought against his violence and tried to twist free, but Malo held her fast, chuckling evilly.

"You want to fight me?" And he laughed as he took another drink from his bottle. "You will lose, Chica."

Reaching within her blouse, he kneaded her heavy breasts with hurtful fingers, pinching and pulling at her sensitive nipples until they hardened in protest.

"I will not fight you, Malo," she whispered, her voice thick with fear as he pushed her blouse off her shoulders to expose her bosom.

"I know." He grinned at her, downing the last of his liquor and tossing the bottle carelessly aside to shatter against the rocks. "Undress, Chica." He folded his arms across his chest as she hurried to please him. "You are getting old and fat and slow," Malo said cruelly as he stared at her plump body. "But I will take you just the same."

Lucia had stood motionlessly through their entire exchange, but when he moved toward Chica, violence obvious in his intent, she hurried to help her friend.

"Malo." Lucia kept her voice a soft purr, hoping to distract him from his purpose.

"What?" he snarled, irritated at being interrupted.

With measured tread, she approached him, her hips swaying seductively. "Malo, I'm jealous. Do you find Chica more desirable then me?" Standing before him, she brazenly met his gaze, thinking he would choose her over Chica.

But his mood was too vicious for even such a sensuous ploy. He was not planning on making love to Chica; he was planning on teaching her a lesson. Making a grab for Chica, he roughly shoved Lucia out of his way, sending her sprawling into the dirt. Knowing that she was helpless to do any more, Lucia was forced to watch as he viciously slapped Chica and then hauled her up tightly against him.

Chica knew that it would be useless to fight Malo. Though he was not a big man, he was strong and it would be a simple matter for him to overpower her. Submitting to his degrading touch without protest, she remained passive in his embrace, hoping that her quiescence would soothe his anger.

But Malo found her submissiveness stimulating, and her

lack of reaction to his savagery only encouraged him more. Forcing Chica to the ground, he freed himself from his pants and fell upon her, seeking her depths and grinding mercilessly into her unwilling flesh. His movements were frenzied as he sought his own release. The sense of having conquered her excited him to climax almost immediately.

When Malo rolled away from her, Chica felt grateful to still be alive. She had known him to kill for less provocation, and she hoped that the storm of his fury was over.

"Lucia!" Malo barked sharply, startling both women, and Lucia hurried to him.

"Yes, Malo?"

"Where's the soap? I want to take a bath," he declared drunkenly as he sat up and began to pull off his clothes. "In fact," he said, leering, "I want you to wash me."

As Lucia went to get the soap, Malo staggered to his feet and splashed into the pool, cursing aloud as the icy water sent sobering chills through him.

"Hurry, woman, before I freeze to death!" he grumbled, losing his footing and sitting down heavily in the knee-deep basin.

Lucia undressed quickly and then went to him with the soap. At his instruction, she began to wash him.

"Where's Chica?" Malo glanced over to where he'd left her.

"I am here, Malo," she answered from the security of the shadows of the night.

"Come here and help Lucia with my bath and be quick about it. I don't want to stay in this water too long."

He was pleased when Chica responded to his order right away. Wading into the pool, she began to scrub his back while Lucia soaped his chest and shoulders.

Malo looked up at Lucia, her breasts so temptingly within reach, and he pulled her down onto his lap, fondling her with undisguised excitement. "Did you think I wouldn't be man enough for the both of you?" he asked, a reflection of his earlier fury in his tone.

"I had hoped you would be," she told him admiringly. "And I was right." Slipping her hand between their bodies, she boldly caressed his engorged manhood.

Grasping her hips, he guided her onto him and held her immobile for a moment so he could enjoy the heat of her body surrounding him. Hungrily, he began to thrust within her, not even noticing when Chica scurried away from the scene of their mating and back into the night's concealing darkness.

Eager to be done with him, Lucia employed all the tricks she'd ever learned to hurry him to completion. And she went well rewarded for her efforts for Malo almost immediately lost himself in the splendor of her lithe body and collapsed against her breast, shuddering in the throes of his own ecstasy.

Long moments passed before Malo recovered enough to put her from him and stagger from the pool. Dressing, he smiled arrogantly to himself. The stupid sluts had thought that he would be incapable! Hah! He'd certainly shown them. Malo was most pleased with his own performance and knew that he would enjoy telling the others of his exploits.

As Lucia stepped from the water and dressed, Malo eyed her coldly. Now that he knew how they had talked about him in private, he would feel no remorse in letting the other men have her, too.

Though they were feeling humiliated and abused from Malo's self-gratifying gropings, the women knew from past experience that it was best to remain silent for now, for his temper had a hairtrigger, and they didn't want to risk incurring his wrath any further. Following him meekly, they returned to the camp.

Malo was more than happy with the way the day had gone. The last of the men had arrived; tomorrow they would begin the last leg of their journey to the gold mine; and he'd just proven to Chica and Lucia just how adept he really was, tequila or no tequila! He hadn't felt this good in ages.

Getting a new bottle of tequila from one of the guards, he swigged the liquor thirstily as he boisterously proclaimed his prowess in having taken both women in such a short period of time. But finally, the tequila began to take its toll and, as Lucia and Chica sought their pallets, Malo passed out cold.

Chica fell asleep quickly, exhausted by her fear and degradation, but Lucia could not rest. She knew that Malo was angry with her, and she worried about what he would do to her when he awoke. Until now, her life as his woman had been fairly comfortable, but Malo could end it all at anytime and turn her over to the men for their plaything. Lucia shuddered at the thought and desperately tried to come up with a way to please him and win back his favor. But much soul-searching revealed nothing. Malo was not a man who enjoyed woman. He used them as long as they suited his purpose and then he discarded them without a thought. Disheartened, she lay back, fearful of what the morning might bring because he did not forget things that happened while he was drunk. Tonight he had not only heard her discussing him but also heard that she had tried to prevent him from harming Chica and, in his eyes, that would be unforgivable.

Chapter Twelve

Rick appeared to be sleeping, but in reality he was wide awake and very restless. The feel of Jennie nestled so trustingly against him was driving him mad, and he wondered how he was going to make it through the night without making love to her. The memory of their time alone together was playing through his mind and the thought of making her his, once again, had rekindled the embers of desire he'd fought so hard to subdue.

Determined to maintain some semblance of control over his desires, Rick pushed his hat back and rolled to his side to look around the cave. Everything seemed settled. The only people awake were the guards: one with Juan and the other by the front entrance. Moving slowly from their pallet, he headed outside into the coolness of the night air. Nodding briefly to the lookout, he wandered outdoors and breathed deeply of the late evening's sweetness.

Thoughts of the past few days kept flashing through his mind as he made his way quietly across the rock-strewn countryside. How had he ever gotten himself into such a situation? It had all seemed so simple when he'd left El Rancho Grando; he would infiltrate the gang, discover their weaknesses and then exploit the situation to free Juan. So simple.

And then Jennie. He shook his head as he thought of her—fighting off Luis and Ray, trying to escape from him, falling from the rocks at the waterhole and then saving him this afternoon during the flashflood. She was beautiful and brave and everything a man could possibly want in a woman. And, Rick acknowledged reluctantly to himself, he did want her. He remembered her passionate response to his lovemaking, and he knew what they had shared had been special, for he became roused, even now at the memory.

The prospect of a cold bath became suddenly very appealing to Rick as he strove to push the stimulating musings from his mind, and he strode in the direction of the pool, confident that a few minutes in the frigid water would solve most of his manly problems. Topping the rise, he made his way to the side of the water and sat down to pull off his boots. Unbuckling his gunbelt, he placed it carefully near the water's edge and then stripped quickly and waded out into the shallow basin.

Lucia had been tossing uncomfortably on her thin blanket when she'd seen Cazador quietly leave the cave. Her eyes followed his progress as he disappeared into the darkness. She had never wanted a man the way she wanted Cazador, and a slow heat began to burn within her as she imagined her body joining with his.

Feeling certain that Malo was going to reject her in the morning, she could see no reason to deny herself one night of passion in the arms of a man she desired. Slipping from her bed, she trailed after him, knowing that the guards would not dare question her motives.

Once she was away from the camp, she darted quickly among the rocks, hoping to catch sight of Cazador, but he seemed to have vanished completely. Pausing, much like an animal at hunt, she waited, breathlessly listening for some sound that would indicate in which direction he'd gone, but the night was silent, revealing none of its secrets. Impatiently then she began to prowl among the rocks and bushes, searching for the tall handsome gunman she wanted so badly, but she found no trace of him. Frustrated and about to give up, Lucia decided to look by the pool and it was there that she discovered him.

Lucia gasped at the sight of him as he stood with his back to her, sleek and sinewy. Bathed in the palest of moonlight, he seemed to her a magnificent warrior, with his broad shoulders and narrow hips. His long legs were well muscled and straight, and she longed to know the feel of his hardened thighs thrusting against hers.

A clamoring, throbbing ache grew within her and she knew she had to have him. Wetting her lips in excited anticipation, she boldly approached the water's edge, eager to see more of his masculine physique.

"You couldn't sleep either?" she asked, her voice low and husky, and she was totally unnerved when she found herself looking down the barrel of his cocked gun. "Wait," she sputtered.

"What do you want?" Rick demanded, glaring at her coldly for a long minute before he pointed the revolver away from her and smoothly released the hammer.

"I—uh." Lucia had known that Cazador was good with a gun, but she'd had no idea just how good. "I couldn't rest and when I saw you leave, I thought you might enjoy some company." Her words were hurried as she sought to reassure him of her intentions.

Rick was in no mood to deal with an aggressive woman right now, but he also didn't want to risk alienating Lucia for he knew that in the future she might be able to help them escape.

"What about Malo?"

"Pah! Malo is—" Bitterly, Lucia had started to speak what was in her heart. But as she began, she suddenly realized that it would not be wise. "What he does not know . . ." Her tone was suggestive.

"Ah, but Lucia. It is my understanding that Malo knows

everything that goes on in his camp." Rick started to walk toward the bank, seemingly unconcerned about his nude state.

Lucia's eyes widened as his movements drew her attention away from his gun and back to his body. He was as splendid as she'd hoped, and her eyes roamed over him greedily, enjoying the sight of his massive, hair-roughened chest and the revealing display of his masculinity. How she longed to touch him and caress him to hardness.

"There is no one here but you and me and I certainly would not tell." She smiled provocatively and walked toward him.

Sliding his gun back into its holster, Rick looked up to find her within arm's reach.

"Do you not find me attractive, Cazador?" she whispered throatily, thrusting her bosom out in a tantalizing gesture.

Lucia reminded Rick of a cat, sinuous and supple, yet possessing very dangerous claws that were kept carefully hidden. "You are a very beautiful woman, Lucia. But I find loyalty an even more attractive quality." He began to pull on his pants, much to her distress.

"Cazador." She reached out and touched his arm, loving the feel of his warm male flesh beneath her fingers. "I would be loyal *to you*."

Rick looked at her calmly as she leaned toward him, her blouse gaping open and giving him a full view of her breasts. At another time, in another place he might have taken her up on her blatant offer, but tonight, immersed in dreams of Jennie and her sweetness, Lucia's brazen ploy left him cold. He knew she was his for the taking and yet he felt no desire for her. Even the sight of her bared bosom left him oddly unmoved.

"I already have one woman, Lucia. What would I do with two?" Rick tried to lighten their conversation, but she was too much in earnest to be dismissed so easily.

"Malo has enjoyed having two of us," she said, hating what Malo had done to her and Chica, and yet wanting

160

Cazador at any price.

"I am not Malo." His voice was icy.

"I know and that is why I want you." She tried to put her arms about him, but he stopped her.

"I'm sorry, Lucia." His answer was final as he finished dressing.

"Some day you will need me, Cazador. You will see," she said haughtily as she turned from him and hurried away.

Rick watched her go, discomfitted by the complex situation he now found himself in. By refusing her advances, he had lost a possible ally, and yet at the same time he had preserved his place in Malo's confidences. Had the trade-off been worth it? He wasn't sure and he knew that only time would tell.

When he had finished dressing, he strapped on his gunbelt and walked slowly back to the campsite, hoping to get at least a few hours' rest before dawn.

Jennie had stirred and come awake quickly only to discover that Cazador had gone from her side. Fearful that she would attract unwanted attention to herself, Jennie lay huddled under the blanket as she glanced quickly around the camp, trying to catch sight of him. There was no sign of Cazador anywhere, and she wondered what could have drawn him away. Keeping her eyes fixed on the cavern's entrance, she waited, worrying that he might be in some kind of danger.

The sight of Lucia who came in from the darkness, flushed and out of breath, took Jennie by surprise. She had seen Malo asleep on his own bedroll and had assumed that Chica and Lucia were both bedded down, too. Watching as the other woman strode confidently across the camp and climbed beneath her own covers, Jennie wondered what she had been doing outside, alone, at this time of night.

It wasn't until Cazador's return, just moments afterward,

that a great fear was born inside of her. Had they been together? Had Cazador found Lucia's dark, slender beauty irresistible? Had he just shared with her the same excitement they had given each other that afternoon? A pain seared within her breast as her mind conjured up images of Cazador and Lucia in a torrid embrace.

Filled with agonizing doubts about this late night rendezvous with Lucia, Jennie pretended to be asleep, and she was glad when Cazador made no move to take her in his arms as he slipped beneath the blanket beside her. She remembered once again his appeal to her to trust him, but he had been asking for her trust with regard to her safety—not her heart. Curling more tightly into herself, she longed for sleep to help her escape from her troubled imaginings.

As he stretched out next to Jennie once again, Rick lay slightly at a distance, taking care not to awaken her. Gazing over at her in the dimness of the campfire light, he was taken once again by the freshness of her beauty, and he was glad now that he'd refused to be drawn into Lucia's intrigue, tempting though the other woman may have been. Settling in, he folded his arms behind his head and once again, sought elusive slumber.

From across the campsite, Lucia covertly observed his movements as he reentered the cave and went to lay down with Jennie. She wondered how the other woman could sleep beside him and not want to make love to him. If he were hers, Lucia knew that she would want him all the time and in every possible way.

All worries about Malo fled her mind as her desire for Cazador became an obsession to her. Lucia knew now that the only way she would have a chance to win him would be to eliminate Jennie as a rival for his attentions. Surely if Jennie were gone, he would come to her because he had not said that he didn't want her, only that he already had a woman.

Lucia knew now what she had to do. Beginning tomorrow, she would do everything in her power to get rid of Jennie. Sighing contentedly, she rolled to her side and began to plan.

Juan lay sleeplessly on his blanket. He was alternately excited at the prospect of being rescued and frightened that Malo might, at any minute, discover who Rick really was.

Tossing uncomfortably on the hard ground, Juan shifted positions and stared out across the campsite. He shuddered as he remembered his darkest hours the day before when he would have welcomed death as a release from Malo's torturous ways. But now that he knew Rick was alive, his desire to live had been rekindled. There was hope.

Juan knew that he would do anything he had to do to survive, and he hoped that he would have a chance to speak with Rick soon, so that he could find out exactly what his plans were. Focusing his gaze on the low burning embers of the fire, he let himself drift, his spirit renewed, and soon he was sound asleep.

Some distance away in the McCaine camp at the mouth of Willow Canyon, a sense of savage frustration ran rampant among the searchers. Sitting restlessly around the campfire, the men were furious at having been thwarted by the storm whose powerful rains had scoured the landscape of all traces of the desperadoes' trail. Even Steve, whose tracking skills were incomparable, had failed to turn up a lead as to the direction the outlaws had taken.

"Steve." Mac's voice was edged with nervous tension.

"Yeah, Mac." Steve had been standing slightly apart from the others, and he drew closer at his boss's call.

"If you were going to guess, where would you say they went? Up the canyon?" Mac needed a sense of direction—purpose. The possibility that he might have lost Jennie forever due to a whim of nature left him filled with bitter rage. He would not give up! He would search for her until his dying day. Never would he abandon her to a fate at the hands of the mercenary outlaws.

"I think so. We'll start checking up there first thing in the morning. They had to have holed up during the rain, so when we finally do find their trail, it should be reasonably fresh."

"They're not going to make too much headway on this kind of terrain," Jake put in.

"No, it'll be slow for them and slow for us," Mac said.

"There are two things we do have to worry about. One is an ambush. These mountains are perfect for hiding out, and if they've got a good vantage point, it would be easy for them to pick us off," Steve said, feeling the unspoken threat in the Superstitions' craggy, looming presence.

"And the other?" Carrie asked, curious.

"The Apache." Steve voiced what the other men already knew. "I haven't seen any sign of them yet, but that doesn't mean they're not out there."

Carrie nodded. She knew well the dangers of the Indians because Mac had been fighting them off and on for years.

Vicious, nomadic killers, the Apache roamed the Southwest, preying upon all who were weaker than they were, Indians or whites alike. So far, Mac had always managed to be the stronger in all of their confrontations and had won from them a grudging respect. That, coupled with the presence of the cavalry, had saved the M Circle C from destruction on several occasions.

An uneasy silence fell over the group as they contemplated the results of a possible run-in with a band of marauding Apache, and the men checked their sidearms as they made ready to turn in for the night.

Carrie rose to say her good nights and was offhandedly waved away by Mac, who was deep in discussion with Steve, Jake, and Todd. Only Todd responded with any warmth to her words, smiling up at her quickly before Mac demanded his attention once again. Her father's treatment of her only added to the total frustration she was feeling concerning the entire day, and she went on off to bed wishing that this ordeal were over and done with.

Climbing beneath her blankets, Carrie lay unmoving, her thoughts dwelling on the time she'd had alone with Todd during the storm and the heated remembrance of his body pressed to hers. She had just fallen asleep when the warmth of Todd's hand on her shoulder woke her.

"Carrie? I'm sorry, I didn't think you were asleep yet."

"That's all right. What's wrong?" Carrie was instantly alert, fearing trouble.

"Nothing's wrong," he told her quickly. "I just wanted to make sure you were feeling all right. That was quite a fall you took this afternoon. How's the cut on your forehead?" Todd had a great desire to brush back the sweep of blond hair that covered her injury, but he refrained.

Carrie's hand immediately went to the sore spot on her brow. "Fine, I think. It's hard to tell without a mirror, but I know it's not bleeding or anything."

"Shall I take a look?" he asked.

"Please." Her tone was soft and seductive, but Todd seemed not to notice as he gently examined her injury.

"You're right. It does look much better. There won't even be a scar."

"Good." She grinned up at him, her eyes filled with longing.

Todd stared down at her for a long moment, realizing that Carrie couldn't possibly know how beautiful she looked, lying before him so fragile and seemingly helpless. Shaking himself mentally, he moved slightly away.

"Well, get some sleep. We'll be heading out at dawn again tomorrow." He stood up and started off to his own bedroll across the campsite from hers.

"Todd?" she called softly, not wanting anyone else to witness their exchange, and he turned to look back questioningly. "Thank you."

He flashed her a quick smile and then went on to bed, himself.

The next two hours passed in slow motion for Carrie as she dwelled on the tenderness of Todd's touch on her forehead. He cared! He had to or he wouldn't have bothered to check on her.

Tossing fitfully on the thin comfort of her bedroll, Carrie finally gave up the struggle to rest. Glancing around she found that everyone was asleep, save the lookout who was posted at the vulnerable side of their campsite. Getting up, she wandered in the opposite direction of the guard, wanting to be alone with her thoughts so that she could plan on how to further attract Todd. Carrie didn't notice that Steve came awake as she moved about the encampment, and his eyes followed her avidly as she disappeared into the surrounding shadows.

Steve was glad that he'd placed his bedroll away from the tight confines of the inner circle of men around the fire. He had hoped for just such an opportunity to be with Carrie, and he rose from his bed to follow her, his body eagerly anticipating her embrace.

"Carrie?" He spoke quietly as he came upon her, some distance from the others.

Startled by his unexpected appearance, she jumped at the sound of his voice. "Steve?" she croaked nervously as she hurriedly turned to face him.

"Weren't you expecting me?" he asked, leering at her with the look of a man who knows exactly what he wants and intends to get it.

"Uh—no, actually." Carrie answered quickly. She had meant to tell him that what had happened between them had been a mistake, but she hadn't quite prepared herself yet for the confrontation. She had hoped to put it off as long as possible.

"Come on, Carrie, You know you've been wanting me all day, just like I've been wanting you." He took her by the

166

upper arm and turned her to face him. "C'mon, baby. I've been needing this since morning."

His mouth swooped down on hers, crushing her lips beneath his in a passionate assault. When he felt the resistance in her, he pulled her closer to him and moved suggestively against her body.

"Steve!" she gasped when he released her mouth briefly. "Steve! Don't!"

Suddenly the touch of his hands upon her caused her to recoil, and she wanted nothing more than to be free of his embrace. But Steve was single-minded in his purpose, and he began to caress her, ignoring her protests.

"You know you like this. Last night you couldn't wait for me," he growled, not paying any attention even as her struggles became real.

"Stop it, right now! I don't want this!" Carrie was careful to keep her voice low for she was worried about what her father would do if he found her in this compromising situation.

Finally, as Steve began to fondle her intimately, Carrie lost her temper and kicked out at him with all her might.

"Damn you, you little—" he started to say as her foot connected with his shin, but he never got to finish his sentence for suddenly Todd was looming over them both, his gun drawn, his face set.

Struggling to catch her breath, she staggered as Steve released her, her eyes filling with tears of mortification.

"Carrie, are you all right? I thought I heard trouble." Todd's expression was wooden as his gaze swung from Carrie's flushed face to Steve's livid one.

"I am now, Todd." She was breathing heavily as she stepped closer to his protective strength.

"Steve? Is there some kind of problem?" Todd asked, holstering his gun.

For a moment Carrie knew real fear as she waited to hear Steve's comment for she was terrified that he would reveal all

167

to Todd, but he only shrugged as he turned to walk away.

"No. No problem. Just a little misunderstanding."

Carrie watched him go, her relief obvious. "Oh, Todd. I don't know how to thank you—"

"You can thank me by never putting yourself in such a compromising position again," he said, his tone a curious mixture of censor and concern.

Hastening to convince him of her innocence, she told him, "But I only came out here to think. I was so worried about everything that I couldn't sleep."

"Men don't always understand why women do the things they do," he said gently. "No telling what Steve thought when he saw that you were out here all alone."

"I won't do it again," Carrie said.

"Good. Now let's get on back and get some sleep." He started to turn back to camp.

"I'm so upset, I just don't know if I can yet." Carrie hoped that her tone sounded helpless and confused. "What if Steve's angry with me or—"

"If you're worried about Steve, why don't you just bring you bedroll over near me. I don't think he'll cause you any more trouble, but just in case."

"Do you mean it? You wouldn't mind?" She brightened at the possibilities sleeping next to him.

"No. I wouldn't mind." Todd smiled at her. "Come on, let's go."

With a guiding hand at her waist, he directed her back toward the encampment, glad that Mac and Jake were asleep and had not witnessed Carrie's latest escapade. Picking up her blankets for her, he spread them out next to his own, his movements stiff as he favored his wounded shoulder.

"There. Now try to get some rest." He sat down awkwardly on his own pallet.

"Todd— Are you all right? Your shoulder—?"

"I'm fine. I just need to lie down for a while. Go to sleep, Carrie." He dismissed her interest quickly.

"You're sure?"

"Good night, Carrie." And his words were spoken with such finality as he rolled over away from her that she hurriedly lay down and pulled the blanket over her shoulder.

Stretched out so close to Todd, she could feel his body heat, and she thought once more of their kiss that afternoon during the storm. It had been so perfect, even under such adverse conditions, and she could just imagine how wonderful it would be to know the full extent of his love and passion. Someday, she promised herself, she would be the woman he wanted above all others.

Todd lay stiffly at Carrie's side, his back to her. He didn't know what was wrong, but his shoulder had suddenly started to throb. Trying to ease the ache, he changed position a little, but there was no lessening of the pain. He knew he should probably have her take a look at it, but he didn't trust himself to let her touch him. The embrace they had shared earlier had been more than enough to convince him of her womanhood, and seeing her just now with Steve—It had taken all of his will power not to knock Steve down. Carrie was such a trusting young woman. She needed someone to look after her and keep her out of trouble. Todd sighed, wondering why he was even concerning himself with her, for after all, Jennie was the woman he loved; the woman he wanted to spend the rest of his life with. Wasn't she?

Shifting his weight onto his back, Todd threw a forearm across his eyes and had to grit his teeth as the piercing pain stabbed through his shoulder again. Breathing deeply, he forced himself to relax, and then he reached quietly for his saddlebags, taking out the small bottle of whiskey he kept there. Unscrewing the top, he levered himself up on his uninjured arm and drank deeply of the potent liquor. As he felt the heat of it burn through him, he hoped that its

169

powerful pain-killing effect would soon relieve his discomfort for he intended to be ready to ride out first thing in the morning with the rest of the men. Determined that there was nothing wrong with him that a few hours' sleep wouldn't cure, he took another big swig and then lay back and closed his eyes, waiting impatiently for the rest that wouldn't come.

Chapter Thirteen

Stained red, as if it had survived some bloody conflict, the eastern horizon yielded to the dawn's first light. Only a few benign white clouds dotted the deep blue expanse of the morning sky, and the bright blooming of desert flowers was the sole reminder of the previous day's tempest.

Lucia awoke. Her first thoughts were of Cazador and how glorious he'd looked when he'd stepped naked from the pool last night. Stretching sensuously, she imagined how exciting it would be to know his passion, and once again the desire she felt for him stirred to life. Unable to stop herself, she glanced in his direction, longing to gaze at him unobserved, but the sight of Cazador, sound asleep, with Jennie held close in his arms, upset her. Jealous fury seized Lucia as she stared at them: the blanket twisted sinuously about their hips, their limbs intimately intertwined. Swearing angrily to herself, she quickly got up and went outside, needing to be away from the sight of the other woman in his embrace.

Lucia's movements through the camp roused Chica and, curious as to her friend's activities, she followed her from the cave.

"Why are you up so early?" Chica asked as she caught up with Lucia.

"I couldn't sleep any longer." Lucia's shrug was expressive. "And I was thinking about Cazador."

"You know that's useless, don't you? Did you see how he was sleeping with her?" she chided.

"I saw," she admitted sullenly. "But it won't last forever. One day, when she's gone—"

"Gone? Where would she go? Obviously, she wants to be here with him and I can't blame her." Chica sighed, thinking of how handsome Cazador was.

"Chica." Lucia faced her friend, her tone almost desperate. "I want him so badly—I've never felt this way before. Will you help me? There's got to be something I can do to attract him."

"I don't think so, not while Jennie's around." Chica paused. "And what about Malo?"

"After last night, do you really think he's going to care what I do?"

"Maybe he will go easy on you. After all, I was the one talking about him and I think I paid the price for that mistake last night. I am still sore."

"I'm sorry. I wish there had been more I could do for you, but—"

"No, don't worry. You helped all you could and I appreciate it. That's why I will try to help you with Cazador, but I'm not sure what we can do."

"I've a few ideas," Lucia began hopefully.

"Like what?"

"First, I could try to make her jealous."

"I don't know that it's possible. The man doesn't even look at us the same way he looks at her."

"What if we just dropped hints suggesting that something was happening between him and me? Do you suppose she'd believe it?"

"There's always a chance," Chica answered. "But so what if she does believe it? What's she going to do? Take another man? There is no one else here who even comes close to being like him."

"No, but I think if we made her life miserable enough, she might change her mind about going home to her father. Surely, we'd be able to find her a horse and help her to get away."

"All we can do is try, but if Jennie is as crazy about him as I think she is, she may not fall for it."

"If that doesn't work, I'll just try to think of something else. And who knows? Maybe he'll grow tired of her in the meantime and give her to the other men like he said last night." Her lips curved in a sneering smile at the thought of all the men in camp having their way with Jennie.

Chica nodded and they headed back inside to begin cooking breakfast. They knew that Malo was eager to be on his way this day, so they were determined not to give him any reason to find further fault with them.

Jennie came awake slowly, feeling decidedly warm and oddly comforted after her long, tormented hours of sleeplessness and it was only when she opened her eyes that she discovered why she was so content. There she was pressed closely to Cazador as if it were the most natural thing in the world for them to sleep together. Upset that her body would betray her and seek his, even during her much needed slumber, she tried to move away from him but as she slid her leg from between his, he stirred.

Though Rick had not fallen asleep until an hour before dawn, he was instantly alert at Jennie's slight movement. "Good morning," he murmured, smiling as his legs entrapped hers once more, and he bent to kiss her lightly.

Jennie held herself stiffly as his lips moved warmly over hers, and Rick assumed it was just because there were others present.

"I trust you slept well?"

"Yes, Did you?" Jennie blurted out, wondering how he could even think of making small talk when he'd been with Lucia last night.

"What little I got," he replied, loving the feel of her pressed

173

so sweetly to him.

"I know," she said sharply.

Rick frowned as he wondered at her mood. "Did I disturb you?"

"No, not in the least," she replied with a bit of haughtiness, unwilling to let him know how much his nocturnal visit with the other woman had hurt her. "Lucia and Chica are already up," she said. She had heard their voices by the fire and wanted to see what his reaction would be at the mention of her name.

But Rick didn't react and that left Jennie puzzled.

"What about Malo?" he asked, as he released her to look over in his direction.

"I think he's still sleeping."

Glancing to where Juan had spent the night, Rick was surprised to find his bed deserted and asked worriedly, "Where's the old man?"

"I don't know."

"You go help the women cook. I'll be back," he said thinking that this would be his opportunity to speak with Juan alone for a few minutes.

"Where are you going?" she demanded as he stood up and checked his gun.

Glancing down at her impatiently, he responded, "I don't owe you any explanations for my actions, Jennie. Somehow, you keep forgetting that." And without further discussion, he strode off out of the cave, leaving Jennie behind, angrily watching him go.

Stepping from the shelter of the cavern, Rick caught sight of Juan, his hands still bound, waiting as his guard spoke with the lookout.

"Mornin'," Rick called out as he approached.

Both guards turned quickly toward him. "Mornin'."

"Any sign of a posse yet?" he asked, letting his gaze sweep the canyon floor.

"No. It's still quiet. Just the way Malo likes it."

"There is a posse?" Juan asked excitedly, playing along with Rick.

"Shut up, old man." His guard jabbed him in the ribs with his rifle butt, doubling him over.

But the lookout only chuckled lasciviously. "Yeah, there's a posse, but they're not coming after you, Peralta. They're after Cazador's woman, but from what I can see, it seems to me that she doesn't want to be rescued. Eh, Cazador?"

"She's happy riding with me." Rick smiled widely, wanting them to believe that he was, indeed, one of them. "But even if she wasn't, it wouldn't matter. I want her, so I'll keep her."

"And we all know why." They agreed with pure male enthusiasm.

"So, the great El Cazador can't even get himself a woman? He has to kidnap one?" Juan taunted, unable to resist the opportunity.

And Rick grabbed him by the shirt front and dragged him threateningly nearer. "How I get my women is none of you concern, old man, and if you weren't taking us to the gold—"

Juan met his eyes steadily. "Ah, but until I lead you to the mine, you will not dare to lay a hand on me!"

Rick released him viciously and turned back to Malo's men. "So there's been no sign of the posse." He paused and then grinned easily. "That's good news. There'll be enough excitement when we get to the gold mine, without having them hot on our tail."

"That's for sure." The guards smiled greedily at the thought of the riches they would soon possess.

"The women have started breakfast. You want me to take him back in with me?" Rick offered, hoping they'd jump at the chance to relax from their watch for a few minutes.

"Yeah, thanks. Go on, old man." They waved Juan away and, holding his side as best he could, Juan followed Rick back toward the cave.

"Is it bad?" Rick asked when he knew they were out of earshot.

"Not too. I've had worse." He grunted. "I am so glad you are alive—"

"Alive? I was never in any danger." He looked puzzled at his grandfather's words.

"They told me that you'd been killed in the shootout at the ranch." Juan choked as he remembered the agony he'd felt when he'd thought Rick dead.

"I didn't even get back to the ranch until long after they'd gone with you," he told him bitterly.

"What are your plans? How can I help?"

"I can't do anything until we're out on the trail. Hold tight 'til then." Rick slowed his pace to accommodate Juan's painful progress. "Come on, Peralta! Let's move." Adding the curt words for effect, he took him by the arm in what looked to be a show of force but what was, in actuality, support for him.

"And the woman?" Juan looked up at him as he posed the question, and he was surprised by the mixed display of emotions that crossed Rick's face before he answered.

"We ran across her on the way in. I had to bring her along as my own to save her. The others—Luis and Ray—wanted to rape and kill her."

"Does she know about us?"

"No," he replied hurriedly. "And I intend to keep it that way."

"Good. We are safe, then." Juan breathed a sigh of relief. "Who is she?"

"Her name is Jennie McCaine. She's Mac McCaine's daughter."

"No wonder you are expecting a posse to follow you. He is a very powerful man. He will not rest until he finds her, and he will be looking for you."

"I know, I know. But I don't intend for McCaine to catch

176

up with me," Rick replied, an edge to his voice. "I know these mountains."

Juan fell silent at Rick's declaration, recalling the time he'd spent here and the circumstances, and they entered the cave without speaking again.

As soon as Cazador had disappeared outside, Jennie reluctantly got up and went to join Lucia and Chica by the cooking fire.

"Chica," Lucia said expressively. "He was wonderful! *Muy hombre!*"

Chica gurgled with knowing laughter. "I can see that for myself."

"But not as well as I did." she gloated. "And when he came out of the water—" She pretended to be surprised by Jennie's appearance. "Oh, Jennie—Good morning."

Jennie took care not to reveal her innermost feelings, but her stomach churned as she recalled that Cazador's hair had been wet when he'd returned to their bed the night before. "Good morning," she said as cheerfully as she could. "What can I do to help?"

They set to work speaking only of inconsequential things until she heard Lucia remark, "Here he comes now."

Looking up, Jennie caught sight of Cazador coming into the cave with Juan Peralta. For a moment, watching them silhouetted against the brightness of the sky, she was struck by how much alike the two men were for they both were tall and slim and carried themselves with a certain pride, but she thought no more of it when she heard Lucia's throaty whisper to Chica.

"I cannot wait until he tires of her, completely."

And the last word burned into her heart—completely. Did that mean he would take her as often as he wanted and then bed other women, too? As he no doubt had last night? The thought nauseated Jennie, but she forced herself to ignore

Lucia's comment.

"Jennie!" Cazador's call drew her attention and she looked up at him questioningly. "Bring Peralta something to eat," he instructed as he escorted the old man back to his own bedroll.

Jennie didn't bother to answer as she hurried to do his bidding.

"I'll take it over, if you don't want to," Lucia offered, eagerly.

"No. I will do it." She cut her off as she carried the bowl of hot food to where they waited.

Juan spoke softly to his grandson as they watched Jennie's approach. "I can see why you wanted no harm to befall her."

"Jennie is beautiful and brave," he answered softly so that no one else would hear.

"She has come with you this far without knowing the truth?" Juan was amazed.

"I couldn't tell her. Knowing would put her in too much danger."

"I agree, but why isn't she fighting you?"

"She did, at first. Now, I suppose she's grateful." The words rang hollowly in his mind and heart. "I did rescue her from Luis and Ray."

"And she knows the alternative to staying with you is rape or death." He nodded slightly in understanding.

"Right." Fleetingly Rick wondered if her response to his lovemaking had been real or an act of desperation.

"Well, if you want Malo to believe that she is your woman, you had better act like it. The man is astute. He will catch any flaw and know."

Rick knew what his grandfather was telling him and, though he had wanted to refrain from making love to Jennie while they were in the midst of the outlaws, he realized now that he could not avoid it.

Walking slowly toward them, Jennie couldn't help but

notice the intensity of Cazador's expression and she wondered at the cause.

"Here's your food," Rick said as she neared.

"You will need to untie me." Juan gestured helplessly.

Rick knelt down beside him and efficiently untied his hands.

"Thank you," he told him with exaggerated, sarcastic politeness, and then he turned to her to take the bowl. "And thank you, my dear."

"You're welcome," Jennie responded. "Is there anything else I can get you?"

"No. No, this is fine." He gave her a warm smile as he began to eat.

Jennie glanced up at Cazador to see if there was anything he wanted. "Would you like your breakfast now?"

"Not yet," he replied curtly. "You can go ahead and eat if you want to."

"All right," she answered as she started back to join Lucia and Chica. Jennie sensed that he was angry about something, but she had no idea what it was.

Rick watched her go, his thoughts troubled. How he wished the whole ordeal was over and they were all safely back at El Rancho Grande. Then he would be free to tell her the truth and all the problems they had would be over. Resigning himself to continued secrecy, he turned his attention back to Juan.

"If I can get a knife to you, do you have a place to hide it?" he murmured in low tones.

"Yes."

"Good, I'll try to figure something out before we leave here." As he spoke, he saw Lucia heading their way carrying two tin mugs of hot coffee.

Lucia had been pleased by Jennie's hasty return and saw the opportunity to insinuate herself into Cazador's company.

"I thought you might like some coffee." She offered them

each a cup of the steaming brew as she joined them.

Juan took the coffee and thanked her. "You have been good to me since I've been in camp here, Lucia, and I appreciate it."

Rick was surprised by his statement. He had thought Lucia to be a selfish young woman, who thought of no one but herself, and suddenly, now, he realized that there was more to her than that.

"Thank you," he said as he drank from the cup.

And Lucia smiled sweetly, touching Rick's arm in a casual gesture that she knew would look intimate to Jennie. "You're welcome. There is plenty more food."

"This is more than enough for me," Juan told her.

"Cazador?"

"I will eat later, with Malo." Rick was glad that she seemed to have no hard feelings about his rejection of her offer the night before.

"I would like to talk with you for a moment alone, if I could?" She looked up at him hopefully and, though he thought better of it, he agreed.

"I can't leave until his guard returns. It would not be safe to trust Peralta untied."

"Ramon is coming now." Lucia indicated the Mexican who was heading in their direction.

Just roused from a short, unsatisfying sleep, Ramon was hung over and not at all thrilled with having to stand guard over the decrepit old man.

"Is it your duty now, Ramon?" Lucia asked.

"Yes. You two can go on. I will watch him," he growled at Rick and Lucia, and they walked away together.

Jennie was sitting by the campfire with Chica when she saw Lucia put her hand on Cazador's arm again with comfortable familiarity. A slow burning anger flared to life as she watched them, and when he looked down at Lucia and laughed at something she said, Jennie wanted to slap them both.

Lucia was very aware of Jennie's eyes upon them and

smiled coyly at Cazador, telling him huskily, "Please—after last night, could we talk outside?" She wanted to convince him that her interest had been momentary so he would let his guard down, and she also wanted to set up a scene to make the other woman suspicious of his motives when he was with her.

Rick studied her for a moment and, sensing nothing threatening in her moves, he nodded his agreement and followed her from the cave. Lucia walked ahead of him some distance, until they were away from the prying eyes of the guard, and then turned to face him.

"I wanted to apoligize."

"There's no need—"

"No, wait, let me finish." she said quickly. "My loyalty does lie with Malo. I wanted you to understand that. And I did not want to cause any trouble for you here in camp."

He met her eyes evenly, his remembrance of Juan's words about her tender care of him during his captivity softening his feelings for her. "There has been no trouble, and you have done nothing to be sorry for."

"Thank you," she said, her tone suitably grateful. "I'd better get back inside. Malo may be up."

And she hurried from his presence, afraid that she might betray the pulsing need she felt for him. He was so handsome, and he'd been so kind. But he stayed with her, his long strides matching her quicker, shorter ones, and they reentered the cave together.

Jennie noted their return and grit her teeth in subdued fury. Why was he humiliating her this way? He had barely spoken to her this morning and yet he had time to spend, alone, with Lucia.

Lucia was smiling triumphantly as she came back to the fire, but she said nothing, allowing her expression to tell Jennie all she wanted her to know.

"Malo is up," Chica said, breaking the tense silence among them.

"I will see to him," Lucia said, sighing heavily and

181

worrying about what he would do to her this morning.

Fixing him something to eat, she carried the hot bowl of food and a mug of coffee to where he sat on his bedroll waiting for her. She approached carefully, not quite sure of her reception.

"I have brought you breakfast." She placed the food before him and waited, nervously, for his reaction.

"I want tequila. Bring me a bottle," he growled as he lifted his nearly empty bottle to his lips, draining its contents and then tossing it carelessly against the rocky cave wall where it shattered on impact.

Hurrying to get him another, she returned quickly and handed it to him. Pulling the cork out with his teeth, he drank thirstily of the liquor and then wiped his mouth with his forearm before looking at Lucia. His eyes narrowed as he remembered the night just passed, and he stared at her long and hard, making Lucia even more tense than she had been.

"What were you doing outside with Cazador?" he demanded, his eyes snaking over her.

Knowing that he had been asleep when she'd left the cave, Lucia knew it was safe to lie to him. "I wasn't with Cazador."

"You came back in at the same time," he charged.

"We were not together, Malo. Why would I want to be with him when I have you?"

"Do you?" He sneered.

And Lucia gasped as she feared the worst. "Malo, please, I would never betray you. You are the only man for me."

Grabbing her wrist in a viselike grip, he pulled her down beside him and slipped his hand within her blouse to toy with her small breasts. "You are lucky that I am feeling generous this morning, you know?"

"You are?" she whispered, fearful of what he might do next.

He jerked her to him, pushing her blouse off her shoulders. "I am," he said smoothly just before his mouth crushed down on hers in a vicious possession that left no doubts as to his mastery of her. "I find that I still want you. So, I will keep you for myself, for now."

Lucia relaxed, secure once more in her position. Raising her arms about his neck, she pressed herself tightly to him. She was not yet ready to make her next move on Cazador and until then, she had to keep Malo happy. "I will be good to you, Malo. I always have been."

But her words were met with quick anger as he grabbed her by the hair and jerked her painfully back, his black expressionless eyes burning in intensity as they roamed over her face and bared breasts. "You have no choice, do you, Lucia?"

She shivered at his coldness but didn't flinch. "But I come to you willingly. Is that not worth something?"

He snorted derisively as he pushed her down on the rough ground and, brushing her skirt aside, he rid himself of his pants and took her there, quickly and efficiently, in front of the others.

"He is an animal," Chica seethed as she turned away. She had been watching and hoping that nothing terrible would happen to Lucia this morning, and now, she knew that her friend was safe. For, if Malo had still been angry, he would not have had sex with Lucia; he would have beaten her.

Jennie, too, averted her eyes from Malo's fervid possession of Lucia's body, and she wondered how the other woman could tolerate his filthy hands upon her.

Though Rick knew that Malo's open taking of her was a common occurrence among outlaws, he was disgusted by it. Taking great care to disguise his emotions, he left the cave and sought out the best vantage point to see if there was any sight of a posse.

Juan, had he been free and in possession of a weapon, knew that he would have killed Malo at that moment. He had developed a caring for Lucia and, though he knew that it was her life, he hated to see her so used.

The other men watched avidly, though, each wishing that

183

there was enough time to vent their lust on Chica.

Lucia lay beneath Malo's pounding body, grateful that he hadn't hit her. She knew from past experience that he would not take long this morning and as soon as he was finished, she would be able to resume her old routine, unafraid of his wrath.

Thinking only of his own gratification, Malo climaxed and then slowly moved off of Lucia's submissive body. Straightening his pants, he shifted away from her and took another drink of his tequila. Lucia sat up and, after pushing down her skirt, she stood up.

"What do you want me to do this morning?"

"Start packing. I want to be on the trail by noon. There has been enough celebrating for now."

"All right."

"Lucia?" His voice was stern as he stood and called her back.

"Yes?" As she turned toward him, Malo slapped her unexpectedly with brutal force, knocking her sideways.

"Remember!"

Sobbing, Lucia nodded as her hand flew to her injured cheek, and she raced from the campsite as Malo looked on, smiling his satisfaction.

Chica had witnessed his savage blow and spoke in low tones to Jennie. "Come on. Let's go wash these dishes and see if we can help her." But as she got to her feet, Luis came up behind her and tried to grab her around the waist.

"Chica!" Jennie warned and Chica turned on him, a knife suddenly appearing in her hand.

"Tonight, Luis. Not now."

Glaring at the wicked looking blade, he smiled quickly and stepped back. "Whatever you say."

Malo roared with laughter at Chica's command of the situation, and Luis scowled blackly at him, determined to make Chica pay for his humiliation when he got her alone that night.

"Thanks," Chica said as she slipped her knife back in her waistband. "He's a cruel one."

"I know. He's an animal," Jennie replied, glad that she had saved her from the other man's lust.

Chica nodded. "Now, let's go see if we can find Lucia."

Carrying the heavy load of dishes with them, they headed for the small pool, watching as they went for some sign of Lucia. After settling down at the water's edge, Chica looked around quickly.

"I will go and look for her. It is not good that she sulk. That will only make him angrier."

"I'll be fine here. Go ahead." Intent on washing the dirty utensils, she didn't hear them coming until they were already at the clearing.

The sound of Cazador's deep voice startled her from her work, and she looked up just as he walked into view, his arm protectively around Lucia's waist as she leaned heavily against him. "Some cool water should help," he was saying as he guided her toward the water.

Jennie stared at him, disbelieving. Lucia had run outside, not so much to escape Malo as to seek out Cazador's protection. She was livid. How had he soothed her? With gentle kisses and soft words? Furious, she wanted to jump to her feet and run away as fast as she could, but she held her ground, all the sweet emotions she felt for him freezing deep inside of her.

Rick stopped briefly as he came face to face with Jennie, but he knew that he had to rely on her trust in him and he continued on, helping Lucia to kneel down by the pool. Lucia was delighted with this unexpected turn of events, and she gloated as she sensed Jennie's surprise and jealous fury.

Chica returned just then, interrupting Lucia just as she planned to make another move on Cazador. "There you are. Are you all right? I was worried." She hurried to go to her friend's aid.

"I will be fine. My lip is bleeding a little, but other than that—"

"I will leave her in your care, Chica." Cazador stood and moved away.

"Cazador?" Lucia's voice was soft with gratitude. "Thank you—for everything."

He nodded abruptly and faced Jennie. "I want to talk to you," he said, knowing she was angry, and he wanted to settle things between them right then.

Jennie glared at him over her shoulder. "I have nothing to say to you."

"But I have something I need to say to you," he answered and his hands were not gentle as he pulled her up to him.

"Let me go!" she hissed, struggling to be free of his restraining grasp.

"I will when I'm damned good and ready." And he stalked off, dragging her behind him.

Rick picked his way through the boulders until he was certain that they were out of sight before slinging her around to face him.

"I think it's time we had a little talk," he told her as he made the mistake of releasing her.

It was all Jennie needed, because she drew back and with full force, she slapped him. Gasping in surprise at what she'd done, she stared up at him, awaiting his answering fury, but Rick only looked down at her, his expression wooden, the narrowing of his eyes the only clue to his inner thoughts. The imprint of her hand was reddening on his tanned cheek, and she felt a mixture of remorse and righteous anger.

"There is no reason for you to be jealous, love," he said quietly, and she found his words so close to the truth that she immediately denied them to herself and to him. "Lucia means nothing to me."

"You think I'm jealous of you and her—?" She laughed coldly. "Hardly."

"Then what the hell is the matter with you?" Rick demanded.

"I'll tell you what's the matter with me! I hate you! You've done nothing but use me and humiliate me. And now you have the gall to bed another woman and then come back and sleep with me!"

"I don't know what you're talking about," he replied levelly.

She looked at him disbelieving. "I'll just bet! I'm tired of all this intrigue! You told me to trust you. Well I don't, not anymore. How can you expect me to trust you when you don't trust me enough to tell me what's going on. You keep me in the dark about everything you're doing and then expect me to blindly accept whatever it is you're up to. Well, I won't—not anymore. I want to know what's going on. Why are you here?"

"Shut up." His words cut violently across her wild tirade.

"I won't! It's time I told you—"

"You won't tell me anything, Jennie McCaine. We are not on the M Circle C, little girl. We're playing things by my rules now, not yours or your precious daddy's."

She looked up at him again, horrified as the helplessness of her situation returned to her full force.

"I hate you!" she seethed, infuriated by her own vulnerability.

"I'm sure you do, after all, I only saved you from Luis and Ray and kept you alive until now."

Suddenly, she looked so frightened and alone that she touched something deep within him.

"Damn you!" he swore under his breath as he pulled her into his arms and sought her mouth with unerring accuracy.

Jennie had been limp in his embrace until he kissed her, and then her fight returned and she tried to jerk away. "Don't you dare! You go with Lucia and then try to make love to me! I hate you, Cazador! I can't stand the sight of you! I don't enjoy your touch! Why don't you go back to Lucia and just let me go!"

But Rick was not to be denied. "But I don't want Lucia. Right now, I want you."

Jennie looked up at him defiantly as she still fought against his dominance. "You can make me do whatever you want, but I won't enjoy it," she said firmly, holding herself rigid as his hands relaxed their firm grip.

"Jennie." Her name was a low groan as he bent to her once again, capturing her lips in a sweet, soft exchange that, had she not been so intent on resisting him, would have left her breathless and panting for more.

Rick felt the resistance in her as he drew her inexorably closer, his hands splayed across the tempting swell of her hips. Pinioning her to him, he moved rhythmically against her reluctant body as he kissed her deeply.

Jennie shivered at his sensual assault. She didn't want to feel anything! She didn't want him to touch her this way. But she was powerless to prevent the surges of heated desire that jolted through her every time his hips pressed intimately to hers.

Trying to think of other things, hoping to keep her mind off the exciting things he was doing to her, Jennie dwelled on his time with Lucia, forcing herself to imagine the other woman in his arms, sharing this love. And she succeeded, too, until Rick slid the blouse she wore over her shoulders and bared her pale-hued breasts to his kisses.

"You're mine," he said hoarsely as he tasted her warm, hard-tipped flesh.

"No, let me go. I hate you!" Her words were a moan and totally unconvincing as her body began to move with his, craving his arousing thrust and the feeling of his hardness as he sensuously ground his hips against hers.

"Liar," he murmured as he met her lips and pulled her roughly to him, the buttons of his shirt cutting into the softness of her bosom.

Finally, when he could stand the torture of needing her no longer, Rick picked her up in his arms and lay her upon the sandy ground. Mindless in his desire, he lifted her skirt and with an eager touch, caressed the inner womanly sweetness of her.

"Please. Don't do this to me. No, I don't want you to," Jennie cried softly as his touch quickly, expertly, brought her to the peak of pleasure.

As the pulsing joy of physical release throbbed through her, tears of humiliation coursed down her cheeks, but Rick didn't notice as he freed himself from his pants and sought the hot, wet velvet center of her warmth. With long, powerful strokes, he moved within her, straining to hold back long enough to please her again.

Unable to resist him anymore, Jennie submitted to his possession, and she was totally unprepared for the tantalizing arousal of his every impaling thrust. She responded in spite of herself, and the fire of her passion for him flared to life and burned heatedly as they soared to the heights of excitement. Beyond thinking, beyond caring, Jennie became a creature of sensuality; seeking him, wanting him, needing his body joined to hers. When their rapturous moment came, they clung together, lost in frenzied abandon, surrendering to love's conquering ecstasy.

Rick lay still for a long moment, thrilling at the feeling of her body's enveloping him so tightly, and it was with deep regret that he withdrew and moved away to straighten his clothing. It was only when he was about to speak that he looked down at Jennie and saw the pain reflected in her eyes. Rick reached out to touch her cheek, but she turned away from his caress and quickly got to her feet, tugging her blouse back in place and smoothing her skirt.

"If there is nothing else, I should go help Chica with the dishes," Jennie said stiffly as she started to walk away from him.

"Jennie—" He tried to take her arm, but she pulled free.

"As *your woman* I have certain *duties* that I must perform." Her words were cold and filled with contempt, and this time when she made to leave, he did not try to stop her.

Rick was filled with a terrible sense of dread as he watched Jennie go. Though he had forced her to respond to him, as he knew she would, he was afraid that he had destroyed something very precious and very fragile that had existed between them.

Sternly pushing all thoughts of their torrid mating and its results from his mind, he headed toward the cave to find out what Malo's plans were for the final trek to the gold mine.

Chapter Fourteen

The first light of day found the posse on the move. According to Steve's instructions, they had divided into groups and were already methodically combing the entrance to Willow Canyon for some sign that other riders had trespassed there. But the storm had been thorough in its fury, and the harsh terrain yielded no telltale traces of previous encroachment.

Afraid of getting in their way, Carrie stayed back from the search area and watched their efforts from a safe vantage point. Following Todd's progress as he scouted with Jake and another ranch hand, she wondered at his strange mood this morning for he had been withdrawn and almost unapproachable. After a few initial attempts at conversation, she had left him alone, fearing that he might still be angry with her for her escapade the night before.

Carrie's hopes had been high when Todd had invited her to sleep so near to him, but they had been cruelly dashed by his indifference, for he had shown no inclination to pursue the heated embraces they had shared earlier in the day. Temporarily at a loss as to what to do next, she wondered just how much longer she could stand being with him and yet never knowing his love.

"Carrie!" Jake's echoing shout drew her sudden attention,

and she quickly raced to her horse.

"Did you find something?" she asked breathlessly as she reined in beside him.

"Steve just did," he told her, pointing in their direction, and Carrie looked farther ahead to where Steve and her father stood.

"What is it? A cave?"

"I'm not sure, let's go find out." Putting his heels to horse, Jake followed the rest of the men up the canyon's rocky incline.

Todd was waiting outside, still mounted, when they finally made their way to the abandoned diggings.

"Were they here?" Jake asked quickly as he swung down out of the saddle.

"Looks that way," he responded brusquely.

Jake glanced up at him, wondering at his surliness, but before he could make mention of it, Mac's call drew him inside. Carrie looked over at Todd, worrying at his paleness.

"Todd, are you feeling all right? You don't look well—" she began, but he cut her off.

"I'm fine," he growled, his features set in an expressionless mask as he tried to control the pain that was wracking his body.

"But—" Carrie continued, concerned.

"I'm all right, I tell you!" Todd barked.

Stunned by his harsh tone, tears stung her eyes, and Carrie blinked quickly to hide her distress as she dismounted to follow the others into the mine, wanting to tell Mac or Jake of Todd's worsening condition.

"Pa—" She tried to get her father's attention as he spoke in earnest with Steve and Jake.

"Not now," he answered sharply, not even looking up.

"But it's important, I think—" Carrie tried again.

Mac glared over at her in the darkness of the shaft. "Didn't I tell you when I allowed you to come along that I didn't want to be bothered by you?"

"Yes, but it's Todd. I think his shoulder is bothering him."
She spoke quickly now that she had Mac's attention.

Mac snorted in disbelief and spoke sarcastically. "My
dear, Todd is a full-grown man. If something's wrong, he'll
take care of it. He doesn't need you, little missy, to mind his
business for him. Now, Steve . . ." He turned back to his
foreman.

Carrie flushed at his cruel, dismissing words and fell silent,
hoping for Todd's sake that he was right.

Todd was relieved when Carrie went inside for he didn't
want anyone to know how badly he was hurting. He was
determined to see this through to the end and would not give
up until Jennie had been found; his own health be damned!

Afraid that his legs would not support him, Todd
remained mounted. With a shaking hand, he pulled a near
empty bottle of whiskey from the saddlebag and drank
deeply of its potent contents. Since last night, he had been
fighting the wracking torment that was pounding through
him and, though he was unwilling to openly admit it, he
feared he was losing the battle. Even the liquor he'd been
consuming in copious amounts was now failing to grant him
any relief whatsoever. His mind in a haze, his body on fire,
Todd struggled to maintain his equilibrium as he heard Mac
and the others coming out of the mine.

"Which way from here, Steve?" Mac's voice jolted
through Todd as he emerged with his foreman by his side.

Steve scrutinized the trail carefully and pointed up the
canyon. "The horse was heading up there and they're riding
double."

"There's only one horse?" Mac's mood brightened
considerably for riding double in this kind of country would
certainly be slow going.

Steve nodded. "Yep."

"How long ago do you estimate they left here?" Jake asked

as he picked up his horse's reins and vaulted into the saddle.

"Late yesterday," he replied, studying the tracks one again before mounting.

Encouraged at the prospect that they might be gaining on them, Mac ordered, "Then let's ride fast!" And spurring his mount to action, he hurried to ride abreast with Steve.

Gritting his teeth against the excruciating pain that seemed to afflict his entire being, Todd stayed straight in the saddle and followed their jarring lead up the steepening trail. It was only after they had been on the rugged trek for over an hour that he could no longer keep up the pretense, and he gave in to the dizziness that had become overpowering in its intensity. Slumping in the saddle, he felt himself falling, and he called out weakly as he rolled slowly from the horse's back and landed heavily on the hard ground.

"Carrie—"

Sensing that Todd's condition was worsening, Carrie had deliberately been riding near him, and she was the first one to come to his aid when he fell.

"Jake! Hurry! Todd's sick." Jumping down lightly from her mount, she ran to his side. Looking up worriedly as her brother and father rode back to her, she told them, "He's burning up with fever and his shoulder's bleeding again. The fall must have opened it!"

"Damn!" Mac cursed, irritated that something else had gone wrong, but he suddenly felt a new dawning of respect for his youngest daughter as he realized that she had tried earlier to warn him that this might happen. "Why didn't he tell us he was ailing?"

"You know how worried Todd was about Jennie, Pa," Jake said as he went to help Carrie. "He wouldn't let anything stand in the way of our rescuing her, not even his own pain."

Carrie was growing angry. She had tried to tell them that Todd was ill, but they hadn't listened to her. And Todd! How could he be such a fool? Why hadn't he just admitted that he was sick? Was it worth risking his own life, just so the search for Jennie could continue? He wouldn't be much good to Jennie dead, she thought bitterly.

"What do you want me to do?" She looked up at her father questioningly. "I have to check his shoulder, and he needs to rest until the fever comes down."

Mac and Jake exchanged worried looks.

"What about the mine? Why don't we take him back there?" Jake offered.

"That's about the only thing we can do at this point," Mac said frowning.

"I'll stay there with him until he's well enough to ride again. Then we can try to catch up with you." Carrie offered bravely.

"All right," Mac said curtly, surprised by Carrie's selfless offer. "Jake, ride along with them and take whatever supplies you think they'll need. Leave an extra rifle and ammunition, too."

Jake hurried to get their provisions, while two of the ranch hands tied Todd on his horse, taking care not to disturb his injured shoulder. Carrie was alternately excited and frightened at the prospect of staying in the abandoned mine, alone, with Todd. While it did offer her the perfect opportunity to prove her love to him, it also left them vulnerable to attack by Indians or anyone else who happened upon their shelter. Steeling herself against such scary thoughts, Carrie bravely wheeled her horse around and, with Jake leading Todd's mount, she began the trek back down the canyon to the abandoned mine.

The dark and uncomfortable dampness of the deserted diggings was hardly inviting, but Carrie knew they had no alternative for Todd was too ill to make it all the way back to the ranch. Working quickly, she arranged a bedroll for him and then, together with Jake, they carried him in and laid him down.

"Jake, while I start a fire, see if you can get his shirt off."

"All right. I've brought in all the medical supplies." Jake indicated the leather pouches he placed near the mine's entrance.

"Good, I'm going to need them." She stared down at Todd briefly, worrying at the grayness of his coloring.

Jake could tell that she was uneasy, so he went to her and put his arm about her in an affectionate embrace. "He'll be fine, probably by morning if he gets a good night's rest."

Carrie sighed and leaned into her brother's strength. "I hope so. It's just that—" She stopped just as she was about to blurt out the truth of her feelings for him.

"What?" Jake asked, wondering what she was about to say.

"Nothing. I'm just glad that I'm here to help," Carrie lied as she started the small campfire.

"We all are. I know Pa is," he confided, carefully stripping the shirt from Todd's inert body.

She looked up, amazed. "He is?"

Jake nodded. "You know he doesn't show much emotion, but I think during this time on the trail, he's come to regard you a bit differently."

Shrugging, she moved away from the small blaze to kneel beside Todd. "You may think he's changing his attitude toward me, but I don't believe it. He's never cared about me, one way or the other, so why should he start now?"

Jake put a reassuring hand on her shoulder. "I don't know, but he was impressed with the way you've ridden this entire time without complaint and now, volunteering to take care of Todd—You're being very brave, Carrie.

Carrie felt a deep surge of affection for Jake. He was a dear man and, although the difference in their ages was such that they had never been particularly close, she knew him to be fair and honest and caring. "Thanks, but I don't feel very brave. Just worried."

"You'll do fine. I've made sure that there's ample water and food."

"All right."

"But, Carrie—"

"Yes?"

"If for some reason, he doesn't improve right away, don't try to leave. Wait here for us. You're relatively safe and protected here."

She nodded, heartened by his concern for her. "I will."

"Well, I'd better get going before they ride on too far ahead of me," he told her as he started to leave.

"Jake—" There was a catch in her voice.

"What Carrie?" Jake paused and looked back as Carrie got to her feet and hurried to him.

"Thank you." She hugged him quickly. "I'm sure we'll be fine."

"I never had any doubts." And with that he was gone, leaving Carrie alone with Todd.

She watched Jake ride off up the winding trail before turning back to Todd. With gentle fingers, she pried loose the blood-soaked bandage and stared with dismay at the damaged flesh. Jarred by his fall, the wound had partially reopened and was still oozing blood. Applying firm, steady pressure, she finally brought the bleeding under control and then administered the medicine and redressed it, packing the wound tightly with clean soft wrappings.

His shoulder cared for, Carrie now turned her attention to his fever, and she lost track of time as she tirelessly sponged his heated body with a dampened, cool cloth. Never wavering in her efforts to bring his raging temperature under control, she hovered over him, ever conscious of his ragged breathing and fitful movements. Drifting in and out of consciousness, Todd tossed feverishly on the hardness of his bedroll, and Carrie wished that they were back at the ranch so she could give him the proper care he so desperately needed.

"Carrie—" It was late in the afternoon when his voice boomed in the silence of their gloomy refuge.

197

"I'm right here." She rose above him so he could see her more clearly.

"Carrie—I love her, you know?" Todd said very lucidly.

"Yes, I know you love her, Todd." She sighed in exasperation. Here she'd been nursing him for hours and his first words to her were about her sister! *Damn!*

"I shouldn't but I do," he continued as if she hadn't even spoken. "Jennie is—"

"It's all right." She tried to soothe him. "Things always seem to have a way of working out."

"I'm worried—Jennie—Got to find her. They might kill her." Todd's anguish was real, and Carrie's heart sank as it dawned on her just how much he cared for Jennie.

"As soon as you're better, we'll go catch up with them. Pa and Jake will find her. Now try to rest."

His next words were garbled as he began to move restlessly, and it was then that Carrie realized that he had been out of his head and hadn't been coherent at all.

With a quieting hand on his heated brow, Carrie spoke to him in low, dulcet tones until he stopped thrashing about and fell into an unsettled sleep. Sitting back on her heels, she let her gaze roam over him, worrying at the dry heat that emanated from him.

Moving to lie down on her own blankets, she sought a few minutes of rest for herself while he was quiet. It disturbed her to see him so helpless, and she hoped that his fever would break soon.

Jennie pulled on her boots and stood up, smoothing the wrinkles from her riding skirt. Tying the long shirt in a knot at her waist, she neatly folded the clothing that Chica had lent her and walked to where she was sitting with Lucia.

"Thank you for letting me borrow your clothes," Jennie told her sincerely as she handed her the blouse and skirt. "It was very kind of you."

"Any time you need them, just ask."

"I will. How soon are we leaving?" she asked, noticing how all the men had gone outside to saddle their horses.

"Probably within a half an hour," Lucia said coolly. "Didn't Cazador tell you?"

"I haven't spoken to him since we were by the pool."

Lucia chuckled throatily as she grinned knowingly at Jennie. "I wish he'd drag me off like that. *Que hombre! I* certainly wouldn't fight him! I would enjoy it!"

Jennie stiffened at the other woman's taunts. "The next time he feels the need to forcibly drag someone off, I'll tell him you're interested."

"You do that!" She laughed even louder as Jennie turned and walked away.

"Go a little easier on her," Chica chided.

"Why should I? She is a fool!" Lucia sneered. "She has such a gorgeous man and she doesn't know what to do with him."

"We would not have that problem, would we?"

"Never." And she looked up to watch Cazador as he reentered the cave and headed in Jennie's direction. "The girl is stupid and I will do all I can to take him away from her."

Busy with rolling up their bedroll, Jennie didn't hear his approach.

"Jennie." Rick's voice caught her unawares and she jumped nervously.

"What?" Though her heart was pounding just at the sound of his voice, she kept her tone curt and cold as she stood up and faced him.

Rick stared down at her, wondering at her thoughts. He knew that things were not good between them right now, but there was no time to explain. They had both wanted what had happened this morning. She was just too stubborn to admit it. Impatient with her arbitrary ways, he spoke more sharply than he meant to.

"We'll be leaving very shortly, so get the bedroll ready and the rest of my gear."

"I know, those are part of my duties, too." She couldn't stop the sneer in her voice.

"Jennie." He scowled blackly.

"Is that all, sir? Or is there something *else* you'd like me to do for you before we pull out?"

"No. There's nothing else *you* can do for me. Just be ready to ride." He began to walk away and then stopped and turned back to her. "By the way, I've managed to get you a horse of your own, so I won't have to be burdened with you. Now, get busy! I'll be back." He stalked forcefully away, his anger evident in his every stride.

Jennie watched him go, feeling strangely bereft. Why, all of a sudden, did she feel like calling out to him and going willingly into his arms? But the fleeting thought of the comfort she would find there was quickly eclipsed by the memory of his possession of her just hours before, and her pride surged forth. He had treated her with contempt, refusing to stop when she'd begged him not to go on, and for that she didn't think she could ever forgive him. He was a callous and unfeeling brute; he had used her without conscience, and no doubt he would do it again at the first opportunity.

She shivered as she remembered the way his hands had touched her and how her own body had responded so wantonly to his every caress in spite of herself. Jennie didn't know what power he had over her, but she knew that she had to escape. For with just one touch, he could make her forget who she was and why she was here.

Shaking herself mentally, Jennie hurried to finish rolling up the bedroll, all the while wondering why his words about being burdened with her had hurt so badly.

They had been riding for over an hour when, at last, they passed the crest of the final ridge. Malo reined in sharply as he faced the jutting magnificence of Weaver's Needle for the first time. Motioning for Juan to ride up alongside of him, he turned to the old man.

"This is the landmark you've been telling me about?" He gestured toward the stark, skyscraping tower that rose menacingly before them.

"That is it," Juan told him calmly, but he was disturbed by the glinting of madness that he'd just witnessed in Malo's eyes.

"Is something wrong?" Rick rode up beside them, his nerves on edge.

"No. Everything is just fine. This is the mountain he had been telling us about. Come, we are getting near the mine, I can feel it! Let's go! You take the lead now, Peralta, and we will follow you," he said, and Juan nodded silently as he directed his horse to the head of the column of riders so they could begin their descent into yet another treacherous canyon.

Rick witnessed the look of pained acceptance on his grandfather's face, and he was once more forced to hide his fury at Malo's greed. Soon, he told himself, soon he would free them from this living nightmare.

Glancing back down the trail they had just ascended, Rick caught sight of Jennie riding with Chica. He had been greatly relieved when he had discovered that there were extra horses in camp, for without Jennie's distracting presence riding double with him, he could keep his mind more firmly on the real reason he was here: to rescue Juan before they got to the gold mine.

Jennie saw Cazador look her way and she deliberately averted her eyes. Though she had thought him cruel when he had told her earlier that he had a horse for her, now, she was grateful. Being away from him this way had given her the time she'd needed to think through her feelings, and she had come to realize just how tenuous her position was here in the camp. She knew with certainty that no one would ever come to her aid for Cazador was too powerful for them to dare to cross. So, if she wanted to get away, she would have to do it on her own. Any trust Jennie had ever had in Cazador had been destroyed by his refusal to heed her desperate plea to stop when he'd taken her, and now her thoughts were only on how to escape his captivity as soon as possible.

As Juan Peralta, Malo, and Rick began the descent into the next canyon, Jennie and Chica reached the top of the ridge and saw Weaver's Needle for the first time. The harshness of it as it rose spikelike out of the desert floor sent a chill of apprehension down Jennie's spine and she shivered in spite of the heat.

"It's ugly!" Chica remarked laughingly. "But I imagine it looks beautiful to Malo."

"Why?" She turned questioningly to the other woman, wondering why anyone would think it pretty.

"Did you not hear them talking this morning?"

"No." Jennie, in truth, had been so preoccupied with trying to figure out a way to flee from Cazador that she had paid little attention to what had been going on in camp.

"The old man told him that once they found that mountain it would be a simple matter to locate the mine. So, we must be getting close."

Jennie nodded, thinking suddenly of Juan Peralta. How sad that this should be happening to him; first to lose his family because of the gold and now— She wished that there was some way she could help him, something she could do. A plan began to take form in her mind.

"How long until we get there?"

"He wasn't too definite on that, but I think the day after tomorrow."

"Then it will all be over," she said distractedly.

Chica answered indifferently. "For him it will be."

"You mean, Malo will kill him?"

"Of course, once he has no use for him anymore."

Jennie was aghast but didn't speak.

Chica shrugged, giving Jennie a sideways glance. "You never did say what happened between you and Cazador after

202

he dragged you away from the watering hole this morning."

"Nothing important," she answered, trying to dodge the question.

"If it was nothing important, why have you been ignoring him all day? Believe me, if you don't want him, Lucia and I will be happy to take him off your hands," she offered happily.

"Feel free."

Seeing a chance to help Lucia, she asked coyly, "You do not care? Lucia will be glad to hear that. You do not mind if I tell her?"

Jennie, for some unknown reason, bridled at her words, but she was careful to keep her expression blank. "Tell her whatever you like. It's of no consequence to me." And with that she kneed her horse to a faster gait, leaving Chica watching her with suppressed excitement.

Rick rode at the head of the line with Malo, and with the passing of each mile his resolve not to fail strengthened. He hated everything about these mountains and the memories they stirred within him.

With slow scrutiny, Rick kept his gaze locked on the craggy peaks and camouflaging boulders, knowing that at any moment, the Apache could appear and devastate their entire group. Tension knotted within him, and he wondered how Juan was holding up under the pressure. He had managed to slip him a small knife earlier in the day, but he knew it would be of little real protection to him if they were attacked.

"Malo." Luis rode up to join them.

"Yes, Luis?"

"How long until we are there? Ray and I are getting anxious."

"No more so than the rest of us," Cazador put in smoothly and Malo chuckled in agreement.

"No need to count your money yet. We will be at least another day on the trail. The old man has grown confused as to the right directions."

"You want me to help refresh his memory?" Luis offered, eager in his bloodlust.

"No, not yet." Malo smiled thinly as he glanced at the old man. "But if we are not there by the day after tomorrow, then I will let you have your fun with him."

Rick grimaced inwardly. He had one day left to plan and then he would have to make his move, regardless.

"Lucia," Chica called out to her in a low voice.

Reining in, Lucia waited for the others to pass her by so she could ride nearer to her friend. "What do you want?"

"I have news for you." Her eyes were twinkling.

"About what?"

"Cazador, of course, what else?"

"Cazador? What happened?" She looked up to where he rode easily at the front of the group with Malo and Peralta.

"I don't know exactly what for sure, but there has been some kind of trouble between them."

"Good! It worked!"

"I think so. She said she didn't care if you wanted Cazador or not."

Lucia's eyes narrowed in anticipation. "But I still have to convince him. Maybe I'll get the chance tonight."

"Will we be camping soon? It is near sundown."

"Malo is anxious to get to the gold mine. I don't think he's even thought about stopping. We'll just have to wait and see."

"There is water up there," Juan told Malo an hour later as they started up another incline. "It should be about the safest place to make camp for the night."

"All right, lead the way." Malo was quick to agree for the heavy shadows of dusk were beginning to fill the canyon with darkness, and he had no desire to get lost in these dangerous mountains during the night.

Juan nodded and urged his horse up the slope at a faster pace, leading them to a small clearing with a clean spring-fed pool.

"Ramon!" Malo called as he dismounted and gestured to Rick to come with him. "Take our horses and water them. Then see to the old man. No fires tonight."

"Yes, Malo." The other man took the reins to Malo's and Cazador's mounts and led them away.

"I have a proposal I want to talk with you about, Cazador," Malo said in undertones that indicated he had something very serious on his mind.

Tensing at this sudden unexpected invitation, Rick warily followed the desperado away from the campsite.

Malo's eyes were alight with avarice when he turned to face Rick. "It occurs to me, Cazador, that we would do well together."

"Oh?" He was cautious and wondering what was on the other man's twisted mind.

"You do need money, don't you?" The outlaw watched him knowingly.

"Of course. Why else would I be here?" Rick gave the answer Malo was expecting.

"I know." Grinning evilly, he continued. "And I have a plan that will make the both of us so rich that we won't have to worry about money ever again." He paused for effect. "Are you interested?"

"I'd be a fool not to be," Rick replied amiably, returning his feral smile.

"Good." Mentally Malo rubbed his hands together. Why, with Cazador at his side, there was nothing he couldn't do. "Now, the way I figure it, we'll be at the gold mine late tomorrow or sometime early the following day at the very latest."

"Yes, so?"

"How good are you at directions? Do you think you could find your way in and out of here again, on your own?"

"Probably." Rick wondered at the plan he had devised. "Why?"

"Because, they are all idiots." Malo nodded toward the camp. "And once they have served their purpose . . ." He shrugged expressively.

"Are you suggesting we take them?"

"Between the two of us, I'm sure we could," Malo told him calmly.

"And then *we* split the gold?"

"That's right and only two ways. Think of it, Cazador— riches beyond all imagination."

Rick's eyes narrowed as he considered the double-dealing proposal with what he hoped looked like real interest. "How do I know that you wouldn't back-shoot me the first chance you get?"

"You don't. We'll just have to trust each other, because once we get rid of the old man, there'll be the two of us left who know the mine's exact location. Two men could make it in here, but one man, on his own, would have no chance. We need each other."

"I'll think about it," he answered quietly, resisting the urge to gut-shoot him right then and there. "And I'll let you know, *after* I've seen the color of the gold."

"You do that. We could do well together, Cazador. With my gold and your gun—"

"Our gold." Rick's smile was deadly as he met Malo's eyes.

"We're thinking more alike already." Malo tried to weasel out of his words for, in that moment, he had known what it must be like to face Cazador down the barrel of a gun during a shootout, and he didn't like the feeling at all.

"I know." And they walked slowly back toward the campsite.

*   *   *

Jennie sat quietly on the bedroll, the calm demeanor she was displaying outwardly totally at odds with the conflict warring within her. She had to get away. She couldn't stay, not after seeing him with Lucia; and then the way he'd treated her afterward.

Her stubborn McCaine pride surged forth, forcing Jennie to deny to herself all the finer emotions he had stirred to life within her. She had not loved him. It had all been a terrible mistake. How could she love someone as ruthless as Cazador? He was a man without conscience, a man without morals, who would take whatever he wanted and damn the consequences.

Well, Jennie thought heatedly, if he wanted Lucia, he was welcome to her, but he darn well wasn't going to have her at the same time!

Looking up, Jennie spied Cazador returning to camp with Malo, and she wondered again at the connection between them as they stopped to talk with the other men.

"Who's on guard duty first?" Malo demanded, and a general rumble of complaint went through the men.

"I'll stand one watch," Rick offered, hoping for the opportunity to speak with Juan.

"I'll take one, too," Luis said quickly. "Let me watch the old man, Malo."

Malo looked at him quickly and then spoke to Rick. "Cazador, you watch Peralta."

"But—"

"Shut up, Luis. You will have your chance if we don't find the mine and, perhaps, even if we do!" he said, and Luis stalked angrily away to take his place as guard at the lookout point. "We will leave at sunup," Malo continued. "Be ready."

As the men dispersed, grumbling among themselves, Rick went to speak with Jennie for a minute.

"I've got first guard duty," he told her as he rummaged through his saddlebags for some jerky. "I should be back around midnight."

"Fine," Jennie answered with little emotion.

"I warned you once before about fighting me," he said softly with considerable menace.

"I'm not fighting you," she replied simply, looking up at him defiantly.

Rick muttered a violent curse under his breath and strode quickly away without another word, leaving Jennie alone to ponder his words.

Juan looked up expectantly as Rick came to stand beside him. "You are my guard?"

"Malo's choice."

"He couldn't have done better." There was a smile in his tone.

"No fires tonight, so I brought you some jerky." Reaching down, Rick untied his grandfather's hands and handed him the dried meat before stepping quickly away to assume a guardlike position.

"Thank you," Juan replied as he gratefully accepted the food. "You have news?"

"According to Malo, we'll be heading out at dawn. He expects us to get to the mine late tomorrow or the next morning. If not, he's going to turn Luis loose on you."

"Ah, Luis." He nodded. "A true *compadre* of Malo's, I think."

"He is vicious but not as smart."

"I will remember."

"Do you want to stretch your legs before you turn in?" Rick felt a deep need to be away from the presence of the others.

"Yes. It will be good to be alone for a while." Juan go slowly to his feet.

"I know," he said under his breath as he directed him from the encampment.

Lucia saw Cazador leading the old man away and, with a fast glance in Malo's direction to make sure he wasn't watching her, she quietly slipped away in pursuit. Pausing behind a massive boulder, Lucia waited for a chance to approach him.

"It will all be over soon," Rick was saying as he stood with Juan a goodly distance from the camp.

"Have you a plan?"

"Tomorrow, I'll know for sure exactly what I'm going to do. Until then, we can continue as we are."

Lucia could not believe what she was hearing. Peralta and Cazador knew each other? What were they up to? Excited by what she had learned, she backed away from them, undetected. Her mind was racing as she wondered how best to use the information. Knowing that Malo would kill him if he found out, she knew she wouldn't tell him. No, she decided, she wanted Cazador and she now had the means to get him. Smugly, she returned to camp and waited for just the right moment to face Cazador with what she knew.

Chapter Fifteen

It was a dark, moonless night, and in the most isolated corner of the campsite protected from prying eyes by the night's ebony mantel, Lucia lay in wait for Cazador. She would have him! And soon! Tense with expectation, she found the thought of being held in his arms arousing and her body was alive with sensual excitement.

Malo had passed out hours before from a combination of tequila and whiskey, and Lucia had then secreted herself in this distant part of the encampment to watch Cazador unawares and to await the end of his guard duty so that she could ·make her move. She knew she should be more cautious, but she didn't care. Driven on by the need to possess him, Lucia dreamed only of his embrace as she gazed at him, committing to memory the leanness of his manly form as he stood sentinel in the silence.

It was well past midnight when Ramon roused to take Cazador's place as Peralta's guard, and Lucia breathed a heavy sigh of relief for she had begun to think that her chance to be with him would never come.

From her vantage point, Lucia watched as Cazador stretched tiredly, and she was overjoyed when he walked, not toward Jennie, but away from camp, back down the trail they had just traversed. Knowing that this would be the only time she could talk with him privately, she slipped from under the covers and moved quickly to follow.

Rick strode wearily down the rocky hillside, his mind racing. Though he needed rest, he knew he would not afford the luxury of sleep just yet. Time was running out. Tomorrow, they would have to make their escape.

Rick thought briefly of Jennie and of how stubborn and uncommunicative she had been today. Worrying that she would fight him when the time came for them to take flight, he knew the only way that things would go smoothly would be for him to tell her the truth. And, Rick decided, he would, but not until tomorrow, when he was certain of exactly what his plan of action would be.

"Cazador!" Lucia's whisper was hushed and urgent.

At the sound of the voice so unexpectedly close by, Rick whirled about, his hand flying to his gun. Making out the form of a woman approaching, he relaxed only slightly as he recognized her. "Lucia?"

"I need to talk to you," she told him coming to stand boldly before him. "It's most important."

"Where is Malo?" he asked warily as he holstered his sidearm.

"He is sleeping. We will not be bothered and it is better that way."

"I have told you I have no need for another woman," he began.

"Ah." Lucia smiled knowingly. "But I told you that one day you would want me, and I think that now, you will."

Rick's eyes narrowed as he considered her. "Oh?"

"Yes, you see, I overheard your conversation with Peralta. I know what you're up to." She reached out and toyed with a button on the front of his shirt.

Rick reacted with a viciousness he had not thought himself capable of, grabbing her forcefully by her wrists and shaking her violently. "What are you talking about?" he demanded.

211

Lucia felt a pang of fear as she looked up into his gleaming, predatory eyes. "I heard you say that tomorrow you would make your move."

"And?" He tightened his grip, uncaring if he bruised her.

"And I know that you are here to rescue the old man." She gasped, as it suddenly occurred to her that he might kill her. Quickly, she searched for a way to turn this moment to her advantage. "I have not told Malo and I don't intend to, unless, of course, you force me into it."

"What do you want?" His tone was cold and deadly.

"You," Lucia said brazenly.

Rick studied her upturned face, trying to read her thoughts. Lucia had the power of life and death over Juan, Jennie, and himself for hours now, and she had chosen not to use it. Did she really mean what she said?

"You see, no one need know. I will even help you if you promise to take me with you when you go for I'm fed up with Malo and the way he treats me." She took a step closer to him, in spite of his fierce expression and the firm hold he had on her. "And I will please you—much better than Jennie." Lucia tossed her head.

"Leave Jennie out of this," he snarled.

"Would you rather I tell Malo the truth about you? Do you know what would happen to your precious Jennie then?" she said.

In disgust, Rick released her and pushed her away, trying to buy himself time to think. "I don't believe you'd do it, Lucia."

"But you can't be sure, can you Cazador?" she answered.

Rick stood motionlessly as she strode back toward him, her hands on her hips, but when she got within reach, he reached out and hauled her up against him.

"I don't like to be pushed or maneuvered, Lucia. If you want to keep me happy, you'll remember that in the future," Rick told her cuttingly before he kissed her, his mouth grinding against hers in an exchange meant to conquer and cower.

Thoughts of Jennie haunted him as he mechanically caressed Lucia. There was no gentleness in his touch. He roughly pushed her blouse from her shoulders, and he felt only a suppressed rage at having found himself in this situation. With precise expertise, he aroused her, his hands exploring her every curve.

Lucia was so aflame with desire for him that she found even the pain he was inflicting as stimulating as the most gentle caress.

"Yes. Oh, yes," she whimpered as his lips left hers to seek the vulnerable length of her neck, arching to him when he lifted her tightly against him.

With eager hands, she sought to inflame him, too, and Rick found himself responding to the wildness of her wanton touch, in spite of his determination not to. When Lucia slipped her hand within his pants to hold and caress him, he growled low in his throat and surged against her, his baser instincts urging him on.

It was only the sound of a slipping rock that thrust them both back to reality.

"What was it?" Lucia said, quickly pulling her blouse up to cover her breasts.

"I don't know," he replied. "But it wasn't Malo. If he'd seen us, we'd be dead."

Lucia shivered at the import of his words. "I will be more cautious in the future." With a bold hand, she reached out to caress him, but Rick grabbed her wrist, effectively stopping her ploy.

"No more. Go back now, while it's safe."

"Tomorrow," she told him with promise. "Tomorrow, Cazador."

Tense from their encounter, Rick watched Lucia go. Though she was a beautiful woman, he was not in any way attracted to her. He hadn't wanted to make love to her and his body's reaction to her manipulations had been only animal instinct. There had been no emotion involved on his part in the embraces he'd just shared with Lucia, and Rick was surprised at the unexpected feeling of guilt he experienced at having physically responded to her in any way. Even though he knew that he had only done what was necessary to assure their safety, the memory of Jennie's tender lovemaking made the other woman's possessive caresses seem somehow sordid.

Thinking of Jennie as he stood there alone in the desert darkness, he suddenly needed to be with her, feeling that her nearness would purge his soul of Lucia's physical extortion. Heading back toward camp, Rick was intent on tasting once again the beauty of Jennie's love.

Luis moved through the circle of sleeping men with a catlike stride. He glanced over to where Jennie was sleeping and knew that by the following night, she would be in his bed.

Climbing into his bedroll, he smiled as he began to plan the best way to reveal to Malo exactly what was going on between Cazador and Lucia. He knew it would be more effective if he let them trap themselves and then claimed Jennie for himself. And, after what he had just seen, he knew that wouldn't be hard to do.

He saw Lucia hurriedly return to her bedroll, and his body hardened as he remembered her bared breasts and the avid way she had been caressing Cazador. Had it not been so late, he would have gone to Chica to seek momentary forgetfulness in the familiar heat of her well-used embrace. Tomorrow, he thought. Tomorrow he would have Jennie all to himself, and Malo would be most pleased with him.

Rick stood on the outer edge of the encampment, scanning all who lay before him sleeping, hoping to find some clue as to who might have witnessed his passionate embrace with Lucia. But no one was stirring; all was quiet.

The fact that there was no disturbance heartened him. Taking a chance that the dislodged stone they'd heard had only been a night animal on the prowl, Rick made his way to Jennie and lay down next to her, pleased that they were some distance from the others.

Jennie had awakened a short time before to see Luis turning in. Knowing that Cazador would be ending his watch, too, she was unable to fall back asleep and was lying quietly beneath her one sheltering blanket, nervously awaiting his return.

Jennie wasn't quite sure what to expect from him tonight. They had been sparring verbally ever since this morning, but she knew that that would rapidly come to an end whenever Cazador chose to end it. All he had to do was touch her and she knew she would be lost. With that knowledge came a deep, abiding fear of him. She didn't want to give in to him. He was cruel and ruthless. He was just like all the others.

At the sound of footsteps, Jennie looked up to see Lucia returning stealthily to her pallet. And when Cazador followed her into camp a few minutes later, she knew why the other woman had been so intent on sneaking.

They had been together! Again! A pain, that Jennie refused to acknowledge as jealousy, tore at her heart. She did not care that Cazador found Lucia more attractive. She would leave just as soon as she could get away and then when she got back home, Jennie decided in a flurry of irrational emotion she would marry Todd—if he would still have her!

Huddling deeper into the warmth of the blanket, she pretended to be asleep as Cazador stretched out beside her. She thought for a moment that she had been saved from a confrontation with him, but then he turned and took her into his arms.

Rick had thought Jennie asleep and had hoped to awaken her softly with gentle caresses and tender kisses. He did not want to argue with her, but the moment he touched her she recoiled from him as if she'd been burned.

"No!" Jennie hissed, trying to wriggle free from his embrace. "Leave me alone!"

"Jennie," Rick snarled, his tone telling her all she needed to know about his mood. "Lie still."

Petrified and knowing that he would have his way regardless of her wishes, she quieted.

"That's better," he murmured as he rose above her to kiss her softly.

Jennie lay impassively as his mouth moved over hers, testing and taunting her. When she didn't respond, he drew back to stare down at her. He was too tired this night to cajole her. He needed her to be loving and giving, not stiff and unyielding. Recognizing the mutinous look on her pale features, his jaw tightened and he spoke caustically.

"If you wish to remain my woman, you had better learn to please me."

"I don't want to be your woman! I never did! You forced me to come with you. You—"

Before she could finish, Rick lost control. And though she struggled against his superior strength, it was for naught as he pulled her forcefully to him. Kissing her with an intensity that had nothing to do with passion, he forced her lips open and savagely raped the honeyed sweetness of her mouth. His hands were almost brutal, unbuttoning her shirt and pushing it down off her shoulders, entrapping her arms at her sides.

When she started to scream, Rick clamped a heavy hand across her mouth. "You idiot! Do you want every man in camp waiting to take his turn with you?"

Though Rick could read the terror in her eyes, she refused to stop fighting him, and he cursed low under his breath as he pinned her to the ground. Knowing the ony way to subdue her would be to force a response from her, Rick began to fondle her breasts, teasing the sensitive peaks to tautness.

Jennie still tried to wriggle away, bucking wildly as she

avoided his touch. but her movements only proved stimulating to Rick, and he threw a restraining leg across her thrashing ones, pressing the heat of his erection against her straining thigh. She groaned low in her throat as she felt the proof of his arousal, and she knew then that he would not be denied.

Rick smiled slightly at her groan and then lowered his head to kiss the soft valley between her silken breasts. With lips and tongue, he traced burning patterns of delight upon her flesh, teasingly coming near but never quite touching the pink crests.

The fire of need he was insidiously stirring to life within her was growing more and more out of control, and Jennie had to force herself to remain rigid, refusing to give into the powerful, heated flashes of desire that were throbbing through her loins. It was heaven and it was hell. He was in total control, using her just as he had this morning, and there was absolutely nothing she could do about it.

Logically she wanted to be free of his embrace. How dare he come to her after having been with Lucia! But her body betrayed her, instinctively recognizing its mate even though she refused to. As his mouth descended to kiss the aching peak of her breasts, she surged wildly up against him, needing the feel of his hardened thighs driving against her.

Lifting his head, Rick's eyes met hers, reading the confusion in their passion-darkened depths.

"I don't want to hurt you, love," he murmured as he moved his hand and stifled anything she might have said with a deep, heart-wrenching kiss.

Jennie was past resisting, lost in the enthralling haze of passion's glory as Rick moved erotically against her.

"Please," she gasped as his mouth left hers.

"Please what, Jennie?" Rick encouraged, wanting to hear the words, needing to know that her vows of hatred earlier had been just wounded pride and jealousy and nothing more.

"Oh, Cazador." She twisted restlessly beneath him, yearning for closer contact.

"Please what, Jennie?" he demanded, stopping all movements, forcing her to answer him truthfully.

Looking up into his handsome face, Jennie knew she could no longer deny her need for him. Her body craved joining with his, no matter what he'd just done with Lucia. Later, she would think about that, but right now she didn't want to think; she only wanted to feel.

"Make love to me." The words were a husky whisper.

"Tell me you need me," he pushed.

Jennie almost balked at his confident tone.

"Now Jennie," he insisted.

"I need you, Cazador."

Grateful for the cover of night, he moved away just enough to help her from the rest of her clothes before going back into her arms. Jennie was surprised that he hadn't shed his own clothing, but at the touch of his hand on her burning flesh, she gave up all pretense of thought and surrendered to his masterful possession.

With long ardent caresses, Rick stroked the satin softness of her flesh, kindling feelings within her that Jennie didn't know existed. Rising above her and unbuckling his gunbelt, he set it nearby and undid his pants. No longer able to resist the seductive, inviting warmth of her, he plunged into her slick, velvety softness, losing himself even as he conquered her.

Jennie accepted the hard length of him eagerly and rocked with him in love's age-old rhythm. Each thrust of his driving hips sent her passion soaring higher and higher until it exploded in a star-burst of ecstasy that sent sparkles of shimmering love-light through them both. Breathless yet sated by their fervid mating, they collapsed in each other's arms in silent splendor.

Though the blackness of the night had provided a

sheltering blanket of privacy for Rick and Jennie, Lucia had been totally aware of their joining. Frustrated and angry, she lay on her pallet cursing the interruption that had torn her from Cazador's arms and sent him back to Jennie for satisfaction. After tomorrow, Lucia thought, smiling to herself, he would no longer need Jennie, for she would take care of him—completely.

Jennie tensed in Rick's embrace as the reality of her situation returned full force. How could she have allowed this to happen to her twice in one day? What was there about Cazador that his very nearness could reduce her to a mindless wanton? Hating herself for her weakness and hating him for pressing his advantage, she turned her fury on him.

"Damn you!" she seethed, pushing ineffectively at his chest to try to rid herself of his weight.

Rick had felt her tense, but he was completely startled by the fury in her voice. He had hoped that the rage she'd felt toward him since the morning had faded, but he knew now it hadn't. And, despite the fact that their lovemaking had been as stimulating as ever, she still refused to openly admit her desire for him.

Rick knew that Jennie was probably jealous of Lucia, but there was nothing he could do to reassure her until they were safely out of camp. For now, he would have to do whatever he deemed necessary to insure their continued well-being and that included his playing along with Lucia.

Shifting his body off Jennie's comforting softness, he looked down at her, making sure his expression was carefully shuttered.

Jennie glared up at him, her frustrated fury shining in her eyes. "How could you do this to me? You knew I didn't want you."

Rick shrugged indifferently as he moved away. "It really doesn't matter to me what you did or did not want. I wanted

219

you, so I took you."

Stung by the reminder of her subservient position, her pride rebelled and her indignation grew. "What's wrong, Cazador? It seems I remember you telling Luis and Ray that you liked willing women. Wasn't Lucia *willing* enough for you? Or have you changed since you joined up with Malo?"

Her accusations enraged him and he fought down the urge to throttle her. Tomorrow, as soon as he had his plan of action finalized, he would tell her the truth and then, at last, she would understand. Knowing that this was no time to get into an argument with her, he calmly adjusted his clothing, strapped on his gunbelt and rolled over away from her to go to sleep, pulling the blanket up over his shoulder.

Jennie was incensed that he could dismiss her so easily, but she felt his refusal to answer her incriminations made them all the more valid in her mind. Angry tears of defeat coursed down her cheeks, and she furiously wiped them away. There was ony one course of action left to her: She had to escape.

Giving Cazador a sidelong glance, she was relieved to see that he was apparently asleep. Jennie knew that if she really planned on getting away it had to be tonight for she was certain that Cazador was tiring of her and that he would turn her over to the other men as soon as he could claim Lucia for his own. Determined to wait at least another hour before she made her attempt, she lay stiffly beside him, fearing that at any moment he would stir and come awake, foiling her plan.

A momentary fear of failure assailed her, but she pushed it firmly aside. She was Jennie McCaine and she would make it. After all, her father was somewhere behind them looking for her, and it would only be a matter of hiding out in the rock-strewn mountains until they found her. The thought of her father's warm loving embrace filled her with a calm confidence and she relaxed. Soon she would be back home again.

Jennie suddenly remembered Juan Peralta and she

frowned worriedly. There had to be a way she could help him. Knowing that it would be useless to try to take the old man with her, she decided that as soon as she made contact with her father she would lead them back to rescue him. No doubt, the posse would be large and well armed, and she was certain that the men of M Circle C could save him.

Chapter Sixteen

It was late and it seemed to Jennie that a heavy pall of silent expectation hung over the small campsite—as if it knew what she was about to attempt. Knowing that she could delay no longer, she girded herself for the next harrowing hours, praying that her escape would be successful and that she would be able to find her father. Taking great care not to make any noise, Jennie slipped unnoticed from Cazador's side and, grabbing a canteen, she disappeared stealthily into the desert's moonless night.

Jennie moved warily to avoid the guard's watchful presence and, though hindered by the oppressive darkness, she began her slow progess down the rocky hillside. Afraid that the guard might hear her, she did not attempt to run until she was well away from the camp. Knowing that she would have to make her best time now while she could move about undetected, Jennie paced herself, running at a steady, ground-eating pace in the direction from which they'd just come, and it was not an easy task in her riding boots. The going was rugged and more than once she lost her footing, but still she struggled on, resolute in her determination to get as far away as she possibly could by sunup.

*   *   *

Dreading the night to come, Carrie stared wearily out across the slowly darkening landscape, her exhaustion clearly evident in every line of her slender body. The afternoon had been long and nerve-wracking as Todd's fever had soared out of control, and though she had labored over him lovingly he had shown little improvement. Even her attempts to get him to take drinks of water mixed with whiskey had met with little success and, more than a few times, she had feared that he might grow violent as he tossed miserably about in his delirium.

Turning away from the sun's fading glory, Carrie was disturbed to find that Todd had ceased his restless movements and was lying ominously still. Hurrying back to his side, she worried at the shallowness of his breathing, and she reached out nervously to touch the dry, searing hotness of his forehead.

As she knelt there wondering what she could do to ease his torment, violent chills began to wrack him. Hurrying to get her own blankets, she spread them over his big body, but their added warmth seemed to give him little relief. Troubled that he seemed to be worsening, Carrie grew desperate for a way to help. Finally, knowing there was no other alternative save body heat, she slipped beneath the covers and put her arms around him, hugging him to her.

Seeming to sense her comforting presence, Todd turned toward Carrie, hungrily seeking her embrace. His agitated movements slowed as he took her in his arms, and he quieted as he held her close. Relieved by his calming, she let herself relax.

"Carrie?" Todd's voice was husky and hoarse.

"What?" She was surprised that he was awake.

"Don't ever move away. You feel so wonderful next to me."

Carrie could hardly believe his words and quickly denied any deep meaning. She was convinced that it was the fever talking and she kept her response light.

"I'll be here as long as you need me, Todd."

His arms tightened momentarily about her and then slackened. "Good, forever," he answered her faintly, before he drifted off into a troubled sleep.

Closing her eyes to envision the joy of it, Carrie allowed herself the extravagance of pretending for a moment that Todd really had meant what he'd said. Her heart filled to bursting with love for him, and she smiled serenely to herself as she imagined him declaring himself and proposing to her ever so gallantly. Carrie had not intended to fall asleep, but somehow her sweet daydreams of loving him had swept her into a lengthy, restful slumber.

When she awoke, Carrie had no idea how much time had passed. Outside, night had claimed the canyon with a vengeance, its blackness forbidding and impenetrable. The fire that had been burning brightly when she'd drifted off was now only a mass of glowing embers. Wanting to stoke it back to life, she tried to edge from Todd's side, but as she stirred and started to move away he roused.

"Don't go," he growled as his arm came about her to pull her to him.

"But the fire," Carrie protested, feeling tortured by his nearness— a nearness that she craved physically and mentally but knew she would never have for her own.

"There's only one fire I'm concerned with," Todd told her as he turned her to face him.

"What?" She turned a startled gaze to him, noticing how feverishly bright his eyes were. "Todd. You're ill. You don't know what you're saying!" Carrie protested as his hands explored her with rousing expertise.

"I know exactly what I'm saying—and doing." He moved closer then, capturing her lips in a blazing exchange.

Carrie shivered under the onslaught of his passionate kiss. This was what she'd always wanted: Todd's kiss; Todd's embrace. Why fight it? And she pushed away all thoughts from her mind of what the morning would bring.

"Oh, Todd, I love you so!" she groaned excitedly as his mouth left hers to caress the sensitive cords of her throat, and she arched against him temptingly. "I've wanted this for so long."

With eager fingers, Carrie began to unbutton her blouse, wanting Todd to touch her, and he pulled back suddenly, to look down at her.

"Your hair is so beautiful," he remarked, running his fingers through her blond, silken tresses. "Just as you are." He dipped his head to kiss her again, more slowly this time. Quivering in anticipation of his total possession, Carrie looped her arms about his neck and hugged him close. The heat of his chest seared her bared breasts and her nipples hardened at the contact. A low moan escaped him and she drew away, her expression worried.

"I'm sorry, Did I hurt your shoulder?" The sudden remembrance of his wound jolted her back momentarily to reality.

"No you didn't hurt me. Far from it." He slipped her blouse from her shoulders and tossed it aside, staring in awe at the perfection of her creamy breasts. With a gentle finger, he reached out to touch each rosy peak, and he smiled when she gasped at the sensation his tender caress aroused within her. "Lovely," Todd murmured as he bent to her, kissing each throbbing tip.

A fire of desire was born within Carrie at the touch of his hot, moist mouth, and she tossed fitfully beneath his sensual ministrations as the tightening coil of her need grew. Holding his head to her breast, she rotated her hips invitingly against the hard heat of his manhood, hoping to bring him to the brink so she could take him deep within her and make him hers.

That one encouragement from Carrie was all he needed, and he rose above her to quickly strip away the remainder of their clothing. Gazing down at the beauty of her slender body, Todd found that she was more gorgeous than he could ever have hoped, and he had never been with a woman who was as responsive and as exciting as she was.

Bracing himself on his elbows, he fitted himself to her feminine softness as she reached down to hold him. Her touch brought him to the edge of mindlessness, and he covered her hand with his as she stroked him in the most pleasurable, knowing way. Gritting his teeth against the exquisite agony of her caress, he fought against the need to take her quickly.

Carrie, sensing that she was now in control, used all of her knowledge to bring him to unending rapture. She wanted him to remember this moment with her for the rest of his life, no matter what happened between them in the future. Encouraging him to lie on his back, she explored him hungrily with greedy kisses, searching out and finding his most erotic zones and teasing him to the peak again and again without giving him the completion his body craved. Moving lower, her lips sought the hardness of his desire, and as she took him within her mouth, Todd jerked in stunned surprise.

"Carrie," he protested groaningly as he grabbed her by the shoulders and pulled her up to him.

"I only wanted to please you, Todd," she told him sensuously. "Didn't you like it?"

With a guttural growl, he kissed her fiercely, and Carrie once again reached down for him, guiding him to her hungry flesh. Raising her hips, she slid down the magnificent length of him, enveloping his heat and hardness in one smooth stroke. At the feeling of him deep inside of her, Carrie lost all semblance of restraint.

"Todd!" she cried out as her body climaxed convulsively and, at the feel of her unbridled passions, he began to move, thrusting forcefully into her as she pulsed around him, her muscles contracting in rhythm with his possession.

Carrie was amazed that Todd understood her needs and, as her first peak subsided, he rolled her to her back without leaving her and took charge of their mating.

Staring down into her passion-glazed eyes, Todd smiled triumphantly. He had never known a woman so exciting. Carrie was a treasure. Withdrawing from her, he stifled her protest with a deep kiss and then began to caress her again, tasting every inch of her, sucking at her breasts eagerly and then moving down to press heated kisses on the silken expanse of her stomach.

Languidly, Carrie allowed him to position her, lifting her hips, and she thrilled to the hot devouring touch of his mouth when he claimed her innermost secrets. Her climax this time was so intimate and so shattering that she sobbed when he released her. He slid up over her to possess her again, giving her no time to think. Surging within, he thrust rapidly, eager to seek that moment of ecstasy he'd been longing for ever since he'd kissed her during the sandstorm.

Carrie, overpowered by his ardent lovemaking, luxuriated in his domination of her, and she lifted her arms to embrace him more closely as his body strained to hers. Shuddering as his excitement peaked, Todd collapsed heavily on top of her, totally spent by their fervid lovemaking.

It was long moments before he had the strength of will to move from Carrie, but even when he did, he brought her with him, holding her close to his uninjured side. Without speaking, they lay together, eyes closed, expressions rapturous, and softly they drifted off to sleep.

The first light of dawn cast a pinkish golden glow to the eastern horizon as Jennie continued to move as quickly as she could across the demanding terrain. With morning's presence threatening to reveal her whereabouts, Jennie started a climb to higher ground, searching for an observation point from which she could view the surrounding area without being seen.

There were numerous rocks and boulders, but she found

none that afforded the protection she knew she would need when Cazador came looking for her. Stopping briefly to take a drink of her treasured water, Jennie surveyed the surrounding area, hoping as the day brightened to catch sight of a more suitable shelter. Her hopes went rewarded for at the crest of the next rise, she spotted a massive, rounded boulder well camouflaged by a huge saguaro cactus and assorted scrubby bushes.

The climb to the top seemed endless as Jennie slipped constantly on the loose, sandy soil, but at last she reached her goal, scrambling awkwardly behind the protective cover it afforded. Breathless from the rugged ascent, she leaned heavily against the monolith until her strength returned. Taking one more quick drink, she sealed the canteen tightly and sought some comfort in her rocky shelter, knowing that it was probably going to be a long wait.

Todd came awake slowly, his entire body aching and his head pounding fiercely. He wondered quickly what had happened, and it came to him then that he'd been feeling weak and had been having trouble sitting his horse. But where was he now? Opening his eyes, he lay unmoving, staring at the rocky ceiling above. The mine? How had he gotten here? Shifting positions he almost bolted when he found Carrie lying next to him, her nude body pressed enticingly to his own unclad length.

Blinking in confusion, he groaned inwardly as he realized that it hadn't been a dream. He actually had made passionate love to her. Dear God! What had he done?

"Carrie?" he rasped hoarsely.

Carrie was instantly awake and she smiled at him as she stretched sinuously. "Good morning."

As her breasts accidentally grazed his chest, Todd started as if he'd been burned. Why had he let it happen? How could he have taken advantage of Carrie when he felt the way he

228

did about Jennie? Feeling very much ashamed, he moved quickly away from Carrie's intoxicating nearness, trying desperately to get himself together. He had to apologize for his behavior; he had to reassure her that he would never let this happen between them again. He was practically engaged to her sister, for heaven's sake!

Carrie was surprised when Todd withdrew from her. The sensuality they had shared just a few hours before had been nothing short of Elysian ecstasy, and she had wanted it to go on forever.

"Todd?" Carrie couldn't stop herself from questioning him.

"Carrie, I'm sorry. I never meant for this to happen." He was nervously reaching for his pants as he spoke.

Despair gripped her. She had given of her love freely, wildly. Never before had she reached the heights of joy that she'd reached with Todd and yet he was denying it all. Carrie had known from the beginning that this might happen, but she'd never really believed it would. She had held onto the hope that after Todd had made love to her, he wouldn't be able to forget her or live without her. Too late she realized the flaw in her plan: No matter how much she loved him, she could not force him to love her—not when he'd already told her of his proposal to Jennie.

"I know," she stated flatly, tears stinging her eyes as she admitted to herself that once again her sister had won.

"It'll never happen again, Carrie. I promise." His words were solemn and earnest as he finished buttoning his pants, and he turned to look at her.

Adept at hiding her feelings, she met his gaze steadily. "Todd, there's no need for you to worry. You hardly took advantage of me. I wanted you as much as you wanted me."

Todd's heart ached as he returned her regard, and grimly he realized how badly he had hurt her. Carrie sensed that he could read her thoughts and it frightened her. No one else had ever been able to see through her very capable defenses;

229

no one until Todd. Nervously moving away, she grabbed her clothes. She felt at a distinct disadvantage with him, and she hoped that by dressing she might regain some of her shattered composure.

Watching her jerky movements as she pulled on her clothes, Todd understood her upset and, though he wanted to comfort her, he knew it would be better if he stayed some distance from her. The attraction between them was far too potent to risk losing control again.

"How do you feel?" she asked, wanting to break the raw tension between them.

"I'm fine," he replied, glad that they had turned the conversation. "What happened?"

"You developed a high fever, so we decided it would be best to bring you back here until it passed."

"How long have we been here?"

"Just since yesterday. I guess your fever must have broken during the night." Carrie said and then blushed, as she remembered their feverish mating.

"Yes," Todd replied distantly as he, too, was lost in the haziness of his memory of their passionate lovemaking. "Well," he continued abruptly, clearing his throat, "I think I'm strong enough to ride now."

"Let's have something to eat and then we can try to catch up with them."

"Fine. What time is it now?"

"Just past sunup," Carrie told him as she moved to the entrance and looked out across the canyon.

"So your father's about eight hours ahead of us?"

"About that," she said as she busily began to prepare some food.

Todd found himself watching Carrie's every move and admiring the snug fit of her pants on her slim hips. He remembered well the way her legs had felt wrapped so sensuously about him, and he knew no matter how hard he tried, he would never be able to deny the physical attraction he felt for her. Distractedly, Todd wondered how he was going to handle these feelings he had for Carrie once he was married to Jennie. It had felt so right, holding her and kissing her and seeking his ultimate pleasure in her lithe body. Forcing his thoughts back to the present, he thanked her as she handed him his meal, and he ate hungrily, forcing himself to keep his attention solely on the food.

Carrie sat down opposite him, saying, "Before you put your shirt on, I want to check your wound one more time."

"All right," he answered, not looking up, concerned that he would have to allow her so close again.

Carrie had hoped to draw him into conversation to ease the awkwardness of their situation, but he seemed determined to ignore her, leaving her feeling rejected and filled with the fear that she had ruined their relationship for all time.

Rick's eyes narrowed as he stared out across the rough, rock-jumbled landscape. Where the hell was she? There had been no sign, no trace, since he'd lost her tracks on the trail about half a mile back.

"Jennie!" His call split the silence of the early morning like a crash of thunder, and once again he urged his horse forward to continue his search.

Rick had been looking for her for hours now, and he was growing more apprehensive by the minute. The sun, warm on his back as he rode slowly over the rugged path, had only been breaking the horizon when he had roused from his restive sleep to find that Jennie had disappeared. At first he'd thought she'd just left the camp to take care of her personal needs, but when she hadn't returned right away, he'd become concerned. And, as long minutes had passed with no sign of her, the memory of the night before had begun to haunt him. He'd acknowledged to himself then that she had been justified in so bitterly admonishing him for he had been almost brutal in his taking of her, forcing a reaction from her body even while her mind had rebelled.

In the cold objectivity of that first morning light, Rick had realized how wrong it had been to use her in that way, but by the time he decided to apologize and set things straight between them, it had been too late; he'd discovered, much to his distress, that she'd already fled the camp—and him.

The initial uproar in camp over her disappearance had ended quickly when it was found that she had taken off, on foot, with only a single canteen of water. Malo had been particularly indifferent, not wanting to be distracted from his quest for the gold mine.

"She was pretty, Cazador, but very stupid," he'd said dispassionately. "She won't last a day in the mountains, alone, especially without a gun."

Rick had had a difficult time keeping a tight rein on his fury. "I'm going to look for her. I'll catch up with you later today."

Malo had shrugged his unconcern, but his expression had revealed that he thought Rick's concern about Jennie revealed a weakness in him. "She is only a woman."

Rick had been hunting for her ever since, alternately angry and anxious. He'd quickly discarded his initial fear that she had wandered off during the night and had been injured—when he'd found that she'd taken a canteen with her. She had planned her escape; there had been no accident.

Enraged that she'd felt the need to flee from him, yet understanding her fear, Rick had continued to search until now. Reining in and letting his gaze roam over the craggy, lifeless peaks, it suddenly occurred to him that Jennie was in hiding. She didn't want to be found, especially not by him! Swearing aloud, he took one last cursory look around and then wheeled his horse in the direction of the camp

Rick was convinced that she was safe and merely concealing herself from him while she awaited the posse's arrival. Torn between the need to keep searching for her and

232

his need to rescue Juan, Rick knew he had no real choice. He was Juan's only hope for survival. Taking one more glance over his shoulder, he spurred his horse to a faster gait, intent on catching up with the outlaws as soon as possible.

Jennie cautiously peeked around the side of the boulder. Cazador was so close she felt almost as if she could reach out and touch him. His expression was so fierce that she caught her breath and slipped back behind the rock's protective cover, praying that he wouldn't find her.

She waited. Each minute that passed seemed an eternity as Jennie silently endured the torture of uncertainty and then, finally, she heard him ride away. Moving from her place of safety to see in which direction he'd ridden, she breathed a deep sigh of relief when she discovered that he had headed back toward camp, apparently giving up his search for her.

As Jennie watched Cazador disappear down the narrow canyon, she felt suddenly bereft and alone, and she wondered briefly what she would do if the posse never came.

Chapter Seventeen

Because Steve and Mac had left their trail carefully marked, Todd and Carrie made good time in their attempt to catch up. They had been riding hard since that morning, and they were excited to find that it had paid off.

"Look! Over there!" Todd slowed his mount and turned to Carrie.

"Do you see them?" Carrie asked as she reined in beside him, staring off into the distance.

"It's the posse!" Putting his knees to his horse, he picked up their pace.

"Should we signal them to wait for us? It'll be dark soon." Carrie did not relish the possibility of spending another night on the trail alone with Todd, especially now that she knew exactly where she stood with him. He did not love her and he never would.

"No. If we fire a shot, we might alert more than just the posse to where we are," he told her ominously. "Come on. We'll have to hurry, if we want to meet up with them before nightfall."

"I'm glad Pa marked the trail for us. We certainly managed to make up for a lot of lost time today."

"That we did, but we're not there yet," Todd said, keeping his gaze on the posse riding far ahead of them, and they rode on steadily, not even considering stopping, as the shadows of dusk began to lengthen.

Falling into a comfortable silence, Carrie shared his conviction to meet up with the men as soon as possible, and she rode at his side, uncomplaining and determined. She was glad that the initial awkwardness she'd felt in Todd's company that morning had faded as they'd shared the turmoil of the day and that the anxiety she'd felt about ruining their relationship had been completely unfounded. Todd had been the perfect gentleman, treating her with the same good-natured temperament that he'd always shown her, and it was almost as if their fervid lovemaking had never happened.

Todd cast Carrie a sidelong glance as they rode abreast, wondering how much longer he could keep up his charade. He had been trying since morning to convince both Carrie and himself that they could ride together and stay in close contact and not be swept away by their passions as they had been the night before. He was finding, however, that it was not as easy as he'd thought it would be.

Carrie had ignited a fire within him, and though he was fighting to keep it carefully under control, at times he felt he was failing miserably. That was why he felt the need to make the desperate dash to catch up with the men of the M Circle C. There they would have no opportunity to be alone again, and her virtue would be well guarded.

He was still angry with himself for having taken her; although, the love he had shared in Carrie's arms had been unlike anything he'd ever experienced in his entire life. It had been enthralling, bewitching, and had it not been for his feelings for Jennie, Todd knew that he would be actively pursuing her, even now. His jaw clenched as he felt the familiar tightening in his loins, and he almost wished that his shoulder was still bothering him, just so he would have something to take his mind off his desires.

When Carrie had doctored his wound before they'd

started out, it had been pure torture for him. Her closeness, her scent, and the feel of her hands on his body had sorely tested his resolve not to touch her again. It had been all he could do just to lie still beneath her ministering hands. Things had gotten so bad that at one point he'd had to stifle a low groan of desire and, luckily, Carrie only thought she'd wound the bandage too tight.

Todd was certain that she had no idea of the agony of physical need that was wracking him, and he wanted to keep it that way. He did not want her to feel threatened by him. What had happened between them had been a momentary aberration, no doubt brought on by his feverish state, and he would make sure that it never happened again.

Steve was the first one to catch sight of Carrie and Todd, and he halted the posse's progress up the narrow canyon to give them time to catch up.

"Looks like your plan worked," he remarked to Mac as he nodded in their direction.

"Good!" Mac was pleased to see Todd back in the saddle and, he thought with surprise, he was glad to see his daughter, too. Riding back to the rear of the group, he waited eagerly for them to traverse the last mile separating them. "Todd! It's good to see you moving again. I can't tell you how concerned we were," he called out in greeting.

"It's all thanks to Carrie, Mac," he replied as he drew up beside him. "She took good care of me."

"Good girl." He found himself smiling benignly at his youngest daughter.

Carrie was stunned by her father's approving look. Never before could she ever remember him being pleased with any of her accomplishments. It gave her a warm feeling inside and she smiled back, somewhat tremulously.

"Have you found anything yet?" Todd asked anxiously.

"No, we're still tracking them. The going was real slow today." Mac shook his head in frustration over the nearly impassable terrain as he looked up at the craggy peaks that surrounded them.

"Well, they can't be traveling too much faster. The land is just too rugged," Todd said, hoping he sounded optimistic.

"That's true enough," he began but was interrupted by Jake's arrival.

"Todd, good to see you. Steve was scouting up ahead, and he's found a small watering hole with some good water in it. He figures if we camp there for the night, we'll be in good shape come morning."

"All right," Mac said gruffly, hating this time every night when he had to stop searching for Jennie. "Tell him to go ahead and set up camp. Maybe tomorrow we'll find her."

Mac slumped wearily in the saddle as his vitality drained from him. Another day spent in fruitless search as God knows what was happening to Jennie.

Carrie was startled when Mac suddenly seemed to trasform before her. No longer was he the dreaded invincible godlike being who had ruled her days and nights with an iron will; instead, she realized that he was just an exhausted old man.

With that knowledge came an entire change of perspective for her. Carrie wished, right then, that she could somehow reassure Mac and ease the weight of his worry, but her feelings of warmth toward him were far too new for her to act upon them. She was still not certain that he would be receptive to any conciliatory advance on her part, and she was fearful that, if she did venture any kindness, he might cut her to the quick with a caustic comment as he had done so often in the past. So, Carrie held her tongue and followed along with their lead as they rode on to the campsite that Steve had chosen for the night.

As darkness descended, Jennie sat huddled in her shelter, miserably aware of what a poorly prepared escape she had made. No blankets, no food, no gun. Away from Cazador's

237

disturbing presence, she wondered how she could have been so desperate to escape that she hadn't thought to bring along the basic essentials for survival. Swearing at her own stupidity, she wondered at her lack of common sense.

What was there about Cazador that caused her to panic and lose sight of all the things her father had ever taught her about staying alive on the desert? Jennie didn't know, but she was sure that death on the desert was far preferable to being passed around Malo's camp from man to man, until they'd had their fill of her. She shuddered at the thought.

As much as she'd thought herself in love with the gunfighter in the beginning, she knew now that she had made the right decision in leaving him. Lucia had made no secret about her desire for Cazador, and it had been painfully obvious to Jennie that Cazador had taken the other woman up on her offer. In her mind, she pictured them in a passionate embrace, his deeply tanned body pressed naked to Lucia's slim welcoming length, and it seared her to the very depths of her soul. Refusing to admit that she still cared for him, she congratulated herself on getting away from him before she'd been made to suffer more of his advances. She did not want Lucia's leftovers. Jennie seethed to herself and tried to push the image of their lovemaking from her thoughts.

Shifting uncomfortably on the hard ground, Jennie was pleased that she'd had enough foresight to conserve her water that day. Originally, she had thought that her father was only a few hours behind in his pursuit of them, but as the day had slowly passed, she'd come to realize that she might have made a drastic miscalculation. Jannie refused to allow herself to think about being stranded out here on foot. Intead, she began to plan what she would do to save herself if indeed the posse did not find her the following day.

When she finally managed to fall asleep, her rest was not an easy one. In her defenseless state, visions of the last few days bombarded her: Luis and Ray, the rattlesnake, the flash

238

flood, Malo, Lucia, and finally, at the center of the swirling vortex was Cazador—His dark, powerful form dominating her every fantasy as her body came alive with the memory of his lovemaking. His words rang in her mind even now: *I wanted you so I took you.* His face swam before her, and she realized in her dream that she had wanted him, too; that she had needed his possession desperately to ease the desire that was burning within her. But in the dream, the passion she felt for him turned to hate as Lucia enticed him away into her lusty embrace. In her dream, Jennie was forced to watch them come together, and she began to toss and turn in protest until she awoke, mentally and physically exhausted from the nightmare.

Sitting up, Jennie clasped her knees to her chest and hugged them tightly, trying to make sense out of the madness of her visions. She didn't want to care what he did with Lucia. She didn't want to care about him! But, she acknowledged to herself in defeat, she did. Cazador had managed to awaken a sensuality within her. She knew no other man would ever satisfy her the way he had, and she wondered how she would possibly be able to find happiness with Todd after having known the exquisite rapture of Cazador's conquest.

Cazador had been the master of her senses, forcing her to the heights of breathtaking ecstasy against her will until she had surrendered all to him and then exacting the most cruel of revenges: making her admit that she wanted him. Jennie shivered as she remembered the ultimate thrill of his total possession, and she knew that she had been right to leave him when she had—before her need for him had become so overpowering that she would have been unable to break away.

Her breasts were throbbing in anticipation of a lover's touch, and Jennie bit her lip to stifle the moan of desire that welled up within her as she imagined his hardness penetrating her softness. Mentally, she shook herself fiercely, driving all memories of Cazador from her conscious thoughts, and then curled up again on the unyielding ground, to await the coming of the new day.

Malo tilted the bottle of tequila to his mouth and drank thirstily, not bothering to wipe away the excess that dribbled down his chin. With shining eyes, he surveyed his camp. Tomorrow it would all be over. Tomorrow, Peralta had assured him, they would reach the mine!

"Cazador!" His raucous call drew Rick's immediate attention.

Rick tossed his saddlebags down on his bedroll and walked to where Malo was waiting for him. "What?"

"You do not seem as excited as the others at the prospect of being rich." Malo had found him to be subdued all day and he wondered at it.

Rick met his eyes coolly. "I have not seen the gold yet. When I do, maybe then I'll feel the need for a little excitement." His words expressed his disdain at the outlaws' heavy drinking and amorous use of Chica.

Malo nodded and held the bottle out to him, but Rick shook his head.

"I'm guarding the old man in another hour, and I want to be in complete control. I don't want to risk losing him, now." He glanced over to where Juan sat, bound hand and foot.

"He's not going anywhere tonight," Malo said and shrugged.

"That's right and I want to keep it that way. There's too much at stake here."

"I agree and I'm glad you're the one guarding him tonight. I know I can trust you to make sure that nothing happens to him."

Rick smiled to himself at the truth of Malo's words. "I plan on taking real good care of him."

"Have you seen any sign of Apache?" He didn't want

anything to go wrong, not when he was so close to his goal.

"No," Rick answered curtly. "Nothing yet."

"Good and let's hope it stays that way." Walking away, his gait was unsteady as he drank again from the bottle of liquor.

Returning to his bedroll, Rick unrolled his blanket and then sat down and made himself comfortable to await the beginning of his turn at guard. He had had no opportunity to speak with Juan today, but he was certain that his grandfather had heard of Jennie's flight. No doubt Juan was wondering what was going on and why Rick had disappeared for so long this morning. Resigned to waiting until the time was right to tell him the whole story, he settled back and tried to relax.

But Rick found no ease as his thoughts turned to Jennie: Where was she? How was she? Was she safe in her father's protective care, as he hoped? Or was she wandering around the wastelands of these mountains, alone and afraid?

Giving up the search for her this morning was one of the hardest things he ever had to do in his life, and had it not been for the very real danger that Juan faced, he would probably still be looking for her. Rick had been convinced, though, that she had been hiding from him, not that she'd been hurt or injured, and it was only that belief that allowed him some modicum of peace.

Looking up, Rick saw Lucia join Malo. He felt confident, for the moment, that she would not tell Malo of his conversation with Juan. Rick had dealt with women like Lucia before, and he knew exactly how to play her. He didn't relish the thought that he might have to have sex with her just to keep her quiet but, if he wanted to maintain his element of surprise, he would do whatever he had to do.

No matter how physically satisfying it would be for him, Rick still found the idea of joining with Lucia unappealing. Having tasted of Jennie's love, he knew he wanted no other. And, he decided firmly in that instant, as soon as he was

241

away from here with Juan he would find Jennie and make his peace with her.

Focusing once again on Juan, he noted the time. Then with professional expertise, he checked his sidearm to make sure that it was fully loaded before heading over to relieve Ramon from his post as Juan's guard.

Luis had been watching Lucia's every move since they had made camp, and though she had not, as yet, made any attempt to speak with Cazador alone, he felt certain that they had set up a rendezvous for later. He could hardly wait for the moment when he would lead Malo to where his woman and his top gun were making it. A sly grin split his swarthy features as he imagined the reward Malo would give him for the information. It bothered him some that Jennie had run away, but he knew he'd be able to buy a bunch of women with the money he was going to make from Malo.

"Ray."

His partner looked up drunkenly from where he sat with a bottle of whiskey. "What do you want?"

"Help me keep an eye on old Cazador tonight. He seems mighty restless since that woman of his took off."

Ray grinned stupidly. "We shoulda taken her while we had the chance. She sure was a looker."

"Well, I want money more than I want her. You can always get women if you got gold, but you can't always get gold if you got women," he said convincingly.

"You speakin' from experience?" Ray laughed and took another swallow.

"I am." Luis smiled. "And I never intend to be in that situation again.

Lucia sat at Malo's side, trying to gauge how much longer it would be before he passed out from the tequila. Though outwardly she presented the picture of the attentive lover who was caring for his every need, inwardly, she could hardly wait for him to fall asleep so she could safely go to Cazador.

Lucia had been caught totally by surprise when Chica had told her the news of Jennie's escape. Delighted that the girl could be so stupid as to leave Cazador, she intended to take up where Jennie had left off. Tonight she would make him hers, and then tomorrow they would figure out a way to steal all the gold just for themselves. Lucia was sure that Cazador would like her idea, and she could hardly wait to tell him of her plan.

"What are you smiling about?" Malo demanded, his eyes sharp on her face in the darkness.

"I was only thinking about how rich we're going to be tomorrow." Lucia turned her full attention back to him before he grew more suspicious at her errant thoughts.

"That, I will." He grinned.

Malo pulled her close for a sloppy possessive kiss and, though the thought of being with him almost made her sick, she submitted to his gropings without protest, knowing that soon she would be in the arms of the man she truly wanted.

Juan watched Rick's approach, pleased that his grandson would again be his guard this night. The day had been a particularly troubled one for Juan, and he longed to speak with him and to be reassured that everything would indeed turn out all right.

Juan's gaze went over Rick as he drew near, and he felt a swell of pride that he had turned out to be such a fine specimen of a man. Tall and lean, his gun worn low on his hip, his movements were confident and easy, reflecting the control he maintained over himself at all times.

Ramon saw Rick coming and was eager to join the other men in their celebration.

"It won't be long now, will it?" Ramon greeted him with a greed-inspired smile.

"No," Rick said, glancing down at his grandfather meaningfully. "It won't be long, now."

"Take good care of him, Cazador. He is priceless." The desperado chuckled cynically at his own humor as he headed across the camp to where some of the others had gathered around Chica.

Rick waited until Ramon had joined them before speaking. "How are you?"

"Better, now that you are here," Juan answered truthfully. "What happened this morning?"

"Jennie ran away sometime during the night," he responded levelly, not allowing any emotion to reflect in his tone. "I went to look for her."

"You didn't find her?"

"Not a trace. Her tracks just stopped about a mile from the campsite."

"You're sure no one forced her to go?" Juan worried that one of the outlaws might have dragged her away against her will.

"No." Rick frowned at the possibility. "She went of her own accord, and she took a canteen with her."

"She is hoping that her father will find her?"

He nodded in response. "I'm sure she was deliberately hiding from me."

"Maybe it is better this way."

"Maybe," he answered distantly, unable to rid himself of the haunting fear that somewhere, out in the oppressive darkness of the Arizona night, Jennie might be in trouble. "We will leave just before the end of my watch. I figure they'll all be passed out by then, and I'll only have to take the one lookout."

Juan nodded in silent consideration, knowing how dangerous the next hours would be for them.

*   *   *

Midnight had long since come and gone when the revelry finally quieted. Most of the men had passed out, overcome by the amount of potent liquor they'd consumed, and even Chica had taken to the bottle to ease the indignity of the outlaws' constant degrading demands on her body. She lay now in a drunken stupor, thankfully anesthetized by the tequila's heady spirits, while Pablo sought his release within the abused, bruised acceptance of her limp form.

As the hours of the night had slowly passed, Luis had watched the men as they had used Chica over and over again, and he had taken a perverted pleasure in the humiliating pain that had been inflicted on her. Unlike Malo, who on occasion showed some kindness toward women, Luis hated them all. He truly believed that they were all whores at heart and that they enjoyed the punishment that he dealt them.

Luis felt a stirring in his loins as he saw Pablo shudder in the throes of his climax, and he collapsed on top of Chica. Anger raced through him as he thought of how close he had come to having Jennie for his own. Once he had his share of the gold, he was going to go look for her and somehow find a way to get at her. Mac MaCaine or no Mac McCaine!

Luis watched with a shuddered expression as Pablo rolled wearily off Chica's inert body and began to pull up his pants. As he staggered to his feet and lurched off into the darkness, Luis let his gaze fall upon Chica.

She lay spread-eagled and helpless on her blanket. The last thought sent a surge of desire through Luis, and his body demanded that he take her, knowing that she was powerless to resist anything he chose to do. He didn't really want her. She was just a vessel to receive his wrath, and he rose from where he had been sitting with Ray, who was now asleep.

Stalking across to her bedroll, Luis stood over her, feeling at once excited and disgusted by the picture she made: her body glowing whitely in the night's covering blackness. Bruises from the other men showed darkly on her breasts and thighs, and Luis was mesmerized as he knelt between her legs.

With hurtful hands, he reached out and pinched at her nipples, hoping to draw some response from her. When she moaned in drunken protest, he smiled wolfishly and lay fully upon her.

"Tell what you like, *puta!*" he rasped in her ear as his hands continued to torment her.

Chica stirred as the pain became unbearable. "No," she groaned as his fingers dug into her tender flesh.

Twisting weakly, she tried to fight him off, but Luis was used to using force to get what he wanted. Grabbing her chin, he held her head still.

"Open your eyes, *ramera!*" he ordered, and his diabolical tone cut through her liquor-induced haze.

Chica stared up at him, terrified. She had never been with Luis before, but she had heard of his reputation. He was known for his cold, ruthless ways with women and more than one had died from his beastiality. The other men, while they did sometimes hurt her, never intentionally set out to cause injury; but Luis was different.

"No, Luis, please, no," she pleaded, her eyes wide and glazed with horror.

"I like to hear you plead, Chica." He laughed low, as he bit at her neck. "Beg me to stop. Maybe, I will."

Biting her lip, she tried to lay unmoving beneath him, but his touch was so manipulative that her body began to respond to him.

Luis smiled to himself as he felt her begin to relax. It always pleased him to taunt women with sensual pleasure before he sought his own excitement in their pain. Though he was not tender with Chica, he did know exactly where to caress her to arouse her sufficiently, and he dipped his head to suck at her nipples, so sensitive now from his earlier cruel assault.

When her hips began to move invitingly against his, he drew away from her and, without speaking, slapped her twice, as hard as he could, rocking her head back and forth with the force of his blows.

"*Puta!* Whore!" he seethed as he positioned her legs to receive him. Letting his pants down, he plunged mercilessly within her.

She was barely conscious, and her groans of agony only aroused him all the more as he thrust rapidly against her. When he reached his peak of pleasure, Luis did not allow himself to collapse atop her; instead, he pulled back and quickly fastened his clothes. Taking one last look at her bruised and swollen face, he got up and walked calmly away, his only regret being that Chica had not been Jennie.

Rick stood his ground, barely in control. The viciousness of Luis's attack on Chica had stunned him, and he was filled with the terrible need to kill the outlaw. After witnessing the way Luis treated women, Rick was relieved that he'd saved Jennie from him, for falling prey to Luis would certainly have been a fate worse than death.

Eager to be free of Malo and his men, Rick looked down at his grandfather who had also been aware of the assault.

"Men like Luis need to be killed," Rick told him in low, determined tones.

Juan nodded. "A man does not mistreat women. Luis is little more than an animal."

"They all are," Rick acknowledged bitterly. "Vicious human animals, and they are far more dangerous than any of the creatures in the wild. Wild animals kill only to survive. Men like these kill and maim strictly for the enjoyment of it."

They exchanged a knowing look as Rick moved a distance away to resume his position as guard.

Lucia glanced over to where Chica lay unmoving on her bed. Carefully extracting herself from Malo's side, she took a canteen and hurried to her friend's side.

247

"Chica." Her words were hushed and filled with worry as she bathed her face with the cool water.

"Lucia," Chica managed in a croaking whisper, "he hurt me."

"I know, I know." Lucia's voice was hard as she gazed down at her.

Chica's cheeks bore the imprint of Luis's rage, and her lip had been split by the force of his blows. Vivid purple bruises covered her breasts, and there were bite marks on the side of her neck.

"Help me dress," she whispered through swollen lips as she tried to sit up. A violent pain tore through her midsection, and she fell back in agony as Lucia noticed for the first time the blood that seeped ominously from between her thighs.

"Chica! You're bleeding." Lucia was frightened.

"I'll be all right. Just give me my blouse. I want to get dressed."

With Lucia's help, she managed to pull on the loose-fitting garment.

"Is there any tequila left in that bottle?" Chica pointed to a discarded bottle.

Hurrying to get it for her, she found it was almost half full, and she handed it to her.

"Thanks." Chica maneuvered herself upright with Lucia's help and then drank quickly of the tequila, almost draining the bottle completely. "Give me my skirt," she said as she managed to stay sitting up by herself. "Someday . . ."

"Someday, what?" Lucia asked worriedly.

"Someday I will see that man in hell." She spoke the words so calmly and with such effect that a chill ran down Lucia's spine.

"It is where he belongs," she said.

There was a silence between them as Chica slowly got to her feet. "I'll be back."

Knowing that Chica wanted and needed to be alone, Lucia

watched her painful progress from the camp. When her friend had disappeared from sight, she returned to Malo's side and tried to rest, but a strange sense of danger seemed to hang over the encampment. Lucia tried to dismiss the feeling as just her own nervous reaction to Luis's brutality and the excitement of the reaching the gold mine tomorrow, but somehow her instincts told her it was more than that. Determined to use even greater caution when she approached Cazador tonight, she settled back on her blanket to wait for the safest moment to search him out.

Chapter Eighteen

It was over an hour later when Lucia finally felt it was safe enough to pursue Cazador. She had seen Chica return to her bed and fall quickly into an exhausted slumber and Luis, too, appeared to be sleeping soundly. Stealthily, she rose and tiptoed quietly from the camp, unaware of the evil, slitted eyes that watched her go.

Rick had hoped he and Juan could make their escape without having to deal with Lucia, but when he saw her creep away from Malo's side, he knew it would be impossible to avoid the upcoming confrontation with her. Pondering the situation, he tried to decide the best way to handle her.

There was no doubt in his mind that she fully intended for him to make love to her, and Rick found the prospect profoundly disturbing. Not that he considered Lucia unattractive for he actually thought her quite pretty in an earthy sort of way; it was just that Jennie was the only woman he really desired. He frowned as he contemplated the thought.

Juan saw Rick frown and wondered at the cause.

"What is wrong?" he questioned softly.

"Nothing," Rick denied hurriedly, not quite ready to discuss his feelings. Kneeling before Juan, he untied his bonds and took one of the lengths of rope. "Don't move. We

250

want to make it look like you're still tied up. I'll be back in just a few minutes."

Stuffing the rope into his back pocket, he stood up and disappeared into the darkness in search of Lucia. She was waiting for him only a short distance away, and Rick had no trouble finding her.

"I had hoped that you would see me leave," she purred. "And come to me willingly."

Lucia was afire with her desire for him; Malo's love-making had, as always, left her unfulfilled, and she was burning with the need to be taken by a real man—by Cazador.

Her eyes went over him hungrily, taking in the breadth of his wide shoulders and the narrowness of his hips. She found him so magnificent that she could hardly wait to see him naked again. Gazing up at him, she searched his face for some sign of emotion, but his expression was inscrutable, his eyes almost cold as they regarded her.

Lucia's heart sank as she realize that he was not feeling the same excitement she was, but the knowledge did not dim her passion. Reaching out to him, she slid her hands up his chest to toy with the top button on his shirt.

"I have been thinking about this moment since last night," she told him huskily as she began to unbutton it.

Rick stood rigidly before Lucia, waiting for the right time to make his move. Though her caresses and words were erotic enough, they left him unaroused. He wanted no woman but Jennie. He needed no woman but Jennie.

It suddenly occurred to him, as he stood there passively accepting Lucia's exploring touch, that he was in love with Jennie. From the very beginning, Jennie had challenged, excited, and enthralled him as no other woman ever had. He thought of the first time they'd made love in the abandoned mine, and he realized that he had fallen in love with her then. The memory of Jennie's virginal surrender that day sent a flow of sensual excitement through him, and Rick vowed that as soon as he could, he would go back to find her and make her his own.

Lucia felt the response in Cazador's taut body, and she smiled up at him as she ran a bold hand over his hardness. "So, you're not as indifferent as you would like me to believe."

Rick wanted nothing more than to thrust Lucia away from him, but he knew his grandfather's life depended on his seemingly willing cooperation with her during these next few minutes. He didn't want to hurt Lucia, but he did need to subdue her. There could be no interference when they made their escape. Knowing that it was almost time for him to act, he took her in his arms and kissed her.

Luis had observed Lucia's secretive flight from Malo's side and noted that Cazador had disappeard from his place near the old man. He felt a thrill of excitement, not unlike the sexual arousal he'd just achieved with Chica. Soon, he would be Malo's most important ally for Cazador would be dead. A wide grin split his dark face and he waited long moments before going to rouse Malo. It would not do to find Lucia and Cazador too soon. When they did discover them, Luis wanted to be sure that they would be in the most revealing position possible.

"Malo!" Luis hesitated touching the other outlaw while he slept for he knew of Malo's tendency to shoot first and ask questions later.

"What?" Malo grumbled, opening one bleary eye to glare at the fool who had dared to awaken him.

"It's important! There is something I must show you."

Sitting up quickly, aware of the urgency in the other man's tone, he looked at Luis questioningly. "What is so important that you disturb my rest? Are there Indians?"

"No, no Indians. Come with me, you have to see this," Luis replied mysteriously, standing up to lead the way.

"This had better be good, Luis, or I just might extract some payment from your hide!" he threatened menacingly as

252

he followed him from the camp, furtively moving off into the night. As they stalked through the darkness, Luis drew his gun, just in case.

Malo was totally unprepared for the sight that greeted him as they entered the small clearing. Cazdador and Lucia were sharing a heated embrace and, luckily for Rick, the tequila slowed Malo's reaction time considerably.

"Lucia?" Her name was wrenched from him as he started to draw his revolver.

A chill of deadly intent curled up Rick's spine, and in the time it took Malo to speak her name, Rick had whirled, pushed Lucia protectively behind him, and pulled his gun. The lightning speed of his draw amazed even Luis who got off only one poorly aimed shot before Rick's blazing volley of return fire knocked the gun from his grasp. Firing with careful precision, Rick sent Malo and Luis scurrying for cover as he backed quickly away with Lucia.

"Hurry. Get the old man, my saddlebags, and the rifles," he ordered curtly over his shoulder, as his continued fusillade pinned the desperadoes behind some rocks.

"Right." Lucia was wide-eyed with terror and excitement as she raced to free Juan. She was surprised to see that he was already up and running toward them, carrying as many rifles and cartridge belts as he could manage.

The sound of gunfire so close by their camp roused the other men, and they were looking around in drunken confusion as Lucia ran into their midst.

"What's going on?" they asked her as the men tried to strap on guns and get ready to fight the enemy, who, at this point, was unknown.

"I don't know, but they told me to get these." Grabbing the saddlebags and other equipment, Lucia ran back to Cazdador, proud of the presence of mind she had just displayed.

Malo, realizing that his men were still drunk from their wild carousing, swore viciously under his breath.

"Luis! We have to catch them before he can escape with Peralta! If they get away from us now, we'll never find them again in these mountains!"

"We'd better get back to guard the horses, then!"

Manuevering their way back toward the encampment, Malo rallied the men and hurried to get more arms and ammunition.

"We can't let them get any horses!" he snarled, snatching up his rifle and cartridge belts. "Ramon! Pablo! Stay with them!"

"What's happened?" Ramon demanded.

"It's Cazador! He's double-crossed us! He's trying to get away with Peralta so he can have the gold all to himself! We've got to stop him!" Malo seethed as he loaded a rifle. "If you see the bastard, shoot him!" He ordered coldly.

As Malo was busy getting his men together, Rick, Juan, and Lucia fled into the night, seeking the highest ground possible so they would have the advantage when it came time to fight. Scrambling up the steep, sandy incline, pausing only to help one another, they struggled ever onward. Rick was surprised by his grandfather's agility.

"I have surprised you, Ricardo?" Juan chuckled in breathless victory as they topped the ridge. "You were afraid I was too old, eh?"

"Nothing you do surprises me anymore, *abuelo*," Rick answered with warm affection.

"*Abuelo*? Ricardo? You are El Cazador, are you not?" Lucia demanded in confusion as they rushed on through the darkness.

"I will explain it all to you later, Lucia. For now, let us just concentrate on getting as far away from Malo as we can."

They stopped for a moment and fell silent, listening nervously for some indication of how close behind them the outlaws were. But only a deadly quiet assailed them, leaving them at once thankful and apprehensive.

"Ricardo, do you know exactly where we are?"

"I can't be positive in the dark, but at sunup I'll be able to tell for sure. By rights, we should be traveling in the opposite direction of the mine, which is just what I wanted to do. I want to lead those fools away from it. If we elude them tomorrow, we can double-back and go out through Willow Canyon." Rick did not want to think about the possibility of making the trek on foot. Though he knew the location of the water holes, there was no way he could guarantee that they would be able to last the distance between them, walking.

Lucia was stunned by his words. Cazador knew where the gold mine was? How could that be? Was the old man really his *abuelo*—his grandfather? And if so, who was he, really? Peralta had called him Ricardo. Lucia suddenly remembered some talk among the outlaws that the old man had had a grandson and that he'd been killed in the shootout at the ranch the day they had taken Juan captive. It all fit: the infamous El Cazador was none other than Ricardo Peralta and, contrary to what Malo believed, he was very much alive.

She was amazed at Cazador's cunning at having been able to infiltrate Malo's camp and then win his trust. No doubt Malo would be furious at being so duped, and he would not rest until he'd exacted a terrible revenge. Unless, of course, Cazador managed to stop him first. Lucia was very much pleased with that possibility, and she determined to do everything in her power to help him.

Chica stood in the midst of the camp's chaos trying to find out what had happened. She had figured out that the old man had escaped, evidently aided by Cazador, but she had not seen any trace of Lucia, and she wondered where the other woman had gone in all the excitement.

"Ramon!" Chica approached where he stood nervously safeguaring the horses. "Where is Lucia? I have not seen her."

Ramon looked at her sneeringly. "You mean she did not tell you of her plans?"

255

"Plans? What plans?"

"She went with Cazador. They took the old man with them, and they've fought their way out of camp, up into the mountains."

"She ran away with Cazador?" Chica was totally astounded.

"What do you think all the shooting was about?"

"I didn't know. No one said anything."

"Well, she's gone with them for now, but don't worry. Malo will get your friend back and when he does . . ." Ramon laughed in prurient pleasure. "I can't wait to see what he decides to do with her."

Chica shuddered as she realized that Ramon was right: If Malo ever did catch up with Lucia, she would be far better off—dead. Making her way back to her bedroll, Chica sat down to wait. There was nothing she could do except to wish her friend good luck in her flight and pray that Malo never had the chance to wreak his vengeance upon her.

Luis and Malo stood in the small clearing, trying to make out in which direction Cazador had gone.

"I think we would be wise to wait for daylight. It is only a matter of a few more hours and then we will know for sure exactly where they went," Luis suggested.

Malo nodded, frustrated and angry. "You are right. We will follow them at first light."

At the thought of their traveling on foot in these mountains, Luis smiled. "Besides, on foot, they will be no match for us. They will be begging for us to rescue them in a day or so, especially if the weather stays hot."

"We must be careful when we fire not to hit the old man. If he dies, we lose everything," Malo said. "We can take no chances with his life, but once we find the gold, then I will take great pleasure in seeing him torn limb from limb."

"I have learned many very effective tortures from the Apache," the other man offered excitedly. "Some I have not yet had the opportunity to try."

"He will be all yours. Luis. And, maybe if we take Cazador alive, I will let you have him, too."

Sharing the love of the bloodlust, they smiled at each other in understanding before leading the men back to the encampment to plan their strategy.

The brightening of the eastern sky was a thing of joy to Jennie. The darkness had seemed an unending nightmare for her, and she needed the reassuring bright warmth of the sun to hearten her.

Throughout the sleepless hours of the night, she could have sworn that she'd heard gunfire, but the sound had been so faint and the winds had swirled it around her in such confusion that she had not been able to tell from which direction it had come. Whether it had been Malo and Cazador or, hopefully, the posse, that was coming after her, she had no way of knowing, but it left her determined to start trying to walk out of the mountains this morning. No longer could she afford to just sit and wait in the naive hope that her father would come. Her water supply was limited, and she had to move while she still had some left.

Getting up from her rocky mattress, Jennie slung her canteen over her shoulder and started back down the hillside to the narrow, winding trail that they had followed on their way in.

The talk among the posse was excited and expectant as the men hurried to break camp.

"Did you hear that gunfire last night?"

"Where did it come from?"

"Got any idea of the direction?"

Carrie listened to their conversations halfheartedly as she mechanically tightened the cinch on her saddle. She thought they were crazy to get so excited over the sound of a few

257

echoing shots. Lord knows, they could have been made by anybody, not necessarily Jennie's kidnappers.

"Are you about ready to ride?" Todd's deep tones fell upon her frazzled nerves like a soothing balm as he joined her, leading his own mount.

"Yes, I'm all set." She gave him a forced, artficially bright smile. "How's your shoulder this morning?"

"It's doing just fine." He flexed his rugged muscles for her.

"What do you think about those shots we heard last night?"

"I don't know what to think. In these mountains it's hard telling where they came from."

"I thought the same thing. But I guess it does give us something to go on."

Carrie hated making stupid small talk with Todd. She thought it was totally ridiculous that she had to stand there and try to think of impersonal, polite things to say, when all she really wanted to do was to throw herself into his arms and tell him how much she loved him. Determined not to betray her inner feelings when he obviously didn't care deeply about her, she swung lightly up into the saddle.

"I guess I'd better ride up and join Jake and Pa." Putting her heels to her mount, she rode off toward where her father and brother stood talking with Steve.

Todd watched her go, his eyes glued to the perfection of her slender body in those tight-fitting pants. He felt the beginnings of passion swell within him, and he fought it down with an effort. What was the matter with him? All night he'd lain awake, torn apart by his unceasing desire for Carrie. Why had she become such an obsession to him? He longed for her to be in his arms, naked against him. Startled by the direction of his thoughts, even now in broad daylight, he swore silently to himself as he brought his errant desire under control.

Mounting his horse, Todd followed behind her, unwilling to let her completely out of his sight—and, he added to himself, his protection.

Jennie was startled as the riders suddenly appeared at the top of the distant ridge and, instinctively, without waiting to see who it was, she dove for cover behind a clump of creosote bushes. Praying that it was her father, she shifted her position and stared in their direction. After taking a longer look, Jennie knew that they weren't Indians and with that knowledge she breathed a heavy sigh of relief. Watching as they topped the rise and started down into the canyon heading in her direction, she suddenly recognized her father's horse and with a spurt of joyous energy, she darted from her hiding place.

"Pa! Pa!" She ran toward them, waving her arms excitedly.

Mac saw her first and, spurring his horse to action, he raced toward her. "Jennie! Jennie, darling!"

To Jennie it seemed an eternity before he reached her side, but when he did, he vaulted from the saddle and clasped her to his chest.

"Thank God, you're all right!" he sobbed as he cradled her close, hugging her tightly, and Jennie returned his embrace, feeling protected in the warm, familiarity of his arms.

"I'm fine. And I'm so glad you're here. I was so worried." She was smiling and crying at the same time.

Suddenly stern, Mac held her away from him. "You're fine?"

"I wasn't injured," Jennie hurried to explain, wiping childishly at her tears.

"What happened? We don't know much except what little Todd was able to tell us."

"Todd? Is he really all right? Did he come with you?" She looked back expectantly toward the posse, and she thrilled to see Jake and Todd riding at top speed in their direction.

"He's doing just fine," Mac confirmed, still holding her

tightly by the shoulders, not quite ready to release her yet. Frowning, he pressed once more. "But what about you? You're really sure you're all right?"

With a gentle, reassuring hand she reached up to touch his cheek. "I'm really sure. In fact, now that you're here, I couldn't be better!" She hugged him tightly again.

"Sweetheart, how'd you manage to get away?"

"I escaped from their camp the night before last."

"And you've been hiding out ever since?"

"I was sure that you'd come."

Mac gazed down into her upturned face, tracing the features he loved so dearly. God, but he was grateful to find her in one piece, and she said she was all right. But still—

"Jennie, darling, are you sure you weren't—injured?" Mac stammered.

"No, Pa, really," She quietly assured him just as Jake and Todd joined them.

"Jennie!" They exclaimed in excited unison as they jumped down from their mounts and ran to embrace her.

Jake got to her first, sweeping her from Mac's arms and whirling her around. He didn't speak until he'd set her back on her feet. "You're all right?"

"Yes." She laughed breathlessly as she turned to face Todd.

Todd was standing silently by her side, his face taut with tension. Without speaking, Jennie left her brother and went to slip her arms around him.

"I thought you were dead," she choked out as she leaned against his massive chest, finding comfort there. "I thought they'd killed you."

Todd was finding it difficult to speak. The guilt he felt over her fate was enormous. He had been utterly useless to her when she'd needed him the most.

"Jennie, I-"

Jennie sensed that something was desperately wrong, and she stepped back to gaze up at him. "Todd, what's the matter?"

"I'm just thankful that you weren't injured." Suddenly, he held her close, his relief at having found her alive and in good health leaving him momentarily stunned. "I'm sorry, so sorry."

"What do you have to be sorry about?" she questioned, frowning as she looked up into his ruggedly endearing features.

"It was all my fault. I wasn't able to help you."

"That's ridiculous!" Jennie protested quickly. "How could you have helped? You'd been so badly injured that I thought you were dead."

"I know but—" he tried to continue, to explain his feeling of uselessness, but Jennie hushed him.

"There was nothing you could have done, Todd. There were three of them and they were well armed and very dangerous."

With deep, abiding tenderness, she pulled his head down for a gentle kiss and at the touch of her lips, his arms came around her, drawing her closely to him. Jennie relaxed in his supportive embrace, hoping to find in Todd's touch that same spark of passion that Cazador had so easily ignited with just a caress. But, Todd's kiss was not anything like Cazador's; Todd's was calm and warm and nice, just like he was. The feeling left her oddly unsettled. Could she be happy for the rest of her life with *calm* and *warm* and *nice*? The question haunted her for a moment until she pushed it from her mind. Of course she could, she told herself sternly. She had vowed to marry Todd and she would do it!

Mac and Jake looked on happily as they kissed, and by the time they finally broke apart, the rest of the posse had managed to catch up with them. Todd kept a guiding arm about Jennie's waist as she turned to speak with all the men and thank them for coming to her rescue. For a moment, he felt almost relaxed until his gaze accidentally collided with Carrie's.

Carrie had deliberately not ridden ahead with her brother and Todd. She had no desire to be a witness to Jennie's triumphant homecoming and even less an interest in welcoming her back personally. Riding at the back of the posse, she'd maintained a low profile as they'd followed the others, and no one bothered to question her lack of excitement at her sister's recovery.

Carrie was glad now that she had stayed back, for when she'd seen Jennie go willingly into Todd's arms, the pain she'd felt was as if someone had stabbed her and viciously twisted the knife in her heart. And then, when Jennie had reached up to kiss him lingeringly, tears of outrage and sorrow had threatened to spill forth. How dare Jennie!

It took all of her acting ability to meet Todd's happiness and relief-dazed glance with mocking indifference, and she could have sworn that he'd been shocked by what he'd seen reflected in her eyes. Forcing her trembling lips into a semblance of a smile, she turned her attention to her sister, relishing for a moment the fact that her sibling looked rather worse for the wear.

"Jennie, I'm so glad we've found you. Everyone was so worried." She mouthed the usual platitudes, trying to give the impression of immense relief.

"Carrie?" Jennie was totally startled to see that her sister was among the posse. "You came, too?"

The thought that Carrie cared enough about her to come along with the posse touched Jennie deeply, and she felt a sudden tenderness for her.

"I couldn't just stay home. It would have been terrible to wait there and not know what was happening," she lied artfully, ignoring Todd who was staring at her intently.

"And she's done very well, too." Mac put in, shocking both his daughters as he smiled up at Carrie proudly.

"How'd you manage to get away?" Todd finally asked, wondering how she'd managed to escape from three armed desperadoes. "If there were three of them—"

"Oh, there were more than three of them. The men that ambushed you were on their way to join up with another gang—Miguel Malo's."

"Malo!" There was a collective gasp, and Jake's expression was suddenly intense. "The man's an animal. How'd you manage to stay alive?"

"It was your friend, Cazador, who helped me," Jennie told him quickly.

"My friend? Cazador? I don't understand. I don't know any Cazador." He tried to sound confused.

Jennie stared at him. "But he said he knew you."

Jake shook his head. "Maybe from years ago, but I sure don't remember him. All that really matters is that he took care of you. I'm certainly grateful for that." He tried to shift the focus of the conversation.

"He protected me from the others by telling them that he wanted me for his own woman," she explained. "And then, the first chance I got, I ran off."

"Thank heaven."

"Where were they headed?" Todd asked, trying to piece her story together.

"They had kidnapped an old man down in Sonora, and they were forcing him to guide them to some abandoned gold mine."

"What was his name?" Jake's tone was suddenly sharp.

"Peralta—Juan Peralta," she answered and then turned to her father. "Pa, we've got enough men here. Could we go after them and try to rescue him? I know they planned to kill him just as soon as they got to the mine."

"We'll go," Jake answered for his father. "I know Peralta."

"You do?" Mac looked at him in surprise.

"From years back," he acknowledged. "How far are they ahead of us?"

"About a day's ride, I guess. It just depends on how much progress they made yesterday."

"I'll go scout the trail," Steve offered, riding on ahead with a few of the men.

"Are you hungry, Jennie?" Mac offered as he took some food out of his saddlebag.

"Famished! When I ran away, I didn't think to take any food. I only grabbed a canteen."

"Here, take the time to eat and then we'll start out again. Hopefully, we'll catch up with them before they have a chance to harm the old man." He handed her some dried meat.

"I sure hope so. I felt so sorry for him, being forced to go back to the mine that had brought such disaster to his family," she told them as she began to eat hungrily.

"All of his sons were killed in an Apache attack when they were on their way out of the mountains with a pack load of gold. Only his grandson survived the assault." Jake explained to the others. "It was a long time ago, but I rode with his grandson, Rick, for a while. And there were times when we stayed at the Peralta ranch." His thoughts turned to Rick and the dangerous game he was playing with Malo. Jennie had said that one of the outlaws had claimed her for his own, and he wondered if it had been his friend. "What was the name of the man who protected you?"

"Cazador. Why?" Jennie glanced at her brother nervously. She didn't want to think about Cazador, not while she was standing, comfortable and secure, with Todd's arm around her.

"Just curious." Jake shrugged and his expression didn't change, but inwardly he smiled, knowing that she, indeed, had been safely guarded from the other outlaws.

"Mac! Jake!" Steve's call as he rode back toward them drew their attention.

"Did you find it?" Mac asked as his foreman reined in beside him.

"Yes. We're ready to ride whenever you are."

"Well, I've finished eating, so we can go now." Jennie didn't want to risk not arriving in time to save Juan Peralta.

"And I'm pretty sure I can direct you to where they camped the night before last."

"Good," Steve told her admiringly. "That'll save us a lot of time."

"Bring up one of the extra mounts and adjust the stirrups for her," Mac ordered, and one of the ranch hands hastened to comply. Then, going to his own horse, he pulled out his rifle and handed it to Jennie. "This could get dangerous and I don't want you unarmed."

"Thank you." Jennie felt much more confident of her ability to face Malo now that she was armed. Shoving the rifle into the scabbard, she mounted easily and rode to the head of the posse to direct Steve to the campsite.

"Let's ride," Jake called and they started off in search of the outlaws.

Rick cursed the dawn savagely as they took shelter behind a barrage of massive rocks. "If only we'd had a few hours more."

"Ricardo, we have done our best." Juan soothed him with confidence and more than a little boastful bravado. "And I think that, between the two of us, we can outshoot any of those outlaws."

As exhausted as he was, Rick had to smile at his grandfather's sense of adventure. "You're right of course," he said.

"I can shoot fairly well, too," Lucia offered, wanting to help as much as she could. Cazador had just saved her life by allowing her to come with him, and she wanted to do all within her power to help him.

"Here." He handed her one of the rifles. "Just be sure to take careful aim. We can't afford to waste any ammunition."

"I'll be very careful." She met his eyes solemnly. "Cazador?"

"What?" His tone was flat, revealing no emotion.

"Thank you for bringing me with you. If you hadn't, I'd be dead by now." Her words were heartfelt, and Juan reached out to pat her hand.

"Everything will be just fine, Lucia, you'll see. We won't let Malo have you." He gave her a fatherly smile.

"You'll be safe," Rick told her firmly.

Lucia felt an inner peace sweep through her, and for the first time in years she felt good about herself. "Thank you."

Rick searched through his saddlebags and, finding some dried meat, gave Juan and Lucia a share. "We'd better eat now while it's still quiet. I figure, since they're on horseback, they'll catch up with us within an hour or two."

Juan nodded in agreement. "I'll take first watch for them. You two go on and try to get some rest. An hour is better than none at all."

Rick acquiesced without comment, knowing that he was near the point of exhaustion. He'd gotten little sleep the night before, and the day just passed had been a tense one, fraught with constant frustration. Quickly finishing off his food, he checked their weapons and then tried to seek a comfortable position that would not leave him at a disadvantage should he need to come awake in a hurry.

Lucia, too, ate without further comment. She still wondered about the relationship between Jaun and Cazador, but she knew it would not do for her to ask again. When they were ready to tell her, they would.

Lucia let her gaze roam over Cazador as he lay resting with his eyes closed. Where before Lucia had thought him as just simply handsome, now she was certain that he was the most wonderful man in the world. There was nothing she wouldn't do for him, she swore to herself, nothing!

Feeling Juan's knowing eyes upon her, she smiled at him softly and then curled up in her own place to nervously await the upcoming confrontation with Malo and his men.

Chapter Nineteen

The solemn determination of the outlaws this morning was at distinct odds with the wild gaiety that had possessed them the night before when they'd prematurely celebrated their arrival at the gold mine. When Malo ordered them to break camp, they moved quickly and efficiently, anxious to be after Cazador and to reclaim their captive guide.

Malo was inordinately pleased with himself, though, as the sun's dawning brightness dissolved the night's repressive gloom. The hours they'd just passed waiting for sunup had been tense and frustrating for them, but he was glad now that they'd been patient. For, having had no time to cover his tracks, Cazador's trail was easily followed, and it would be a simple matter for them to track him down in the daylight.

Filled with an undying hatred for Cazador, Malo watched as his men saddled their horses and made ready to leave. Cazador would not get away with this. His thoughts were vicious as he dreamed of the revenge he would wreak on the gunman who had dared to betray him.

And Lucia—Her name was a curse in his mind. She would pay, the little *puta*, he would see to that! And he would enjoy every moment of her torture! Leave him for Cazador, would she? An evil, leering smile distorted his face as he imagined the terrible things he would do to her as she begged for mercy.

Dismissing all thoughts of Lucia from his mind, Malo concentrated instead on Cazador's ambitious plan to kidnap Peralta and have the gold all to himself. No wonder he hadn't been eager to agree to Malo's double-cross of the other men.

Malo had to admire Cazador for taking the chance, but it was a gamble that he was going to lose. He had worked too hard to let the gunslinger take what was rightfully his. He would have that gold yet!

As he swung up into the saddle, Malo glanced at Luis who had approached to ride beside him. He was not quite sure if he trusted him or not. There had been something too easy in the way he had handled the scene with Cazador and Lucia last night. And if there was one thing Malo hated more than a double-cross like Cazador had pulled, it was a sly treacherous snake in his camp. He would keep an eye on Luis, just in case.

"Let's ride," he ordered, urging his horse forward up the incline in the direction Cazador had fled, leaving Luis to follow behind in his dust.

"Ricardo." Juan's insistent call was hushed yet urgent, and Rick came awake immediately. "They are coming."

Rick moved to kneel beside his grandfather, his body tense as he watched their approach.

"If only we'd had more time to cover more of our tracks," Lucia whispered, terror gripping her as she was sure that she faced certain death. There were only the three of them against Malo and all his men!

"Have faith, Lucia," Juan answered softly, giving her hand a reassuring squeeze. "There are only five of them, and we have the element of surprise on our side."

She smiled tremulously and, remembering the religion of her childhood, she crossed herself and said a quick Hail

Mary under her breath.

"We'll wait until they're almost directly beneath us before we fire. We don't want to waste any ammunition. We've barely got enough as it is." Rick's tone was curt as he mentally calculated their odds. He knew that if they could end the confrontation quickly, they would have a very good chance of winning. But, if it dragged on for any length of time, there would be little hope of victory for them. Their water supply was limited to the three canteens that Lucia had brought along and they had no food. Accuracy and speed were the two factors that would determine if they were to live or die, and Rick prayed that he would have both when the time came.

Lucia watched as Malo and his men rode ever nearer, and she shivered in spite of the early heat of the day.

"Cazador!" She grabbed his arm nervously. "Please, don't shoot Chica!" Lucia pointed to where her friend rode at the rear of the column.

Rick nodded but didn't speak. Levering his rifle into position, he waited for just the right moment to fire. Bracing himself beside Rick, Juan also took careful aim.

"Lucia, I want you to stay down and out of sight for now," Rick ordered as she started to pick up her firearm and join them.

"But I want to help!"

"You heard me. I don't have time to worry about you. If you stay down, I'll know you're all right."

Huddling down miserably, yet pleased that he cared enough to be concerned about her, she held her breath as she heard the sound of the horses' hooves clattering over the rocks below.

Luis and Malo studied the abrupt ending to Cazador's tracks.

"They're somewhere very close by. I can feel it," Malo

growled as he looked up, his eyes scanning the ridges and outcroppings of rock on the mountainside above them.

"See anything?"

"No, but I think we'd better split up." He studied the narrowing passage of the canyon ahead of them. "This is the perfect place for Cazador to attempt to ambush us. It is the place I would choose if I was the one being hunted."

"He's not that good!" Luis scoffed, and had they been standing on the ground, Malo would have backhanded him.

"He is very good and you would do well to remember that, fool," Malo fired back. "He has Peralta, does he not? We are done with underestimating him."

Luis bristled at Malo's insult but knew better than to cross him, and he held his tongue.

"Ray—Pablo—I want you two to search this section," Malo ordered, and they quickly began to ride forward, their eyes constantly on the abruptly rising hillside. "Chica will ride down the middle." He smiled at her derisively. "Since Cazador liked Lucia, maybe he would like Chica, too."

The men all laughed at his comment and watched as she kneed her horse on, her knuckles whitening as she held onto the reins in pure terror. Chica had never considered her life useless before, but she knew now that to these men, she was less than human. Vowing to herself to get away from Malo at the first opportunity, Chica lifted her head almost regally and rode forth to face the unknown.

"Ramon—Luis—You two check the far side."

Luis stiffened at the order. He did not like being shunted off like some underling, but he went along with Malo for now, knowing that is was the only way he could get to the gold.

"Damn!" Rick cursed. "They've divided up. There's no way we'll be able to get them all at the same time."

"We will take these two, first." Juan gestured to Pablo and Ray. "And that will even the odds considerably."

He nodded in agreement, knowing that there was no other

alternative open to them, and he took careful aim with his rifle, squeezing the trigger with professional ease.

The sound of the shots reverberated through the canyon, echoing far across the countryside, alerting all within hearing distance to the shootout.

Though they had aimed as carefully as they could, when the volley was fired everyone below headed for cover. Ray, alone, was hit, knocked from his mount by the force of Rick's bullet, and he sprawled lifelessly in the dust, blood seeping from the death-dealing wound in his chest.

"There were two people firing at us!" Luis gasped as he leaned breathlessly against the boulders that formed a natural bulwark, below and across from where Cazador had hidden.

"And Lucia must be one of them!" Malo's expression was malevolent as he fixed his gaze on Cazador's hideout above them, gauging its strength and hoping to find a breech in its defenses.

"How is Ray?" Luis asked Pablo as the other man joined them.

"He is dead. The bullet took him through the heart." Pablo was sweating and his hands were shaking. "That could have been me." He nodded toward where Ray lay in the dirt.

"Malo!" Ramon called from the far end of their protective cover where he stood sentry, rifle in hand. "Do you want me to try to work my way up behind them?"

"No. Not yet."

"But we could get this over with in a hurry."

"Ah, but wouldn't it be much better to let them suffer a while?" Malo's lips thinned in a satisfied smirk. "They have no food and very little water."

"We just don't want anything to happen to Peralta," Luis began and Malo's sharp look silenced him.

"It is much more likely that the old fool would be killed in a wild shootout."

"That is true," Ramon agreed.

"We will wait for now and see what they intend to do next." He seemed to relax a bit. "For, after all, we have plenty of food and water enough to last at least a week."

In accord, the four men settled down in their secluded fortress to see what move Cazador intended to make next.

Jennie sawed back on her reins and turned quickly to her father.

"Did you hear that? Steve! Which direction did those shots sound like they came from?"

"They were pretty faint, but I think they came from this way." Steve took the lead, picking up the pace, but always with cautious intent. He was too experienced a tracker to rush foolheartedly into the unknown.

Todd followed close behind Jennie and Mac, but not before he glanced back to make certain that Carrie was all right. When he saw that she was riding safely with the rest of the ranch hands, he hurried after Jennie.

Todd's eyes traced her feminine form as she rode fearlessly ahead with her father. Jennie was tall and gently rounded, a direct contrast to Carrie's slender, petite beauty. He admired the expert way she handled her horse but thought at the same time that Carrie had done well riding with them, too. Jennie had felt so good in his arms, and she had actually kissed him! Carrie fitted into his arms perfectly and when their bodies mated . . .

Todd gritted his teeth as he realized the game his mind had been playing, subconsciously comparing the two beauties. He was going to marry Jennie and that was that. He didn't know why Carrie kept haunting him. What had happened between them had been an accident, and he had promised her that it would never happen again. But why then was she constantly on his mind? Why did his body yearn for her touch? And why was he constantly worrying about her and checking to make sure that she was protected?

He couldn't have Carrie; he had already proposed to Jennie. And just as soon as she would have him, he was going to marry her.

Turning his thoughts to the danger they might be facing at any time, he put his heels to his horse and rode up closer to Mac.

Carrie rode silently with the armed men. Her thoughts were in a turmoil as she watched Jennie leading the way like some Valkyrie and Todd riding so close behind her. At least, she thought with some relief, there had been an extra horse for Jennie so she didn't have to ride double with Todd.

She wondered if there was anything at all she could do to take Todd away from her sister, but she knew it was a useless cause. If he had proposed to Jennie, then he meant to marry her.

Carrie sighed as she acknowledged the truth of the situation. She had hoped by making her play for Todd and showing him how much she loved him that she would win his love, but all she'd done was make a miserable mess of everything.

Not that Todd looked particularly miserable, Carrie thought with irritation, for he had been fawning all over Jennie ever since they'd found her hours before.

Carrie supposed it was natural for a man, when he loved a woman, to want to be near her all the time, but it didn't lessen her pain as she was forced to watch them together—talking and smiling—knowing that once they returned to the ranch it would only get worse. Carrie began to plan a trip back East again. She knew that she would never be able to stand idly by and watch as Todd married Jennie—not feeling the way she did about him.

Keeping her thoughts on St. Louis and New York and possibly even New Orleans, she lost herself in daydreams of glamor and excitement and allowed herself to forget, for the moment, Arizona, the desert, and Todd.

"Have they moved?" Lucia asked as Rick and Juan peered from their vantage point.

"No. Not yet."

"Where is Chica?"

"She didn't hide with Malo and the others. She rode in the opposite direction, down the canyon."

"Good. She's safe then." Lucia was glad that Chica had not been caught in the crossfire.

"For now."

"What are we going to do?"

"Wait until dark. They've got us pinned down and they know it. If we try to move in any direction right now, we're dead."

Lucia paled at his bluntness. "We can't just sit here. You know how limited our supplies are."

"We aren't going to. As soon as it gets dark, we're going to move again. Malo's expecting me to shoot it out with them, not make a run for it." Rick's smile was not pleasasnt as he thought of the outlaw's surprise in the morning when he discovered them gone.

Juan agreed. "Do you want to head back the way we came?"

"It's more familiar territory for all of us. I think we might make better time if we go back. I know it's the most direct way out of these mountains."

"You know these mountains that well, Cazador?" Lucia looked at him questioningly.

Rick's gaze was serious as he met Lucia's searching eyes. "Yes."

"But how?"

"I suppose it is time for the truth between us now. We are, it seems, in this together." He exchanged knowing glances

274

with his grandfather. "I am Ricardo Peralta, Juan's grandson."

"But—Malo accepted you as El Cazador. How can that be? He would not make such a foolish mistake." She was confused by his astounding revelation.

"I am El Cazador, too," he explained, leaving her even more befuddled.

"But why? You had a family and—"

Rick's expression darkened when she mentioned "family" for the memory of his father's and Antonio's useless deaths still had the power to cause him great anguish.

"It's a long story and one better not retold," Rick said solemnly, exchanging a look of mutual pain with Juan. "I was very young and foolish, and at the time, I thought living by the gun seemed a good way to spend the rest of my life."

Juan looked quickly away from him, remembering the pain he'd felt when Ricardo had told him of his decision to leave El Rancho Grande. He could still envision the tense scene between them when Ricardo had approached him one afternoon in his study.

"Grandfather?" he had said in a deadly, monotonic voice as he'd come to stand before his massive desk.

"Yes, Ricardo? Is something wrong?" Rick hadn't been himself since his return from the mountains, but Juan had held onto the faint hope that his strange mood would pass as he came to accept what had happened.

"I have something important to tell you."

"Yes?"

"I am leaving."

Juan had looked up at him in astonishment. How could he leave? He was the sole heir!

"It is impossible," Juan had stated in his usual gruff style. "You are needed here."

"Grandfather, this time I am not going to obey you blindly. I have to go. I cannot remain here. Not any longer.

I'm sorry." And Rick had turned and left the room without a backward glance, leaving him standing there, alone, speechless.

After Rick had gone, his own life had become a living hell. A broken, lonely old man, he had lived alone in the big hacienda and had turned the running of the ranch over to his foreman. The vigor and excitement that had once possessed him had drained away, leaving him bitter and miserable. He'd felt he'd had no reason to go on, no reason to exist.

Juan smiled now as he recalled the day Ricardo had come back to El Rancho Grande. Ah, the thrill of seeing him again after all those long solitary months! And Rick had changed in so many ways. No longer was he the carefree young boy Juan had chosen to remember. Instead, he had become a man: strong and hard and, if his reputation was anything to believe, ruthless.

There had been no awkwardness between them upon his return. Juan had eagerly accepted him back, and Rick had been enfolded in his love once again.

"From the reputation you managed to build, it must have been exciting," Lucia was saying as Juan brought himself back to the present.

Rick shrugged, not wanting to discuss those years any further. "Let's just say that I had to be very cautious about who I turned my back on."

The silence of the seemingly endless afternoon fell heavily upon them as they waited for nightfall, drinking sparingly from their canteens and keeping a careful watch on Malo to make sure that he did not attempt to rush them.

They were a part of the land: the bronze, suntanned lengths of their meagerly clad yet powerful male bodies blending perfectly with the rawness of the desert terrain. They stood in unmoving spendor near the top of the ridge, listening to the wind and reading its message with an accuracy that was shared only by the beasts of the wild. They did not speak but remounted their barebacked ponies and rode swiftly in the direction of the gunfire.

"Damn." Steve muttered under his breath as sundown spread its possessive shadows across the land. "We can't go any farther tonight."

"But Steve! Juan Peralta might be in trouble!" Jennie desperately wanted to come to the old man's aid.

The foreman turned to Mac for his opinion.

"Jennie, darling, I'm sorry, but Steve knows best when it comes to tracking." At his daughter's crestfallen look, he hastened to reassure her. "But we'll ride out again at dawn. All right?"

She nodded briefly, but her expression reflected her concern.

"Don't worry, sweetheart." Jake rode up beside her. "We'll make it in time."

"I hope so, Jake," she told him as she gazed about at the rugged terrain that surrounded them, wonderng at the shots that had been fired, and, yes, worrying, in spite of her determination to put him from her mind, about Cazador.

"We're stopping for the night," Mac directed as they searched out a suitably protected area to use for their campsite.

Once the site was chosen, they settled in quickly and, this night, they built a small, warming fire. They ate in relative quiet, each person lost in thought as they stared into the flickering flames.

Carrie sat across the campfire from Jennie and Todd, watching in concealed frustration as he appeared to cater to her every whim. She controlled herself admirably while they ate, but when they stood up and moved off for a moment alone away from the revealing brightness of the fire's light, she knew she had to get away. Excusing herself, she went to lie down, hoping that sleep would claim her exhausted body and give her the rest she so sorely needed.

Jennie sighed as she stared out at the myriad of twinkling stars. "It's hard to remember how cruel this land is when the nights are so beautiful." She felt secure with Todd's comforting presence beside her.

"Jennie," Todd said as he pulled her easily into his arms. "I was so worried about you."

"I know all the trouble I put everybody through and I'm sorry," she said.

"But you have nothing to be sorry for!" he countered and lowered his head to kiss her softly. "Jennie."

His lips moved gently over hers, testing her response, before deepening their embrace. Jennie gave herself up to his kiss, wanting to enjoy his touch, hoping for the same explosion of desire that Cazador had wreaked in her senses, but the caress of Todd's mouth was only pleasant, stirring no exciting emotion within her. Frightened by the thought that only that despicable gunslinger could excite her, Jennie panicked. Looping her arms about Todd's neck, she sought his mouth more fervently, pressing closer and wriggling her slender hips suggetively against his.

Todd was surprised by her sensuous moves and wondered at her behavior. Was this the same woman who'd responded so coolly to him back at the ranch? It seemed to Todd that he had longed for this moment for an eternity and yet now that he had Jennie, willingly in his arms and very responsive, he felt oddly unaroused by her eagerness.

"Oh, Todd." Jennie leaned back to look up at him. "When I thought you were dead, it was just terrible. Todd—"

"What?" He was gazing down at her, admiring her dark beauty, yet thinking how much more perfectly Carrie had fit against him. Maybe, he thought with hope, there was still a chance he could be with Carrie. Maybe Jennie still didn't want to marry him and, in due time, he could somehow extricate himself from this very delicate situation.

"If your offer is still open, I'd love to marry you."

Todd was caught momentarily dumbfounded. As reluctant as she'd been to accept his proposal back at the M Circle C, he had not been expecting this total about-face in her attitude.

"Er, of course," he answered as quickly as he could, so she wouldn't think that he had any doubts.

"Oh, good!" Jennie hugged him tightly. "Shall we tell Pa right away or wait until we can tell both him and Hildago together?"

"I think it would be better if we wait until we get back to the ranch. Then we can make a real celebration of it. How does that sound?"

"Fine," she agreed and for some reason, she felt a sense of relief.

Carrie had been unable to rest. No matter how tired her body was, her mind was still racing, filled with thoughts of Todd and Jennie. Try as she might, she had not been able to wipe out the picture of them in a warm, loving embrace from her memory.

Desperately needing to be alone for a while, she wandered a short distance from the encampment. Carrie had not wanted to run into Jennie and Todd; in fact, at the moment they were probably the last people on earth that she wanted to see, but as she rounded a small boulder she found them in an intimate kiss.

Agonizing pain tore through her heart and with it a renewal of her hatred for her sister. Carrie knew she should move away and allow them their privacy, but for some reason she stayed, watching as Todd held her so tenderly after the kiss had ended and watching how Jennie gazed up at him with such undisguised adoration. It was then that she heard her sister's words, and her greatest fears were confirmed.

"If your offer is still open, I'd love to marry you."

Fleeing hurriedly, Carrie moved silently through the night, seeking out a hiding place where she could shed the tears that demanded release. Blinded by her anger, eyes downcast, she rushed on, and it was only when she heard someone call her name that she stopped.

"Carrie!"

Wiping furiously at her eyes, she glanced back to find Steve coming after her.

"What do you want?" she demanded of him sullenly.

A knowing smile split his face, "What do you think? I saw you leave camp and I thought you might be missing me— now."

"What's that supposed to mean?" Carrie challenged, facing him angrily, her hands on her hips.

"You know you shouldn't be out here alone, and since your boyfriend is going to be busy with Jennie, I thought you might have time for me."

She groaned inwardly at his words. Had her feelings for Todd been that obvious? Did everyone know how she felt? Were they all laughing at her now that Jennie had returned to claim Todd? With as much dignity as she could muster, she met his gaze levelly.

"I'm sorry, Steve, but what we had is over."

"You little bitch!" he seethed, reaching out to grab her by her forearm. "Is that your game? Use any man available until a better one comes along?"

"No! I'm not like that at all!" she denied hotly.

"Hah!" he snorted derisively as he gave her a violent shake and then released her. "Then why have you been so hot after Todd since we've been on the trail. Don't think I haven't watched you two. Don't think I don't know what went on when you went with him back to that mine."

Carrie gasped and Steve smiled coldly.

"You may have the others fooled, but I know you, Carrie."

"No you don't! I—"

Steve mocked her viciously. "I should have followed my instincts in the beginning and never touched you. You mean nothing but trouble for a man." Giving her one last disgusted look Steve turned and walked away.

Carrie stood unmoving as the harshness of his words settled over her. Had all the things he'd said about her been true? Was she really the way Steve had perceived her? Did she use men? Her tears began to fall freely as she leaned against a nearby boulder. She had never thought of herself that way. She had always thought that she was just having a good time. It had never occurred to her that her behavior might hurt someone else. She had been so sure that no one cared about her that she had given little thought to the results of her actions, living only for the day and nothing more. Little else had truly mattered to her until Todd.

When once again she was in control, Carrie made her way quietly back to her bedroll. This time, sleep came quickly.

Jake lay on his back staring at the night sky, his arms folded behind his head. His thoughts were serious as he pondered the wisdom of his earlier decision not to reveal Rick's identity. He did not want his friend to be mistaken for one of the bandits, and he knew he should speak with Mac and Steve about him in the morning. They would probably catch up with them soon, and he wanted to make sure that Juan and Rick both came out of this uninjured.

Rick's disguise, Jake mused, must have been very effective for Jennie had seemed convinced of his status, and she was certainly no fool. He wondered idly, just before he drifted off to sleep, what his little sister's reaction would be when she found out that El Cazador was really Peralta's grandson and his own good friend.

Chapter Twenty

The night's black grip tightened on the mountains, strangling all light from the land. Its hold was unrelenting and while some cursed its power, Rick, Juan, and Lucia gave thanks for its coming.

The absence of the moon both hindered and helped them in their flight. Without its guiding brightness, they made very slow progress across the difficult terrain, yet the lack of that light is what made their escape possible. Staying close together, they crept along at a snail's pace across the rock-strewn mountainside, taking care that each footfall was on solid ground. The huge saguaro cacti loomed grotesquely above them as they clawed their way across the arid land, and Lucia could barely control her tremors of fear as each monstrous shape took menacing form in the darkness. All precaution was taken to avoid any unnecessary noise that might accidentally alert Malo.

They had been on the move for long hours when it happened: The flat supportive rock that had first served Rick and Juan so well shifted under Lucia's slight weight, and she fell heavily, tumbling wildly some distance down the rocky slope.

Lucia was surprised by her fall, and she couldn't stop the cry of terror that escaped her as she lost her balance. The stones and grit cut at her flesh as she careened downhill, and she almost fainted from the pain that shot through her when a craggy rock stopped her reeling plunge.

Lying breathless, Lucia found that for the moment she couldn't move, and she lay perfectly still as the world tilted dizzily around her.

"Juan. Wait here," Rick told his grandfather as he dropped the guns and ammunition he was carrying and ran to Lucia's aid.

"Be careful!"

Rick's answering nod was lost in the darkness as he raced to her side.

"Lucia!" His words were hushed yet filled with urgency as he knelt beside her. "Can you move?" he asked when he saw that she was conscious.

"Yes, I think so," she whispered, her breathing strained.

"Let me help you." As gently as he could, Rick slipped a supportive arm behind her shoulder and tried to lever her into a sitting position.

"Ah." The low cry was muffled as she hid her face against his chest. "My side—When I hit the rock—"

"Lay back." Rick lowered her as gently as possible down flat on the ground. "Does it feel as though something is broken or bruised?"

"I don't know. Let me catch my breath and I will try again. We must hurry and go on. They might have heard my cry and they'll know." Lucia drew a ragged breath.

"Don't worry about Malo right now. Just take it easy for a minute."

Her eyes were filled with tears as she gazed up at his night-shrouded features. How gentle this man was. Malo would have derided her at her clumsiness and left her behind if she couldn't keep up; yet, Cazador was caring for her and worried about her, even though she was the one who had gotten him into all this.

"I'll be all right," she declared staunchly, determined not

to cause him any further trouble.

With a reserve of strength she didn't know herself capable of, Lucia sat up slowly and then managed, with his help, to get to her feet. Bracing herself against Cazador's helpful arm, she stood swayingly for a moment before standing alone. Though her side was throbbing and she had difficulty taking a deep breath, Lucia managed a victorious smile at him.

"See, I told you. Now, let's go before Malo has a chance to catch up with us." Bravely she started up the incline on her own, but her strength failed her on the arduous climb.

Rick tightened his supportive grip on her and gently helped her to sit down. "Wait here. I'll go back for Juan."

Lucia sat, her head bowed in agonizing defeat, as he hurried off to get his grandfather. When she heard the sound of their footsteps returning, she looked up in their direction.

"I'm sorry." She felt guilty and she was more than a little worried about what they would do when Malo came after them.

"It was an accident, Lucia, something that couldn't be helped. We'll just stay down in the canyon. It should make for easier traveling for all of us," Rick explained. "Do you think you can try it again?"

"Yes." Lucia stood up and, with Rick's help, they started down the hill this time.

"Malo!" Ramon's agitated call pierced the sleeping outlaw's dreams of revenge.

"What?" he snarled coming awake abruptly.

"There was a noise. It sounded like a woman crying out," he explained hurriedly, not wanting Malo to be angry with him for disturbing his rest.

"Do you think it was Lucia or could it have been Chica?" Malo sat up slowly, yawning.

"Chica—" Ramon frowned. "I had never thought of her.

In fact, I haven't seen her since this afternoon."

"No loss," Malo said. "Get Pablo and the two of you scout Cazador's position from opposite sides. Try to draw his fire, if you can. I want to be sure they're still up there."

"Right." Ramon moved to awaken Pablo, giving him quick directions as to what to do.

"Where is Luis?"

"I am here," the other man called out from the concealing darkness just before he stepped close enough to be seen. "What is the matter?"

"Ramon just heard a woman cry out. He and Pablo are going to climb up there to check on Cazador," Malo said and then turned to the two departing men. "Remember! No shooting! I don't want to take a chance of hitting Peralta."

They nodded as they disappeared into the night.

"Do you think it might have been Lucia?"

"Who knows?" Malo shrugged. "But at this point, we can't be too cautious."

"Why would she scream? She went to Cazador willingly, didn't she?" Luis pushed.

Vicious hatred surged through Malo as Luis's words reminded him of Lucia's unfaithfulness, and it took all of his meager willpower not to shoot him.

"Yes, she went to him," he ground out and then added with savage amusement, "but maybe she got more than she bargained for, eh? Maybe Cazador is not as nice to his women as I am."

And they both chuckled cruelly at the thought of Lucia, suffering at Cazador's hands.

Ramon climbed quickly up the rocky slope. He was angry that Malo had ordered him not to shoot for he felt certain that this was the perfect time to attack Cazador. Surely, the old man would be tied up, and if Lucia had cried out— Well, he knew what they must be doing.

Seeking cover behind a craggy outcropping, Ramon dropped to the ground and slithered forward on his stomach to within fifty feet of Cazador's hideout. Stopping all motion, he lay still, listening for some sounds of activity coming from the gunfighter's camp, but there was no discernible noise. Frowning, he scrambled on, trying to work his way above them.

Pablo, too, had been moving ever closer to their mutual goal, scurrying from cactus to rock for safety. Reaching the pinnacle of his climb and wanting to draw Cazador's fire, he threw a rock in the direction of the shelter.

The sound of the stone's hitting the boulder and bouncing away was magnified in the silence of the night, and both Ramon and Pablo were astounded when there was no movement from within the protected natural walls of the hideout. Confused but resolute in their purpose, they tried again, this time Ramon tossing the stone, but again there was no response.

Emboldened by their luck so far, the two desperadoes ventured nearer, pausing occasionally to listen for some indication that Cazador was still there, but the night was quiet, revealing nothing. Their nerves stretched taut, they began to circle behind the refuge. They had not expected to be able to get this close, and as they rendezvoused above the hiding place, they were uncertain as to what to do next.

"Why hasn't he fired at us?" Pablo wondered aloud as he joined up with Ramon.

"I don't know, but something isn't quite right here." Ramon frowned.

"That's what I was thinking," Pablo agreed. "Do you think we should go tell Malo that he wouldn't shoot at us, or should we move down closer to get a better look?"

"We'd better check it out before we go back," he replied uneasily, his hand unsteady as he inspected his revolver to make sure it was loaded.

"Malo said not to fire at them."

"If you think I'm walking into Cazador's camp, unprepared, you're crazy."

Pablo watched for a moment as Ramon cautiously began making his way, gun in hand, down toward the hideout, and then he went after him.

They covered the final distance almost in slow motion, measuring each movement to insure themselves against an unexpected attack by Cazador, but there was to be no sudden assault. In the tomblike hush of the night, they burst into the shelter to find it long deserted. The discovery that Cazador had abandoned his camp and slipped away without a trace, left them both astounded and furious.

"They must have already been on the trail when I heard Lucia call out," Ramon concluded in disgust.

"We'll catch them easily now. They are, after all, still on foot," Pablo added in relief.

"We'd better let him know. I'm sure he's wondering what's taking us so long."

"Malo!" Their call in unison immediately drew Malo and Luis's attention.

"What?" He was incredulous that his men would call out to him in such a tense situation. Were they fools to give away their positions that way?

"Cazador's gone, Malo," they yelled, and he cursed violently.

"Gone? Where the hell did he go? And when? Get down here now!" he thundered.

Pablo and Ramon raced back to camp, knowing that their leader would be in a rage over being outsmarted again.

"You say you heard a woman cry out. Which direction did you think the voice came from?" Malo demanded of Ramon when they had returned.

"It was hard to tell. You know how things echo out here, but I think it came from there." Ramon pointed in the direction they'd just come that day.

"So, he's doubling-back, is he?" he said thoughtfully to

himself. "That must be where the mine is. I'll bet he's planning on heading there next! How many hours until sunup?"

"Two at the most," Pablo supplied.

Malo nodded. "At first light, we move out. I want Cazador by high noon, and I don't care what the cost. We've been too nice in our dealings with him so far. Now, we're going to start to play by our rules."

Jennie lay wide awake on her bedroll. She had expected to sleep soundly now that she was back under her father's protection, but it was not to be. Ever since she had returned from her time with Todd, she had done nothing but toss and turn.

Her thoughts were in a jumble and Jennie had to admit that she was scared. Had she done the right thing in accepting Todd? She genuinely cared for Todd, but the cruel thought that she was using him crept into her mind. She quickly denied it to herself, but still the lingering doubt about her lack of passionate response to his kiss haunted her.

Why was Cazador the only man who'd excited her in that way? Why couldn't she feel the same passion for Todd? Jennie had no answers, but she knew that her future did not lie with a gunslinger. Most probably, she reasoned, he didn't even have a future. Why after they caught up with them, he'd probably be—A chill of panic raced through her soul as she considered the possibility that Cazador might be killed in the upcoming shootout. No matter what had happened between them, Jennie realized that she didn't want to see him dead.

Irritated with herself for even thinking about him, Jennie rolled over in a huff and sought elusive sleep. Her eyes closed and she rested until the sudden tormenting thought occurred to her: What if she were pregnant with Cazador's child? She bit back a groan. In all of her wildest imaginings she had never before considered it, and now that she had promised herself to Todd—She swallowed nervously and ran her hand over her stomach. Could she possibly be? The answer was unescapable. Yes, she could very well be.

Jennie shivered. Pregnant by an outlaw. And no doubt he was probably a wanted man, too. An agony of misery overtook her as she remembered his touch and his kiss. Never again would she experience such bliss. She had loved him when she'd given herself to him, but it had all been one-sided. He had taken all she had to offer and then turned to Lucia for more. He had given her nothing in return for her love. Nothing except maybe his baby.

Curling up on her side, she wept silently in the night, knowing that it would be at least another week before she'd know the truth of her condition.

Rick shifted Lucia's weight in his arms as he and Juan continued their trek through the canyon. Since Lucia had fainted from the pain of her injury, he had been forced to carry her, and the extra burden had slowed their pace considerably. Exhaustion was clearly evident now on his haggard features, but there was no time to stop and rest for the morning sun was already casting its rosy glow across the dark blue sky.

"Juan," Rick called out in subdued tones. "See that ledge?" He indicated a broad, flat rock protruding from the canyon wall some distance ahead of them. "What do you think?"

"If we have time to make it up there and then get our tracks covered, it might work." Juan paused for a moment to study the only viable shelter nearby.

"I don't see anything else. Not down this low." His gaze scoured both sides of the narrow canyon searchingly.

"Let's go." Juan led the way up the mountainside, struggling under the weight of the rifles and extra ammunition.

They advanced on the ledge slowly, each foot of ground they traversed seeming like a mile. When they finally reached it, both Rick and Juan were breathing laboredly from the arduous climb. Juan rushed to unload the gear he'd been carrying and then helped Rick lay Lucia down.

"How is she?"

"I don't know," Rick answered as he reached for a canteen. "She must have broken a rib when she fell."

Lifting her head slightly, he tilted the water to her lips. At the touch of the cooling liquid, she stirred and opened her eyes, blinking in surprise to find Cazador leaning over her, his expression grave with concern.

"Lucia? Are you all right?"

"I'm not sure. What happened?" She glanced nervously around her.

"You fainted," Juan explained drawing nearer.

"Oh." Lucia tried to change positions, but pain jolted through her and grasped her side. "It's my side."

"Let me take a look," Juan offered.

"I'm sorry I caused you so much trouble," she said, wearily as she closed her eyes against the probing agony of Juan's gentle fingers.

"It looks like you've broken a rib or two," he told her, drawing away and pulling out the knife Rick had given him earlier. "I'm going to cut away some of the hem of your skirt and use the material to bind you."

Lucia nodded quickly and lay unprotesting as he ministered to her, wrapping the wide strip of cloth tightly around her just beneath her breasts.

After pausing only long enough to catch his breath, Rick moved off to camouflage their trail as best he could. He was on edge with fatigue, and yet every nerve in his body was strung tight as he constantly kept watch for some sign of Malo.

As he worked, Rick thought briefly of Jennie and wondered at her safety. By now, he reasoned, she was with her father and well on her way back home to the McCaine ranch. In his heart, he finally acknowledged that he was glad she'd run away when she had for he had serious misgivings about their ability to survive this next encounter with Malo.

Yesterday they'd had the advantage of position and surprise, but today—Rick knew he was outgunned and, in his present precarious location, he also knew that he could easily be outmaneuvered. A heavy sense of foreboding swept through him, and his years as a hired gun had taught him not to ignore his feelings. Hurrying back to his grandfather, he hoped for once that his instincts were wrong.

The sun was shining brightly, wiping away all vestiges of the night's shielding darkness, as Rick made his way up to the ledge. Juan had been watching him as he'd tried to destroy their trail, and he smiled warmly when Rick rejoined him.

"You've done well. We have a good view and we will know as soon as they're near," Juan said, trying to cheer him but also sensing his anxiety.

"I hope I've done enough," he replied distractedly, his thoughts on Malo and the impending, unavoidable showdown. "How's Lucia?"

"I'm much better," she called softly and Rick went to kneel beside her.

"Good. They'll be catching up with us soon, so I want you to stay right where you are. Don't try to move. Juan and I will handle everything."

"You won't let me help?" Her dark eyes were anxious as she reached out to touch his arm.

"I appreciate your offer, but as badly as you're hurt, there's not much you'd be able to do. It'll be easier on us not to have to worry about you." Rick knew she was worried, but there was little he could do or say to encourage her.

"All right," Lucia said meekly, knowing that he was right.

Rick nodded impersonally and started to stand, forcing her to release his arm. "Rest easy," he told her as he walked off to stand by Juan.

"We might as well try to relax while we can." Juan glanced at Rick's strained features and knew that they were sharing the same worries.

"You go ahead. I'll just stand watch," he encouraged, knowing that the older man had to be more tired than he was.

Sensing that Rick needed some time alone, Juan went to sit under the small overhang near Lucia, keeping a loaded rifle balanced carefully across his lap. Rick checked their firearms once more, verifying their state of readiness, and then positioned himself at the best vantage point from which to watch for Malo's approach.

Almost an hour had passed before they rode forth into the canyon, and Rick spotted them right away.

"Get down!" Rick called out to his grandfather as he quickly stretched out flat on the rocky shelf. He grabbed his rifle and, bracing himself on his elbows, he took aim, carefully judging the distance they'd have to travel before they'd be within his range.

"Where are they?" Juan asked as he crawled up beside Rick.

"There." Rick pointed out the four riders who were splayed out across the canyon, heading their way.

Juan nodded but didn't bother to answer as they both concentrated on making the best first shot they could.

"I just saw something!" Ramon shouted to Malo and pointed toward the ledge where he'd seen the sun glint off their rifle barrels. "Up there!"

"All right, this has got to be them!" Malo grinned in victory as he reined in. "We're going to split up and try to stay out of his range of fire. Ramon—Luis, you two ride up to the top of the ridge and then shoot down at them. I don't know what kind of cover they've got from above, but I doubt

292

that it's much. Pablo and I will work our way along the other side." Malo's smile widened for he was pleased that finding them had been so easy. "Now let's ride! I want to get to that gold mine, today!"

Rick glanced over at Juan. "They've seen us."

Juan put a reassuring hand on his shoulder. "It is not over yet. If they are out of our range, then we are certainly out of theirs."

"For right now, anyway," Rick commented, and his eyes narrowed as he followed Malo's advance. Steadying himself, he watched their oncoming maneuverings with the practiced, cool detachment that had earned him his reputation, and all thoughts of possible defeat were banished from his mind as he focused only on killing Malo.

Chapter Twenty-one

It was still dark, but the morning star, shining brightly in the blackened heavens, offered proof that the new day would soon be dawning. While Jennie and Carrie slept on, the men of the M Circle C gathered together in a tight group to discuss their plans for continuing the chase.

"There's something I've hesitated to tell you," Jake began, knowing that he could delay no longer in revealing the truth about Rick.

"Jake?" Mac looked at his son quizzically. "What is it?"

"It's about one of the outlaws—Cazador."

"What about him?" Mac's voice cut through the momentary silence, as he wondered what his son knew about the bandit who'd held Jennie captive.

"He's the one who had Jennie, right?" Todd asked.

"Yes," Jake answered and quickly went on to explain. "And although he is known by the name El Cazador, he is, in reality, Ricardo Peralta—Juan Peralta's grandson."

"What?" The question rose from all the men.

Jake nodded as he continued to speak. "I ran into Rick in Mesa Roja the night before Jennie disappeared. He told me that Malo had raided their ranch in Sonora and kidnapped his grandfather."

"But why?"

"The Peraltas used to have title to these mountains, and supposedly there's a very rich gold mine located in here, somewhere. Anyway, Malo heard that Juan was the only one who knew the location, and he was forcing the old man to lead them to the mine."

"But how does this Cazador thing fit in?"

"Rick was riding as a hired gun at the same time I was. He helped a posse track down a killer one time, and they thought he was so good that they nicknamed him El Cazador—the hunter.

"After the word got out about how quick Rick was on the draw, though, every fast gun artist in the Southwest started looking for him. He gave it all up a few years ago and went back to live with his grandfather, but after the raid he resumed his identity in order to infiltrate Malo's gang and win his confidence."

The men listened intently to Jake's explanation, and they were stunned by what they'd just learned.

"You're serious?" Mac's expression was incredulous as he looked at his son.

"Very. He swore me to secrecy that night in town, otherwise I would have told you sooner," Jake replied, glad now that he'd revealed Rick's true identity to them.

"Then we do know that Jennie was protected while she was with them," Todd added thoughtfully.

"Completely," Jake assured him, confident of Rick's ability to keep his sister safe from the likes of Malo and his gang.

They exchanged looks of relief and then settled down to business.

"So you think that all the shooting that's going on may be your friend Rick trying to escape from Malo with his grandfather?" Steve ventured.

"I'm almost positive. When I spoke with him in town, that was his plan."

"All right," Mac said as he stood up to pace nervously

about. "We owe Rick Peralta, and I intend to see that we pay him back for safeguarding our Jennie."

"Good." Jake was glad that they were all in agreement. "We'll ride out at sunup."

Todd went to wake the women while the others prepared to break camp.

"Carrie?" His voice was husky as he stared down at her. In repose, he found her even more attractive, and it was only with a fierce effort on his part that he didn't reach out to touch the silken length of her blond hair.

"What?" Carrie came awake slowly. Her dreams had been of Todd and their passion-filled moments together, and when she opened her eyes to find him standing over her, a knowing smile curved the fullness of her lips. "Todd." His name was a caress, and she longed to pull him down to her for a morning kiss.

"We're breaking camp now. It's almost dawn." His tone was gruff as he tried to hide his conflicting emotions.

The sound of his indifference sliced through Carrie's mellow mood like a knife. Struggling to a sitting position, she glared up at him. "Fine. I'll be ready to go when everyone else is."

Todd wanted to say more—to pull her into his embrace and kiss her pouting mouth, but he knew it was impossible. Turning on his heel, he made his way across the encampment to where Jennie lay, still sleeping.

"Jennie." Again, as he watched her rouse from sleep, he was amazed at the difference in the two women. It bothered him greatly that he didn't feel that same overwhelming sense of desire for Jennie that he felt for Carrie, but he dismissed it from his mind. Why was he so concerned? He had loved Jennie from afar for years and, at last, she had agreed to marry him.

"Todd? Good morning—I think." Jennie woke quickly and sat up, staring about her into the darkness. "Are we breaking camp?"

"Right away. Jake wants to be on their trail again as soon as it's light."

"I'll be ready," she told him as she stood up and stretched wearily. Though she had finally managed to fall asleep, it hadn't been until the wee hours, and what little rest she'd gotten had been filled with torturous dreams of Cazador and Malo and Lucia. "Thank you."

Todd nodded, not knowing quite what else to say to her, and hurried off to get his own gear ready.

They had been riding for over an hour when a sudden volley of shots fired just over the next rise halted them. Pausing just below the crest of the next hill, they regrouped, quickly plotting what to do next.

"Whoever it is, they're right over there," Steve said, restraining his restive mount with a firm hand.

"We'd better take a look before we go any farther," Mac ordered as he reined in next to his foreman.

Jake nodded as he joined them. "I'll go up first on foot so I can see what's going on.

"All right," Mac agreed.

"Steve, you want to come with me?" Jake asked as he dismounted and retrieved his rifle.

"Sure," he answered, pulling his rifle from its scabbard and checking to make sure it was loaded, before following Jake up to the top of the ridge.

"Where are they going?" Jennie asked as she rode forward to join her father and Todd.

"Since Jake knows what Peralta looks like, he's going to see if he can pinpoint him," he explained. "You'd better ride back with Carrie and stay there. I don't want you in any more danger."

"But Pa, I've been riding back there all morning!" she protested, outraged at being left behind. "Let me go with you! I know what Juan looks like, too, and I can shoot as well as most of these men."

"Jennie, I don't have the time or patience to fight with you.

We've worried enough about you these past few days to last us a lifetime. Now, stop arguing with me and get back there." His face reflected his steadfastness of purpose.

Jennie knew that expression well and looked quickly to Todd for support, but he was in full agreement with Mac.

"Go on, Jennie. We want you to be safe."

She found his attitude equally as irritating and angrily turned her horse around, heading back to where her sister patiently waited.

"They didn't want you with them?" Carrie couldn't resist the jibe.

Jennie shot her a quick, questioning look, but Carrie's carefully schooled features revealed nothing. "No. Pa said I should stay back here where it was safe." She added the last word in disgust.

Carrie bit back a smile, pleased that they had been relegated to the same status. "Don't worry. I'm sure they'll be able to handle it without you."

"I don't doubt that for a minute," Jennie replied, ignoring Carrie's sarcasm. "It's just that—" She stopped, catching herself before she revealed too much of her real feelings: her concern for Cazador.

Would she ever be able to forgive herself if anything happened to him during the shootout? Wild thoughts raced through her mind. He had never hurt her. He had protected her when the others would have raped and possibly murdered her. Did she want him to die just because he had found Lucia attractive?

"Just that what?" Carrie's curiosity was aroused now.

"Oh, nothing." Turning away from her sister, Jennie focused on Jake and Steve as they climbed the steep hillside, leaving Carrie to wonder at her cryptic remark.

Staying low and close together, the two men finally reached the summit. Crawling forward on their stomachs, they crept unobserved to a vantage point that gave them a panoramic view of the embattled canyon below, and from where they lay, they had no trouble spotting the combatants.

"There! On the opposite wall from us, up on that flat rock—that's Rick and his grandfather," Jake told Steve excitedly as he spotted Rick and Juan firing across the canyon at the outlaws who had them pinned down on their ledge.

"It looks like there's someone laying down behind them. A woman?"

"I don't know."

"You're sure that's the Peraltas?" Steve wanted no mistakes made when they rode into this fracas.

"Positive, and it looks like Malo's got them pinned down real good. Look." Jake indicated a place near the Peraltas where Luis and Ramon were working their way down from the top of the ridge. "There's a couple of them trying to move in on them now."

"Damn! We'd better hurry!"

Drawing quietly back, they hurried down the slope to where the others waited.

While the sounds of the sporadic gunfire echoed eerily around her, Chica rode slowly back the way she'd come. The trail she'd followed in hopes of finding a way out of the mountains had ended in a box canyon, and she had been forced to retrace her steps in order to save herself.

As Chica neared the site where Malo had been stalking Cazador, it surprised her to find the spot deserted. She had automatically assumed that the gunshots were coming from there, and she wondered what had happened. Had Cazador managed to make an escape? Was Malo still chasing him?

Urging her horse up the far slope, Chica went to investigate the place where Cazador and Lucia had been hiding, and she was greatly relieved not to find them lying dead in the dirt. They had gotten away! But to where? Glad that she carried a rifle with her, she hurried in the direction of the shooting, hoping to be of some help to her friend and possibly gaining some revenge of her own.

Mac and Todd and the rest of the men were waiting anxiously for Jake and Steve's return.

"What did you see?" Mac demanded as they raced back down the hillside.

"It looks like he attempted the escape, but Malo caught up with him," Jake explained as he faced them. "They've got him pinned down across from us about a half mile up the canyon."

"We're going to have to be careful," Steve put in. "Things could easily get confusing once we get caught up in the middle of this."

"We'll divide up," Jake instructed the men. "Steve will take half of you and attack the men on this side, while I work my way around and try to pick off the ones who have Peralta trapped from above."

"Be sure not to shoot at the people up on the ledge. That's where the old man is, and it looks like there's a woman up there with him, too."

Jennie had been hanging on their every word, and at the mention of a woman, she wondered if it was Lucia or Chica.

"There should be two women with them," she added, urging her horse closer to where her brother sat, giving directions.

"We only saw the one, and she looked to be injured in some way." Jake frowned at her news. "We'll just have to be careful."

"Everyone ready to ride?"

The men all nodded as they pulled their rifles from their sheaths and prepared to do battle.

"Jennie and Carrie!" Mac's voice cut through her thoughts of following them, and she looked up somewhat guiltily. "You stay here."

With that, they were gone, splittng up into two groups and riding cautiously toward their respective targets.

Rick got off his final rounds in the direction of the two men who were lodged in the rocks above him before seeking better shelter to reload. Juan was still holding his own, firing at the outlaws directly across from them, and though his shots were well taken, the outlaw's cover was too protective to allow for a good hit.

As bullets were ricocheting viciously about them, Rick wondered seriously for only the second time in his life at his chances to elude death. As logically as he could, he tried to calculate the most aggressive move he could make in order to shock Malo and perhaps gain an advantage, but the desperadoes' constant barrage allowed him little time to formulate a plan or make a move.

"Ricardo!" Juan's call was low yet imperative.

"What?"

"I'm running low on ammunition."

Knowing that the end was near and knowing that there was no way to avoid it, Rick scrambled back to his side. "If you want, I can tie you. That way they'll think I stole you from them in order to get the gold for myself."

Juan's eyes misted at his offered self-sacrifice. "Ricardo." His voice was hoarse with emotion. "If I am to die, it will be fighting by your side."

Their gazes locked, and Rick clasped his grandfather's shoulder in a moment of total love and devotion. Then smiling undauntedly, he added, "But we are not dead, yet!"

"You have a plan?"

"Only not to give up easily!" And with that he grabbed his revolver, determined to do everything within his power to save them.

"Cazador, can I help?" Lucia called out, knowing that Malo's men were pressing in on them.

"Here." He slid a loaded weapon to her. "If they get passed me, you're going to need it."

And then, in a lightning move that stunned both Juan and Lucia, Rick ran from their refuge, firing automatically in the direction of the outlaws who were in the rocks above him. Darting quickly from cactus to rock, Rick continued to run, constantly seeking a better angle from which to shoot. Juan had resumed shooting, too, providing the necessary distraction Rick needed to advance on the desperadoes' position.

The brazenness of Rick's charge shocked Ramon and Luis. They fired at him rapidly, but their shots missed their mark time and time again as he zigzagged across the landscape and finally dove behind a pile of rocks, safely out of their line of fire.

"Cazador will not get away from me this time!" Luis swore to Ramon. "You circle back to get the old man away from Lucia, and I'll take care of him."

Ramon moved away hurriedly, thinking that it would be a simple matter to outsmart Lucia and recapture Juan Peralta. No doubt, Cazador had him tied up anyway, so all he had to worry about was disarming one woman. Confident of his eventual success, Ramon worked his way nearer to the outcropping.

At first, Chica had concealed herself a safe distance from the scene of the action, but when she saw Luis come out of hiding to chase Cazador, she knew the time was right for her to seek her vengeance. Unnoticed by the others, she moved ever nearer.

Finally, Jennie could stand it no more. Though the men had been out of sight for some time, the gunfire had not abated; if anything, it had grown more intense. Her nerves stretched to the breaking point. She knew she couldn't sit back and wait any longer. Kneeing her horse forward, she headed toward the crest of the hill.

"Jennie! You're supposed to stay her with me!" Carrie reminded her.

302

"I can't stand not knowing what's going on over there!" Jennie shouted as she continued on. "What if they need my help?"

Carrie debated for only an instant before the thought of Todd's being in danger spurred her to action. Putting her heels to her mount, she hastened after her sister.

Jennie paused briefly at the top of the rise to get her bearings. She had heard Jake say that Juan was on the far side of the canyon, and she spotted him right away, lying flat on a ledge, halfway up the steep wall. He was armed with a rifle and shooting at the bandits who had positioned themselves opposite him.

"Is that Juan Peralta over there?" Carrie asked, pointing in his direction.

"Yes, that's him," Jennie replied, her eyes scanning the rugged terrain for some sign of Cazador.

And, as if her thoughts conjured him up, she caught sight of him, then, as he darted across the sloping hillside, running away from Juan. Jennie wondered why he was running from the old man. Surely, as one of Malo's men, he should be trying to get to Juan. What had happened? What was going on?

"I'm going down there!" she told Carrie, her expression fierce with determination.

"Well, I'm not staying here by myself!"

"Then get your gun ready. We might need it," Jennie stated, pulling her rifle and urging her horse forward toward the action.

When Rick dropped down out of sight behind a boulder to reload his revolver, it gave Luis the opportunity he needed to shift his own position. Racing at top speed, he circled around behind Rick and waited for him to show himself.

Unaware that the outlaw had moved, Rick charged boldly forth from his temporary shelter, firing in the general area where Luis had been before.

Jennie stiffened in the saddle as she spotted Luis among

the boulders. Anxiously she glanced around for some sign of Jake and his band of men, but they were just now topping the ridge and were too far away to be of help.

"Cazador!" Jennie screamed his name in terror.

Luis grinned in silent victory as he stood up behind Rick and aimed his rifle at him.

Putting her heels to her mount, she galloped toward him, her gun drawn and ready. Time stood still in that horrible moment and her throat constricted in terror.

Rick thought he heard someone call out to him. Glancing about he caught sight of a horse racing at breakneck speed in his direction, and he wondered who it could be. It was then that he looked up the hillside and saw the riders appear directly behind Juan's position. Jake! Rick thought excitedly. It had to be Jake! A surge of fresh resolve soared through him, and he started to signal to his friend when he recognized Jennie's voice and heard her horrified words.

"Behind you!"

Rick dove sideways just as Luis pulled the trigger. There was no pain, only a brief moment of time suspended when the world reeled sickeningly around him. He did not see Jennie's stricken face or hear her anguished cry as he pitched forward to lay still in the dirt.

Luis never felt the bullet that slammed into his back and threw him violently to the ground, and Chica climbed down proudly from the top of the rock from where she'd taken her aim at him. She had not known that her shooting ability was that accurate, but she was more than pleased with the results. She had gotten there in time. She had shot Luis full in the back just as he'd fired at Cazador.

Making her way down to where Luis sprawled facedown, she stood victoriously above his lifeless body, oblivious to the fight still going on around her. All she cared about was that he was dead. He would never hurt her again and even better, he would never have the opportunity to hurt anyone else.

Having just run out of ammunition, Juan was forced to look on in helpless horror as Luis had crept up behind Rick and aimed with deadly accuracy at his back. He stood, calling out to Rick, but in the noise and confusion of the moment, Rick did not hear his warning. In heartsick agony, he watched as his beloved grandson fell and lay motionless.

Oblivious to the riders coming up behind him, Juan's only thought was to get to Rick as soon as possible. Climbing from the ledge, he ran as quickly as he could down the rugged slope, unmindful of any danger or threat to his own life. Ricardo needed him.

Jake's men had cleared the top of the rise and descended on the ledge, effectively trapping Ramon as he made his way cautiously toward the refuge in his effort to recapture Juan. Taken totally by surprise, Ramon had no time to flee their unexpected assault, and he was shot down as he turned to fire back at them.

Jake had looked up just in time to witness Rick's shooting and to see Juan spring from the outcropping and start down the steep incline toward him.

"Help the woman," he told Todd and the rest of his men. "Rick's been shot."

Spurring his horse to action, Jake urged him after Juan.

"Juan, climb up. I'll take you down to him," Jake offered, stopping his mount by the old man.

"Jake? Jake McCaine?" Juan peered up at the young man before taking his offered hand.

"Yes, it's me," he answered, helping him into the saddle behind him and starting off quickly in Rick's direction.

"Thank you. Thank you. You got here just in time, but Ricardo's been hit," Juan told him nervously.

"I know," he answered as he expertly guided his horse down the slope. "I hope he's all right."

They fell silent then, each lost in his own worries about Rick as they traversed the rocky hillside.

305

Malo and Pablo saw Steve's men coming and had enough time to get away. Vaulting onto their horses, they raced quickly from the scene, giving no thought to those left behind. To them, the important thing was saving their own necks. They didn't recognize the men who were after them, but they didn't want to wait around to find out who they were, either.

Fleeing as quickly as possible, they rode like the wind in the opposite direction, but the posse stayed on their trail and would not be discouraged. Hoping to confuse the determined band, Malo and Pablo split up, each taking a different canyon, but again the men of the M Circle C would not be put off. Dividing up themselves, they continued to pursue the escaping desperadoes, resolute in their desire to bring them to justice.

Chapter Twenty-two

The sound of Luis's shot reverberated through Jennie's mind and, as if in a nightmare, she saw Cazador fall under the bullet's impact. A scream of rage tore from her throat. Filled with an all-consuming hatred, she took careful aim at Luis, but before she could pull the trigger, he pitched forward and fell, the wound in his back gaping.

Grateful that someone else had saved her the trouble of killing him, she threw herself from the saddle and, rifle still in hand, raced to where Cazador lay.

"Cazador!" she cried as she knelt carefully beside him, her eyes lovingly tracing his pale, almost lifeless features. "Oh God, please! You can't let him die!" Jennie muttered aloud as she discovered the blood flowing freely from the head wound he'd suffered.

With gentle fingers, Jennie located his pulse at his throat, and she relaxed a little when she found that its beat was still strong and regular. Carefully examining his scalp, she was even more relieved to find that the bullet had only grazed him.

At the sound of approaching hoofbeats, Jennie looked up to find Carrie sitting on her horse staring down at her.

"Who's he?" Carrie asked, amazed to find her sister tending a wounded outlaw.

"This is Cazador." Unaware that the very tone of her voice plainly revealed the depth of her feelings for him that moment, Jennie could only think of the urgency in stopping his wound's bleeding. "Quick, Carrie—I need bandages. Do you have any with you? He's bleeding badly."

Reaching into her saddlebags, Carrie pulled out the bandages she'd brought for emergencies and tossed them to her.

"Why are you so worried about him?" Carrie asked astutely.

The implication of her words was not lost on Jennie, and she flushed deeply as she caught the wrappings and turned back to Cazador.

"I'm not, really. It's just that he's the one who helped me."

"Where's Todd? Aren't you even the least bit concerned about what might have happened to him?" she probed, anxious to know more about Jennie's true feelings.

"Of course, I am," she snapped hotly. "It's just that I saw Luis shoot Cazador and I was afraid that—" Jennie stopped quickly, not wanting to even consider the possibility of his dying. "Can you bring me a canteen?"

Carrie dismounted. "Here." She held the container out to her. "Can I do anything to help?"

"I don't know yet. I've got to get this bleeding under control."

"Is he going to live?"

"I think so." Jennie dampened one of the clean cloths and held it to the wound. "The bullet just grazed him."

As she applied the steady pressure, Rick groaned low in his throat. A thrill of relief soared through her at the thought that he was coming around, and in her happiness she almost reached out to caress the leanness of his cheek. It was only Carrie's restrictive presence that helped Jennie maintain control over her warring emotions.

How could she still care about Cazador so much? Jennie tried to reason it out, but while her mind told her that she didn't love him—he was an outlaw, a desperado, and he wanted Lucia—her heart told her that the feelings he'd awakened within her would never die. She loved him.

"Cazador? Can you hear me? Say something," she encouraged softly.

Carrie moved away as she heard a rider coming, and she looked up just as Jake reined in nearby. An old man she assumed was Juan Peralta was riding double with him.

"Jennie! Carrie! How is he?" Jake demanded as he first helped Juan down and then swung out of the saddle himself.

"It's a head wound, Jake." Jennie looked up, making sure to keep her expression carefully blank. "But—"

"Damn!" Jake swore as he stared at Jennie's bloodied hands, and remorse flooded through him. He had tried so hard to get to Rick in time and now—Coming to kneel at his side, he searched his friend's face for some spark of life.

At Jennie's words, Juan suddenly seemed to age. His eyes were filled with unspoken sorrow and grief.

"Ricardo," the old man murmured painfully, reaching out to touch Rick's shoulder.

"But, it's just a graze," she said, finally managing to finish her sentence.

Jennie was surprised by Juan Peralta's show of deep concern for him. And she wondered why he had called him Ricardo.

"Only a graze?" Her brother lifted hopeful eyes to hers. "Let me have a look."

Jake lifted the cloth and checked the injury that Jennie had so painstakingly cleaned.

"It doesn't look too bad, Juan," he told him reassuringly. "I think he's going to be all right."

Transformed in that instant, Juan smiled brilliantly at Jake and Jennie and then hurriedly turned his attention back to Rick.

"Rick!" Jake barked insistently when Rick groaned again.

"Jake, why do you keep calling him Rick?" Jennie

questioned and then realized that they had known each other. "So! You did know him," she accused, but before her brother could offer any explanation, Rick stirred and opened his eyes.

The pain in his head was nearly blinding, but somehow Rick managed to keep his eyes open. The first person he saw silhouetted against the brightness of the late morning sky was Jennie, and in spite of the agony pounding in his head, he thought she looked particularly beautiful. Rick wanted to speak to her—to tell her how worried he had been about her, but Jake's forceful inquiry cut through his romantic haze.

"Rick, damn it!"

Frowning, he rolled his head slightly to get a look at his old friend. His voice a husky growl, he answered, "I thought I told you to stay out of this."

Jake gave him an undaunted grin. "You did, but since when do I ever listen to you?"

"Thanks, Jake." Rick spoke the words humbly, closing his eyes for a moment as he thought of how close he'd come to death.

"Are you all right?" His voice was sharp and Rick looked up again, scowling.

"I will be when you stop shouting. I've got one hell of a headache."

"Sorry." Jake grinned, not in the least repentant.

Rick lifted a hand to rub at his forehead and then tentatively touched the bandage. His lips quirked in a crooked vestige of a smile. "Luis came damn close, didn't he?"

"I'll say," he agreed, recalling the heartstopping moment when they'd seen the outlaw shoot him down. "We saw it all, but we were too far out of range to help. And then when Jennie told us it was a head wound, we thought you were dying."

"Ricardo." Juan breathed easier now that his grandson was conscious and lucid.

"Grandfather." Rick reached out, and Juan clasped his hand firmly in his own. "Thank God, you're all right."

"I'm fine, thanks to your friend here. Jake got to me just in time."

"What about Lucia?"

"She is uninjured, too," Juan supplied.

"Good." He breathed easier.

Jennie stiffened at their conversation. Rick? Grandfather? She didn't understand.

"What's going on here?" she blurted out suddenly, unable to keep quiet any longer.

"Jennie," Jake began patiently, "I'd like you to meet my good friend Rick Peralta. Rick this is my sister, Jennie."

"I know," he answered, turning to look up at her and giving her a quixotic half-smile.

"Peralta!? You?" she stammered, her dark eyes widening in shocked anger. "Why didn't you tell me?"

"I asked you to trust me, Jennie," Rick replied.

"Trust you!" she seethed, standing up and backing away. "But how could I?"

Rick Peralta, indeed! He had made a complete fool out of her! He had used her! She had been nothing more than a pawn to him in his plot to rescue Juan.

And, as she remembered his concern about Lucia, Jennie grew even more embarrassed. While he had been unconscious, she had acted like a lovesick fool and, to her dismay, Carrie had witnessed it all. Glancing nervously at her sister, Jennie was mortified when Carrie gave her a knowing smirk.

Todd and his group of men rode up just then, and Jennie was grateful for the interruption, but her relief was short-lived. For, as she looked up to greet them, she spotted Lucia, safely ensconced on the back of Todd's horse. Well, she though angrily, if Cazador wanted Lucia, he could damn well have her. Refusing to give in to the urge to scream out her frustration, she lifted her chin proudly and smiled her welcome at Todd.

Todd dismounted quickly and then turned to help Lucia down, settling her gently on the uneven ground. Jennie gritted her teeth at his gentlemanly display but said nothing as he started their way, his arm solicitously around Lucia.

"What happened?"

"Rick was shot," Carrie told him quickly, and she was surprised by the reaction from the Mexican girl.

"Rick? He was injured?" Lucia asked and at Carrie's answering nod, she broke painfully away from Todd's supporting arm and hurried to where Rick lay.

Jennie was livid. So! Even Lucia knew his real identity! Probably everybody in the whole wide world had known who he was but her! She watched in barely concealed disgust as Lucia knelt by Rick's side. Unable to stand any more, Jennie started to go back to her horse, but Todd's next statement stopped her.

"Is he going to be all right?" Todd asked with real concern.

"He should be," Jennie replied, hoping her words reflected indifference.

Todd nodded and then, realizing that both Jennie and Carrie had disobeyed the specific orders their father had given them, he frowned.

"Jennie—Carrie—" His tone was firm as he looked back and forth between the women. "I thought we'd told you to stay behind where it was safe!"

"We were worried about you," Carrie said quickly in all honesty.

"But you could easily have been hurt down here in the midst of all the gunfire." Todd's expression was almost stern.

"Well, we weren't!" Jennie snapped in exasperation. "Now let's go and see if we can help Pa."

"In a minute. I want to speak with Rick first," Todd told her as he approached the other man.

"Rick? I'm Todd Clarke."

312

"Yes, I remember you. How's your shoulder doing?" Rick struggled to sit up, but fell back as dizziness washed over him. "Help me up, Jake," he asked, irritated at his own weakness.

But before Jake or Juan could help him, Lucia was there supporting his shoulders and aiding him in his attempt to sit up. Rick looked up quickly, wanting a moment to talk to Jennie alone. He knew she was angry, and he wanted to make peace with her. But as their gazes met, Lucia pressed closely to his back and leaned over his shoulder to ask huskily, "Are you comfortable now?"

To Jennie, Lucia's move looked just like the deliberately seductive ploy it was, and she turned away from him, refusing to answer the plea in his eyes.

"My shoulder's doing fine, thanks to Carrie. Are you going to be all right?" Todd asked worriedly, noting the sudden, strained look on his face.

"Sure, thanks. I'm just a little groggy," Rick replied, frowning.

"Well, I just wanted to thank you for taking such good care of our Jennie. I know we all appreciate it. We were very worried about her." Todd slipped an affectionate arm about her slim waist and drew her to his side.

"There was no doubt that I'd take care of her. She is, after all, Jake's sister." Rick's reply was casual but his eyes narrowed as he wondered at the relationship between the two.

"Well, I'm especially grateful to you," Todd said as he looked down at Jennie with open adoration.

Rick's expression was shuttered, revealing nothing of the inner turmoil. What claim did Todd Clarke have on Jennie? In the beginning, she had told him that they were just friends. But was there more to it than that?

He tried to stand for he wanted to meet Todd on his own terms, but a wave of agony pounded through him, forcing him to sit back down. A groan escaped him and he leaned forward, bracing his throbbing head in his hands.

"Carrie, you have some medicine with you, don't you? Why don't you finish wrapping Rick's wound for him?" Jake asked.

"Sure, I'll get it right away." Carrie was glad to get away from Todd and Jennie for a while.

At the sign of Rick's obvious pain, Jennie wanted to rush to him—to soothe him and hold him to her. But she knew she couldn't. Whatever had existed between them was over. Holding herself ramrod straight, she tried to shift slightly from his possessive hold.

"Jennie? Is something wrong?" Todd asked, wondering at her attempt to move away from him.

"No, nothing's wrong." She smiled up at him a little too brightly. "Since he's going to be all right," she said, indicating Cazador, refusing to use his name. "Why don't we go after Pa and Steve?"

"All right. I suppose you'll be safe enough riding with us," he said reluctantly. Then, turning away from her, he spoke to Jake. "We'll meet you back here. Men? Let's ride."

The hands from the M Circle C were more than ready to help track down the other bandits, and they reined their horses around, ready to follow Todd's lead.

"Jennie—wait." Rick looked up quickly, protesting her leaving.

"Jennie," Todd said softly as they were walking away, "I think Peralta wants to talk to you."

"He's just a little late with his explanations, and I have absolutely no interest in anything else he has to say. Let's go."

Todd was surprised by the vehemence of her statement but said nothing.

Without looking back, Jennie moved to her horse and swung quickly into the saddle. She waited in seeming impatience for Todd to mount up, too, and then they rode off with the rest of the posse in the direction that Steve and Mac had taken earlier in their pursuit of Malo and Pablo.

Carrie stood silently by, wondering at the entire exchange between this Rick Peralta and Jennie. There had been far too many undercurrents in the words and looks they'd exchanged for her to believe that there was nothing going on between them. Especially after the way Jennie had cared for him.

Carrie, with an effort, controlled the smile that threatened. Maybe, just maybe, there was still a ray of hope for her with Todd.

Returning with the medicine, she busily set about bandaging Rick's head.

"Thanks." Jake welcomed her help. "Oh, Rick, by the way, this is my younger sister Carrie."

Rick looked up at Carrie and was impressed by her loveliness. "You're one lucky man to have two such gorgeous sisters, Jake."

Carrie was instantly charmed by Rick's flirtatious words.

"Why thank you," she told him, giving him a warm smile. "Now, let me see what I can do to ease your headache."

"Jennie?" Todd called to her after they had ridden a distance from the others.

"What, Todd?" There was an unusual tenseness to her tone.

"What happened between you and Rick Peralta?" Carrie had not been the only one to sense the undercurrents between them.

"What makes you think anything happened?"

"You acted almost rude to the man," he answered.

Todd had known Jennie for many years and in all that time, she'd never been anything but gracious and well mannered.

Jennie shrugged but didn't reply.

"Jennie." Todd was choosing his words carefully, trying to keep his concern from showing.

She glanced over at him quickly and, reading his sudden anxiety in his expression, she almost panicked. Had Todd somehow sensed how confused her feelings were?

"What?" Her voice reflected a steadiness that she was not feeling.

Todd gazed off across the distance. "You've been acting so strangely. I was just wondering—Did Peralta hurt you in any way while you were with him? I mean, there I was thanking him for taking care of you, and if he—"

"No," Jennie put in quickly, totally relieved that Todd hadn't picked up on her inner distress. "He didn't hurt me."

"Oh." He relaxed a bit. "Well, good. But, what about—" He wanted to ask her why she'd been so cold to him then, but her next words cut him off.

"I don't want to talk about Cazador or that time. It's better off just forgotten. If you've got any more questions, ask him. He seems to be the one with all the answers!" And with that, she spurred her horse sharply, picking up her pace considerably and leaving him to follow.

Lucia sat back and watched with concealed pleasure as Jennie rode off. Her side was aching and she was tired, but none of it mattered. They had won! They had defeated Malo. They had rescued Juan. And now Rick and the gold would be all hers

She sighed contentedly, thinking of how concerned he had been for her safety and how he had carried her when her strength had failed her. A small smile curved her lips. Now, there was absolutely no reason why they couldn't become lovers—or more!

Dreaming of the day when she would, at last, experience his full possession, Lucia glanced over to where Rick sat, deep in conversation with his grandfather and Jake. In spite of her own injury, she still felt a thrill of desire course through her as her eyes roamed hungrily over him. When they had told her that he'd been hurt, she'd thought she was going to die. Rick and Juan were the only men who'd ever shown her the least kindness, and if anything had happened to them—She shook her head, denying the thought. Leaning back, she closed her eyes, hoping that a little rest might ease the ache in her side.

"There. I'm finished," Carrie told Rick as she efficiently tightened the bandage around his head. "How does it feel?"

Rick managed to give her a wry smile as he gingerly touched the side of his head. "It's fine. Thanks."

"I'm going to put these away," she told them, gathering her supplies. "I'll be back in a minute."

With Jake and Juan's help, Rick slowly got to his feet and then leaned against a nearby boulder to steady himself.

"That's better," he told them as he took a deep breath and glanced quickly around. The pounding in his head had lessened and, now that he was thinking clearly again, he asked. "Who shot Luis?"

"I don't know," Juan told him. "We saw him fall right after you were wounded, but I'm not sure who did it."

"I shot him," Chica told them as she rode slowly toward them. She had hesitated in coming forward, wanting only to flee the nightmare of her past, but logic told her that she would need help to escape the confusion of these mountains.

"Chica!" Lucia exclaimed happily, getting up and running to her. "We didn't know what had happened to you! Thank heaven you're all right! You shot Luis?"

She nodded her answer. "I was behind him, and when I saw him sneaking up behind Cazador—"

"Thank you, Chica," Rick told her earnestly.

Her smile was almost feral as she looked at him. "It was my pleasure, believe me."

All but Jake well understood Chica's meaning.

"Now, if they can catch up with Malo," Lucia said.

"Do you think we should go after them and try to help?" Rick offered. "If you've got any ammunition, I think I can ride."

"No, there's no need. We'll wait here for them. Pa will catch them." Jake said.

"Good," Lucia remarked fiercely, knowing that her life would be useless if she ever chanced to run into Malo in the future.

When Carrie returned, she brought all the food she'd been carrying with her.

"Thanks, Carrie. It's been a while since we had anything," Rick told her.

"I thought it might have been." She flashed Rick a warm smile as she divided the supplies among them.

Carrie found him very attractive, and she wondered briefly what it would be like to be his "captive". Smiling to herself, she glanced at him quickly as he settled himself on the ground to eat. He certainly was a fine specimen of a man.

Carrie wasn't quite sure what had happened between Rick and Jennie while they were on the trail together, but she was determined to find out. She knew that Jennie felt something for him, for she'd never seen her sister that worried about anyone ever before. And there had been too much tension in the way they'd been verbally sparring for them not to be attracted to each other.

Determined to find out, she sat down next to Rick.

Settling down a short distance from the others, Lucia took the time to explain everything that had happened to Chica.

"You mean he is really the old man's grandson?"

"Yes, and he risked everything to save our lives," she told her excitedly. "Now that Malo's gone, I suppose we'll continue on to the gold mine." Lucia continued to weave her own fantasy.

"Are you sure? The story I heard was that the Peraltas never wanted to return to that mine again."

"He would be a fool not to go, now that we are so close."

318

Looking up, Lucia grew furious as she watched Carrie fawning all over Rick. She scowled angrily.

"What's wrong?" Chica asked.

"That bitch! Doesn't she know he's mine?"

"Lucia," her friend said. "Is he yours? I get the feeling that Rick Peralta belongs to no woman."

Refusing to believe that, she gave her an irritated look. "He may not be mine yet, but he will be. You didn't see how he helped me and took care of me."

Chica knew that Lucia was deluding herself, but she held her tongue. It was a lesson that had to be learned through experience.

"Whatever." She gave an eloquent lift of her shoulder. "But do not make a scene. Rick Peralta is not the same man as El Cazador. He is a gentleman. You would do well to remember that."

Lucia looked confused. "You do not make sense, Chica. Of course, he is the same man. And he wants me, I know it!"

"Very well, but do not underestimate the blond. She is interested in him and she is a lady."

She snorted her derision at Chica's last statement. "What lady would wear men's trousers? I do not think she is a lady."

"Maybe, maybe not, but she will not be as easy to discourage as her sister."

"About that, you are right," she said as they recognized Carrie as a worthy rival. "This one knows men."

And sitting back, they continued to eat in silence.

Chapter Twenty-three

The familiar rhythm of the horse's gait helped Jennie to relax as they rode onward at the steady, ground-eating pace in search of Mac. The sun's pulsing heat on her shoulders was soothing to her frazzled nerves, and she turned her face to the wind to enjoy the wild gentleness of its caress. Closing her eyes briefly, she could almost pretend that her life was normal again—that the last few days had never happened.

Jennie was still a bit bewildered by everything that had occurred. One moment it seemed that she had been happily enjoying her morning ride, and now she was tracking murderous outlaws and engaged to marry Todd.

Glancing at Todd as he rode along beside her, Jennie sighed. She liked him, admired him, cared about him—but, damnit, she thought, she didn't love him. As much as it angered her to admit it, Rick was the only man she loved, and now, because he hadn't been honest with her, it was too late.

Not that he cared, Jennie thought nastily. He seemed perfectly content with Lucia. Hadn't he chosen Lucia over her while they were in camp? Hadn't he rescued Lucia along with Juan? The memories still had the power to hurt, and Jennie forcefully tried to dismiss all thoughts of Rick from her mind.

Todd was the man she was going to marry, and they would live happily ever after, she decided firmly. Happiness was, after all, just the way you looked at things. Todd was tender, warm, and affectionate. He owned a good-sized ranch, and he would make an excellent father to their children.

Suddenly, the thought of Todd's hands on her body chilled her. Would she be able to respond to him? His kiss and embrace had been pleasant but not exciting. Would he be able to take her to the heights of passion she'd experienced in Rick's arms? In her heart, Jennie knew the answer and she became melancholy. What she had shared with Rick had been special—a once in a lifetime experience and it would never come again.

"There they are!" Todd shouted as he caught sight of Steve heading in their direction.

Todd's loud call ripped through her thoughts, and Jennie was glad for the distraction. She had no business being unhappy. She had just been rescued from a fate worse than death; they had managed to save Juan and, in the process, they had broken up one of the most dangerous outlaw gangs in the territory. It was all cause for celebration, not depression. Turning her full attention to Steve's approach, she smiled widely and waved her greeting to him and his men.

"How'd you do? Where's Pa?"

"We got one of them," Steve told her, indicating Pablo, who was tied up and riding in the back under heavy guard.

"And Malo?" Jennie asked, worriedly.

"Mac went after him. Malo and this one split up when they found out they couldn't lose us real easy." He grinned. "How'd you do?"

"We got both of our men, but Rick Peralta was wounded," Todd told him.

"Is he bad?"

"No, just a graze, but he's going to have a headache for a while, I think."

"Lucky for him."

"It was. He came very close to being dead," Todd went on.

Jennie was about ready to scream. Why did they have to talk about Rick? Everytime they mentioned him, she remembered the horror of watching him fall beneath Luis's bullet.

"Which way did Mac head?" Todd was asking as Jennie pulled herself back from that devastating memory.

"We'll have to backtrack a bit. They took off down a side canyon about a mile or so back."

"Let's go. He may need us."

After directing two of his men to take Pablo back to where Jake awaited their return, they set off again to locate Mac. It wasn't long before they did find him and his men—frustrated, angry, and cussing.

"Mac!" Steve and Todd called out to him as he was searching the steep, rocky slope of the canyon.

"Did you lose Malo?" Todd asked as they joined up with his group.

"Yes, damnit! One minute he was there and the next he just disappeared!" Another savage curse exploded from him. "Malo couldn't have vanished off the face of the earth! He's got to be here somewhere!"

"Where did you last see him?" Steve asked, his eyes raking over the rock-encrusted rise.

"Right in this area, about forty-five minutes ago," Mac told him in disgust.

"All right. Call off the men and I'll see what I can do." Steve dismounted and handed his reins to Todd before starting to comb the stone-ridden ground for some clue as to Malo's disappearance.

They watched with interest as Steve studied the numerous tracks, slowly working his way into an ever-widening circle. Finally, in frustration, he gave up.

"I don't know, Mac. All I can pick up here are the ranch horses. I don't see any sign of Malo's mount at all." Steve's expression was troubled. "Are you sure this was the area?"

"Positive," Mac said firmly and his men nodded their agreement. "Well, I guess I lost him." His flat tone reflected everyone's mood. Looking up at Todd then, he asked, "How'd the rest of you do?"

"Steve got his man and we took care of both of ours."

"Anyone hurt?"

"Only RickPeralta."

"What happened?"

"One of the outlaws worked his way behind him and tried to back-shoot him. Luckily, Jennie yelled to him, and he moved just in time so the bullet only grazed him."

"Good girl, Jennie." Mac beamed at his daughter. "How's Carrie?"

His question surprised Jennie. "She's fine. She stayed behind to take care of Rick."

"Good." Mac was pleased that almost everything had worked out for the best. "What about the other two outlaws that you took care of?"

"We got them both. They're dead."

Mac nodded his approval. "But I'm still damned angry that I lost Malo. He was the one I really wanted. I just wish I knew where he'd gone."

Malo waited until the posse had disappeard from sight before making a move toward freedom. He had known that the McCaines might be on Cazador's trail, but he had not thought that they would ever catch up with them. Realizing that it must have been the gun battle that had given away their position, he cursed himself for his own stupidity.

Malo was angry at being thwarted so close to his goal, but he refused to give up on his quest. He wasn't quite sure just what he was going to do yet, but he knew he was going to get that gold, one way or the other.

Mounting his horse, he started off in the same direction as

the McCaine men. He had no intention of revealing himself to them, but he was determined to find out if Juan Peralta had survived the posse's attack. And, if he had, then there was still hope that he could get to the mine.

Jennie grew more and more tense with each passing mile as they headed back to meet up with Jake. Her fate taunted her like a cruel and twisted joke. For the next three days—and nights—she was going to be in very close contact with Rick. There could be no avoiding it, though she wished she could. She was caught well and good in a strangling web of emotional pain.

A pang of despair gripped Jennie's soul as she wondered if Rick would be sleeping with Lucia during that time. She fervently hoped that she wouldn't be made to witness their desire for one another for it had been hard enough for her to tolerate Lucia's attentiveness to him that afternoon. Jennie wasn't sure what she'd do if she was forced to watch as the wench crawled into Rick's bedroll with him.

Shaking off these infuriating thoughts, Jennie tried grimly to get control of herself. It would not do to let Rick know how she felt. She was engaged to Todd now and that was the way it was to be. She would not humiliate him by allowing her feelings for Rick to overrule her common sense. The choices had been made; the matter had been settled.

As the rendezvous point came in sight, she drew a deep, ragged breath and prepared to face the situation bravely. She was a McCaine and she would carry herself as one. Unconsciously squaring her shoulders, Jennie knew she was as ready as she would ever be to face him again.

For all that Jennie imagined it would be a traumatic event. Their return to the meeting point was anticlimactic. As much as she worried about trying to avoid him, she found the effort totally unnecessary. Rick was completely engrossed in talks with the other men and did not once look in her direction.

Jennie knew that she should have been relieved at having been spared his attentions, but instead, she found herself oddly irritated that he could ignore her so completely. And when Rick seemed to make a point of seeking out Todd and conversing with him at length, she grew especially angry. He had no business speaking with her fiance! What could they possibly have to talk about, anyway? Jennie knew a moment of sudden panic when she thought that Rick might be telling Todd everything that had happened between them, and when she looked up, her expression was pale and worried.

It was at the particular moment that Rick glanced up, too, straight at Jennie. He had been trying his damnedest to ignore her, but when he saw the worried look on her face, he knew he had to speak with her, if only to reassure her of his gentlemanly intentions. Excusing himself, he walked casually toward her.

"Jennie." His voice was deep and mellow, and just the sound of her name upon his lips sent a sensuous shiver down her spine.

"What?" She jumped as he touched her arm.

"I'd like to talk to you for just a few minutes, if I could?" He sounded courteous and thoroughly civilized and nothing at all like himself.

"Well, I really need to speak with Todd," she lied, not wanting to be with him.

"This won't take long." He still sounded cordial, but she just didn't trust him.

"No, I don't think so." She started to walk away, but his hand snaked out and grasped her upper arm in a formidable grip.

"Jennie, I don't ask nicely twice. Let's go. Unless, of course, you want to make a scene right here?"

"All right," she consented quickly, angry at having been blackmailed into agreeing.

"If you'd always been this compliant, we wouldn't have had our misunderstandings," he told her cryptically as he led her slightly away from the others. "Jennie."

"What do you want?" she demanded sharply, glaring up at him.

"I noticed that you seemed concerned about my speaking with Todd and—"

"I'm not in the least concerned with anything you do," Jennie told him loftily.

"Then you wouldn't care if I told Todd about our more intimate moments together?" He had wanted to be patient with her, but her hardened, indifferent attitude was grating on him.

"You wouldn't dare!" she gasped at his emotional blackmail.

"Jennie, my love," he began slowly. "You above all people should know how much I'd dare." Rick watched as all the color drained from her face, and he felt a sickening lurch in his vitals as he realized that she really did care for Todd.

"You," she hissed, barely able to control her rage. What game was he playing? Why was he tormenting her this way? Surely he didn't want her anymore? He'd made that perfectly clear long ago. Tears stung her eyes, and she blinked them back with an effort.

Rick noted her distress and was suddenly contrite for having cause her so much pain. "You've no need to worry, love. I may not have been the perfect gentleman while we were with Malo, but contrary to what you may think, I do know how to treat a lady. What happened between us was very personal, and it will remain that way."

Jennie knew she should be pleased by his discretion, but for some reason his whole attitude enraged her even more. How dare he play the perfect gentleman with her after all that had happened! What a mockery this entire scene was! She knew what he was really like. Suddenly, Jennie wanted to strike back at him, to dent that calm, civilized veneer he was now presenting to the world.

"Thank you," she replied with cool disdain. Keeping her expression critically dispassionate, she looked him up and down before managing a semblance of a sweet smile. "I do appreciate it. I find it's always best not to dwell on past errors in judgment and to learn from one's mistakes so they aren't repeated."

Then without another word, Jennie turned on her heel and left him standing there, staring after her. The only sign of Rick's inner torment was a slight tensing of his jaw as he watched her take Todd's arm and smile up at him beguilingly before leading him away in her father's direction.

Juan let his gaze sweep nervously over the craggy hills that surrounded them.

"We'd better start on back right away," Juan said to Mac just as Jennie and Todd joined them. "It's still light yet so we should be able to cover some miles before sundown."

"Are you up to it?" Mac asked, knowing how rough the past few days had been on him.

"All I want to do is leave these mountains. I won't rest easy until we're back out on the desert." He spoke so earnestly that the others were startled.

"But why?" Mac wondered at his anxiety.

"Jake didn't tell you the whole story?"

"He told us about your kidnapping. Is there more?" Todd questioned.

Juan ran a weary hand over his eyes, as if to block out the memory. "It was long ago, yet it seems like only yesterday." He sighed deeply before he went on. "I discovered the gold mine myself in my younger years, but I only made occasional trips because of the danger. The area that the mine is in, you see, is sacred ground to the Apache." Juan sounded exhausted as he continued to explain. "But then, when we had suffered a few setbacks on the ranch, my sons Rodrigo and Antonio—Ricardo's father and uncle—led an expedition to the mine to get more gold. They took many workers with them and mules to pack the ore out. And from what Ricardo told me, they did well."

"Rick went with them?" Jennie couldn't stop the question.

327

"Yes, he was young then and eager for the excitement." Juan's eyes were burning with emotion as he met Jennie's currious gaze.

"What happened?"

"The Apache attacked them just as they left the mountains. Ricardo was the lone survivor of the massacre."

Jennie could not stifle the gasp that escaped her. Suddenly, his tense moods and uncomfortable silences made sense to her. It had been a living hell for him to return here, and she had caused him nothing but trouble the entire time.

"They are near—even now—watching," Juan said looking up once again at the jagged peaks. "We would do well to leave here as soon as possible."

"You don't want to go back to the mine?" Mac asked.

"Never! It has been a curse on my family and the cause of nothing but death and destruction," he stated vehemently.

"Then let's ride," Mac ordered. "How close are we to the next watering hole?"

"I'm not sure," Juan answered. "But Ricardo will know. He learned these mountains well. Ricardo!"

As much as Rick wanted to stay away from Jennie, Juan's call forced him to join in the conversation.

"How far are we from the nearest water?" Mac questioned, knowing that their supply was running a little low.

"We're about a half day's ride from the next basin. We should make it by noon tomorrow."

"Good." Mac was pleased with the news. "Do you know of a better location to camp tonight? I thought we could get a few more hours of traveling in."

Rick glanced up at the sun to judge the lateness of the hour. "There's about four hours of daylight left, so I think we'd better head for higher ground. Some place that would be easier to defend just in case there is any trouble."

"Then let's go back out the way we came in and see what kind of campsite we can find," Mac said and, giving the order to the men to get ready to move out, they headed for their horses.

The ranch hands were all eager to be home, and there were no complaints as they swung back into the saddle after an already arduous day. Chica and Lucia were mounted on Luis's and Ramon's horses, and they began the long, return trek to the M Circle C.

Malo was very cautious as he made his way down the canyon. He knew how lucky he was to still be alive, and he was not about to take any chances when he was so outnumbered. He would wait until the odds were more in his favor.

Malo had no trouble catching up with the posse and, unobserved, he worked his way up the slope to near its crest, seeking a secluded spot from which to survey their movements. It pleased him to see that Juan Peralta was still alive, for as long as he was healthy there was a chance for his plan to succeed.

As he studied the people below, Malo was shocked to see that Cazador was moving freely about in their midst. How could that be? He was the one responsible for Jennie McCaine's kidnapping in the first place. Why would the men who'd rescued her befriend Cazador?

Confused, he searched anxiously for some sign that Luis or Ramon had survived the assault, but when he saw Lucia and Chica mount up on their horses, he knew that they'd met their end. Only Pablo had been taken alive, and he was under heavy guard. Angry over the frustrating situation he found himself in, Malo sank back out of sight, cursing the fate that had brought Jennie McCaine into his camp.

Knowing that he would have to bide his time and wait for the right opportunity to make his move did not sit well with Malo. He wanted the gold and he wanted it now. He was glad when the posse began to move out on their way back up the canyon, and he determined that he would stay with them all the way, for there was no doubt in his mind that they would now be heading for the gold mine.

Again Malo waited until they were out of sight before venturing forth from his hiding place. Pacing himself, he followed them at a safe distance, taking great care to stay just out of sight and all the while wondering at Cazador's connection with the McCaines.

The campsite they picked that night was near the top of a ridge and well protected on two sides by massive rock formations. Though the men of the M Circle C did not expect any more trouble from Malo, the ever present threat of a possible Indian attack prompted them to post a watch. The darkness had fallen like a comforting blanket of peace, and since it was no longer imperative that they conceal themselves completely, they took the luxury of building a small fire.

The evening passed in a celebration of sorts for the posse because they had accomplished their goal in rescuing Jennie. Bottles of whiskey, hoarded until now, were passed around, and their mood was generally light.

Standing with Jake a short distance away from the camp, Rick was tense and on edge.

"Here." Jake thrust a bottle of whiskey at him. "You look like you could use a drink."

"Thanks," he replied gratefully, drinking deeply of the potent liquor.

"Is your head hurting?"

Rick looked up questioningly. "No, why?"

"I just thought that might be the reason why you're being so quiet tonight."

"No, I guess I'm just anxious to be out of here." He rubbed tiredly at the tense muscles of his neck as he glanced in Jennie's direction.

He loved her, yet after the harsh words they'd exchanged that afternoon, he wondered if there was any hope for him to win her. She had acted almost as if she hated him. But no matter what Jennie might say, Rick could not forget the way she responded to him when they'd make love. Try as she might to deny the attraction, they shared a very powerful physical bond.

When he heard Jennie laugh at something Todd said, Rick looked quickly in her direction and then scowled blackly. Somehow he had to win her trust and her love. He couldn't bear the thought of another man touching her or holding her.

Unable to stand there and watch anymore, he started to walk away into the night. "I need to walk around a little bit. I'll talk to you later."

Jake was surprised by his abrupt departure. "Sure." And it wasn't until later that he realized that Rick had taken the bottle with him when he'd gone.

"Walk with me, Jennie?" Todd asked as he gazed down at her in the flickering light of the fire.

He had been sitting between Carrie and Jennie all evening and the strain was getting to him. He knew he had to get away from Carrie's magnetic sensuality or go crazy. Damn! he thought with a vengeance. He should never have touched her, never have surrendered to his desire to have her.

"Of course," Jennie said, and Todd breathed an inward sigh of relief as he hoped that Jennie's kisses would drive the memory of Carrie's torrid loving from his mind.

As Carrie watched them go, she was barely able to keep up her pretense of nonchalance. All night she had stayed by Todd's side, engaging in light conversation with him and Jennie while subtly trying to remind him of their time together. In frustration, she realized that it hadn't worked. He seemed friendly enough but had not responded to any of her ploys.

The thought that he really might not care frightened her. How could she go on living if he married Jennie? Determination rose anew within her: She could not, would not give up. She loved Todd and she would do everything she could to get him.

Walking together from the camp, Todd glanced down at Jennie. "Has something been troubling you? You've been quiet tonight."

"No, not really. I guess I'm just a little tired."

"It was an exciting day, but I am just really glad that it's all behind us now, so we can get on with our lives." He stopped once they were out of sight and pulled her into his arms.

Jennie's smile was soft as she looked up at him. "I know. It seems like I've been living in some sort of limbo."

"Well, that's all about to end," he told her just as his mouth claimed hers.

Todd wanted their embrace to be passionate. He wanted to feel the flames of desire for Jennie. He wanted to lose himself in her love. But the kiss they shared was only pleasant. There was no heightening of his senses as he held her tightly to him.

Jennie wanted Todd's touch to ignite her desires, just as Rick's had, but it did not happen. She got angry with herself then for even thinking of him while she was in Todd's arms. It seemed a betrayal of his goodness, and guilt washed over her in heavy, choking waves.

Jennie knew that she had to stop dwelling on the past and concentrate on her future happiness. Todd was her future, not Rick. Throwing herself into the kiss with increasing gusto, she gave up her dreams of Rick's lovemaking and sought only to please Todd.

*　　　*　　　*

"Rick?" Lucia called out softly. She had been watching him all evening and waiting for a time when she could find him alone.

Rick had walked some distance from the campsite in hopes of being alone for a while, and he wondered in irritation how she'd managed to find him.

"I'm over here, Lucia," he called out into the darkness.

"I've been looking for you." Her tone was sultry.

"Why?" He chose to ignore the suggestiveness in her voice.

"Why do you think?" she taunted, coming to stand before him.

"Lucia," he began, wanting to discourage her once and for all, but she was not about to be discouraged easily.

"I want you, Rick," she told him throatily. "I have since the first time I saw you in Malo's camp."

Deliberately, she lifted a shoulder so her blouse slipped down and revealed the swell of one breast. "You want me, too. I tasted it in your kiss that night."

Rick had no desire to hurt Lucia, but the last thing he wanted to do was to make love to her. The only reason he had pretended an interest in her in the first place had been because of her threats to expose his relationship with Juan.

"Lucia." He started again to tell her the truth as painlessly as possible. But before he could go on, she stepped closer, pressing against him, and then she linked her arms behind his neck.

"Kiss me, Rick. I want you so."

Rick closed his eyes for a brief second, wondering wildly what he would do if it were Jennie saying those words. The reality of the situation had a firm grip on him, however, and he tugged Lucia's clinging arms away.

"No, Lucia."

"No?" She looked up at him, questioningly. No man had ever turned her down before.

"I don't want you, Lucia."

"But the other night—" She started to say.

"There were other circumstances involved in what happened the other night," he sasid coldly, knowing it would be the only way to stop her passionate pursuit.

She was stunned by his revelation, and it hurt her to realize that he had only shared her embrace because of her threat. Never one to give up easily, though, she gave him a seductive smile.

"But, I can make it good for you. I will be your woman now that Jennie—"

At the mention of Jennie, Rick almost lost his temper. "Lucia. I do not want another woman. That time with Malo is over. You would do well to find yourself a man who could love you."

"But you're the one I want. I could make you love me."

"I'm sorry, Lucia." He shook his head in denial as he spoke.

"I thought you cared about me."

"You showed kindness to my grandfather when he needed it most, and I was grateful to you, but, Lucia, it was never more than that."

Lucia bitterly nodded her understanding. Her dreams of having his love and the gold were shattered, and she turned to walk away.

Chapter Twenty-four

Tiny pinpricks of heavenly light spangled the night's ebony face with a magical, mystical twinkling. Jennie stood alone in the darkness, so intent on her troubled thoughts that she did not notice the beauty of the star-dusted sky.

She had told Todd that she'd needed some time to compose herself, and she'd remained behind in the privacy of the small clearing long after he had broken off their embrace and returned to join the others. Jennie had needed some time alone to deal with her wayward feelings. While her mind was logically dictating that she marry Todd, her heart was still longing for Rick.

Though a tear of sadness slipped from the corner of her eye, she didn't bother to wipe it away. The pain of seeing Rick and being near him was proving almost unbearable. Yet, somehow, someway, Jennie knew she would have to get over him. She had her own life to live, and she couldn't waste it in mourning for a love that obviously had never existed. Sighing heavily, she finally felt more in control, and she turned to start back to camp.

After Lucia left him, Rick stayed alone in the darkness, thinking of Jennie and drinking heavily from his bottle of whiskey. He couldn't get her out of his mind this night. The memory of her wanton response to his lovemaking flowed through him, and with the rememberance came the all too familiar stirring in his loins. God, how he wanted her. He could still remember the taste of her and the silken feel of her satiny flesh beneath his hands.

Rick wondered at her feelings for Todd Clarke. Did she let him hold her and kiss her? His hands knotted into fists of anger as an image of Jennie in Todd's arms assailed him, and only the consoling thought that Jennie had give him her greatest gift—the gift of her innocence—soothed Rick. Being the type of woman she was, he was sure that she would never have come to him so willingly in the abandoned mine if she had cared for someone else.

Rick thought briefly of her sharp words that afternoon and smiled. Try as she might to deny what was between them, Rick knew that the union they'd shared was overpowering and lasting. Draining the last of the liquor from the bottle, he tossed it thoughtlessly aside and started back to the camp, resolving to himself once again that she would be his.

As he moved quietly through the night, he was startled to come upon Jennie alone in a clearing, staring up at the clear, night sky. Standing a short distance from her, Rick let his hungry gaze sweep over her. She was a beautiful woman, and he knew that he wanted to spend the rest of his life with her— loving her.

"You are very lovely," he murmured, the deep resonant sound of his voice shattering the peace of the night.

Jennie gasped at his unexpected intrusion. "What are you doing here?"

"Would you believe me if I said I'd been looking for you?" he asked thoughtfully.

"No," she scoffed. "You didn't even know that I'd left camp."

"Jennie," he told her solemnly. "I've known everything you've done since we made camp."

A thrill soared through her, but she fought against it.

"I've got to go back now," she stammered as she attempted to walk past him.

Rick was anxious for a moment alone with her, though, and he reached out to grasp her arm.

"Wait, Jennie. Don't go. I want to talk with you."

"I really don't think we have anything left to say to one another." Jennie tried to pull away, but he held her fast in an unyielding yet painless grip.

"Well, I think we do."

"Look," she said with exaggerated patience. "You have Lucia and I have Todd . . ."

"What are you talking about?" Rick frowned down at her. "I've never 'had' Lucia. She doesn't mean anything to me, and I don't believe for a minute that Todd means anything to you."

"It doesn't matter to me what you believe! Let me go!"

"Not until we've settled things between us." He pulled her closer.

"There's nothing left to settle," Jennie said hotly.

"Oh, I think there is. All this concern about Lucia. Was she the reason you ran away?" When she refused to meet his probing gaze, he asked again. "Jennie? Why were you concerned about Lucia?"

"She made no secret of the fact that she wanted you, and you were with her so often."

"It was not what you're thinking."

"Hah!"

"I admit she wanted me to love her, but, Jennie," Rick said, releasing her arm and tilting her chin up so that her eyes met his. "I didn't take her."

Jennie's confusion showed plainly on her face and when she didn't speak, Rick went on:

"The first time she came to me was the night when I brought you back from the pool. I had wanted to make love to you so badly that it hurt. That's why I went back up to the basin to take a cold bath. I thought it might help to bring my desire for you under control. You see, Jennie, I didn't want to take you there with all the others around."

Jennie looked up at him quickly as he continued to explain.

"What we shared in the mine was so special. I felt that if I'd made love to you in camp, I might somehow cheapen our feelings. Do you understand what I'm trying to say?"

She nodded nervously as his hand slid warmly to the side of her neck, the intimacy of his touch thrilling her.

"Lucia evidently had been watching me, and she followed me out to the pool. She was even bold enough to proposition me, but I turned her down." His thumb caressed the wildly beating pulse at the base of her throat.

"But what about all those other times when you were alone with her?" Jennie could not easily forget the many occasions when Lucia had flashed her a knowing, victorious look.

"My refusing her only made her more determined, and she decided to try another tactic."

"You mean she didn't give up?"

"Hardly. Somehow she managed to overhear a conversation I'd had with Juan, and she approached me one night on guard duty to tell me that unless I bedded her, she was going to Malo with the news of what I was up to."

Jennie gasped in outrage that the other woman would do something so despicable. "How could she do such a thing? If she loved you, why would she try to hurt you that way?"

Rick smiled tenderly at Jennie. "Lucia doesn't know the meaning of love, Jennie. There's a big difference between the beauty of what we shared and what she was wanting from me."

Jennie frowned at his statement and then looked shyly away as she whispered in a barely audible voice, "Did you do it?"

"No, thank heaven. But not for a lack of trying on her part. Luckily, the first night we were interrupted and then the second night when she cornered me, Malo found us."

"My God, you're lucky to be alive!"

"I know." He gave her a lazy grin.

"What happened?"

"I managed to get the drop on Malo and Luis, and that's when we made our escape."

"So that's why Lucia was with you? And that's how she came to find out your real identity?"

Rick nodded and then realized what Jennie had been thinking. "You thought that I'd confided in her? That I'd gone to her willingly?"

"Yes."

Rick wanted to pull Jennie into his arms and declare himself, but he also didn't want to move too quickly with her. They had been at cross purposes for a long time now, and he wanted to straighten everything out before they went any further.

"If I had left her behind, Malo would have killed her—but only after he'd tortured her first." He paused. "Lucia's not a bad woman at heart. She's just led a very difficult life."

"I'm so glad we came along when we did."

"So am I. We were just running out of ammunition when your father and Jake arrived." Rick stopped as he gazed down at her. "Did I ever thank you for calling out to me? You saved my life, Jennie. If you hadn't yelled, I have no doubt that Luis's shot would have taken my head off."

"I'm just glad that you're all right," she murmured.

"Are you, Jennie?" His eyes bore into hers, seeking the truth. "Really?"

It was the moment of reckoning, and Jennie instinctively knew that there would never be another chance for complete honesty between them. Her thoughts were jumbled. There were so many things to consider. Her heart cried out that she should tell him everything, yet her conscience seemed to be telling her that Todd should have her loyalty.

Rick seemed to understand her confusion and he smiled

indulgently. "I know you think that you hate me for keeping my identity a secret from you, but I had my reasons. Believe me, it would have been much easier to confide in you and enlist your help, but I wanted to make sure that you were safe."

"How could lying to me keep me safe?" she demanded with renewed indignation.

"If Malo had happened to find out about me and had even suspected that you might be involved in some way, your life would have been worthless. But as my captive, he would have kept you safe just so he could ransom you back to your father. As a kidnapping victim, you were worth a lot of money, Jennie."

"Oh." She hated to admit it, but he was making sense.

"There were so many times when I'd wanted to tell you the whole truth," he said softly, yet earnestly. "But even now, knowing how you say that you feel about me, I'm still certain that I did the right thing. You're alive and well."

A sweet silence hung between them as everything he'd been saying began to take root in her heart. It all made sense, beautiful, wonderful sense, and her spirits soared.

"I had finally decided to tell you everything, but when I woke up that next morning, you'd run away." Rick scowled slightly as he remembered the temper he'd been in that morning and his subsequent fruitless search for her. "Why did you leave me, Jennie? You'd told me that night that you needed me. And then you were gone."

"I thought you were going to give me to the other men. I'd overheard Lucia and Chica, and I felt certain that you were growing tired of me."

Jennie lifted luminous eyes to him as she realized how Lucia had planned the whole thing just to get rid of her. Lucia had wanted Rick for herself, and she'd used every trick she'd known to convince her that Rick was losing interest in her.

"Tired of you?" Rick was completely amazed. "Couldn't

you tell? Good God, woman, I couldn't get enough of you."

At that news, Jennie wanted to launch herself into his arms and hug him wildly, but she controlled the impulse.

When Jennie didn't respond to his revelation, he went on: "That last night I'd needed you so badly—" He dropped his hand away from her as if suddenly he couldn't bear to touch her.

"Was that the night when Lucia threatened to reveal you to Malo?" she asked.

"Yes. I had needed your sweetness, your love. And then when you resisted me—" Rick glanced at her, his expression a bit shamefaced. "I'm not sorry that I made love to you, but I do apologize for forcing you to respond to me. I want more for us than mere physical gratification."

"You want more? For us?" Jennie's heart filled with joy. Was he really saying what she thought he was saying?

"I guess I'm not handling this as well as I could, but, Jennie," Rick said, suddenly very serious, "I've never in my life said this to another woman before. I love you. I've loved you from the beginning."

"Oh, Rick." As the mellow sound of his voice and the magic of his words mesmerized her, Jennie swayed unconsciously toward him, lifting her hands to brace herself against the broad expanse of his powerful chest.

"I love you, too."

Her words, so breathlessly spoken, were all the encouragement Rick needed and, bending to her, his mouth moved sensuously over hers, parting her lips and drawing the very breath from her body. Jennie gasped at the intimacy of the exchange and started to draw back, but Rick refused to free her.

"Oh, no, my love. I'm not about to let you go. Not after everything we've been through."

Rick sought her lips again, and this time she met him eagerly, matching his intensity in a devouring kiss.

All thoughts of Todd and her commitment to him were

341

wiped from her mind as Rick moved erotically against her, showing rather than telling her of the strength of his desires. Arching to his hardness, reveling in the feel of him, Jennie responded instinctively to his sensuous summons.

How she'd longed for this moment. How she'd dreamed of it! Rick loved her. The touch of his hands was ecstasy as he cupped her buttocks and lifted her hard against his thrusting arousal.

"Jennie." Her name was a passionate groan as his lips left hers and caressed the sweetness of her throat.

She whimpered her excitement as her nipples hardened in anticipation of his caress. Rick felt the taut peaks against his chest, and he shuddered at the excitement their touch roused in him. Drawing a ragged breath, he ceased all motion and, releasing her hips, he let her slide slowly down the length of his body.

"Rick?" Jennie was on fire with her desire for him as she rested full against him. She needed him and she wanted him, now. "Rick, what's wrong?"

She tried to pull his head down for a kiss, but he resisted her efforts. "Stop, Jennie." His tone was more curt than he'd meant it to be, and her eyes reflected her hurt. "Darling, don't look at me that way. I'm trying to stay in control of the situation and—"

Suddenly realizing why he'd stopped, she smiled to herself. Wickedly deciding to test that control, she began to unbutton his shirt.

"Jennie, for God's sake, stop that," he growled, his jaw tightening as she slipped her hands within to explore the hair-roughened expanse of his chest.

He gripped her upper arms, intending to push her away, but when she leaned forward to kiss his heated flesh, he gave up the thought. Rick could not see the smile of victory that curved her mouth as she trailed sensuous kisses across his chest and then stood on tiptoes to nibble seductively at his throat. Looping her arms about his neck, she again tried to pull him down to her and this time he surrendered, meeting her in a heart-stopping kiss that told her everything she needed to know about his desire for her.

Rick broke off the kiss but didn't release her as he looked around for a more secluded spot to share their love. He longed for the softness of a bed, but if they were to enjoy each other to the fullest this night, he knew their comfort would have to suffer a bit.

"Come with me," he growled, leading her behind a massive boulder farther from the campsite, and Jennie went with him eagerly.

Hidden in the night's enveloping darkness, he kissed her once more and drew her close as he leaned back against the rock. With great pleasure, he unbuttoned her shirt and spread it apart to reveal the glory of her breasts, hard tipped and aching for the touch of his lips. Jennie's knees threatened to buckle when Rick moved to kiss her breasts, and she leaned weakly into his strength as his warm mouth tugged gently, yet erotically, at her throbbing nipples. Burning desire pulsed through her as he intimately loved her breasts, and Jennie could not control the urge to move against him, her hips seeking the hard, masculinity of his own.

"Love me, Rick, please," she begged, unable to bear not being a part of him any longer.

At her fervently whispered plea, he held her from him for a moment and gently stripped away her clothing. Standing before him, Jennie gloried in the knowledge that Rick wanted her. She felt powerful yet womanly as she moved back into his arms. pressing her nude body to his fully clad one.

"Now, Rick," she demanded throatily as her hands caressed him through his pants and then deftly undid them to hold him more boldly.

"I need you, darling," Rick told her seriously. "Now and always."

Then lifting her hands to his shoulders, he picked her up and turned around. Jennie clung to him nervously as he balanced her weight against the boulder and guided her legs about his waist.

"I wish we had a bed, love."

"It doesn't matter to me, Rick. I just want to be with you."

Her eyes widened in stunned surprise as he stepped closer and fitted his body to hers. Their gazes locked as he slid deeply within her, and all concept of time vanished as they stared at one another, memorizing the beauty of the moment. It was a rapturous reunion of flesh and spirit and one that had, for too long, been denied.

His lips sought hers as he began to move, and Jennie held tightly to him, reveling in his every thrust. The novelty of their position both amazed and excited her, and she matched his movements with ardent enthusiasm. The words of love they whispered were as heated as their mating as each sought to heighten the other's passion.

The end, when it came, was a rapturous burst of pleasure that left them spent, yet sated.

Jennie clung to Rick's neck, weak in her sensuous satisfaction. Never before had their joining been so wonderful, and never before had her love for him been so deep.

Rick stood unmoving, his eyes closed as he dwelled on the joy Jennie had just given him. He had not known love could be so perfect, but with her it was.

Gently, he helped her slide from his body, and he kissed her passion-bruised mouth softly when she stood before him once again. Quickly rearranging his own clothing, he picked up her things and, in continuing silence, helped her to dress. As she finished putting on the last of her clothes, he held his hand out to her and she took it trustingly.

"As soon as we get back, we'll be married," Rick said with calm confidence.

"Oh, no." Reality crashed around Jennie with a vengeance.

"Sweetheart? Is something wrong?" He turned her to face him, noting worriedly her paleness and her stricken expression.

"How could I have done this?" Jennie was mortified that she could have forgotten Todd and her promise to him.

"Done what? Jennie! Tell me what's wrong." Rick wanted to help and his hold on her shoulders tightened.

Hanging her head in self-condemnation, she couldn't look up at him.

"Jennie!"

"I can't marry you," She finally managed to way, the words choking her in their bitterness.

"Why the hell not?" Rick was totally confused. One moment they were loving each other and sharing that bliss, and now she was telling him she couldn't marry him?

"It's Todd," Jennie whispered. "I've already accepted his proposal."

"You what?" Rick was incredulous.

"He had proposed to me before I met you—when we were at the ranch."

"You told me he was just your friend," he challenged.

"He was—is—but when I got back, I was so upset that I accepted his offer."

"You accepted a marriage proposal from a man you don't love?" Releasing her, he stared down at her condemningly.

"How was I to know I would ever see you again?" she cried helplessly. "I thought you didn't want me."

"And that justifies marriage to a man who can't possibly make you happy?" he demanded brutally.

"Todd's a good man and I'll be happy with him."

"You mean you intend to go through with it?"

Jennie fell silent, not knowing what to do. "I don't want to hurt him." She raised tear-filled eyes to Rick. "He's such a good man. He's kind and generous and—"

"Spare me the litany of his finer points," he interrupted her angrily. "If you're so worried about hurting him, what do you think you're going to do to me if you marry Todd?"

Jennie was trapped, faced with making a decision she didn't want to make. She looked up at Rick, but in his anger he had suddenly become a cold and forbidding stranger and she grew frightened.

"Jennie, love." Rick read her mood accurately and softened. She was frightened and confused and he was determined to help her, not make it harder on her. "I love you and I want you for my wife. You love me, too, don't you?"

She sensed the change in him and met his eyes, reading there his tender concern.

"I do love you, Rick."

"Do you think it would be wise to marry another man, feeling as you do about me? What we share is so unique. We can't give it up, Jennie. I won't let you." He framed her face with the comforting warmth of his hands. "Have you made love with Todd?"

"No! How could you even think such a thing?" She gasped and Rick smiled as victory was his.

"I just wanted to prove a point. You've known him for years, yet never wanted to make love to him. Do you think we could have denied our attraction for that long? We belong together, Jennie. You're mine," he said fiercely.

"I know."

"Good. I'll be right there, whenever you need me," he quietly assured her.

"I'll tell him as soon as I can, but I can't be cruel about it."

"I wouldn't expect that from you. I like Todd, too, but not enough to let him have you." Rick grinned.

They moved together, holding each other in a cherishing embrace as the strength of their love surrounded them and bound them together for all time.

346

"We'd better be getting back," Rick finally told her, regretfully. "I'll try to stay away from you until you can get this all straightened out with Todd, but I don't guarantee that I'll be successful."

"I wouldn't want you to be too successful!" She kissed him quickly and then stepped away from the circle of his arms.

Leaving their protective hideaway, they started back to the camp to face their future together.

Carrie tossed restlessly on her blanket. Try as she might she had not been able to fall asleep, and she was growing more and more frustrated by the minute. It had been bad enough to have to sit back and watch as Jennie and Todd had disappeared into the night for some time alone, but ever since, her mind had refused to cooperate with her heart and had been conjuring up the image of the two of them making love.

Shifting uncomfortably again, she stared off into the darkness and was delighted to see that Todd was returning. She watched him as he quickly went to his bedroll, lovingly admiring the strength of his big body and remembering all too well how perfectly they had fitted together when they'd made love.

Carrie stifled a groan as she thought of his big hands exploring her body, and heat flushed through her at the remembrance of his touch. How exquisite it had been to be possessed by him. Her nipples hardened in longing, and a throbbing ache grew between her thighs.

Rolling over, she closed her eyes, trying to force all thoughts of Todd's tender lovemaking from her mind, and it was then that she realized that Jennie had not returned with him from their tryst. Why had Jennie remained behind, alone, in the darkness? Had she and Todd shared such a passionate embrace that she'd had to have time to pull herself together before coming back to camp? That possibility irritated Carrie greatly, and she turned to face Jennie's bedroll, waiting to see how long it was before she returned.

It was a long time later when Jennie finally appeared within the circle of the campfire's light, and Carrie watched with avid interest as she went straight to her bedroll. She would have thought nothing of the length of time her sister had supposedly been alone if Rick hadn't followed her into camp from the same direction a short time later.

So, Jennie had been alone in the dark with Rick Peralta, had she? All her earlier suspicions about their relationship flared back to life, and Carrie couldn't suppress the excitement she felt at the possibility that there was something going on between them. Anxious for morning to come so she could find out more of what was going on, she closed her eyes and courted the sleep that had eluded her for so long.

Chapter Twenty-five

The Apache had moved swiftly and silently in their pursuit of the white men, and as darkness fell across the land they chose their position carefully to allow them the best advantage from which to keep watch. They waited through the night; their anticipation growing at the thought of all the horses and guns they could claim when they defeated these hated intruders. Though the hours passed slowly, their patience never wavered, and as the sun began to rise, they readied themselves to persevere in their quest.

Having elected to take the last watch, Todd stood alone now, rifle in hand, at his vantage point high above the canyon floor. The hours he'd just spent on guard duty had been long and tedious, and he was glad that it was almost daylight so they could start on their way home again.

Glancing toward the place in camp where Jennie lay sleeping, he reflected on the few minutes of privacy they'd shared the night before. Though she was a beautiful, responsive woman and he cared a great deal about her, he knew now that something was missing in their relationship. Had he never tasted the joys of love with Carrie, he probably would have gone through his life blissfully ignorant of the fact that there could be more, but since he'd touched her and loved her, things would never be the same for him.

No matter how hard he pretended that everything was fine, it wasn't. It was Carrie he wanted; Carrie he needed with an undying passion, and yet, he was caught in the awkward position of being engaged to marry her sister. It was an engagement he could hardly break. Jennie had just been through so much. How could he leave her if she needed him?

Todd cursed himself for having allowed the situation to come to this, but Jennie had been so vulnerable when they'd been together that first night back that it had been impossible for him to recant his proposal. So, now they were engaged, and he knew he would have to make the best of it. Todd only hoped that he would be able to keep his desire for Carrie under control.

Carrie stirred and came awake just as the sky brightened from black to a deep shade of purple. Her rest had been fitful all night, filled with dreams of Todd and Jennie, and she was glad that dawn was near to put an end to the misery of her mind's disquieting fantasies.

Though no one else was up and about, Carrie could lie still no longer. It was then, when she started to rise, that she noticed that Todd was not asleep in camp. Looking nervously around, she finally spotted him up at the lookout point, taking his turn at sentry duty. Thrilled at the possibility of having a few moments alone with him, she slipped quietly from her bed to make her way quickly up the narrow trail.

Todd saw her leave the campsite, and he hoped that she wouldn't come to him. Though they had continued their relationship under the guise of their old friendship, he knew now that things had been too drastically altered between them to keep up the farce for long. How could he continue to hold a tight rein on his emotions when she was always near? He couldn't wait until they got back to the ranch for maybe then the tension he was feeling would ease.

"Good morning," Carrie greeted him, her voice still husky from sleep, and Todd reluctantly turned to face her.

His eyes devoured her as a wave of longing washed over him: her sleep-flushed cheeks, the shining paleness of her hair, the curve of her hips beneath the clinging, tight pants. He wanted her badly and, he acknowledged to himself, he loved her. No other woman had ever had the power to arouse him the way Carrie did.

"Good morning, Carrie." He tried to sound pleasant yet casual. "You're up early."

Her heart was pounding, and all she could think of was throwing herself in his arms. Suddenly tired of constantly hiding her love for him, Carrie wondered what he would say or do if she just came right out and told him how she felt.

"I didn't sleep well last night." She looked up at him, her gaze tracing his rugged yet endearing features.

"Why did you have trouble sleeping? It was safe. We had guards posted all night. Were you worrying about something?" he asked, noticing how perfectly her mouth was formed and remembering how it tasted beneath his. Shaking himself mentally, he tried to concentrate on what she was saying.

"Yes, I was.—" Quickly, impulsively, she made her decision. "I was thinking about you and remembering—"

"Remembering?"

"Todd—" Carrie paused briefly over her next words. "Todd, I really do love you. That short time I spent with you in the mine was the most beautiful experience of my life. I just can't go on this way any longer—pretending that what I feel doesn't really exist."

She was instantly frightened by what she'd blurted out, but she hoped that he would understand. Taking a deep breath, she looked up, meeting his eyes unflinchingly. She was not ashamed of her emotion. Far from it. She wanted him to know that.

Todd was stunned by her declaration, and he stood rooted in place as her eyes blazed into his. She loved him! His soul filled with happiness at the thought. He wanted to pull her into his arms and kiss her senseless, but a fleeting thought of Jennie held him immobile.

"Carrie—I—" he stammered, wanting to tell her his most heartfelt sentiments yet fearful of the repercussions.

Realizing that she'd put Todd in an awkward position by being so open with him about her feelings, Carrie was contrite. She hadn't wanted to embarrass him.

"Look, I've embarrassed you and I'm sorry. I love you too much to ever want to make things difficult for you. I just wanted you to know how I felt, that's all. And, maybe if things ever change between you and Jennie—" She hurried to go before she made the mistake of saying any more.

The sight of her leaving him spurred him to action.

"Carrie."

The deep sound of his voice stopped her flight, and before she knew it Todd was there, beside her, taking her by the shoulders and turning her to face him. Without speaking, he drew her closer, crushing her to the hardness of his chest.

"Ah—Carrie." His words sounded tortured to her, but she lost track of the thought as his mouth found hers with unerring accuracy.

Of their own volition, her arms looped around his neck, and she held on tightly to him, never wanting to let him go. Their coming together was explosive, and their passions flared in a fury of ecstasy.

Todd was out of control from the moment her lips touched his. How could he have denied his love for her? She was the woman he wanted, the woman he needed. His hands skimmed over her, splaying across her buttocks and pulling her hips more tightly to his so she could feel the affect she had upon him.

"Please Todd," she whispered, eager for the thrill of his hands upon her.

"What the hell is going on here?" Mac's low, violent curse

shattered the glory of the moment for the lovers, and they both looked up guiltily as their passion drained sickeningly from them.

"Mac—" Todd was having trouble speaking.

Mac had been coming up to relieve Todd as lookout, and he had been totally unprepared for the sight that had greeted him. If it had been Jennie in Todd's arms, he would have delicately made his excuses and left them alone for a while, but when he'd recognized Carrie in Todd's arms, he'd been livid. How could he have been so stupid to think that the girl might have changed? She had always been the cause of trouble, and he'd been a fool to forget that. He should never have trusted her or even given her the benefit of the doubt.

She is just like her mother! Mac thought, his expression thunderous. All the more gentle feelings he'd been developing for her died, buried beneath the smothering weight of his bitterness against a wrong long ago committed.

Carrie wanted to plead her case, to explain to him that she loved Todd, but Mac's well-remembered condemning glare choked off her words before she could utter them.

"Have you no pride?" he said. "What kind of a game are you playing?"

"I can explain everything, if you'll—"

"You can't possibly justify what I just witnessed!" he coldly interrupted.

"Mac—" Todd began, but Carrie cut him off.

"No, it's all right, Todd. I'll go." Quickly, she hurried away, shaking with the force of the emotions that assailed her.

"Carrie! Wait!" Todd called, wanting to soothe her and to tell her he loved her.

"You had better just make certain that Jennie doesn't find out about this indiscretion of yours! I don't want her hurt! She's been through enough." Mac gave Todd a withering look before he turned to stalk away.

*   *   *

Not wanting to lose track of the posse, Malo roused himself from his fitful sleep at first light. He was certain that today they would be going to the gold mine, and he would be dogging their trail the entire way! Excited at the prospect, he edged cautiously from his hiding place to see what was going on in their camp, and he noted with pleasure that they were just preparing to move out. Wanting to be ready to ride when they did, Malo saddled his horse and mounted up.

He was taking one last glance around the steep canyon walls, when he saw the Indians, crouched among the rocks, watching the posse with avid interest. Malo was so startled by the sight of them that he sat unmoving for a moment, fearful of drawing attention to himself. He knew how vicious the Apache could be, and he had no intention of being anywhere nearby when they attacked the McCaines.

Malo wheeled his horse around in the opposite direction and fled, all thoughts of the gold forgotten in his determination to save his own life. There were any number of ways he could get money, but riches would do him little good if the Apache got hold of him first.

Rick's casual manner as he strode across the camp to where his grandfather was speaking with Jake belied the tension that was building within him. It wasn't often that he experienced this disquieting sense of forboding, but he knew enough to trust his feelings. Honed to uncanny accuracy during the old days, his instincts had seldom proved wrong, and right now they were telling him that all was not what it seemed to be; that the peace that surrounded them would not last.

"Something is troubling you, Ricardo?" Juan immediately noticed the grimness in his grandson's manner.

"I'm not sure," he answered, scanning the surrounding hillsides, his hand resting on the butt of his gun.

"What is it, Rick?"

"Just a gut feeling. It could be nothing, but —"

"I learned a long time ago to trust your gut feelings. You think there are Indians around?"

"I hope to hell not," he answered. Then, glancing up at the craggy cliffs once more, he asked, "How soon can we start out of here? With any luck and a lot of hard riding, we should be able to get past Weaver's Needle today and be out of the mountains tomorrow."

"I'll check with Mac," Juan said as he saw him returning to camp.

Rick nodded as Juan hurried off to meet with the elder McCaine. Turning to Jake, he said, "Let's make sure there are no stragglers. If there are Apache out there watching us, they'll be after our horses, our guns, and our women."

"We'd better send out advance riders, too. It never hurts to take extra precautions."

"I'll go," Rick volunteered. "I know the land—and the Indians."

"Then I'll ride with you."

"All right." Rick was glad for Jake's company. "And let's stay together, just in case. It'd be too damned easy to pick us off if we're out there alone."

Saddling their horses, they paused to check their weapons and then mounted.

"Ricardo! Where are you going?" Juan came back to his side after ending his conversation with Mac.

"Jake and I are going to ride out ahead to see what we can find. Have everyone follow as soon as you can."

"We will. Mac says they'll be ready to go in ten minutes."

"Good, and tell them to keep close together and to keep their rifles ready. If there are Apache out there watching us, they won't attack as long as they think we're better armed than they are."

"I'll tell them. Ricardo?"

"Yes?"

"Be careful." His words were solemn as he dreaded an encounter with Indians.

Flashing him an encouraging smile, he said confidently, "Always." He started to ride away and then stopped, turning back to meet his grandfather's gaze unflinchingly. "There will not be another massacre." Turning to Jake, he asked, "You ready?"

"Whenever you are."

"Let's go then." They urged their mounts forward.

"Rick! Jake!"

Rick heard Jennie's call and reined in as he saw her heading toward him. He had been hoping for the opportunity to speak to her before he left, but he knew that he couldn't approach her. He was glad now that she'd taken the initiative, but she looked so worried that it was all he could do not to dismount and hug her to him.

"Where are you going?" Her dark eyes were filled with concern as she glanced questioningly from Rick to her brother.

"We're going to scout the trail to make sure it's safe." Rick tried to sound impersonal, but he was finding it nearly impossible. All he could think of was the night before and how perfect it had been to hold her and caress her.

"But why? Malo never sent out advance riders."

"Malo was a fool," Rick said derisively.

"Do you think he's still around?" She had suspected that the outlaw might be stalking them in hopes of somehow getting Juan back.

"He could be, but I'm not worried about him right now. It's the Apache I'm worried about," he told her honestly. "We've been lucky so far not to run into any of them."

"I know." Jennie remembered what Juan had told her about the massacre, and she knew how much courage it was taking for Rick to ride out with Jake.

"You'll take care?" She wanted to touch him, but she knew

356

it was impossible just yet.

"Of course. When you follow us, make sure everyone stays close together."

"I will."

Then, unable to resist, he leaned nearer, his tone low and urgent. "And talk to Todd!"

Jennie nodded and then watched as he and Jake rode slowly from the encampment. Staring after him, she was lost in the memory of their lovemaking the night before. She had completely forgotten Juan's presence until he spoke.

"So, you love my grandson, do you?"

His question was so astute that she flushed guiltily. "Is it so obvious?"

"Only to me. I know Ricardo well and, though he has not yet spoken to me of his feelings for you, I can tell that he does care, deeply." Juan's smile was tender as he looked at the beautiful young girl whom he was certain had won Rick's heart.

"We haven't told anyone yet. There are problems." As she started to confide in him, Mac walked up, interrupting her.

"We're heading out right away and with any luck, we'll be back at the ranch by the day after tomorrow," he told them with forced cheerfulness.

"It'll sure feel good to be home. I'll bet Hildago is really worried about us."

"I'm sure she is," Mac said, knowing how much she loved Jennie and how concerned she'd been about her disappearance.

"Hildago?" Juan asked.

"She is my housekeeper," he explained quickly, though he did not like using that term for the woman who'd come to mean so much to him. "And you will meet her soon. She is a wonderful woman, and she's been with us for years, ever since the girls were young."

"I will look forward to it with pleasure," he replied gallantly as they walked to where their mounts were saddled

357

and waiting.

Todd did not immediately return to camp after his encounter with Mac. He stayed on at the lookout point, trying to get his thoughts together. He knew Carrie had been right. He couldn't go on trying to hide his true feelings any longer. Carrie was too important to him to allow her to be hurt that way. And, while Mac's condemnation had been justified at the time, Todd knew that it was imperative that he straighten things out as soon as possible. Leaving his post, he headed back, intent on making peace with Carrie.

As he entered their encampment, Todd saw that Jennie was busy talking with her father and Juan, so he took the time to approach Carrie.

"Carrie, I need to talk with you." He came up behind her as she was tightening the cinch of her saddle. All he wanted to do was to tell her how much he loved her and let her know that at the first opportunity he was going to break off with Jennie.

"Todd." She was startled by his unexpected approach.

The last thing Carrie wanted to do was talk to him right now. She knew exactly what he was going to tell her, and she was in no mood to listen. Carrie knew that he loved Jennie. She supposed she'd always known that, but in the depths of her heart she had hoped that her love would be enough for Todd. Obviously, she acknowledged to herself now, it wasn't.

"Well?" Todd asked again, waiting for her to respond. "Will you talk with me for a few minutes. What I have to say to you is very important."

Glancing in her father's direction, she grimaced as she remembered his critical words. "After what just happened between us, I really don't think we should be anywhere near each other."

"But Carrie, this is important."

"I think I've heard it all before, Todd," she answered flatly. "And, frankly, I don't want to hear it again. If we just stay away from each other maybe everything will work out all right."

Refusing to look at him, she swung up into the saddle and started to ride away. But Todd was undaunted by her coolness, and he reached out to snare the bridle, effectively halting her horse's progress.

"Damn it, Carrie! What happened just now was—"

"I know, a mistake." She gave him an exasperated look. Casting a quick look in her father's direction, she groaned. "Now, let me go, damnit! My father and Jennie are looking this way!"

Todd quickly released his hold on her horse and she rode away from him, leaving him feeling completely frustrated. With firm resolve, he knew that he had to talk with Jennie, and soon.

Realizing that everyone was about ready to leave, he hurried to his mount. Shoving his rifle into its scabbard, he swung into the saddle and started off to join the others.

"Todd?" Jennie's call beckoned him to her side.

"Good morning, Jennie. Are you all set to go?" he asked as he reined in beside her.

"Yes, I'm ready." She smiled at him warmly and then looked puzzled. "Were you and Carrie arguing just now?"

"No," he replied quickly. "Why?"

"Oh, I don't know, I guess I thought you looked angry."

"No. I wasn't angry. We were just having a difference of opinion." Todd hurried to change the subject. "Where did Rick and your brother go?"

"Rick seemed to think that it would be wise to have someone riding in advance, so he and Jake went on ahead."

At that moment, Mac signaled for everyone to gather around, and they were forced to discontinue their discussion.

"We're going to head out of here as fast as we can. Rick

seems to think there's a good chance that there may be Indians around, so let's keep our eyes open and make tracks."

A murmur of agreement went through those gathered there, and they willingly followed Mac and Steve from the campsite, heading in the direction of home as fast as the rocky terrain would permit.

"I'm going to ride with Mac for a while," Todd told Jennie a short time later. He had wanted to talk with her, but he was certain that this was not the time or place. When he finally did break the news to her about his feelings for Carrie, they would have to have some privacy.

"All right, I'll just stay back here with Juan and Carrie."

Todd managed to keep his expression bland as he glanced at Carrie, but she was looking the other way, seemingly oblivious to his interest. Sighing to himself, he rode forward to join Mac and Steve.

Chapter Twenty-six

The Apache were watching the posse's every move, and as soon as they saw Rick and Jake ride out ahead of them, two braves were dispatched to go after them and kill them. They knew that, as a group, the whites were a formidable, well-armed force. So they planned to pick off as many of them as they could individually before making their assault on the main party. Armed with rifles stolen from previous raids and their deadly bows and arrows, they kept pace with Rick and Jake, waiting for the right moment for an ambush.

Rick and Jake rode carefully down the steep slope into the canyon, their full attention on the rocky peaks that surrounded them. It was quiet—too quiet—Rick thought, and he was uneasy as they neared a place where the trail passed between two massive boulders. As they drew closer to the opening, his horse trembled unexpectedly as its nostrils flared in a sudden awareness. Rick neatly controlled the animal as it pranced sideways, but its nervousness only served to confirm his own suspicions.

"Jake," he muttered low under his breath as he slowly slid his revolver from the holster and held it close against his thigh.

Jake noted his action and followed suit. "What is it?"

"There's something in the wind. Up ahead." He nodded in the direction of the passageway. "I think we've got some company."

"What do you want to do?"

"The same thing we did that time the sheriff was after us in El Paso and we were in a hurry to get out of town. Remember?"

"How could I forget?" Jake would have laughed at the reference if the situation hadn't been so serious.

"If the Apache are here, they're probably waiting for us at the far end. Take it fast and stay low."

Though Jake's grin was easy, it did not hide the dangerous glitter in his eyes. Pushing his hat more firmly down on his head, he took up the reins in a tight grip.

"Ready?"

"Whenever you are."

Time seemed suspended for a moment and their nerves stretched taut as they guided their jittery mounts forward. Once inside the narrow channel they raked their spurs over the horses' flanks, pushing them to a dead run down the trail.

At the sound of the approaching horses, the braves crouched on top of the rocks at the end of the passage, waiting for the white men to emerge. The blades of their knives flashed wickedly in the brilliance of the morning sun as they prepared to launch themselves at the riders, knock them from their mounts and fatally stab them before any shots could be fired to warn the others.

Though both Rick and Jake were leaning low over their horses' necks as they neared the end of the passageway, only Rick made it through the attack unscathed. Jake was torn from his saddle by the force of the warrior's body plowing into his, and in the resulting confusion his revolver flew from his grip and was lost. When he hit the ground, he rolled to the side to avoid the Indian who was diving toward him. Jake felt a brief, searing pain in his upper arm but had no time to worry about it as he scrambled to his feet and pulled his own knife from its sheath in his boot.

Jake had learned knife fighting from some of the best during his years of brawling in saloons, and he felt calm and in control as he faced his foe evenly armed. Lunging toward the Apache's unprotected shoulder, he slashed him viciously and watched with obvious pleasure as blood welled from the wound. They thrust and paried, testing and pushing until Jake finally managed to slip a leg behind his opponent's and trip him. The warrior lost his balance, falling heavily, and Jake was upon him, driving his blade deeply into his heart, ending his life.

Rick had managed to escape the initial attack, and he wheeled his horse around so he could get off an accurate shot at the Indian who was chasing after him. Firing rapidly, the force of his bullets ripped into the brave's chest and sent him sprawling lifelessly in the dirt.

Panting for breath, Jake pulled his knife free of the Indian's body and wiped the gore from it. His expression was a mixture of victorious male animal and disgusted civilized human being. He stood up slowly and then, after glancing down at the body, he walked away.

"You all right?" Rick asked as he led Jake's horse back to him.

"I think so."

"What about your arm?" He indicated the blood that was flowing freely from the wound on Jake's left arm.

"Oh." He seemed surprised to find that his arm was bleeding heavily. "See if you can tie it up for me and then we'd better head back. There's no way Pa and Steve could have missed hearing those shots, and they'll be wondering what's happened to us."

"I just hope they were the only ones within hearing range." He paused as he listened carefully for some sound that would indicate the presence of more Indians.

"You think there could be more of them?"

363

"I'm sure of it." Rick looked coldly at the two dead Indians. "These two were probably sent to get rid of us, while the rest of them concentrate on the posse."

"Let's hurry then. We need to warn them."

"We'll go as soon as I fix your arm. You won't be any good to me if you pass out from a loss of blood."

Dismounting he tied their mounts to a nearby bush and took an extra bandanna from his saddlebag. Applying pressure to the bloody gash, he tied the cloth tightly to stop the flow of blood.

"That should hold you until we get back."

"Thanks." Jake flexed his arm as if to test its strength. He was about to say something more when the sounds of gunfire echoed sharply about them. "Oh, no. Let's go."

Vaulting onto their horses, they raced back the way they'd just come, filled with a sense of dread in what they were going to find.

Though Jennie and Carrie had been riding side by side since they'd left camp, they had had little to say to each other. Carrie thought Jennie seemed very preoccupied, and she wondered if it was because she knew about her rendezvous with Todd. Casting a sideways glance at her, she sighed. Jennie was beautiful and she could easily understand why Todd felt as he did about her.

Her resentment of Jennie flared again to life as Carrie wondered why it was that her sister always ended up with exactly what she wanted. Ever since they were little, Jennie had consistently been the one who earned the praise and received the rewards; while she, herself, had seldom been on the receiving end of anything except Pa's temper and impatience.

After a while, Carrie had learned to accept that things would always be that way, and though she made an outward show of not caring, deep inside it still hurt. Mac's condemning words earlier when he'd caught her with Todd had severed any and all hope she ever had of having a normal relationship with him. For a time, while they had been riding with the posse, Carrie had hoped that he might have been coming to like her, but she knew now that it was impossible. No matter what she did, in Mac's eyes it would be wrong.

Looking up, her gaze fell upon Todd, and she watched him hungrily as he rode with Steve and her father at the head of the posse. He was the only man she would ever love, and she just hoped that one day, she would, somehow, get over him.

Carrie would have been totally shocked if she'd known what Jennie was really thinking about. True, she seemed preoccupied, but that was because she was lost in her daydreams of Rick. As they rode on with the warmth of the sun beating down on them, her mind was summoning forth images of the night before: of making magical, passionate love to Rick and of his subsequent proposal.

Jennie knew that her life would have been perfect at that moment had it not been for the confrontation she was going to have with Todd. Logically, she knew it would be better if she waited until they got back to the ranch to break off their engagement, but two more days of pretending that her love for Rick didn't exist seemed an eternity.

Jennie was glad now that she and Todd hadn't told anyone about her acceptance of his proposal. That way, Todd would be able to save face for no one need ever know, save Rick, that there had been an engagement in the first place. She hoped he wouldn't be too hurt by her actions, and that maybe someday, he would be able to understand and forgive her for having been so impulsive on her first night back.

The sound of distant shots startled them, and Jennie and Carrie exchanged worried looks as Mac halted the posse.

"Do you suppose it was Jake and Rick?" Carrie asked.

"It must have been them. The shots came from their

direction!" Jennie answered, her concern evident.

"Do you think they're in trouble?"

"It sure sounded like it. That wasn't a warning shot we just heard," she said sharply.

"I know." Carrie glanced up nervously at the craggy hills that encircled them.

The Apache warriors heard the shots being fired, too, and immediately knew that something had gone wrong. Realizing that the posse had been alerted to their presence now, they knew they had to act and act quickly. As they swooped down on the posse, their screeches reverberated menacingly throughout the canyons and gorges.

Firing with deadly accuracy, the Indians had hoped that the whites would panic and scatter, but Mac had warned his men, and they were ready for the attack when it came. Returning their shots with equal, if not superior expertise, the ranch hands sought protection at the nearest possible shelter and stayed as close together as possible. Not wanting to give the warriors any chance to break through their defenses, they covered one another judiciously and tried to make sure that each bullet found its mark.

Jennie and Carrie were riding near the back of the posse when the assault came, and they fled to safety together behind a good-sized boulder a short distance from the men. Using all the training Mac had taught them over the years, they stayed low and chose their targets carefully.

"You're good!" Jennie looked at Carrie with surprised respect after she'd managed to hit one of the Indians.

"Thanks," Carrie answered, not taking her eyes off the attacking savages. "I guess Pa was right when he told us that it was important that we learn how to shoot."

"He sure was," she replied, turning back to the fighting. Taking precise aim, she squeezed the trigger and her shot missed the Apache brave she targeted by inches. "Damn!"

Carrie got off another two rounds before she had to stop to reload. She had squatted down with her back to the rock to slip the cartridges into the chamber, when a furtive movement on the slope behind them caught her eye.

"Jennie! Look out!" Raising her rifle, she fired the one and only bullet she'd managed to load.

At the sound of Carrie's warning cry and shot, Jennie threw herself sideways just in time to see the warrior fall dead behind them.

"Oh, my God—Carrie—" Jennie's eyes were wild and unbelieving as she stared at the dead Indian.

"You all right?" she asked quickly as she looked from the Apache's lifeless body to her sister's pale face.

"I think so, thanks to you." Jennie hugged Carrie. "You saved my life, Carrie."

"You'd have done the same for me." Carrie replied the standard answer quickly, but suddenly as she said the words she realized that they were true. Jennie was her sister and, despite all the jealousy and anger she sometimes felt toward her, there was love and caring there.

A bullet whizzed closely past them, and they quickly broke apart. Jennie took up her rifle again and started to fire again as Carrie finished reloading her own weapon and then joined her.

"Look! Where are Todd and Steve going?" Carrie saw them making their way behind the rocks, away from the others.

"I don't know, unless maybe they're going to try to sneak around to the side and get a better angle on the Indians. Then when Rick and Jake make it back, we should have them hemmed in on three sides."

"I hope Todd's careful!" She spoke so emotionally that she drew a curious look from Jennie.

"Carrie—" Jennie wanted to question her about Todd and the scene she had witnessed between them earlier, but there was not time as another wave of Apache rode at them, firing viciously.

Hidden behind a jumbled barricade of rocks, Steve and

Todd were ready and waiting for the renewed assault, and they let loose a barrage of gunfire that caught the Indians by surprise. Forced to fight on two fronts, they were suddenly divided in their pursuit of the white men and retreated quickly to regroup and plan a new strategy.

Casualties had been light among the men of the posse so far, and Lucia and Chica were hastening to aid those who had been hit.

"Steve! Todd! You two all right?" Mac called up to them from the position he was sharing with Juan.

"We're fine," Todd answered.

"Do you see any sign of Jake or Rick?"

"No, nothing yet."

While Carrie felt relief at hearing the sound of Todd's voice and finding out that he was uninjured, Jennie felt troubled. There was still no sign of Rick.

"Jennie, is something wrong?" Carrie asked, noticing her strained expression.

"I was just worrying about Jake—and Rick."

"You love Rick Peralta, don't you?" she asked astutely.

Jennie regarded her sister for a long moment before answering her straightforwardly, "Very much, but how did you know?"

"I suspected it from the first. You were so worried about him when he was shot. I'd never seen you that concerned about anybody before."

"I've never felt this way before."

"Then why did you accept Todd's proposal?" Carrie couldn't stop herself from asking.

"How did you know about the engagement? We hadn't told anyone yet."

"I know, because I overheard you that first night you were back in camp." Her words came out almost bitterly.

"Oh—Carrie?" Jennie sensed her upset.

"What?"

"Do you care for Todd?" She tried to search her eyes for an answer, but Carrie looked quickly away.

"Why do you ask?" She avoided the question, keeping her gaze locked in Todd and Steve's direction.

"When we were breaking camp, I saw the two of you together, and it looked like you were having an argument," Jennie said.

"No. We weren't arguing," Carrie said quickly, wanting to deny it.

"I asked Todd about it, but he denied it, too," Jennie went on.

"What would we have to argue about?"

"That's what I was wondering. Do you love him?"

"Jennie, that's not a fair question. He's your fiance, for God's sake!" Carrie blurted out, not wanting to dredge up the agony of her own feelings. No matter if Jennie was in love with Rick or not, she was still engaged to Todd.

"Carrie, can I be honest with you?"

They considered each other for a long moment before Carrie answered, "Yes."

"In the beginning, I tried to deny my love for Rick. I thought he was an outlaw and that I would never see him again. That's when I accepted Todd. By the time I found out who Rick really was, it was too late."

"How does Rick feel about you?"

"He loves me and he's asked me to marry him after I break off with Todd. So, I'm going to end the engagement as soon as I can," she explained.

Carrie was secretly thrilled by the news.

Jennie continued: "I care about Todd and don't want to hurt him, but I think, in the long run, I would hurt him if I did marry him. I could never love him the way I love Rick."

"I understand," Carrie told her, and, in truth, she did.

"But will he?"

"I don't know, Jennie, but I think it's time I was honest with you, too. I love Todd very much."

"You do?" She brightened considerably.

"I have for a long time," Carrie confided and then grimaced as she remembered the scene earlier with Mac.

"And this morning—that little discussion you witnessed—well, I had finally made the mistake of telling him."

"So, that's what Todd was so upset about," Jennie said thoughtfully.

"Yes. It was bad enough that I'd made a fool out of myself by telling him how I felt, but then he kissed me and—"

"He kissed you?" Jennie was delighted.

Carrie flushed guiltily. "Yes and Pa caught us."

"Oh, no!" She groaned, easily imagining what Mac had said to them.

"And if that wasn't enough, Todd cornered me a little while later and wanted to talk."

"But that's a good sign."

"Not with Pa watching. He'd been furious at me and I didn't want to make things worse. Besides, Jennie, I know how much Todd loves you. The last thing I wanted to do was discuss it!"

"He might have had another reason for wanting to talk with you."

"No, I doubt it. It's you he loves, Jennie, not me." She forced down her jealousy and turned back to watch for the Indians.

Jennie frowned, remembering Todd's evasive response to her earlier question about Carrie. "But he kissed you! Certainly you didn't force him to!"

Carrie did manage a small smile as she remembered the heated embrace they'd shared before Mac's untimely arrival. "I know, but he probably was just feeling sorry for me."

"Hardly." Jennie dismissed the notion. "Todd's too much of a gentleman. He wouldn't kiss you unless he wanted to."

Carrie's spirits lifted at the thought, but before they could say any more, the Apache struck again, their bloodcurdling shrieks piercing the silence and sending spine-tingling chills of apprehension through them.

Rick and Jake were riding as fast as possible in their

effort to get back to the posse, but it was slow going over the rocky, steep trail. Rifles ready, they topped the final ridge just in time to see the Apaches advance.

"Where's Jennie?" Rick asked immediately as his gaze scoured the scene for some sign of her. "I don't see her."

Jake glanced at him questioningly, wondering at his concern, and then pointed out Jennie and Carrie where they had taken cover. "She's down there with Carrie."

"Oh, good." Reassured, Rick breathed easier when he spotted her below.

"What do you think?" Jake asked, as they quickly tried to calculate the best way to trap the Indians and guarantee victory.

"We'll have to take them from behind. It looks like Todd and Steve have worked their way around one side, so with our help we can almost box them in."

"Good. Ready?"

"Let's go!"

"Keep firing!" Mac called out as the warriors relentlessly pounded their positions, swooping in again and again, coming closer to breaching their positions with each try.

Todd and Steve were so busy firing on the main thrust of the assault that they failed to notice the Indian who was creeping up on the rocks behind them armed with a bow and arrow. He took them completely by surprise when he let out his war cry and took aim at Steve.

"Todd!" Steve turned, gun in hand, but he was too slow for the agile, merciless warrior.

The Apache's aim was murderous and exact as he released his death-dealing arrow. It took Steve full in the stomach and he doubled over, frantically clutching at the brutal shaft. Filled with bloodlust, the warrior faced Todd just as he managed to get off a shot at him.

"Jennie!" Carrie gasped as she realized that Todd and Steve had stopped shooting. "Something's wrong! Something's happened to Todd. I'm going up there!"

Grabbing a cartridge belt, Carrie crouched low and began to run in Todd's direction.

"Not alone you're not! I'll come with you." Jennie was determined not to let her sister face such danger by herself.

Two of the warriors spotted them and were starting to close in just as more gunfire erupted behind them.

Rick and Jake came riding down the canyon, making as much noise as they could and firing as rapidly as their pace would allow. They were overjoyed when the Apache, realizing that they were now really outnumbered, fled the scene. The two who were following the women broke off their pursuit, too, and raced away after the other fleeing members of their party.

Some of the men from the ranch mounted up and gave chase for a time, but they knew better than to get caught in unfamiliar territory in small numbers. They turned back as soon as they were certain that the Indians were, in reality, leaving the area completely.

From their location, Jennie and Carrie couldn't see Rick and Jake, and they weren't aware that the Apache had broken off the attack entirely. They were only grateful for the moment of calm as they rushed on to aid Todd and Steve.

"Oh, God," Jennie groaned as she reached their cover first. "How is he?"

"How is who?" Carrie cried as she pushed past Jennie expecting to see Todd wounded or worse. But her fears were unfounded for Todd was bending over Steve's motionless form, pierced so obscenely by the Apache's arrow.

"What happened?"

"The Indian came in behind us," he told them, pointing to the Apache who lay dead some distance away. "Steve didn't have time to shoot before he got him in the stomach."

"Oh, no." Carrie knelt beside Steve, feeling for a pulse at his throat and finding only a faint one. "Jennie, he's still alive. Should we try to pull the arrow out?"

Jennie joined her. "We have to do something. Todd, can

you get it out? Maybe we can stop the bleeding then."

"I'll try." Todd's reply was hoarse with emotion for he had seen men gut-shot before, and he already knew the outcome.

They watched grimly as Todd carefully pulled the vicious, iron-headed arrow from Steve's nearly lifeless body. He never regained consciousness as they struggled to save him, stripping his shirt away and trying to stem the almost violent flow of blood from the gaping wound. But their ministrations were not enough.

"You can stop now, it's too late," Todd said softly. "He's dead."

Sickened by the loss, Jennie and Carrie stood up and moved away, and Todd slowly followed them.

Carrie's eyes were luminous and tear filled as she turned to Todd, standing so unapproachably beside them, and suddenly she knew she had to be near him. His life had been spared and that was the only thing that mattered. He was alive.

Sobbing out her anguish, she threw herself against him. "Thank heaven, you're all right. I was so worried about you."

Todd's expression was stony as he looked up at Jennie. He wanted nothing more than to hold Carrie tenderly and reassure her, but he hesitated for a moment in returning her embrace for Jennie was standing there. She felt so sweet against him that his heart finally won out, and his arms closed around her in a cherishing hug.

"Everything's all right now. Carrie, darling, don't cry. I love you, sweetheart. Please," he murmured, his eyes closing at the joy of having her near. But it was then that he suddenly realized what he'd just said—and in front of Jennie.

Todd's expression was tortured as he looked to Jennie, but Rick's call interrupted the moment, and Jennie raced to answer him.

"Jennie!"

"We're up here!" she shouted back, running out into the open to signal to him, leaving Todd alone with Carrie.

Thinking that Jennie was rushing away because she was upset, Todd released Carrie without a word and went after her to explain. Following her from behind the rocks, he came up behind her.

"Jennie, I'm sorry—I—" he said apologetically, expecting her to be angry, and he was totally dumbfounded when she faced him and smiled brightly.

"Todd. It's all right." She tried to assure him, but he was embarrassed and not listening.

"I didn't mean this to happen. I didn't deliberately set out to fall in love with Carrie. I—" He went on until Rick appeared.

"Jennie?" Rick asked warily as he eyed them both. He wanted to grab her and hug her tight, to confirm to himself that she was uninjured, but Todd's presence held him immobile. "You're all right?"

"I'm wonderful," she gurgled as she went to him and kissed him fully on the mouth.

"You've told him?" Rick asked quietly, looking at Todd for affirmation.

"I was trying to, but he wouldn't stop telling me how much in love he is with Carrie." She grinned. "Todd. What you said about falling in love is true. You can't plan it. You have no control over it."

"You— and Rick?" Todd asked in sudden understanding, and his mood lightened as he looked from one to the other.

She nodded, and then slipping from Rick's arms, she hurried to Todd to kiss him on his cheek. "I'm sorry, too. But Carrie loves you very much."

Their eyes were warm as they smiled at each other.

"I know. More than I deserve."

"Hardly." Jennie laughed. "You'd better go get her. I imagine she's feeling pretty anxious right now."

Todd leaned down to kiss her softly and then hurried away to tell Carrie the good news.

Chapter Twenty-seven

Carrie watched, disheartened, as Todd hurried after Jennie. She was confused by his unexpected declaration of love, and she wondered if he'd really meant it or if he had just been trying to comfort her. Surely, she reasoned, if he had meant it, he wouldn't have rushed away to speak with Jennie without so much as a word of explanation. No, she concluded sadly, Todd had only been trying to reassure her and make her feel better. Of course he loved her, as a friend.

Blinded by sudden tears, she stumbled away, seeking some peace and solitude. So much had happened in such a short period of time, and she just didn't want to face any more. Carrie wandered aimlessly, paying little attention to her direction. She didn't really care where she went, as long as it was away from everybody else.

"Carrie?"

She heard his distant call but didn't respond. There was no further need for them to talk. He'd said it all when he'd chased after Jennie.

"Carrie?" Todd's call sounded more worried, and she knew she'd better answer or he'd alert the entire posse to her disappearance.

"I'm over here," she answered dully, not at all enthused about the upcoming conversation.

Todd sighed in relief as he heard her reply, and he headed quickly in her direction. When he found her, she was gazing quietly out across the barren canyon.

"Carrie, I—" He touched her shoulder to turn her around, but she shrugged off his hand.

"Please don't touch me, Todd. Not now. Not until we've talked." Carrie turned to face him of her own accord. She had taken the time to school her features into an emotionless mask, and she was now as ready as she would ever be to hear him out.

Todd was struck by the coldness in her expression, and he wondered at it. Hadn't she heard him say that he loved her? Wanting to crack her icy veneer, he grinned at her.

"At last, you've agreed to talk to me." He sounded victorious. "I've been trying to talk to you all morning, if you remember."

"I remember."

When she didn't respond to his gentle baiting, Todd continued quickly: "Carrie, darling, I love you. I was about to tell you that this morning, but then Mac showed up. I'll never forgive that man for his bad timing," he muttered under his breath, and he was pleased when he noted a flicker of warmth in her eyes. "Anyway, when I tried to tell you again later, you practically ran me down with your horse. And now, when I've finally got everything just about straightened out, you look like you're not believing a word that I'm saying!"

Carrie's lips began to curve in a semblance of a smile, and her eyes misted with gentle emotion.

"Talk to me, Carrie." He lifted a warm hand to caress her cheek. "Tell me what you're thinking. Tell me that you love me."

Carrie leaned against the heat of his hand, loving his touch, craving more from him. "I love you, Todd Clarke," she admitted, gazing up at him in open adoration. "I love you with all my heart."

Gently, wanting to savor the preciousness of the moment, he leaned to her, and their lips met in a delicate exploration of their desires. It was heavenly to Carrie, and she sighed as tingles of delight coursed through her. Shivering under the impact of his soft, sensuousness, she took a step closer.

"I think we've finished talking," she murmured as their lips parted and then met again. "You can touch me now."

"I love you," Todd growled happily and pulled her tightly to him, marveling anew at how perfectly she fit to him—as if they belonged together.

He kissed her then with all the passion she'd known him capable of, taking her mouth in a searing possession that blended them together in a swirl of undying love. Unwilling to break apart after having been denied this closeness for so long, they shared kiss after kiss, each more exciting than the last, until the demands of their bodies that they do more forced them to break apart for a moment.

"Did you speak with Jennie? Is everything all right?"

He nodded as he pulled Carrie back into his arms, lacing his hands behind the small of her back and holding her intimately against the rigid strength of his thighs.

"I still can't believe everything worked out this well. She understood everything. In fact, she's fallen in love with Rick Peralta."

"I hope they're going to be as happy together as we will be." She smiled up at him lovingly.

"Will you marry me, Carrie?" he asked solemnly.

"Yes. Yes. Yes!" she told him happily, throwing her arms around his neck and hugging him tightly. "Did you ever have any doubts?"

They drew back to regard each other seriously for a minute before Todd dipped his head and kissed her sweetly. Carrie was enraptured by his tenderness, and she found it amazing that for such a big man, Todd could be so gentle with her.

"God, you feel good in my arms," Todd told her thickly as

he ended the kiss.

"It's heaven for me, too." Carrie pressed eagerly to him, loving the fact that she was free to touch and hold him. "I've wanted this for so long, loved you for so long," she murmured to him between passionate kisses.

It was long minutes later when they regretfully drew apart.

"We'd better get back and see how the others are." He returned unwillingly to the harshness of reality.

"I know," Carrie said hesitantly, thinking of her father and how he would react.

Todd read her thoughts exactly and squeezed her hand reassuringly, bringing it to his lips. "Don't worry about Mac. I'll handle him."

Her love for him was obvious as she gazed up at him, and he couldn't resist kissing her one more time before they started back, ready to begin their life together.

When Todd had left to search for Carrie, Jennie hurried back to Rick and went straight into his arms.

"I was so worried about you." She gazed up at him, her eyes filled with the remembered pain of not knowing how he was or where he was. "We'd heard the shots and then when you didn't come back right away—" Jennie shivered as she thought of how terribly empty her life would have been without him. "What happened?"

"There were Apache waiting for us."

"You're all right, though—and Jake?"

"Your brother's fine. He's with your father now."

"Is it over? Are the Indians gone for good?"

"They're gone," he assured her.

"Thank God." Jennie leaned weakly against him, enjoying the comfort of his strength.

"When Jake and I first spotted you, you were down where it was safe, by the others. Then by the time I got there, you were gone. Why did you run up here?" Rick held her away from him and stared down at her, his eyes hard as he demanded an answer. He had known in those few minutes of thinking her missing a stark terror unlike anything he'd ever felt before, and the memory of Antonio's battered, tortured body had relentlessly assailed him as he'd searched for her. "You don't know the hell I just went through, thinking that the Apache had dragged you off somewhere!"

Jennie's soft smile and teasing words eased his unspoken fears. "So, you're the only one who's allowed to carry me off?"

Rick frowned at her attempted humor and pulled her closer. "You'd better believe it."

He kissed her passionately, then, wanting to relieve the tension that had been building within him.

"But why did you come up here?"

"Todd and Steve were positioned here, and then suddenly during the fighting, Carrie realized that something had gone wrong and that they weren't shooting anymore. She was determined to find out what had happened and help them if she could. I followed her because I didn't want her to go alone."

"Steve's here, too? I didn't see him." he questioned.

Jennie's tone was low as she glanced back toward the rocks. "Steve was killed. He was still alive when Carrie and I got here, but there was nothing we could do. He'd taken an arrow in the stomach."

"I'm sorry." Rick was solemn for he knew Steve had been a good man and well respected by Mac and the other ranch hands.

"I'd better go tell Pa."

"We'll get some of the men up here to help." His arms tightened around her supportively.

She nodded and, slipping her arms about his waist, she closed her eyes and rested her cheek against his chest. Only in the safety of Rick's embrace did she feel completely protected, and her expression reflected her inner bliss. How she loved him! And she knew she'd be eternally grateful that he hadn't been injured.

Rick stood perfectly still, cherishing the intimacy of the moment. There was something so elemental about their embrace that he didn't speak. Jennie was his! At last! It seemed to him that a great weight had been lifted from him when she'd told him of Todd's love for Carrie. No longer did they have to conceal their feelings. No longer did they have to steal each precious kiss.

It was only the sound of Jake, Mac, and Juan calling out to them that shattered the sublime peace and broke them apart.

"They must be worried." Rick released her slowly. "We'd better let them know that we're all right."

After bending to her for a final kiss, he stepped away and they walked out to meet the others.

"Jennie! Thank heaven! What happened? Where's Todd and Steve?" Mac demanded as he came upon them.

"Steve's been killed, Pa," Jennie told him straight out, not knowing any other way to tell him the sad news.

"Steve? How?" Jake asked quickly.

"One of the braves managed to sneak up on them during the main part of the attack."

"And Todd? He wasn't injured, was he?"

"No, he's fine now." She cast a sideways smile at Rick.

"Well, where is he?" Mac asked, catching her look at the younger Peralta and wondering at it.

"He's with Carrie right now, but I'm sure they'll be back soon," Rick put in smoothly.

"And just what are Todd and Carrie doing together? I warned her—" Mac thundered.

"I see you have managed to straighten everything out," Juan interrupted, smiling widely at Jennie.

"It's turned out better that I ever could have hoped," she assured him serenely as she gazed adoringly up at Rick.

Mac's frown was perplexed as he looked from Juan to

Jennie. "Jennie? What's he talking about?"

"Jennie and I are in love, Mac," Rick stated boldly.

"You two? But what about Todd?" Mac was stunned by Rick's revelation and looked at Jennie uncertainly.

"Todd's in love with Carrie, Pa," she told him gently.

"Todd? And Carrie?" He scowled, remembering the scene between them that morning.

"Yes, and they're working everything out between them right now," Jennie continued quickly.

"But Todd had proposed to you," Mac protested.

"That was before I'd met Rick. I could never consider marrying Todd now."

"Mac," Rick began respectfully as he put an arm around Jennie's shoulders and drew her to him. "With your permission, Jennie and I would like to be married as soon as possible."

"Of course. Whatever makes Jennie happy."

"Oh, thank you, Pa!" She went to him quickly and hugged him enthusiastically.

Mac could only shrug and return her embrace with fatherly affection. "This is all a little confusing, but as long as you're content . . ."

Jake grinned widely at Rick. "I thought you were overly concerned about my little sister when we were riding back in."

"I've been overly concerned with her for longer than that. I just managed to keep it hidden until now," he returned, relaxing now that the issue was finally resolved.

"We'd better see to Steve—and the others," Mac said when he'd let Jennie go.

The stark intrusion of reality cast a tempering pall on the gathering.

"There were more injuries?" Jennie asked quickly.

"One other man was killed," he told her grimly. "And there were two wounded. Lucia and Chica are helping them now."

"I still have some bandages in my saddlebags, so I'll go see if I can do anything." Jennie started down to where the rest of the posse was gathered.

"Fine," they told her as they went to take care of Steve.

Lucia and Chica were each tending one of the injured men when Jennie made her way to them.

"I have more bandages if you need them," she offered as she joined them.

"Thank you." Chica took some of the clean cloths. "His is only a minor flesh wound, but it is bleeding heavily."

"Lucia?"

Lucia glanced up, barely managing to conceal the malice she felt toward Jennie. How dare Rick choose her!

"I don't need any more," she answered curtly. "This one is not badly injured at all."

"Good." Jennie was so busy concentrating on the injured man that she missed the flare of smoldering hatred in the depths of Lucia's eyes.

Relieved to find that the men would soon be back on their feet, she left them to the other women's care and went in search of Rick. When they had finished with their nursing chores, Lucia and Chica wandered away from the main group.

"Lucia, when are you going to give up?"

"What do you mean?" She gave Chica an innocent look, but her friend only snorted in disbelief.

"I can tell how you feel about Jennie."

"And how is that?" she replied sharply.

"You hate her. Why, you can barely contain yourself when she's around."

"You are right, Chica. I do hate her, more than I've ever hated anyone!"

"But why don't you just forget about Rick?"

"I can't forget about him. Rick is the only man I've ever loved, and he doesn't want me, all because of her!"

"Surely, you can't hold her responsible for Rick's feelings.

She did not tell him not to care for you."

"Pah! But if she had not been around, he would have come to care for me. I know it!" Lucia swore.

"Lucia, you're fooling yourself. He is Ricardo Peralta, not Cazador the gunfighter. I told you before that he was not like the others."

"All men are alike," Lucia told Chica smugly.

"You are wrong, Lucia. Give up your anger. We are free of Malo now and we can go home. You are still young and pretty. We'll go back and—"

"And what? Become some other man's whore?" She snarled viciously as she thought of the village they'd come from and how poor everyone had been. "I want more than that!"

"Anything would be better than the life I had. I am just thankful that things have turned out so well."

"So well? What do we have? Nothing! Not even a man to protect us! While she—" Lucia looked over to where Jennie stood, waiting for Rick to return. "She has everything!"

"Your bitterness and envy will be the end of you, Lucia." Chica was thoroughly disgusted with her and without another word she walked away.

She didn't bother to reply or even look up as the other woman left. What did Chica know about anything anyway, Lucia thought arrogantly. Chica had been a *puta* her entire life and she would probably die one. But she, herself, had no intention of ending up that way. She was going to be rich one day, no matter what.

Jennie watched quietly as Rick and Jake carried Steve's body down from the rocks. Mac had decided that it would be best to bury the dead here in the mountains, and some of the other ranch hands were busy digging the two necessary graves.

Juan noticed that Rick seemed to withdraw suddenly, and

when he didn't return to Jennie's side, Juan followed him a distance from the site.

"Ricardo? You are troubled?"

Rick was startled to find that his grandfather had come after him. "It will pass."

"What is it?"

He signed deeply before speaking. "I had thought that there would be a great sense of victory for me in conquering these mountains—and the Indians." Rick's eyes were haunted. "But it doesn't bring back my father—or Antonio."

"I know," Juan said in a sympathetic tone.

"Even after all this time, the pain is there," he continued. "I still remember clawing Antonio's grave by hand out of the damned rocky ground, almost as if it were yesterday." His jaw was clenched, his hands knotted into fists of agony at his sides.

"Ricardo, there is good to be realized from all this."

When Rick looked skeptical, Juan went on.

"You have faced your most terrible fears, Ricardo, and you've won."

"It's a hollow victory. It means nothing."

"It means everything. You have grown into a man your father and uncle would have been proud of. I know I am." Juan put a consoling arm about his shoulders. "But you must remember that you are alive and there is purpose in that."

A shudder wracked Rick as he fought to get control of his own personal hell. "I know."

"For so long, I, too , wondered why it had all happened, but is is not for us to know—not in this life, anyway. Do not allow the past to have power over you. Put it from you and be done with it, once and for all."

Rick knew Juan was right. Since the time of the massacre, he had been living in limbo. At first, he'd taken to the hard, fast life, hiring out his gun in the subconscious hope that someone, somewhere would be faster than he was, but it was not to be. The cynicism had followed and then his return to the ranch when there had seemed nothing left to seek. Now, he understood the demons that had been driving him and, at last, he could lay them to rest.

He had a future. Jennie was his future and, together, they would create beautiful tomorrows as numerous as the stars in the night sky.

Rick smiled at Juan as the tension drained from him. "It is good to be done with it."

And Juan only nodded, but he understood—completely.

Carrie and Todd emerged from the rocks and headed back down to where the posse had regrouped. Secure in Todd's love and devotion, Carrie was no longer fearful of her father's reaction. Bravely ready to face him with the news of their engagement, she smiled happily up at Todd.

"Ready?"

"Absolutely."

"Do you suppose Jennie told him already?"

"I don't know, but I imagine we're going to find out very shortly."

Mac saw them approaching and wondered what to say. He'd certainly made a fool out of himself that morning when he'd berated them so cruelly, and he knew he would have to apologize.

Mac had always liked and respected Todd, and he knew it would be a pleasure to have him in the family. He thought briefly of his own desire to have Todd and Jennie marry, and he realized how ridiculous he'd been to try to force the issue. After all, did it really matter which daughter he married as long as he joined the family?

And Carrie: Thoughts of her competence overwhelmed him. She had ridden the entire distance without complaint; she had fought the Apache with admirable courage, and she had gone after the man she loved with equal determination, even bearing up under the tongue-lashing he'd given her this morning. Mac felt a sudden sense of pride and realized that she was more like himself than he'd ever admitted.

Facing them, he smiled and didn't bother to wait for them to speak.

"I believe I owe you an apology."

Carrie almost gaped in surprise for she had never heard her father apologize to anyone for anything.

"You've spoken with Jennie and Rick." It was a statement not a question.

"Yes, I did, and I realize how wrong I was this morning. I no doubt made things more difficult for you and I'm sorry."

"I did want to mention to you how terrible your timing was." Todd chuckled good-naturedly.

"I can well imagine." Mac was pleased that there were no hard feelings between them.

"Carrie's consented to marry me, Mac."

Mac nodded his agreement as he looked at Carrie for the first time as *his* daughter and not Eve's.

"Be good to her, Todd." His words were filled with intense emotion.

"Oh, I will. I love her very much."

"And I love Todd, Pa."

Mac did not know why he felt it was necessary, but in that moment he wanted to hug Carrie. He went to her almost hesitantly and felt a thrill of happiness soar through him as she met him in the tender embrace.

Carrie was totally surprised by her father's attitude, but she was grateful for it. She had given up all hope of ever knowing his affection, and she found it hard to believe that it was finally happening. Never before had she ever felt so loved and so wanted. She had Todd. She'd made peace with Jennie and now, at last, her father. Contentment settled over her, and she relaxed in the joy of it.

Chapter Twenty-eight

It was near noon in Mesa Roja and the sun, high in the cloudless sky, was sharp and harsh in its relentless splendor. The heat was oppressive, and the streets were dust-choked as the stagecoach rumbled into town and drew to a halt in front of the stage line office.

Silas Stratton, the clerk for the line, pushed his wire-rimmed glasses up on top of his head and rushed nervously out to greet the arriving coach.

"Glad to see you made it through, Ab," he called up to the driver Ab Colter.

"Slick as a whistle. No trouble at all," the burly driver replied as he swung the strong box down to him.

"How are you doing, Ted?" Silas asked the man riding shotgun.

"I am glad to be here. I been thinkin' about Dolly's Saloon for the last fifteen miles!"

Silas laughed as the two men climbed down from the driver's bench. "Any passengers?"

"We got one." Ab nodded and the clerk hurried to open the door and let down the stage's step.

"Welcome to Mesa Roja," he began and his mouth hung open as a lovely lady emerged from the coach's shadowed interior to take his proffered hand.

"Why, thank you for your kind assistance," the woman said softly in a cultured voice as she stepped lightly down.

"You're more than welcome, ma'am," Silas stammered as he stared at the beautiful woman standing before him.

In all of his forty-nine years, Silas had never before seen a woman as pretty as this one, and she was a lady, too, he could tell. Her clothing spoke of wealth and taste even as it accentuated her curvaceous figure. Her voice was well modulated and pleasant to listen to, and she was, in Silas's opinion, just plain gorgeous. Her blond hair was done up in a prim bun that not only added to the regal aura about her but also served to emphasize her classic, delicate good looks.

"Sir?" She was asking, politely.

"Uh—yes, ma'am?" Silas silently cursed himself for acting like such a fool.

"If you would be so kind as to direct me to the nearest hotel?" she continued, the sound of her voice enthralling him.

"Of course! We have only one here in Mesa Roja, ma'am," he explained, eager to help. "It's right over there."

The woman looked in the direction he had pointed and noted the two-story frame structure. "Thank you, sir."

"Name's Silas, ma'am. Silas Stratton. If you need anything, just let me know."

"Of course, Mr. Stratton," she replied, smiling coolly. "Now, about my trunk?"

"I'll have it sent right over!" He hastened to please her.

"Again, my thanks, sir. Good day."

Silas watched until she'd disappeared inside the hotel before turning to Ab and Ted. "She certainly is a looker!"

"I'll say," Ab answered. "But she's been real quietlike the whole trip."

"Do you know her name?"

"Nope. She never seen fit to tell us."

Silas was disappointed, but he knew he could find out later from his friend who worked in the hotel.

"Well, you boys have a good time in town tonight. You aren't scheduled to leave until sunup."

"Join us for a beer, Silas?' they asked.

"I'd love to, fellas, but I can't right now. If you're still at Dolly's when I get finished here, I'll stop off and have a few with you."

"See you then."

Wondering who the mystery woman was, Silas looked up once more in the direction of the hotel and then turned regretfully back to work.

She entered the small area that served as a lobby for the hotel and glanced around with distaste. How provincial! Soon, however, it would all be over, and never again would she have to suffer such tedious surroundings.

Oh, how she wished Andre was still with her! Things would have been so much easier with him by her side. Why, she wondered angrily for not the first time, had he been so careless and gotten into trouble with the law back in Santa Fe? Now, instead of helping her make a fast fortune, he was stuck behind bars in that dismal jail for God knows how long, forcing her to go out on her own.

Sighing to herself, she assumed her dignified manner and approached the deserted counter. After waiting long minutes for someone to come, she gave up and rang the small bell.

"Yes— What can I do for you?" A harried-looking, middle-aged woman came rushing out from the back, wiping her hands on her apron. "Oh, hello."

"Yes, hello," she said disdainfully. "I'd like a room, please."

"Of course." The proprietress turned the register around for her to sign. "Dollar-fifty. In advance."

Opening the drawstrings of her purse, she extracted the correct amount. "Here you are."

"Fine." She looked the newcomer up and down, amazed that such a fine lady would be staying in Mesa Roja. Then, pushing the key to a room across the counter, she said, "I'm Sally Bates. If you should need anything just let me know."

"I will, thank you. My trunk will be sent over from the stage office soon. I'd appreciate it if you could have it taken up to my room."

"Certainly, Miss—" She started to turn the book to read her name.

"*Mrs.*," she said pointedly, as she took the key. "Mrs. Mac McCaine."

Sally stared dumbfounded at the woman across the desk but didn't say another word as the woman calling herself Mac's wife smiled sweetly at her and then disappeared up the stairs to the room she'd just rented.

Eve couldn't stop the laughter that erupted once she was in the privacy of her room. She'd loved it! The look on the woman's face would keep her amused for months—no, possibly years, to come.

Judging from Sally Bates's response to her, it seemed to Eve that no one knew Mac was married. A delighted smile curved her perfectly shaped lips. What fun it was going to be appearing on Mac's doorstep after all these years and demanding her rightful place by his side. My, my, she could hardly wait to see him again. It had been so long.

A loud knock at her door drew her from her reverie, and she opened it widely to admit the young boy carrying her trunk.

"Just put it there at the foot of the bed," she said and then handed him a coin for his trouble.

"Thanks, lady." He beamed. "Can I do anything else for ya?"

"Yes, if you would— What's your name, boy?"

"My name's Billy, ma'am."

"Well, Billy, if you would tell Mrs. Bates that I'd like a

bath brought up here as soon as possible, I'd sure appreciate it."

"I'll tell her on my way out, ma'am."

"Thank you."

Eve wanted to strip off all of her clothes and just relax, but she knew she couldn't until the bath had arrived. Taking the time to survey the room, she grimaced. Though it was clean, it was definitely not up to her usual standards. She was not accustomed to staying in such coarse surroundings, and she could hardly wait for her interview with Mac to be over so she could be on her way.

Eve was pleased that two young girls arrived then with her bath, dragging the tub into the room and then hurrying back to carry in large buckets of hot water.

When at last they had gone, Eve locked the door and began to undress. She felt filthy from the long, stifling hours of confinement in the stagecoach and could hardly wait to soak in the soothing comfort of the hot bath. Searching through her trunk, she found the vial of her favorite bath salts and perfumed the water before stripping off the last of her underthings. Placing a towel within reach, she stepped eagerly into the tub and relaxed in the luxury of the scented liquid.

It was over a half an hour later when she roused enough to wash. She released her thick, golden mane from its bun and then shampooed it, too, scrubbing at her scalp until she was sure it was clean of all the dust and grit. Mac had always lover her hair, and she wanted to make sure that it looked its best when she came face to face with him again after all this time. Rinsing the soap from her hair, she stood up in the tub, enjoying the feel of the water which cascaded off her body.

Shimmering and sleek, Eve stepped from the tub, wishing that Mac could see her now. She had been so young and inexperienced when she'd left him. To this day, it still amazed her that she had had the courage to do it. Everything had all seemed so complicated then, but now, she realized it had really been a simple thing to do. She had walked out and never looked back. Never, that is, until Andre had ended up in jail and she had rapidly run out of money.

That was when she'd heard the story of the wealthy Arizona rancher named McCaine. Discreet inquiries on her part had revealed everything she'd needed to know about Mac and his successes and, in short order, she'd been on her way *home*.

Thinking of the home she'd fled so long ago, Eve could only frown. She certainly hoped that Mac had built a better house, for what they'd been living in when she'd left him had been little better than a hovel. It wasn't often that she thought of the time when she'd been a wife and mother, for she'd buried those memories along with the memories of all the other miserable things that had happened in her life.

Eve refused to acknowledge to herself that she could be the mother of a son in his twenties and two daughters who could probably rival her in size right now. She found the thought terribly depressing, but she supposed she would have to see them when she met with Mac.

She dried herself and then wrapped her wet hair in the towel, turban style, before going to stand before the small mirror over the washstand. Eve was certain, as she stood in front of the reflecting glass, that she was much prettier than when she'd left. She had pampered herself over the years, and there was not an ounce of flab on her slim body. Her breasts were full and tempting and her hips as slim as ever.

Mac had always been enamored with her, sexually, and she knew a lot more now about how to please a man than she'd known then. A sensuous smile curved her lips as she imagined Mac's response to her return. Would he curse her for leaving him and then make passionate love to her? That had always been the pattern of their fights when they had been together. He had thought that everything could be smoothed out between them by having sex, but after three children she had wised up. What had been wrong between them could never be fixed. While they were great in bed, that was the only thing they did well together.

No, she had done the right thing in leaving Mac. She had spent the last years enjoying life. There had been bad times in the beginning, but once she'd met Andre, she'd never regretted a moment of her freedom or the price she'd paid for it.

She and Andre had traveled from one town to the next, working their little ploy on unsuspecting men and then skipping town with whatever money they could sweat out of them. Some called it a badger game, but Eve thought it just fun. She had enjoyed enticing the men and then watching their horror when her *husband* caught them in a compromising position.

What a shame that Andre had had to shoot that stubborn one in Santa Fe. The man had told them that he wasn't going to pay up; that he was going to the law instead. That was when Andre had lost his temper. The law had caught up with them, and though the shooting had been in self-defense, there had been no witnesses, save herself, to give testimony. So now her lover was languishing in jail, and she was here, doing her best on her own, to end up comfortably wealthy.

She didn't know what kind of settlement she could get out of Mac, but she was going to try to convince him to make it a big one. And, if he didn't pay up, well, she'd learned a few tricks over the years, and she'd just have to make his life so miserable that he'd do anything to get rid of her.

Feeling much refreshed and very determined, Eve put on clean clothes and a suitable gown. Then, checking her purse to make certain that the letter was still there, she left her room.

There was no one at the front desk again when Eve descended the stairs, and she wondered idly how the place managed to stay in business.

"Mrs. Bates?" she called out as she waited impatiently

before the counter.

"Yes, ma'am?" Sally again hurried out from the back room.

"I was wondering if you could recommend somewhere to dine and also a way that I might get a message delivered to my husband."

"Oh, uh, sure. The best eating place is right down the street. You can't miss it. And as for your letter, I can have Billy run it out to the ranch for you, if you like."

"That would be fine," Eve responded sedately. "Have him meet me at the restaurant."

"I'll get him for you right away, Mrs. McCaine," Sally told her respectfully as she watched her leave.

"Thank you."

Eve located the small restaurant without any trouble and had just finished ordering from the basic, boring fare when Billy came rushing in.

"Mrs. Bates said you had an errand for me to run," he told her anxiously, as he stood at her table, hat in hand.

"Yes, Billy, I have a letter I need delivered, and I was wondering if you could handle that for me?"

"Yes, ma'am. Where do you want me to take it?"

"I'd like you to ride out to the M Circle C and make sure that Mr. Mac McCaine gets this. All right?" She opened her purse and took out the envelope.

"Right away."

"Make sure Mr. McCaine is the one who gets it."

"Yes, ma'am. But what if he's not there for some reason. Do you want me to leave it or bring it back?"

"You may leave it."

"All right."

"How long do you think it will take you to ride out, drop it off and get back here?"

"Shouldn't take more than a couple of hours, ma'am."

"Fine." Eve handed him a silver dollar. "This is for making sure that the letter gets there, unopened. There will be another one for you when you get back. I want you to come to my room at the hotel as soon as you return."

"Yes, ma'am!"

"You may call me Mrs. McCaine."

"Yes, ma'am, Mrs. McCaine," he answered quickly, surprised to learn that her name was McCaine, but he thought that she must be some kind of relative coming for a visit.

Eve handed him the letter. "I'm sure I can trust you to do your very best."

"I will and I'll come to you the minute I get back!" And with that Billy raced from the small restaurant, intent only on earning that other silver dollar.

After stuffing the letter protectively inside his shirt, Billy got his horse and began the trek out to the McCaine ranch. Though the day was hot, he pushed his horse to the limit so he could get back and get his other dollar. That lady sure was nice—and rich! Never before had he earned so much money running errands in one day, and he hoped she stayed in town for a long time to come.

Billy had been out to the M Circle C on numerous occasions, yet it never failed to impress him when he rode through the main gate. The adobe exterior of the big, main house appeared dazzlingly white in the brightness of the afternoon sun and stood in vibrant contrast to the red-tiled roof. By Billy's standards it was as near a castle as he would ever see, and he felt important now that he had business to conduct here.

Having spent the morning cleaning a house that didn't need cleaning, Hildago had finally given in to her exhaustion and had lain down to try to get some rest. Since Mac had ridden out with the posse all those days ago, she had been existing in a living hell. She'd been unable to sleep or eat. All she'd been able to do was think, and her thoughts

395

had been anything but pleasant.

It had been bad enough having to worry about Jennie's safety and the men who were trying to rescue her, but when she'd discovered that Carrie had followed them, she'd nearly been distraught. Carrie had never shown any inclination toward ranch living, and there she was, in the middle of a posse of rough men, looking for outlaws! Hildago shuddered at the thought, and she could only pray that it would soon be over, for the longer it dragged on, the more serious her concern for them grew.

"Hildago!" The houseboy, Benito, called from outside the closed bedroom door, and her thoughts came back to the present.

"What is it?" she called out, rising quickly from the bed.

"There is a rider coming!"

Excited, yet filled with a sense of sudden dread, she rushed from the room.

"Which direction?"

"From town," he told her, dogging her footsteps as she raced through the house and out the front door.

Stopping in the shade of the veranda, Hildago watched warily as the rider drew near.

"Is it one of our men?" Benito asked.

"No, I don't think so." She shaded her eyes against the brilliance of the sun. "It looks like that boy Billy from in town."

She said no more until the boy had reined in at the hitching post.

"Welcome to the M Circle C, Billy."

"Thank you, Miss Teran," he said greeting the McCaine's housekeeper courteously. "I've got a message here." He fumbled with the buttons on his shirt and finally extracted the missive. "It's for Mr. McCaine."

"Mac or Jake?" she asked as she stepped from the veranda.

"Mr. Mac McCaine."

"Well, Mac isn't here right now, but if you like, you can leave it with me, and I'll see that he gets it."

"Thank you. I'd appreciate that."

"Why don't you come in and have a drink before you start back to town?"

"I'd like that, ma'am." Billy slid down from his horse's back and looped the reins around the post. "It was a hot ride."

"Fine, come on in."

When he had settled at the table in the kitchen with a cooling drink, Billy asked, "Do you know how soon Mr. McCaine will be back?"

"I really don't, Billy. We had some trouble here on the ranch, and he's ridden out with some of the men to take care of it."

"Trouble?" His eyes widened at the thought.

"Yes. I suppose I might as well tell you so you can let the others know in town. Jennie was kidnapped by some outlaws, and Mac went after her."

Billy was stunned by the news. "Miss Jennie?"

"Yes, but I'm sure they'll bring her back safe and sound." Hildago tried to sound confident.

"I sure hope so. Miss Jennie is a real nice lady."

"That she is."

"How long they been gone?"

"Over a week now." The worry crept back into her voice. "So I'm hoping that they will be back soon."

"I'll tell her that, then," he said more to himself than to Hildago.

"Her?"

"The lady who sent the letter," he told Hildago guilelessly.

"Do you know her name?" She was suddenly suspicious. If the letter was for Jake, she wouldn't have given it a second thought, but a letter from a woman for Mac?

"She said her name was Mrs. McCaine. I guess she's one of their relatives or something," Billy answered nonchalantly.

Hildago felt as if her whole world was crashing at her feet. Dear God! *Mrs. McCaine?* It couldn't be. Not after all this time.

"Is something wrong, Miss Teran?" the boy asked as he stood up to leave.

"No, Billy. Nothing's wrong. I'll make sure Mac gets this as soon as he returns home." She walked slowly with him to the door.

"Thanks for the drink."

"You be careful on your way back to town."

"I will."

Hildago stood on the veranda, watching until Billy had ridden out of sight before turning back into the house. Her mind was in a whirl. Her heart was aching. She looked down at the envelope she was still holding in her hand. Could it be? Would she have dared to come back after all this time? Hildago knew deep in her soul the answer to that: Eve McCaine would dare anything!

She longed to tear the letter into shreds, but she knew that it would not change anything. If Eve was back, then she had a reason for being here, and Hildago knew with certainty that reclaiming the husband and children she'd deserted so long ago was not it.

Briefly she considered going into town, but she was afraid that she might miss Mac's return to the ranch, and she didn't want to take the chance. As difficult as it was going to be for her, Hildago knew she would have to wait and let Mac handle it when he got home.

Cursing savagely at the fates that had been so cruel to them, she placed the letter on his desk in his office. Hurrying from the room, she shut the door tightly behind her as if to block the letter's entrance into their lives.

Chapter Twenty-nine

Eve stood in the middle of her room, staring at the numerous gowns she'd just spread out on the bed, trying to decide which one to wear when she had her momentous meeting with Mac. Frowning thoughtfully, she picked up a low-cut evening gown. The dress, a creation of shimmering watersilk, fit her superbly, but as she held it up, she realized that this dingy hotel room was hardly the place to appear in such a fancy dress.

No, when she came face to face with her husband for the first time after all these years, she wanted to be the type of woman he liked: soft and clinging and helpless. Sorting through her other gowns she finally selected a very conservative pale blue one which she was certain would appeal to Mac. It made her seem fragile and very feminine, and she knew it would be perfect.

At the sound of a horse, Eve rushed to the window, thinking that it was Billy returning from the ranch, but to her disappointment, it was not. The man she saw riding slowly down the middle of the street was a disheveled, ominous-looking Mexican, and she drew back quickly before he caught sight of her. Dismissing him from her mind, she busied herself with repacking her things as she waited to hear from the boy.

*   *   *

Malo was hot and thirsty as he rode into Mesa Roja. Exhausted from his desperate flight to safety, he was only concerned with finding the nearest saloon and washing the dust from his parched throat with something stronger than the stale water he'd been drinking. Stopping at the livery, he dismounted and handed the reins over to the man who came out to meet him.

"What can I do for you, stranger?"

"Bed him down for the night and feed him extra," Malo instructed curtly as he pulled his rifle from the scabbard and swung his saddlebags over his shoulder.

"Right. That'll be twenty-five cents."

Malo counted out the money. "Where's the nearest place to get something to drink?"

"That'll be Dolly's, 'bout two blocks down."

"I'll be back tomorrow," he told him curtly and headed toward the saloon.

Though he was tired, Malo was also filled with a great sense of relief. He'd made it! That first day after he'd spotted the Indians, he'd almost ridden his mount into the ground in his desperation to get away, but when he'd realized that they weren't chasing him, he'd finally slowed his breakneck pace. The last few days crossing the desert had given him plenty of time to think and to plan, but for right now, all he wanted was a good bottle and a good night's sleep.

It was late afternoon when Billy tied his horse in front of the hotel and hurried inside, anxious to collect the second half of his wages. The lobby was deserted, as usual, and he climbed the steps to Eve's second floor room without hesitation and knocked on her door.

Eve opened the door promptly for she had seen him ride up and she was expecting him. "Billy, I'm so glad you're back. Come in and tell me how it went. Did Mr. McCaine get the letter?"

Taking off his hat, he entered the room and waited as she shut the door behind them. "No, ma'am. He was gone. But I did leave the note with Miss Teran. She's the housekeeper, and she said that she'd make sure he got it."

"That was the right thing to do." Hiding her disappointment, Eve asked, "Did this housekeeper say when she expected him to return?"

"No, ma'am. She said that there had been trouble and that he'd ridden out over a week ago and that she didn't know when he'd be getting back."

"Trouble? What kind of trouble?"

"She said something about Miss Jennie being kidnapped."

"Kidnapped? But why? By whom?"

"She really didn't say. Miss Teran just said she'd been taken by some outlaws and that Mr. McCaine had gone after her."

"Outlaws? But how would they have gotten her?" Eve wondered out loud.

"I don't know, Mrs. McCaine. That was all she told me."

"Yes, well . . ." Eve hurried to get him the money she owed him. "If you should hear any more about this, you let me know right away. All right, Billy?"

"Yes, ma'am. I'd be glad to." He took the money excitedly and started for the door. "And thanks again, Mrs. McCaine."

"You're welcome," Eve told him distantly, as she let him out of the room.

When he'd gone, she locked the door behind him and sank down on the bed to think. What was she going to do? Her funds were running dangerously low, and she knew what little money she had wouldn't last for more than another week—If Mac didn't get back before then. Refusing to worry about something before it actually happened, she dismissed the thought. Mac would be back and when he did show up, she was going to get everything she needed from him.

Since there was nothing more she could do right then, Eve

401

decided to lie down and rest for a while, but as she stretched out on the lumpy bed, she thought of what Billy had just told her. Jennie had been kidnapped.

Getting up, Eve went to her trunk and rummaged through her belongings until she found what she was looking for: a small gold locket. Frowning, not having the remotest idea why she felt it was necessary, she opened it and stared down at the two young faces pictured there in the miniature portraits. Jake and Jennie. She felt little emotion as she gazed at their pictures, and she wondered idly why she'd ever bothered to save the charm. Snapping it shut, Eve put it away, but as she moved to sit back down on the bed, she couldn't help wondering what her children looked like now. She had some idea of the coloring of the older two, but Carrie— She hadn't seen her youngest since infancy. Shrugging it off as unimportant, she lay down again and closed her eyes.

Dolly's saloon was reasonably quiet as Malo entered, and he stood silhouetted in the doorway for a long minute just to make sure that it was safe. Finally, when no one paid any particular attention to him, he ambled toward the bar.

"What'll it be?" the barkeep asked gruffly.

"Tequila—a bottle," Malo told him as he moved to the deserted end of the counter.

"Let's see the color of your money."

At any other time, he probably would have shown him the barrel of his gun, but today Malo was too tired to take insult. Flipping a coin on the counter, the bartender grunted his satisfaction that the man had means and set a glass and bottle in front of him.

"Name's Ed. You're new in town, aren't ya?"

"Yep."

"Stayin' long?"

Malo eyed him coldly. "I don't like nosy people, and it

seems to me you must be about the nosiest person in these here parts."

Ed shrugged indifferently, "Not nosy, just interested."

"I don't like interested people, either."

"Right." He turned to go, but Malo stopped him.

"I need a room. You rent 'em here?"

"Sure do. Seventy-five cents."

"Here." He shoved more money across the bar.

"Take your pick," he said. "At the top of the stairs."

"I'll be needin' a bath, too."

"There's a bathhouse right up the street."

He nodded and, picking up the bottle of tequila and his gear, he started up the stairs.

Malo chose a room facing the front and, after stowing his saddlebags and rifle, he paused to take a deep drink of the burning liquor. There was nothing he wanted to do more than drink himself insensible tonight, but first he was going to have that bath. Making sure to lock the door behind him, he left his room a few minutes later, bottle in hand, heading, almost eagerly, to the bathhouse.

The sun was dipping low in the west as he headed back to the saloon, feeling much better for having bathed and shaved, and he finished off the whole bottle of tequila. At Dolly's the evening was just getting into full swing. A fumble-fingered piano player was attempting to bang out a boisterous tune, and the ladies who plied their trade there had just begun to emerge from their rooms and came downstairs to greet the men.

Malo entered the saloon unnoticed and he was glad. The fewer people who knew he was around, the better. Sidling up to the bar, he ordered his usual from Ed, who served him this time without saying a word.

"It's true, I tell you!" Silas Stratton was saying with emphasis to those gathered around him at the far end of the bar. "Billy rode out there today, and he heard it from Hildago herself."

403

"But how could it have happened?"

"I don't know any of the particulars," he continued, feeling very important for having been the bearer of such exciting news. "All I know is that she told Billy that Jennie had been kidnapped and that Mac and some of his men had gone out to rescue her."

A low growl of nervousness spread through the men. "Whoever it was must have been stupid! You just don't mess with Mac McCaine or his family!"

As he listened to the men of the town, Malo realized bitterly that they were right. If Cazador hadn't brought the damned McCaine girl along, he would have had his gold by now! The thought of Cazador struck a nerve with him, and had he not been certain that the Apache had already killed him, he would have been planning a way to get even with the double-crossing back-stabbing bastard!

"I know. I wish I knew the whole story, but I guess we'll just have to wait until they get back. Surely, Mac or Jake will fill us in," Silas continued.

Malo was tempted to snort in derision and tell them that their precious McCaines wouldn't be coming back; that the Indians had taken real good care of them. But he held his tongue. They'd find out soon enough.

"Why did Billy ride out to the M Circle C?" someone else questioned.

"Now, that's strange, too," the stage clerk told them in a confiding tone. "This lady arrived on the stage today, and she registered at the hotel as *Mrs.* Mac McCaine."

"But Mac's wife is dead!" one of the men pointed out, scoffing at the thought.

Silas looked indignant. "I'm only telling you what Sally Bates told me, and that's how she registered—Mrs. Mac McCaine." He paused to take a drink of his beer. "It'll sure be interesting to find out what's going on with the McCaines when they all get back."

The talk moved on then to other subjects, and Malo's attention waned until he caught sight of one of the girls working her way across the room toward him. She was attractive enough, but when he thought of Lucia, his desire for a woman disappeared.

"Hello," she said throatily, her eyes roaming over him knowingly. "Buy me a beer, big guy?"

At another time, Malo would have delighted in strangling her for he did not tolerate any remarks about his height, but tonight, in this town, he refrained.

"No." His answer was cold and final as he turned his back on her.

"Your loss," she said and, giving him a disgusted look, she wandered off in pursuit of more willing prey.

Malo drained his drink and then started upstairs, wanting only to get a good night's sleep.

It was noon and Eve was bored. She had deliberately slept late that morning just so the day wouldn't seem so long, but now that she'd breakfasted late, there was absolutely nothing to do. She wanted to scream. Even the men in the town were dull! There hadn't been a handsome one among them, and she had been looking!

Frustrated and disgusted, she flopped down on the bed. What in the world was she going to do with herself until Mac showed up? A sudden idea occurred to her, and she got up quickly and headed downstairs to find Mrs. Bates.

"Mrs. Bates?" Eve called as she waited again at the front desk.

"Yes, ma'am?"

"I was wondering if you could have the young boy, Billy, come up to see me, please? I have another job for him."

"I'll get him for you right away, Mrs. McCaine."

"Thank you," she said demurely and then went back upstairs to await the youth's arrival.

She didn't have long to wait for he arrived within ten minutes, eager to do her bidding.

"Mrs. Bates said that you needed me?" he asked when

she'd opened the door.

"Yes, I was wondering if you could drive me out to the McCaine ranch today?"

"Sure! But I'll have to rent a buckboard."

"Fine, do you know how much it'll be?"

"No, but we won't have to pay 'til we get back anyway. I'll be right back to pick you up." And jamming his hat on his head, he raced toward the stables.

The ride to the M Circle C was as tedious as she'd remembered it to be, but when they crested a small rise and the ranch house came into view, Eve caught her breath.

"My, my," she murmured, admiring the size and splendor of Mac's home. "He certainly has done well for himself, hasn't he?"

"Excuse me, ma'am? Did you say something?" Bill asked.

"Oh, no, nothing important. Listen, I don't want to go all the way down to the ranch."

He looked at her as if she were crazy. "You don't?"

"No. Not if Mac's not there."

"But you're family, aren't you?" He was clearly confused.

"Yes, but I don't want to impose until I've had a chance to renew my association with them. It's been quite a few years since I saw them last," she told him, wanting to quell his questions.

"Oh."

"We can go on back now, if you don't mind."

"Well, sure, Mrs. McCaine, whatever you say." And he efficiently turned the horses around and headed back toward town.

Later that afternoon, in the privacy of her room, Eve was glad that she'd taken the time to ride out to see the ranch. It had helped her to formulate a plan, and she now knew what she would do if Mac didn't show up before her money ran out. A sly smile lifted the corners of her mouth as she tried to imagine the town's reaction when she boldly ensconced herself as the *lady of the manor*, so to speak. Eve knew that

406

Mac's homecoming would be a delight if he found her comfortably settled in his house. For sure, Eve knew that she would have the upper hand in that situation. Glad that she now had something to look forward to, she settled in to maintain her dull vigil in town, almost hoping that he wouldn't show up right away.

Malo sat in the back corner of the saloon with his feet propped up on a nearby chair and a half full bottle of liquor in his hand. Mesa Roja, he'd decided, was a very boring town. He'd been up and down the main street twice this morning, but aside from seeing a fancy-looking woman riding in a buckboard with a young boy, there had been little going on.

He sighed as he took another swig of the tequila. If he'd still had his men with him, he would have given serious consideration to raiding the McCaine ranch. But he knew that without some help to back him up, there was no point in trying to attack a good-sized spread like the M Circle C for there were, no doubt, many well-armed men around just for the purpose of defending against such assaults.

Malo knew he should probably be heading back to Mexico for it would be there that he would find men to ride with him, but he was in no particular rush as long as his money was holding out. Also, he found the thought of sticking around until the news came about the McCaines intriguing.

Settling back in his chair, Malo drained the rest of the liquor in long, hungry gulps and signaled the bartender for another bottle. Yes, he decided, he would just sit it out here in Mesa Roja for a while and take it easy. He thought of the woman who'd approached him last night and smiled. He was definitely feeling more mellow today, and maybe tonight he'd take her up on her unspoken offer. Yes, maybe he would.

Chapter Thirty

Her emotions in turmoil, Hildago stared down at the small portrait of Eve. It was now two days since the letter had arrived, and for those two days, Hildago had been miserable. Why had Eve McCaine come back after all these years? The question haunted her day and night. Hildago wanted to think that her reason was money, but a niggling doubt remained: Could there be something else?

When Hildago had come to work for Mac, she had thought him a widower. Sensing a great pain buried deep inside him, she had attributed it to having lost his beloved wife. Many times she had come upon him staring at the portrait of the lovely blond woman, an odd expression on his face.

In the beginning, Hildago never suspected that there was anything more to it, but once they'd become closer, Mac had finally told her the whole truth and she'd been shocked. How could Eve McCaine just up and leave her family? To this day, Hildago had never been able to understand. She had been glad when Mac had decided to keep the truth from the children, for she believed it was better that they think their mother dead than to know that she'd run off.

But now, Eve was back, and Hildago was worried about how Mac would handle it. Was there still a flicker of love buried beneath the hate he'd professed for her all these years? She shivered at the thought and turned away from Eve's smiling picture.

"Hildago! Hildago! Senor Mac! He is coming!!"

At Benito's excited call, Hildago rushed out onto the veranda to see Mac riding her way. Frightened when she saw that he was coming in alone, she ran desperately toward the main gate.

"Mac! Oh, Mac!" she cried. "Where are the others? Where is Jennie?"

Mac reined in quickly and swung out of the saddle to embrace her comfortingly. "We got her back," he told her happily as he gazed down at her beloved face. "They'll be along in a few minutes. I just rode ahead to have a few quiet minutes with you."

"You are all right?" She looked him over anxiously.

"Hot and dirty, but fine." He grinned and kissed her soundly. "I missed you."

"And I missed you!" Hildago hugged him. "Everyone is all right then?"

Mac's happiness faded as he related what had happened to Steve and the other ranch hand. "We had a run-in with the Apache. Steve was killed, Hildago, and another man."

"I'm so sorry." Her eyes saddened at the thought of two such brave men dying so prematurely.

Mac nodded. "We buried them in the mountains."

"You've been in the mountains all this time?"

"Yes, the outlaws were after a gold mine, and we had to track them down up in the Superstitions."

Hildago shivered at the thought. "Those mountains are dangerous."

"Very," he said before kissing her once again.

Then, after he gave his horse over to Benito, they started to walk toward the house.

"You must tell me everything!" she insisted.

"Well, we will have some company staying with us for a

while," he began.

"Company? Who? Todd?"

"Yes, I'm sure Todd will be staying." He paused for effect. "At least until the wedding."

"Wedding? Jennie finally agreed to marry him?"

"Jennie did finally agree to get married—but not to Todd," he said to tease her.

"Then who?"

"His name is Rick Peralta and he's an old friend of Jake's. You'll like him. He'll be staying with us, along with his grandfather, Juan."

Hildago sighed her exasperation. "How did you meet these men?"

"The outlaws who took Jennie captive," he said as they crossed the veranda and entered the shadowed coolness of the house, "had also taken Juan Peralta captive. He supposedly knew the location of a gold mine, and they were forcing him to lead them there. Rick was trying to rescue his grandfather and had worked his way into the gang—Miguel Malo's by the way—as one of the gunslingers."

"So, this fiancé of Jennie's is an outlaw?" Hildago exclaimed.

"No, not really. He just pretended to be one in order to help Juan. Anyway," Mac went on, "he was taking care of Jennie, too, but she didn't know who he really was, so the first chance she got, she ran away from him. Luckily, we showed up right afterward and found her and then, at her insistence, we went after Malo to rescue Juan."

"And you did," she concluded for him, beaming her pleasure at his successes. "Did you kill Malo? They say he is a vicious dog."

"No. We tried. We got all of his men, but he somehow managed to slip away from us."

"And the Indians?"

"They ambushed us when we were on our way back."

She nodded and asked no further questions.

"So, how are you? Did you do all right while we were gone?"

"Oh, yes. Everything ran smoothly. My only concern was you," Hildago answered quickly, not yet ready to tell him about the letter. There would be plenty of time to bring that up, later.

Going to the liquor cabinet, she poured him a glass of whiskey and handed it to him.

"Thank you." He sighed deeply as he took a drink.

"You look like you could use more than one."

"Just tired, that's all. It's been hell." Mac's tone was solemn.

At the sound of horses nearing the house, they went back outside to greet the others.

"I suppose I should tell you this before you start worrying about Todd's feelings being hurt over Jennie's engagement to another man."

"Tell me what." She was practically wide-eyed as she looked up at him. "There's more news?"

"Well, Todd's going to marry Carrie." Mac was thoroughly enjoying giving her the good news.

Hildago was momentarily stunned. "Todd and Carrie? But I thought he was in love with Jennie!"

"So did he until he was alone with Carrie on the trail." He was smiling widely. "You know, that girl is a lot like me in some ways."

Hildago was speechless at this unexpected praise of Carrie. She didn't know what had happened during the time they were on the trail together, but she certainly knew that whatever it was, it had been for the best. Never in all the time she'd known Mac had she ever heard a kind word from him for his youngest child.

"And you're pleased about this?" she asked, still disbelieving the changes that had occurred.

"Very. They love each other very much, Hildago. Just as Jennie and Rick do." He looked down at her tenderly. "You'll see. Here they are now."

411

"Jennie!" Hildago hurried from Mac's side to hug Jennie as she reined in at the hitching post and dismounted. "Thank God, you're all right. I was so worried. I prayed and prayed."

"I'm fine, Hildago, and I'm so glad to be home." Jennie turned and gestured to a tall, handsome man to come forward. "I have someone I want you to meet. Hildago, this is Rick. Rick, this is Hildago."

"So, you are the one who has stolen my Jennie's heart?"

"I hope so." He grinned, slipping an arm around Jennie's waist as he met her gaze openly. "I know she has stolen mine."

Pleased with his answer, Hildago smiled her approval. "This is your grandfather?"

"Yes, Juan. Grandfather, this is Hildago."

"My pleasure," Juan told her courteously.

"And these ladies are Lucia and Chica," Mac added.

"It's nice to meet all of you," she said cordially. "Now, where are Carrie and Todd? Mac tells me that they have news for me, too?"

"We do," Todd announced as he stepped forward with Carrie by his side. And then he asked teasingly, "How do you feel about double weddings?"

At that everyone laughed and then started inside, glad to be back to civilization.

"Carrie McCaine! I intend to have a word with you!" Hildago gave her a mock stern look as they moved to enter the house. "Just riding off and leaving me like that without a word! I was worried sick about you!"

"But everything turned out just fine, Hildago," Carrie smiled at her in spite of her menacing tone.

"Better than fine," Todd added as he pulled Carrie close for a quick kiss.

"Oh! You're impossible!" She laughed. "Let's get everybody settled in, and then I want to know everything that happened."

"Mac?" One of the men called out to him before he could go inside.

"What is it?" Mac stepped back out on the veranda.

"What should we do with him?" He indicated Pablo, who was still riding with them, tied up.

"Lock him up in one of the outbuildings for tonight, and we'll take him into town, tomorrow."

"Right." The rest of the hands rode off then in the direction of the bunk house.

Lucia heard the instructions and smiled to herself as she followed the others indoors where they settled in the main sitting room to relax after the long trip.

"It certainly feels good to be back." Mac groaned contentedly as he sat in his favorite chair. "I want everyone to feel at home, so make yourselves comfortable. If you don't see what you want, then just ask for it," he told them happily.

Hildago set the servants to preparing a meal and then rejoined them. "We'll probably eat in about an hour."

"Oh, good." Carrie got up from where she'd been sitting beside Todd. "That gives me time for a bath."

"I'll have the girls prepare the water for you," Hildago offered.

"Thank you." She gave Todd a quick kiss and started from the room. "I'll be back in a little while."

"Chica—Lucia? Would you like me to show you to your rooms so you can freshen up before we eat?" Hildago asked them.

"Thank you, that would be very nice," Chica said gratefully, but Lucia only nodded, her attitude toward Hildago almost sullen.

"Do you have clean clothing?" she asked as she led them down the hall toward the guest bedrooms.

"No ma'am, we don't"

"Then I'll have one of the serving girls bring you something to wear," Hildago offered as she opened the door to a spacious cool bedroom that opened both into the main

413

house and into the courtyard formed by the U-shape of the ranch house. "Take your pick. This room or the room across the hall." She hurried to open the other door to an equally comfortable room.

"I'll take this one," Lucia proclaimed as she settled on the bed in the room opening onto the yard.

"This one will be fine for me," Chica said easily, moving into the other. "Thank you, Hildago."

"Would you like to bathe?"

"It would be heaven!" Chica laughed.

"Good. I'll have the girls fix you a bath, too, then."

"Thanks so much."

"You are guests here. Relax and enjoy. I'm sure after all that time you spent with the posse, you need a little rest." Hildago was sympathetic. "Whenever you feel like it, join us."

Chica nodded as the older woman left them.

"Lucia! Isn't this wonderful! Look at this house! It's beautiful, isn't it?" She was enchanted with this glimpse of ranch life, but Lucia only stared at her, her eyes hard and cold.

"Of course it's beautiful! And look who it belongs to! Jennie." Lucia spat her name, seething with jealousy.

Chica gave her an exasperated look. "You're stupid and what is worse is that you do not realize it!"

As Chica disappeared into her room, shutting the door behind her with emphasis, Lucia shrugged her indifference and rose from the bed. She hated Jennie McCaine with a passion, and before she left this place she was determined to make her pay—one way or another. Feeling angry and restless, she wandered out into the courtyard to await the coming of the servant girls with her bath.

"Since we do have so long before we eat, I think I'll bathe, too," Jennie was saying as Hildago returned from seeing the other two women to their rooms. "Rick? Would you like to get cleaned up?"

His eyes glinted with a delightful answering wickedness that only she witnessed as he thought of their getting *cleaned up* together. "It sure couldn't hurt." He grinned easily when she looked quickly away.

"Pa, I'll show Rick to one of the guest rooms and then we'll meet you back here for dinner."

"Fine." Mac waved them on, and Rick rose slowly from where he was seated to follow Jennie from the room. "Your grandson is a good man," he told Juan when they had disappeard from sight. "They'll do well together."

Juan nodded in agreement after watching them go. "Indeed."

Walking slowly down the cool expanse of the hall to the men's quarters, Rick slipped an arm about her waist and stopped, pulling her to him.

"Your idea about showing me to my room was wonderful." He smiled softly. "I've been needing to do this for hours." With slow precision, he lowered his head to hers and claimed her mouth in a raging kiss of pure passion.

Jennie, too, had been longing to be near him, and she clutched at his shoulders for support as she swayed against him. Hands cupping her hips, Rick pressed her to his body, letting her feel his bold response to her tantalizing nearness. A low moan escaped her as she wriggled against his hardness, wanting all of him—not wanting to wait.

But the sound of Jake and Todd who followed after them drove them apart.

"Where's my room?" he asked quickly as he released her.

"Right down here. I'll give you one that opens onto the courtyard." She smiled at him conspiratorily as she opened the door to a large, airy bedroom furnished in massive, masculine tastes.

"That's good?"

"My room just happens to open onto the courtyard, too." She gazed up at him, trying to keep her expression innocent, but the sparkle of excitement was unmistakable in her eyes.

415

"That sounds inviting." Rick closed the door quickly once they'd moved inside.

"I would certainly hope so." Jennie turned to him and looped her arms behind his neck.

"I can hardly wait for bedtime." Rick growled in anticipation, shifting his lower body closer to hers.

"I know." She pouted. "It's been so hard being so close together and not being able to—"

"To what?"

"To kiss you." Jennie pressed a soft kiss on his mouth. "Or touch you." She ran a hand lightly down his chest. "Or— make love to you."

"I know. You can't imagine how many times during the last two days I've wanted to drag you off behind a saguaro cactus!" He rested his forehead against hers.

"Probably about as many times as I wanted to do it to you!" A throaty laugh gurgled from her.

"How soon can we be married?" he asked quickly.

"How about tonight?"

"How about yesterday?" Rick gave a rueful laugh.

"We can talk to Pa and Hildago about it at dinner. I'm sure he'll help us all he can."

"Good. The sooner we're married, the better. I want you with me every moment of every day." He kissed her deeply. "And night."

As the fires of their desires threatened to flare out of control, they moved reluctantly apart.

"Nice," he remarked approvingly as he followed her to the open french doors and looked out across the courtyard. "Which room is yours?"

Jennie shivered as he came up close behind her. "That one." Jennie pointed out her bedroom, her heart racing at the thought that in a few hours she would be slipping silently through the dark to spend the night with Rick.

As his arms came around her, he told her huskily. "I'll be waiting for you tonight."

Leaning back against him, she sighed. "I love you, Rick.

Very much."

"I know, love," he said softly, as his lips sought the sensitive cords of her neck.

Jennie arched at the touch of his mouth, her body aching for union with his. "Oh, Rick."

Turning in his embrace, she rubbed sinuously against him as their gazes locked in understanding.

"Tonight." His voice was deep with promise.

"Tonight." She answered that promise.

Rick was tempted to take her then for his passion was nearly overwhelming, but he carefully held himself in check. He did not want a heated, frenzied joining. Instead, the next time they made love, he was determined to relish every moment.

With mesmerizing slowness, he bent to her, his mouth finding hers in a soft pledge of the delights to come. They broke apart only when the sound of Todd and Jake out in the hallway intruded into their consciousness.

"I'd better go." She sighed.

"I'll meet you in the sitting room." He walked to the door with her.

Jennie reached up to kiss him one last time and then hurried from the room.

Lucia moved quickly back into her room from where she'd stood unobserved on the patio. So! Jennie planned to sneak into Rick's room tonight, did she? Lucia's mouth curled into a sneering smile as a devious plot to spoil their happiness began to take shape in her mind. With any luck at all, she mused, after tonight Jennie would no longer want Rick and then he would be free—free to come to her.

Loving the feeling of being back home, Jennie made her way peacefully through the house, marveling that everything had turned out so well. Wanting to speak with her sister, she paused at Carrie's room and knocked on the closed door.

"Carrie?"

"Come on in, Jennie," she called out.

Jennie entered the room to find Carrie, her hair damp,

wearing only a silken dressing gown, seated at her dressing table.

"You already took a bath?"

"Yes, I didn't want to keep Todd waiting," she told her excitedly. "Oh, Jennie, I can't believe it! Isn't it wonderful! You have Rick and I have Todd."

"I really am glad things worked out between you," Jennie told her sincerely.

"So am I. He's the most wonderful, thoughtful man in the whole wide world!"

"Todd is a very special man. You're very lucky to have him," she answered.

"And you, Rick! He's absolutely gorgeous, Jennie."

"I kind of think so, too." Jennie laughed as she started from the room. "Well, I'd better hurry and get my bath, too."

Her spirits were light as she entered her own room, and she was pleased to find that Hildago had already had her bath arranged. Quickly stripping off her filthy clothes, she stretched tiredly before stepping into the perfumed, heated water. Enfolded in its welcoming warmth, Jennie sighed in pure, heavenly pleasure and lay back to enjoy the bliss of the moment.

Rick—Rick—Rick— Her heart was filled with love for him as she rested in the steaming bath. She thought of the time they'd spent together when she'd thought he was El Cazador, and she smiled, He had been trying so hard to protect her, and all she had done was make things more difficult for him. Well, Jennie decided, she would have the rest of her life to make it up to him. Starting tonight!

The thought of spending the entire night in his embrace thrilled her, and she hoped that they could be married soon, so they could be together every night. Her lips curved sensuously as she imagined the hours to come. True, they'd have to suffer through a long dinner with every one else, but then, when things got quiet, she and Rick could finally satisfy their desire.

418

Chapter Thirty-one

The delicious meal Hildago arranged seemed gourmet fare after the food they'd existed on during the trek, and everyone ate heartily, enjoying each other's company and the sense of peaceful intimacy that came from finally being home.

"What do you suppose happened to Malo?" Todd asked as they moved into the sitting room after dinner.

"I was wondering that myself," Mac replied, pouring whiskey for the men. "I can't help but think that he ran into the Apache before we did."

"If you want, Pa, I'll take Pablo into town in the morning," Jake offered.

"That'll be fine. I've got a lot of work to catch up on here at the ranch." He glanced over to Chica and Lucia. "In fact, Jake, why don't you plan on escorting Chica and Lucia, too, and then you can make all the arrangements for their transportation back home. Would that suit you ladies?"

"Yes, thank you," Chica answered quickly, but Lucia only gave him a curt nod.

"Fine, we'll take care of it first thing in the morning." He looked to his daughters, his eyes twinkling. "I think there's only one other matter that needs settling, now."

"What's that, Pa?" Jake asked.

"Well, the small matter of weddings has yet to be discussed." He smiled widely at his offspring.

"Grandfather and I have to return to El Rancho Grande as soon as possible, and I would like to take Jennie back with me—as my wife." Rick spoke to Mac, but his eyes were on Jennie.

Lucia listened to his words and was barely able to suppress the smile that threatened. Rick might think that he was going to marry Jennie, but if she had anything to do with it, the wedding would never take place.

"If that suits Jennie, then it's fine with me," Mac said. "What about you, Todd? Carrie?"

"We'd like to marry soon, too," Todd answered.

"Well, why don't you and Rick ride into town in the morning with Jake and speak with the preacher? Then we can be more definite about making plans."

"Sounds good. What time do you want to go, Jake?"

"Why don't we plan to go early, right after breakfast. That way, if there is a stage due in, Chica and Lucia won't miss it."

"Since we'll be leaving so early, I think I'll go on to bed then," Chica said as she rose to leave the room. "Mr. McCaine, thank you for everything you've done for me."

"You're more than welcome," he answered.

"Yes, thanks," Lucia told them as she stood up and quietly followed the other woman from the room.

With only the presence of family, the mood became more relaxed, and they passed the next hours in easy companionship.

Jennie, however, sitting so closely to Rick on the sofa, thought the evening would never end. She had been surprised by the rush of desire she'd felt when she'd returned to the sitting room and had seen him for the first time wearing some of Jake's clothes. The whiteness of the shirt he'd borrowed from her brother had only served to emphasize his darkly tanned good looks, and the slim-fitting black trousers clung tightly to his muscular thighs. Jennie's pulse had been racing as she'd gone to him, and throughout the entire meal, she'd been hard put to keep her manner nonchalant. Now, as she sat beside him, their positions looked casual, but in reality, they were anything but, as the heat of his leg pressed tightly to hers and the accidental brushing of his arm against the side of her breast kept her constantly aware of his nearness.

All Jennie could think of doing was losing herself in the power of his passionate possession and yet, she had to sit there calmly and pretend that she wasn't on fire with desire for him. Finally, when she could stand it no more, she forced a yawn and moved to excuse herself.

"If you don't mind." She tried to sound exhausted when, in reality, her body was feverishly alive. "I think I'm going to call it a night. I can hardly wait to sleep in a bed again."

"I know the feeling." Carrie laughed. "Somehow a bedroll just isn't as comfortable."

Leaning down to give Rick a quick, rather chaste kiss, Jennie left the room and the others soon followed. When, at last, everyone had retired, Hildago and Mac made their way slowly to the master bedroom, their arms around one another's waists.

"You were quiet tonight. Is there something troubling you?" Mac asked, having noticed how subdued she'd been all evening.

"I'm just glad you are home, Mac," she told him simply, still not ready to tell him about Eve's message. "I was lost without you."

"I'm glad to be back, too. There's nothing I like better than coming home to you." Closing the door behind them, Mac leaned down to kiss her and they came together in a passionate embrace.

"I need you so much, Mac."

Hildago had been worried all night. She knew she had been wrong in not telling him right away about the letter, but she hadn't wanted to ruin the happiness of the evening. And

421

now, when the time was as right as it ever would be to tell him the bad news, she selfishly wanted to share in his loving just one more time before the pain of Eve's return ripped everything apart. She wanted to show Mac how much she really needed him. Then, she thought, she would be able to handle whatever happened with Eve.

Their lovemaking was wild and tinged with Hildago's desperation as she strove to please him in every way she could. And when he finally entered her, she cried out her pleasure, feeling, at last, complete as he filled her with his love.

Mac was surprised by her fervid response, and he cradled her to him, caressing her gently until, sated, he finally drifted off in sleep.

Lucia paced her darkened room, clutching the note she'd written to Rick and waiting impatiently for the moment when she could set her plan into action. She had heard Jennie return to her own chamber some moments before, and she was now anxiously anticipating Rick's return to his bedroom.

Stalking to the french doors, Lucia once again glanced out across the courtyard and was pleased to see that Rick had, at last, retired for the night and was standing in the open patio doorway of his room, slowly unbuttoning his shirt. Her eyes feasted on the sight of him as he stripped off the garment, and she drank in the beauty of his rugged, male frame as he turned away and disappeared back inside. Lucia shivered in excitement as she imagined that very soon he would be coming to her, wanting the love that only she could give him.

Hurrying across the room, she moved out into the hallway and went in search of a servant to do her bidding. Finally locating a young maid busily straightening the sitting room, she called out softly to her.

"Excuse me."

"Yes, ma'am? Did you need something?" the servant asked attentively.

"I was wondering if you could take a note to Rick Peralta for me?"

"To Rick Peralta?" The girl's eyes grew round, reflecting her speculation at the content of the missive that Lucia was holding out to her.

"Would you have the time to take it to him? It is only a note of thanks. He rescued me from Malo, and I wanted him to know how grateful I was." Lucia hoped she sounded earnest enough.

The maid's expression softened, and she smiled as she took the letter. "Of course. I'll do it right now. The men have only just gone to their rooms, so I'm sure he'll still be awake."

"Thank you. It's very kind of you." Lucia smiled warmly and started back to her room, taking care to keep her exuberance from showing.

For the third time in as many minutes, Rick strode to the patio doors and glanced out across the court in the direction of Jennie's bedroom. Though he knew she had to be discreet and wait until she could leave her room unobserved, it did not lessen the agony of his eager anticipation. God, how he wanted her! Each passing minute seemed an hour as he waited for her to come to him, and he wondered how he'd ever existed without her.

Rick had thought Jennie an uncommon beauty when he saw her dressed only in riding clothes. But when she had joined him for dinner, he had been amazed at her transformation. Clad in more feminine attire, she was positively gorgeous! The gown she had worn was far from revealing, but her innate sensuality had been enhanced by its very softness of style.

His heart had been thundering in his chest through the long meal and then, when they'd been forced to linger in the sitting room—well, suffice it to say that it had been more a chamber of horrors than a family's parlor. With her nestled so gently, so trustingly against him, it had been all he could do not to take her right there in front of everybody! The feel of her hip pressing so close to his and the brush of her breast against his arm had strained his control to the very limit. He had been more than relieved when Jennie had made her excuses and gone on to bed for it had given him the opportunity to leave, too.

Now, here he stood alone in the darkness, remembering the sweetness of loving her, and his patience was wearing thin. He was just about ready to throw caution to the wind and go get her when the knock sounded at his door. Mumbling a curse under his breath, he stalked across the room and threw wide the portal.

"Yes? What is it?" he asked more sharply than he'd intended.

"I just have a note for you, sir." The maid held Lucia's letter out toward him.

Rick frowned as he took the offered missive from her. "A letter? Yes, well, thank you."

"Yes, sir."

Turning back into his room, Rick closed the door and moved nearer to the lamp so he could read the mysterious note.

Rick
   It is important that I speak with you at once. Meet me in sitting room.

Lucia

Scowling, he tossed the letter onto the table near the nightstand. The last thing he felt like doing was talking to Lucia, but he was afraid that if he didn't go, she would be brazen enough to come to his room. And if there was one thing he didn't need, it was Lucia knocking on the door when

424

Jennie was in his bed. Rick looked out across the courtyard one last time to make sure that Jennie wasn't on her way and then, after pulling on a clean shirt, he left his room to see what it was Lucia wanted.

Lucia had been observing his every movement and the moment he left, she made her move. Wearing only a dressing gown that one of the maids had given her earlier in the day, she darted across the patio and into Rick's bedroom. She made fast work of rumpling the sheets on his bed and then quickly threw off her wrapper and snatched up the shirt he had earlier discarded.

Clad only in a seductive nightgown, Jennie silently left her chamber and made her way toward Rick's. Her excitement was great as she remembered the bliss of his embrace, and she quickened her step, eager to be in his arms once again. She noted with pleasure that he had left the french doors ajar, and she slipped into the room, softly calling out his name.

"Rick?" Jennie was totally unprepared for the sight that greeted her, and she stood in numbing silence, staring at Lucia. The other woman was standing at the foot of Rick's bed wearing only his shirt! "Lucia! What are you doing in here?" she demanded as she stepped farther into the chamber, not wanting to believe her eyes but knowing the damning evidence could not be denied.

"Now—Don't be upset—Rick didn't mean for this to happen—I was supposed to hurry." She groaned with fake remorse.

"What are you talking about?" Jennie was outraged.

"I came to thank him for all of his help—and, well, I guess we just got carried away." Lucia deliberately stumbled over her words so that they sounded more believable. "I know how much he loves you, and I wouldn't want to cause you any trouble—"

"Cause me any trouble?" She glared at the barely clad woman with distaste. "You haven't caused me any trouble.

You may have just saved me from making the biggest mistake of my life. Where is Rick?"

"Oh, he, uh—" Even as she spoke the door opened and Rick walked into the room, totally unaware of the maelstrom that was brewing.

"Jennie—Lucia? What the—"

But before he could continue, Jennie raged toward him, more angry than she'd ever been in her life.

"Why you—" she seethed and without hesitation, she drew back and slapped him full force. Blinded by tears, Jennie stormed away, leaving Rick watching her in stunned bewilderment. Coming face to face with Lucia, Jennie felt no regret as she gave her a hearty shove backward that sent her sprawling obscenely on the bed. "You want her? Well, you've got her!" And with that Jennie fled the room.

Not wanting to give Rick time to think, Lucia moved sinuously off the bed and came to stand before him. "Rick— I'm so sorry."

"What the hell is going on here?" he thundered, trying to brush past Lucia and go after Jennie.

"Wait, Rick, I'll explain." She grabbed his arm and momentarily halted his progress.

Easily shaking off her grip, he glared down at her, understanding for the first time what a conniving bitch she really was. His movements reflecting his barely controlled violence, Rick picked up her discarded dressing gown and threw it at her. "Cover yourself and get out of here!"

"No, please, let me tell you—"

"Tell me what?" He sneered viciously. "How you tricked me into leaving so you could play out this charade in front of Jennie?"

"But, Rick! I know I can please you!" she pleaded desperately as she realized that instead of winning him for her own, she had just lost him completely. "I love you!"

"You don't know the meaning of the word! Get out of my sight or I swear I won't be responsible for my actions!" Rick turned away from her as she stripped off his shirt and nervously tugged on the wrapper.

"Rick?"

"Go." His voice was flat and emotionless as he fought to control the fury that raged within him.

Lucia stared at him helplessly for a moment and then fled the room.

When Rick was sure that she'd gone, he drew a shaky breath and nervously raked his hand through his hair. Now what was he going to do? He knew he had to go after Jennie—to explain everything and try to make her understand, but the little scene Lucia had just staged had been so convincing.

As he glanced blankly around the room, he spotted the note on the table and grinned broadly in relief. Picking it up, he raced after his love, determined that their night of ecstasy not be ruined by Lucia's selfish plotting.

"Jennie!" Rick spoke in low harsh tones as he tried to open the courtyard door to her room that was now locked tightly against him. "Jennie, let me in. I have something I have to show you!"

"Go away." Her answer was hushed yet full of venom.

"Jennie, this is important. You know that I love you. How can you doubt that after all we've been to each other?" Silence greeted his declarations. "Jennie—I don't want to, but if you don't open this door right now, I'll break it in."

Jennie glowered at the locked doors resentfully and then slowly climbed off her bed. She had no doubt that Rick would do exactly what he threatened, and she did not want to risk waking the rest of her family. With a trembling hand, she unlocked the portal and opened the doors slightly to glare out at him.

"What do you want?" she asked in a tight voice.

"Jennie—" he began, but she cut him off quickly.

"I thought you said you had something to show me? Well? What is it?"

"Here. Read this." He handed the note to her and the moment she released the door to take it, he shouldered his way into her room.

"I don't want you in here!" Jennie protested as he walked passed her.

"Read it, Jennie. Then tell me you want me to go and I'll leave."

Jennie unfolded the sheet of paper and read it quickly before looking back up at Rick. "What is this?"

"Lucia sent that to me to get me out of my room so that she could sneak in."

"What are you talking about? I saw her there, wearing your shirt—and in your bed." Tears stung her eyes as she remembered the trauma of finding the other woman in his room.

"Jennie, love, nothing happened. It was all a ruse."

"How can you say that?"

"For God's sake, sweetheart! I wasn't even there!" Rick could see that his last statement had made an impact on her, and he pushed his advantage. "Lucia's never made any secret of the fact that she wanted me, you know that. I guess she thought that if she could drive a wedge between us, I would turn to her."

"How do I know that you didn't meet her in the sitting room and then take her back to your bedroom?" Jennie challenged, her eyes glittering with unshed tears.

"Why would I have taken her to my room when I knew that you were due there at any minute? Think, Jennie. Does any of it make sense? I'd waited all day just to hold you. Do you really think that I would have traded a lifetime of love with you for a brief moment of lust with Lucia?"

"Oh, Rick!" A shiver of emotion went through Jennie as she realized how close she had come to throwing away her love, and Lucia's note dropped unheeded to the floor as she went to him. "I love you! I didn't want to believe it, but—"

"Hush, darling." He soothed her, relief flooding through

428

him as he held her close. "It's all over now."

"I'm sorry I didn't trust you."

Rick drew back to look down at her, savoring her beauty. "I love you, Jennie. I couldn't let anything come between us. I don't know what I'd do if I ever lost your love."

"You'll never have to worry." She sighed, nestling against him. "I'll never doubt you again."

Rick bent to her then, his mouth meeting hers in a flaming kiss that rendered them both breathless. Without speaking another word, he swept her up into his arms and strode from her room, not stopping until he'd entered his own. Carrying her to the bed, he lay her gently down before quickly turning out the lamp.

"I love you, Jennie." His tone was husky with excietment as he shed his shirt and then quickly joined her.

The room was dark, save for what little moonlight streamed through the windows, but to the lovers it made no difference. Theirs had become a world of all the senses, not just sight.

Sighing, she reached out to him, caressing the leanness of his ribs. "And I love you. Rick?"

"What?"

"I'm sorry I slapped you." Her words were heartfelt.

"Hush, darling. It's not important. What's important is here—and now." Trapping her hand, he held it over his heart, and she could feel its powerful rhythm. "I want you, Jennie. I've been aching to hold you like this all day."

Moving brazenly closer, she smiled and teased, "Did you only want to hold me?"

"Actually," he confided, his eyes darkening in passion as he finally gave full vent to his long-supressed desires, "I did have something a little more exciting in mind."

"Oh? Show me," she murmured as his mouth found hers in a long lingering kiss.

Her love for him was so great and her need for him so overpowering that she gave herself over to him with no reservations. It had been so long since last they'd loved. Her hands were never still as he shifted closer, and she clung to him weakly as his lips descended to press heated kisses on her breasts through the gossamer material of the gown. When Rick slid one leg erotically between hers, Jennie gasped and arched against the enthralling hardness of his male frame.

"You are so lovely," Rick said, drawing back to stare down at her. "So lovely." With a single finger, he traced teasing patterns over her nipples where his kisses had left the filmy cloth damp, and she moaned low in her throat at his play.

"Rick, please, love me," Jennie begged, wanting to feel his welcoming weight upon her and the surge of his manly power filling her aching emptiness.

Rick gave a low answering chuckle but made no move to possess her fully, yet. He had been waiting too long to rush the moment, and he wanted to savor every second of it.

Gently, he stripped the gown from her and, after tossing it carelessly aside, he kissed her again, pulling her full-length against him. Jennie moved restlessly as his every arousing touch drove her closer and closer to the edge of bliss.

Rolling Jennie on her back, Rick trailed passionate kisses along her throat and then dipped lower to claim her breasts, drawing each throbbing peak into his mouth in turn and suckling them gently until she cried out her pleasure. Tossing feverishly beneath him, Jennie wrapped her legs about his hips, straining ever nearer as his mouth continued its play, and she arched to him in uncontrollable ecstasy when he moved lower to explore the essence of her womanhood.

Her climax was shattering, pulsing through her in waves of rapture that left her pliant to his will. Rick didn't want her to be a mere recipient of his passion; he wanted Jennie to share in his excitement. Easing himself from her, he shed the rest of his clothes before joining her once again on the bed. Fitting himself to her intimately, he rubbed his hips sensuously against hers, wanting her to feel the passion in him.

"Jennie."

She opened her eyes and gazed up at him with open adoration.

"Love me, Jennie," he murmured thickly and kissed her again.

A contented languor had stolen over Jennie, yet at the insistent feel of his arousal pressed to her, something elemental and wanton stirred to life within her. She wanted to satisfy him as perfectly as he had pleased her. Jennie reached down to caress him with knowing hands and then urged him over onto his back. Using the same pattern of teasing kisses, she brought him to the peak of fulfillment with her lips and tongue before moving over him to take him deeply within her body.

As Rick's hands guided her hips, they strove for completion together, their movements frenzied with their desire. Suddenly, no longer content to be on the bottom, Rick shifted positions and pulled her under him, driving forcefully into her soft, wet warmth. Jennie reveled in his taking command and, wrapping her limbs around him, she held him close as he thrust against her. Each ardent stroke stoked the fires of their passion higher, until, in a burst of ecstasy, the flames of desire erupted into glowing beauty. Clasped together, they drifted; their hearts pounding in unison, their souls joined forever in love's perfect promise.

Lucia was frustrated and furious as she sat alone in her room. How dare Rick throw her out of his room without even giving her a chance to explain! It didn't matter to her that he had been right in his accusations. What mattered was that she knew now just how truly hopeless her desire for him was.

Lucia realized that after tonight she would never be able to face Rick again, and she knew that she had to leave. And leave she would, she decided in anger, but not the way Mac

431

McCaine wanted her to go—shipped back to Mexico to live out a fate worse than death. No, she was going on her own terms. She would go now and she would take Pablo with her.

Lucia was certain that it would be easy to rescue Pablo for McCaine had made no mention of having someone stand guard on him tonight. The most difficult thing she had to do, she realized, would be in getting to the horses, but with Pablo's help, she knew they would make it.

When Lucia heard Rick cross the courtyard in pursuit of Jennie, she tried to listen to their conversation, but once he entered her room it had been impossible to distinguish their words. It was only a short time later that she heard footsteps outside on the patio again, and she rushed to her doorway to watch in impotent fury as he strode purposefully back to his chamber carrying Jennie in his arms.

Jealousy ate at Lucia as she watched them disappear into his bedroom and she momentarily forgot her plan to leave. Her hatred of Jennie overwhelmed her. Why should Jennie have everything that she, Lucia, had always desired?

Beyond reason, Lucia slipped from her room and entered Jennie's. Filled with envy, she stared about her. From the silver comb and brush set on the dressing table to the expensive furniture, the room bespoke of the McCaine's wealth, and resentment built within her. Savagely, she pulled all of Jennie's dresses from her wardrobe and threw them on the floor. With equal glee, she set about dumping out all the contents of the drawers in her chest and then followed with pulling all the bedclothes from the bed.

Feeling much better for having vented some of her anger, she started to leave the room, but then paused as her gaze fell upon the silver brush and comb set. With malicious intent, Lucia stripped the pillowcase off Jennie's pillow, determined not to leave empty-handed. Snatching up the brush and comb, she dropped them into the pillow slip and also tossed in a silver-framed portrait. Rummaging through Jennie's clothes, she picked out two dresses to take along with her and then quietly sneaked out of the room by way of the hallway door, once more intent on her original purpose.

Lucia remembered seeing the gun cabinet in the hall near the front door, and she went directly there for she knew she would need at least two rifles plus sidearms for both Pablo and herself. Silently turning the key that had been carelessly left in the lock, Lucia swung open the case door and chose the weapons. Shoving extra cartridges into her makeshift bag, she hurried from the house, eager to free Pablo and be gone.

Her movements furtive, Lucia crept near the bunk house, hoping to overhear in the conversation between the men inside exactly where Pablo had been locked up. She carried only a pistol with her, having stashed her bag near the stables, and she was poised, ready to take flight should anyone discover her presence.

The men of the M Circle C, however, were exhausted this night, and the last thing they were expecting was for someone to cause trouble right there on the ranch.

"Who d'ya think's gonna get Steve's job?" one man asked as they sat around the table in the center of the room.

"Probably Sandy or Jerry, 'cause they've been working here the longest," another added. "But it really just depends on Mac."

"What are they going to do with that outlaw we got out back."

Lucia was relieved at the mention of Pablo and, remaining motionless, she continued to listen attentively.

"Haven't heard, but I'm sure they ain't gonna let him sit around here long. They'll probably take him into town and turn him over to the law tomorrow."

A murmur of agreement went through the men gathered there.

"I hope they do, because as long as we've got him locked up out there in one of the tool sheds, I keep thinking that maybe Malo will show up."

"Nope. I think we've seen the last of him."

Their conversation continued, but Lucia didn't care. She had found out where Pablo was and that was all she needed to know. Slinking away into the shadows of the night, she tried to figure out which of the outbuildings was the one holding him. Darting from shed to shed, she checked each one until she finally found him.

"Pablo?"

"Lucia?" His answer came excitedly from inside the windowless shelter.

"It is me. I'm going to try to get you out of there. Do you know where the key is?" she asked as she noted the big padlock on the door.

"On a nail—around on the side of the building some-where."

Lucia quickly located it, smiling at her victory. Unlocking the door, she swung it open slowly.

Pablo emerged cautiously from the blackness of the interior. "Is it safe?"

"So far. Come, we must hurry so we can be far away from here by sunup. They were planning to take you into town tomorrow real early, so they will come looking for you then."

"Put the lock back on, just in case somebody comes out to check," he instructed. "Do you have horses?"

"No, not yet. I'll need your help for that, but I did manage to steal some guns."

"Good." Pablo was pleased. He didn't understand why she would be helping him, after the way she'd run off with Cazador, but he wasn't about to argue with being rescued. There would be time enough later to find out her motives. "Where are the stables?"

"This way. Come on!" Lucia directed, taking care to keep her voice low as she led the way, and Pablo hurried after her.

Lucia took him first to where she'd hidden her booty. After giving him a rifle and gun and holster, they entered the stable expecting trouble and were amazed to find that there was no guard posted. Even the old man who lived in a room off to the side slept soundly the entire time they were inside. They led the mounts they'd picked some distance from the stable before mounting up.

"Lucia." Pablo gave her an admiring look. "Remind me to thank you properly sometime."

"You can thank me properly by making sure we get out of here alive," she told him sharply.

"But why did you do it? After you ran off with Cazador, I would never have suspected that you would want to help us—me—"

She snorted disagreeably. "Cazador is not who you think he is, and I did not find out until it was too late. The infamous El Cazador is, in reality, none other than Juan Peralta's grandson, Ricardo Peralta."

"What?"

"That's right. He just rode along with us until he found the right time to try to help the old man escape."

"But why did you go with him?"

She shrugged, "At the time, I thought he was smarter than Malo, and I figured I would be better off with him. Now I know I was wrong, but it's too late."

"Maybe not," Pablo answered mysteriously.

"What do you mean?"

"For all that they may think Malo's dead, I've got a feeling he's very much alive somewhere."

"But how do we find him?"

"That I don't know, but if we could locate him again—knowing what we know now—"

"But where would he have gone? Mesa Roja?"

"Probably. And then he'd make it his business to find the nearest saloon," Pablo answered.

They nodded in silent agreement and rode off in the direction of town.

Hildago could not sleep. The long hours of the night had

435

been slow to pass, and she lay beside Mac, still restless. She knew she should wake him and give him the news, but she didn't want to disturb his badly needed rest. Unable to stay in bed any longer, she rolled away from him and sat up on the edge of the mattress, preparing to get up.

"Where are you going?" Mac's sleep-husky tones startled her, and she gasped. Mac sat up and stared at her questioningly after hearing her gasp. "Hildago? What is it?"

"Nothing—nothing, really," she protested too quickly, rising from the bed and hoping to break the link of intimacy between them, but Mac came after her.

Earlier, when she had been so quiet, Mac had suspected that something was troubling her, but she had denied it. Now, he was sure of it, and he wanted her to share whatever it was with him. Maybe he could help.

"Darling, I've never seen you this way before. Tell me what it is. I'm sure I can help. You know I love you."

Hildago faced him, then. Her dark eyes were wide with worry, her features pale at the thought of the news she was about to give him.

"It is something that I have to tell you that has me upset. If I could avoid this, believe me, I would. But there's no way."

Mac was completely at a loss to understand what she was talking about. "I don't understand—"

"I have to give you something. It's in your study." Moving to the foot of the bed, she picked up her dressing gown and shrugged it on while Mac hastily pulled on his pants.

Without saying another word, Hildago headed through the darkened house straight to Mac's study. She paused only long enough to light one lamp before picking up the envelope and holding it out to him.

"This came for you while you were gone." She was careful to keep the emotion out of her voice.

"What is it?" He frowned as he took the missive from her. "Who's this from?" Looking down at it, he suddenly blanched. "No, it can't be, not now!"

436

In one vicious motion he ripped the sealed envelope open, pulled out the single page letter from within and began to read silently to himself.

> *My dearest husband,*
> *I have been hoping for a reconciliation between us for some time now and can only pray that you have, too. I have missed you, darling, and am waiting anxiously to hear from you.*
> *I am staying at the hotel in town, but would much rather be with you and my children. Please come as soon as you can.*
>
> *As always*
> *Eve*

"My God!" He breathed shakily, sinking down into the chair behind his desk. When he looked up at Hildago, his expression was at first bewildered, but it soon changed to enraged. "My God! The woman must be crazy!"

"Then it was from Eve." Hildago sighed.

"Here! Read it for yourself!" He thrust the sheet of paper into her hand as he stood up and began to pace the room.

Hildago read the letter and looked up at him, stricken. "She can't mean this."

"Who knows with that woman?" He ran a hand nervously through his hair as he tried to figure out what to do. "The hell with it." He swore violently. "I'm going into town right now!"

"But, Mac! It's the middle of the night!" She tried to stop him, fearful of what he might do in his frenzy of anger.

"You're damn right it is!" He looked at Hildago. "And that's exactly why I'm going, now. I doubt she'll be expecting me at this hour."

And with that he hurried from the study and headed back to their bedroom to finish dressing. Nervously, she watched him go, and in her heart she said a prayer that somehow, everything would all turn out all right.

Hildago followed him after a moment, hoping that there was something she could say that would help to calm him, but she knew by the expression on his face that it was useless. Resigning herself to the fact that Mac had to handle this in his own way, she said nothing until he strapped on his gunbelt and prepared to leave.

"Mac, what should I tell Jake and Jennie and Carrie?"

"You won't have to tell them anything because there's nothing they need to know. I'll be back long before sunup, so don't worry." He checked his sidearm to see if it was loaded and then slid it neatly into the holster as he started from the room.

"Mac!" Hildago cried desperately. She wanted to run to Mac and cling to him so she could keep him from leaving, but she refrained with great effort. "Please, don't do anything foolish."

Mac only looked at her with a studied coolness and then, without a word, left the room.

Chapter Thirty-two

"I will stay here," Lucia whispered to Pablo as they hid behind the stable in Mesa Roja. "They will be looking for us in the morning, and the fewer people there are who have seen us together, the better."

"All right," Pablo said, knowing she was right. "I will check out the saloon and come back for you."

"Good. I will be waiting," she answered, glad now to be in town and away from the threat of discovery by the McCaines.

Pablo moved easily out into the street and headed for Dolly's. The crowd at the saloon was thinning out as he entered, and he made his way across the smoke-filled room to the bar.

"Whiskey," he ordered, tossing a coin across the counter to the barkeep.

Ed set up the stranger's drink and pocketed the money. "New here, aren't ya?"

"Just passin' through." Pablo turned his back on the inquisitive bartender as he surveyed the room, hoping for some sign of Malo. "I'll probably be moving on in the morning."

Malo had been sitting at his favorite table in the corner, entertaining himself with several of the girls who worked in the establishment when he saw Pablo enter. He didn't know by what stroke of luck his *compadre* had escaped death at the hands of the Apache, but he was glad. Without appearing to be too much in a hurry, he dismissed the women and ambled to the bar.

"Pablo?" He ventured.

"Hey! *Compadre!*" Pablo knew better than to use his real name. "I did not know you would be here!"

Malo shrugged. "I got tired of riding so I settled in here for a while. What brings you to Mesa Roja?"

"At last, I am heading home." He sounded relieved without giving too much away.

"It has been so long since we've had a chance to talk. Let's get a bottle and share a drink!" Malo clapped him on the back.

"I would like that."

"I already have a room. Bartender! A bottle of whiskey!" Malo paid for the proffered liquor and then led Pablo up to his room.

When they were secreted in his bedroom, the door locked behind them, he embraced Pablo heartily. "It is good to see you, my friend. I had thought you dead."

"And I you. How did you get away from Mac McCaine?"

"There was a small cave. I hid there until they turned back and then I followed them out," Malo explained. Then growing curious, he asked, "How did you get away from the Indians *and* the McCaines?"

"I have Lucia to thank for being free tonight."

"Lucia?" His expression hardened at the mention of the woman who had betrayed him. "The *puta!* I will see her in hell!"

"Do not be so hard on her. She realizes now how wrong she was," Pablo said.

"She does?"

"It is a long story and one I'm not sure you want to hear."

"What do you mean?"

"Cazador."

"What about him?" Malo was instantly curious. He had wondered what lies Cazador had told the McCaines in order to ride so freely in their midst.

"The infamous El Cazador is really Ricardo Peralta, the old man's grandson!"

"He what?" Rage surged through him.

"Cazador is, in reality, Rick Peralta. He joined up with us just to rescue his grandfather."

"He played me for a fool!" Malo took a deep swig from the bottle of whiskey, and when he looked up at Pablo his eyes were cold and deadly. "I will kill him. He cheated me out of the gold and my woman! No man does that to Miguel Malo and gets away with it!"

Pablo nodded, understanding his fury. "Lucia didn't find out who Cazador really was until it was too late, and by then she knew that you wouldn't take her back. She was trapped."

"It was by her own choice. Do not expect me to care about her, Pablo. You would be asking too much," Malo said as he tried to figure out a way to get even with Cazador/Peralta. He could not believe he'd been so stupid! Why, he had even promised Cazador half of the gold. No wonder the gunman had been so reluctant to commit himself! It had already been his gold! He glanced up at Pablo quickly. "Where is Cazador now?"

"At the McCaine ranch."

"That is where Lucia rescued you from?"

"Yes. She was staying in the main house."

"She was?"

"Yes. They had accepted her as one of them. She risked everything to free me. She even stole the guns we have and helped me to get the horses."

"And she is here? Now?"

"Yes. She is waiting down by the stable."

Malo took another drink from the bottle and then handed the bottle to Pablo. "If she has been in the McCaine house, she knows everything that is going on. Go and get her and bring her to me."

Pablo chugged a good portion of the liquor and then asked, "You will not hurt her?"

"No. I will not hurt her," he said flatly. "But what I am going to do is get even with Ricardo Peralta. I do not like to be made to look the idiot, and he is going to pay for his attempt. I will need Lucia's help, so you can tell her she will be safe with me."

"She will be glad." Pablo started from the room.

"Pablo, bring her up the back steps."

"Right."

"And Pablo?" Malo waited until the other man looked to him. "How did you get away from the Apache?"

"It was Rick Peralta and Jake McCaine. They circled around behind the Indians and drove them off."

Malo did not want to hear about what a great Indian fighter the man was. "Go," he said with disgust. "Get Lucia. We have much to plan."

Pablo quickly left the room to find Lucia and bring her back.

Eve lay, wide awake, in her bed at the hotel. The day had been long, hot, and tedious, and though she was exhausted, sleep would not come. Tense and on edge, she had retired early in hopes that blissful rest would relieve the feeling of disquiet that had been haunting her, but the solitude and darknes in the room only intensified her anxiety.

Giving up the effort to sleep, she left the bed and moved to stand at the window, staring out across the deserted streets of Mesa Roja. Though she was not one given to introspection, Eve wondered how she had ever come to this. She was a beautiful, sought-after woman, and yet here she was alone, nearly broke and growing more desperate with each passing day. She knew her bad times were all Andre's fault. Why, if he had just stayed out of trouble with the law, they would be together somewhere right now, enjoying life and each other.

The thought of Andre and his passion-filled lovemaking

filled Eve with frustration. It had been so long since she'd been with a man. Had it been another town, she would have considered taking a lover, but she couldn't risk the scandal. Not here in Mac's town.

Groaning at the thought of remaining celibate, she stumbled to her trunk and searched through her things until she found what she was looking for: the small silver cask filled with her favorite brandy. She had intended to nurse the expensive liquor along, but tonight she no longer cared. She needed relief from her thoughts and her body, and from long experience she knew that only drinking could help. Tilting the flask to her lips, she drank deeply, wanting to achieve mindlessness as quickly as possible.

Going back to bed, she plumped the pillow and, using it for support, she settled herself back against the headboard, brandy in hand. She thought idly of Mac as the liquor's potency eased her worries, and she wondered what he looked like now. He had been a handsome man years ago, but at that time she had wanted more from life than a good-looking husband. Stlll, she mused, they had been good together in bed, and she found the possibility of bedding him now most interesting. Eve took another drink and smiled as she imagined using her body to bend the arrogant Mac McCaine to her will. Pondering the thought, she relaxed and closed her eyes as a pleasant wave of forgetfulness washed over her.

The night was beautiful, silvered by the moon's clear brightness, but Mac took little notice as he rode toward town at a vicious pace. Though his horse was lathered and straining, he kept on, clearheaded in his purpose.

Eve. Her name screamed through his mind. He had loved her so much and she had betrayed him. To this day he didn't understand why she'd gone. He had given her everything: his life, his love, his children, and she had walked away from it all. And she had never looked back, at least, not until now.

A tremor of emotion shook him as he remembered the fateful day when he'd returned from working the few head of cattle they'd owned to discover Eve's absence. He'd been a wild man at first, searching everywhere for her. She had been so beautiful and he'd been so afraid that something terrible might have happened to her. In the beginning, it hadn't occurred to him that she might not want to be found. Only after long, agonizing fruitless months of trying to locate her did he realize that she really had deserted him and their three young children, that she had meant everything she'd written in the note she'd left. That was when the bitterness had nearly consumed him.

Hildago had come into his life then, to care for Jake, Jennie, and Carrie, and what had begun in his heart as gratitude to her, over the years, had blossomed into love. Though she was a completely different kind of woman from Eve, she offered him the undying devotion and tender support that he'd needed to build the M Circle C into the successful ranch that it was today.

Hildago was, in truth, his life's partner, and now that Eve had returned, he was going to make sure that whatever ties still existed between them were severed. He wanted nothing whatsoever to do with Mrs. Eve McCaine, and the sooner she left town, the better.

Mac worried briefly that Eve might attempt to contact the children, but he put that from his mind. Somehow, he would have to convince her that they were not interested in meeting with her. He had taken great care to erase her from their lives, and he wanted to keep it that way.

As the lights of Mesa Roja appeared on the horizon, Mac slowed his breakneck speed for he did not want to cause any undue attention to himself when he reached town. What he had to handle would be best kept quiet. Everyone believed his wife to be dead and he planned to maintain that facade.

"Lucia?" Pablo's call was almost a whisper.

"I am here." Lucia stepped from behind a small shed. "Did you find Malo?"

"Yes. He has a room over the saloon, and he wants to see you," Pablo told her urgently.

"He does?" she asked warily. She had known Miguel Malo for too long to trust him in this matter.

"Yes," he confirmed. "I told him everything, and he wants to talk with you. He promised me that he wouldn't hurt you."

"Ha!" She was more than a little frightened at the prospect of seeing him again.

"Lucia," Pablo said, touching her shoulder, "I will not allow him to lay a hand on you. I will protect you, should the need arise. All right?"

Her eyes glowed with gratitude and she nodded her agreement. Leading their horses, they headed for the saloon, being careful to stay out of sight. It was then that they saw him.

"Look, Pablo!" Lucia hissed, nervously. "It's Mac McCaine!"

"Ah, *Dios!* How could they have found out so soon?"

"What are we going to do?"

"Let's watch first and see where he goes. Then, if there is time, we can warn Malo."

Tying their horses, they crept through the shadows to watch Mac's progress through town.

Mac was glad when he found the streets deserted, and he reined in calmly in front of the hotel and dismounted with a seeming casualness that belied the tense anger within him. The town was quiet except for the raucous music coming from Dolly's, and he strode slowly toward the hotel entrance, he thought, unobserved.

"The hotel?" Lucia looked at Pablo, confused.

"The sheriff's office is farther down the street. Why would he have gone into the hotel?"

"Maybe he's not after us," she murmured hopefully.

"I don't know, but I think we'd better tell Malo right away. Since no one has seen us together yet, we can get you into his room, and we should still be safe," Pablo said. "Come on. Let's go."

The small lobby of the hotel was unattended as usual with only a single lamp burning low, but it was all the light Mac needed as he reached the desk and flipped the register open, searching for Eve's signature. He cursed under his breath as he saw *Mrs. Mac McCaine.* Damn Eve! Now the whole town would be wondering about her. Noting the room number, he rushed up the stairs.

Mac located her room with little difficulty and, after trying the knob and finding the door locked, he put his booted foot against it and, uncaring that someone might hear, he pushed. The lock gave with a splintering groan, and the door flew open, banging loudly against the wall.

Eve had finally managed to fall asleep after having drained her flask of all its precious contents, and she was caught totally by surprise by Mac's precipitous entrance into her room. The crash of the door brought her bolt upright in bed, and she stared in horror at the shadowed figure of the man who stood framed in her doorway.

"Who is it?" Eve whispered, but he didn't speak to her. Instead, the man turned to the few peole who'd appeared in the hall.

"It's all right, folks. The lock just stuck. Go on back to bed," the man said.

Eve recognized his voice and she watched uneasily as he stepped slowly into her dimly lighted room and forced the broken door shut behind him.

"Mac," she whispered, and her eyes widened as he crossed the room to stand at the foot of her bed.

His expression was wooden as he stared down at her, and though Eve was tempted to hide from his glaring presence, she faced him boldly, the liquor she'd consumed giving her extra courage.

"Well, I'm certainly glad you finally managed to get here," she told him brazenly, and she was pleased to see the stunned flicker of emotion that crossed his face. "And, Mac McCaine, I certainly hope that you plan to pay for the damage to the door. You could have knocked, you know."

Eve let the covers she'd been clutching to her drop to her lap, revealing the lace and silk bodice of her gown.

"Shut up," he said flatly, trying not to look at the outline of her breasts beneath the satiny gown. "I want to know why you're here."

"Why, Mac," Eve began coyly, "I thought I made that perfectly clear in my letter. I'm back. I want to be with you and my children."

"Why now, Eve? After all this time?"

Eve knew she'd won a small victory when he used her name, and she decided to press her advantage. Shrugging, her gown straps slipped from her shoulders, exposing the tops of her full breasts, and she smiled to herself as his gaze lingered on the smoothness of her alabaster flesh.

"Is that as important as the fact the I am here—now?" Eve leaned toward him to give him a better view of her bosom. She remembered how enamored Mac had always been with her body, and she hoped to awaken those feelings within him again. "Mac," she said throatily, "I've missed you."

Mac couldn't seem to tear his gaze away from the glory of her breasts, and as the memory of their time together came flooding back, heat surged through his body. He remembered the taste of her and the smell of her and the endless hours they'd spent making love.

Eve read his reactions correctly and moved to kneel before him. "Mac, did you miss me, too? Maybe, just a little?"

She wanted to break the rigid control he had over himself and entice him to take her right then. She had been longing for a man, and she knew that Mac would certainly be able to satisfy her.

Eve smiled up at him, her eyes smoky with desire. "Show me how much you missed me, Mac. Show me."

She started to reach out and touch him, but Mac wanted to stop her. He didn't want anything to do with her, and he grasped both of her forearms in a steely grip.

"The only thing I want to show you is the way out of town," he ground out, his jaw clenched against the desire that was burning through him. Eve saw the reaction his body was having to her nearness, and she laughed huskily. "Why fight it, Mac? You know you want me. You always have and you always will." And she allowed the gown to fall then, revealing to him the beauty of her hard-tipped breasts. "Touch me."

His iron-willed control snapped as she bared her bosom to him, and he shoved her back on the bed. In a vicious motion, he ripped the gown from her body and then stood over her, enjoying the sight of her sprawled naked before him. Mac knew he should leave. But the temptation she offered was too much, and if she wanted to act like the slut she was, then he would treat her like one. Following her down on the bed, he covered her nude body with his fully clad one.

Eve smiled with satisfaction, knowing that she could push him to the limits and still come out the winner. No wonder she had left him before: He was so predictable. She gave up her thoughts, though, as he began to explore her body with rough, almost angry caresses that she found very stimulating. This was certainly not the old Mac she'd remembered. Moving sinuously against him, she encouraged him in all the ways Andre had taught her. Eve wanted to prove to him that he couldn't resist her, and then she knew he'd give her everything she wanted.

Mac was on fire with desire as he caressed her. This was Eve, the woman he had loved beyond all reason. He remembered everything about her: the texture of her skin, the sensitivity of her breasts, and the way her softness surrounded him when he plunged deep within her.

Rational thought returned with a vengeance as he realized what he was doing. Shocked that he had lost control of himself, he jerked himself away from her, getting to his feet and stepping away from the bed.

"Mac, why did you leave me?" she purred, holding out a hand to him invitingly.

"Get up and get dressed. You're leaving here right now."

"Oh, good. Are you taking me out to the ranch?" Eve asked, thinking that he wanted more privacy for their more intimate reunion. "We would have more privacy there, I'm sure."

"The ranch?" Her words washed over him like ice cold water.

"Of course, and then once I'm all settled in, we can talk." She stretched languidly on the bed.

"You'll never set foot on my ranch."

"What?" She was startled into reality by his words.

"You heard me," he said calmly as he looked down at her with a mixture of disgust and condemnation. "Now, get up and clothe yourself, woman."

"But you wanted me. And we are still married," she said as a shiver of apprehension shook her.

"That's a mere technicality as far as I'm concerned. Now that I know where you are, it will be a simple matter to start divorce proceedings."

"You'd divorce me?"

"I'd have done it long ago but I didn't know where you'd gone."

"But I don't want a divorce. Think of the scandal."

"Don't you think it's a little too late to worry about scandals? You're the one who left me with three children to raise, remember? And you're the one who returned unannounced and signed the register Mrs. Mac McCaine."

"How can you be so cruel when I've come back to you so

449

willingly." She tried another ploy, forcing tears and looking up at him pleadingly.

"I'm not being cruel, Eve. I'm just stating the facts."

"But you want me. I could feel it in your embrace just now."

"You are sadly deluding yourself if you think that I want you back in my life. What happened between us just now could have happened with any woman who bared her breasts to me and taunted me the way you did. I used you as I would use any whore."

She realized then that she had greatly underestimated him and that it was too late to correct the damage she'd done.

"I want to see my children. If you don't want anything to do with me, maybe they will." She was desperate for another angle to gain a place in his life.

Mac had been expecting her to bring up Jake and Jennie and Carrie, and he was ready for her. "They have absolutely no desire to see you. They know that you deserted them. They know that you never once tried to make contact with them when they were growing up. And they know what kind of a woman you really are."

"I want to hear them say it."

"No. I won't have you upsetting them any more than you already have. You will be on the next stage out of Mesa Roja, and I am personally going to put you on it."

Driven to the wall by the hopelessness of her situation, she came back at him viciously. "I won't go meekly, Mac. I'll create a disturbance in this town like they've never seen before, and when I'm through, your good name will be ruined."

Mac regarded her dispassionately. "I'll be back for you at sunup. Be packed and ready to leave."

Turning his back on her, he quietly opened the door and stepped out into the hall, closing the broken portal behind him.

Chapter Thirty-three

Pablo knocked softly on the door to Malo's room, and he was relieved when it was opened quickly.

"Get inside with her," Malo ordered, keeping his voice down, and they hurried in.

He stared at Lucia for a long minute, his dark eyes roaming contemptuously over her before turning to Pablo.

"Malo, we just spotted Mac McCaine riding into town," the other man told him hastily.

"What?"

"Mac just rode into town. He tied up in front of the hotel and went inside."

"Why would he be going to the hotel at this time of night?" Malo was puzzled.

"I don't know, but I think we'd better find out in a hurry." Pablo was worried. "If he is after us, then we're going to have to get out of town as soon as possible."

"Since he is alone, I'll go down to the bar and see what I can find out. He's never seen me close up, so there won't be any danger that I'll be recognized. You two wait here." Malo strode hurriedly from the room.

There were only a few patrons left in the saloon, and they were gathered around the bar, listening intently to something Ed was saying. As Malo approached, the conversation

451

lulled, but only to allow Ed to serve him. As soon as Malo had picked up his drink of tequila and started to a table, they began again.

"I heard him, I tell you! I was right outside the door!" a little man was saying with emphasis.

"Eavesdropping." One of the other men laughed.

"So what?" the man challenged and then went on to defend himself. "I work in the hotel and it's my job to know what goes on over there."

At the mention of the hotel, Malo started paying close attention to their words.

"So, Ace, what you're telling us is that the woman registered over there as Mrs. Mac McCaine really is his wife, Eve?" Ed asked, incredulously.

"That's right," Ace answered proudly. "Why, I told you just the other day that she had young Billy deliver a letter out to the ranch addressed to Mac, and then she hired him to drive her all the way out there. But strangest thing of all is once they reached the ranch, she didn't go in. She told him to turn around and go back to town."

"But Mac's claimed for years that Eve was dead. If she was still alive, why did he lie?"

"I don't know, but even his children believe her to be dead. Jennie and Carrie used to talk about her all the time whenever they came into the store," added the shopkeeper, who'd been listening avidly to the conversation.

"I know. Even Jake believes his mother is dead. But why would Mac keep her existence a secret from them?"

"What did you hear, Ace, exactly?"

"I heard him ask her why she'd come back after all this time, but I couldn't make out much after that."

The rest of the men nodded their interest.

"He's coming this way, now!" someone announced softly, and the group quickly dispersed around the room, oblivious to Malo's studied exit up the stairs.

He didn't bother to knock as he reentered the bedroom,

and his unexpected appearance startled Lucia and Pablo.

"Well?" Pablo demanded. "What did you find out?"

"He's not here looking for us." Malo smiled as a plan began to form in his mind. "There seems to be some kind of mystery going on around here concerning McCaine and his supposedly *departed* wife."

"What are you talking about?"

"From what I understand, Mac McCaine's always been considered a widower, and yet while he was gone some woman showed up in town and registered at the hotel as Mrs. Mac McCaine." He frowned. "In fact, I think I saw her the other day."

"Wait!" Lucia said quickly, remembering the picture she'd taken from Jennie's room. "I think I may have a portrait of her." Rummaging through the sack she'd brought up to the room with her, Lucia finally found it. "Is this her?"

"What are you doing with this?" Malo asked as he took it from her.

She shrugged indifferently. "I didn't want to leave there empty-handed. The frame is silver, I think."

Malo stared at the picture of the much younger Eve. "Yes, I think this is the woman I saw the other day."

"So?" Pablo wondered what he was planning.

"If this really is his wife and if what I just heard downstairs is true, I think I've just found a way for us to get even with Ricardo Peralta."

"How?" Lucia asked eagerly.

"Evidently McCaine told his children that she was dead when, in truth, she was very much alive." Malo grinned evilly.

"You mean they don't know about her?"

"No, and that's why I think we've got the perfect chance to lure them into town."

Lucia's eyes were alight at the prospect of seeing Jennie suffer. "I'll send a message out to the ranch addressed to Jennie, begging her to come to town and sign it from

453

her mother."

"Do you think Rick will come with her?" Pablo asked.

"I'm sure of it," she declared bitterly.

"Well, if he does, then we'll ambush him when he gets here. And if he doesn't, we'll ride out to the ranch while the rest of them are in town. Maybe with a little forceful encouragement, he can be convinced to take us to the mine." Malo was pleased with the thought.

Mac entered the saloon, wanting only to pass the next few hours in solitude. The run-in with Eve had upset him more than he'd let on, and he needed time to get his thoughts together.

"Give me a whiskey, Ed," Mac ordered, sidling up to the bar.

"You got it, Mr. McCaine. How's it goin'?" Ed asked amiably enough, but Mac looked up at him sharply.

"Fine," he answered brusquely.

"You got Jennie back safely?"

"You'd heard?"

"Hildago sent word into town."

"Of course." He sighed and took a deep drink of the whiskey. "We just got back today. It was some chase, but everything turned out all right."

"What happened?"

"Some of Miguel Malo's men took Jennie captive."

"Malo was in the area?" The bartender was shocked by the news, and he would have been even more shocked to know that that very same gunman was staying upstairs.

Mac nodded as he took another drink. "I took a posse out from the ranch, and we rescued both Jennie and another captive he had in camp."

"But did you get him? He's about the most dangerous outlaw around."

"We got everybody but Malo. In fact, I've got one of his

men locked up out at the ranch now. Jake will be bringing him in to the sheriff in the morning."

"Do you think Malo's still around?"

"I don't know. Last I saw of him, we were up in the Superstitions."

"It's easy to lose a man in those mountains," Ed said. "Did you have any trouble with the Indians?"

"A small party of Apache attacked us on our way back, but we managed to run them off."

"Well, I'm glad you made it, and it's good to know that your daughter's all right. Most of the folks around town were worried about her."

"You can tell them she's doing just fine." Mac finished off his drink and pushed the glass back toward Ed. "Pour me another one."

"You staying in town tonight?"

"Yes, I had some unfinished business to attend to that couldn't wait until tomorrow."

"Would you like a room for the rest of the night?"

"No. There's no need, but thanks for the offer. I think I'll just settle in at a table and relax for a while."

"Sure thing, Mr. McCaine. You want the bottle to take with you?"

"Yes, thanks." Mac picked up the bottle of liquor and made his way to a table in a deserted corner of the saloon.

Oblivious to the curious glances of the other patrons, Mac refilled his glass again and downed it quickly as his thoughts turned to his encounter with Eve. Mac was glad that he'd come to his senses and had broken off their torrid embrace, and he wondered, somewhat guiltily, how he could have let things get out of control that way. He knew what kind of woman she was, and he knew he didn't love her, so why had he allowed himself to touch her?

Though he wanted to deny the answer that came to him, Mac knew he couldn't. He had always found Eve's blond beauty stimulating, and he remembered well how near to

455

perfect their lovemaking had been. He had wanted to see if that spark of passion still existed between them, and he'd been very disappointed to find out that it did. No matter what she'd done, he still found her exciting, and the thought upset him even as it stirred him.

Downing another glass of whiskey, Mac stared, unseeing, across the saloon. He would put Eve on the first stagecoach out of Mesa Roja tomorrow. There was no way he was going to let her cause trouble for him here in town, and there was no way he was going to let her near Jake, Jennie or Carrie. She'd made her choice years ago and now she had to live with it.

Firm in his resolve, he felt some of the tension leave him, and he sat back in his chair. Glancing out the window of the saloon, he was surprised to find that from where he sat, he could see the window to Eve's room in the hotel. Grimly, he kept his eyes fixed on that softly lighted portal, wondering what her thoughts were as she readied herself to leave town.

Eve was stalking angrily about her room, trying to figure out what to do next. The Mac McCaine she had just dealt with had been a different man from the one she'd known before, and she realized now, with unfailing certainty, that she had been the loser in that encounter. He had had the upper hand between them from the moment he'd shoved in the door. There had been little she could do to change it.

Knowing that Mac fully intended to put her on a stagecoach out of town the next day, Eve sat down heavily on her bed. She did not doubt for a moment that he was serious about divorcing her, too, and she knew that somehow, she had to get a financial settlement out of him. Eve tried to think of a way to convince him to pay her enough money to live comfortably. If he wanted her gone forever, as he said he did, that was just fine with her, but he'd have to be willing to pay for her continued absence.

456

The eastern horizon was slowly brightening as she lay back on the bed, and she hoped to get at least a few hours' rest.

Hildago stood at the window of the bedroom she shared with Mac, gazing out at the rising sun as his parting words echoed grimly through her mind. *I'll be back long before sunup, so don't worry.* It was certainly easier said than done, expecially since she knew he was with Eve.

Eve. Just the thought of her stirred resentment within Hildago. Mac's wife had had everything: a loving husband, three beautiful children, and a secure future. Yet she'd given it all up. Hildago shook her head, unable to comprehend a woman and mother who could abandon her family so easily.

Turning away from the lightening morning sky, she returned to their bed, hoping to get some rest. Mac loved her, she was sure of it, and just as soon as he could he would come home to her. The fact that he was late in returning from town, she chided herself, did not mean he was with Eve.

Yet the remembrance of the heartache he'd suffered those first years after Eve's desertion brought to mind just how deeply he had loved her. Her heart heavy with worry, she curled on her side and closed her eyes. He would be back, Hildago tried to convince herself, and everything would be just as it always had been between them for surely Mac would not allow the other woman's unexpected intrusion to ruin the beauty of their life together.

At the first blush of morning light, Rick came awake. He smiled at the sight of Jennie sleeping so peacefully next to him, and he lay still savoring the privacy of these last few minutes before he had to awaken her to return to her own room.

Rick was well versed in the art of lovemaking, but he had

never known it could be so completely and totally satisfying. The night he had just passed with Jennie had been more exciting and more beautiful than anything he'd ever experienced before. Now, as he watched her sleep, he remembered the feel of her bucking, silken hips beneath him, and his body roused, ready once again to taste of her loving delights.

With gentle fingers, he reached out to caress the softness of her breast. "Jennie, love."

Jennie's lips curved into a warm smile as she opened her eyes to gaze upon Rick. "Morning."

"Morning," Rick answered, raising up on his elbows to look down at her, tracing with his eyes the loveliness of her features. He bent to her slowly and kissed her tenderly.

"I wish it was still night," she said throatily as she slipped her arms up around his neck. "Then we'd have time to—"

"To what?" He grinned, moving over her nude, supple form and pressing the heat of his burgeoning desire against her thighs.

Jennie's eyes sparkled at the prospect of one more moment of bliss in his arms, and she pulled his head down to hers for a flaming kiss.

At her blatant yet unspoken invitation, Rick positioned himself between her legs, and as she reached down eagerly to guide him, he sought the sweetness of her womanly sheath. Their mating was breathlessly frenzied as they sought only to please each other with each caress and kiss. They lay together afterward, touching and being touched, whispering endearments to one another. Rick would have been contented to stay with her in bed for the rest of the day, but he knew that Jennie had to return to her own bedroom.

"Rick?" Her voice was a soft purr as her hands indolently explored the hard-muscled strength of his chest.

"Yes?" The mood was so tranquil that he didn't even want to think about breaking it.

"I have to go. It's dawn," Jennie told him, regretfully.

"I know, love," he said sympathetically. "Lord, how I wish you could stay."

"Soon."

"Yes, very soon. I'll talk to your preacher today as soon as Jake, Todd, and I go into town," he said as she finally stirred and sat up.

After one last, lingering kiss, Jennie stood and pulled on her dressing gown. "You're leaving early, aren't you?"

"That's what Jake said last night." Rick got up and took her in his arms.

"Then I guess I'd better go back to my room so I can get dressed and meet you at breakfast."

"Hurry," he ordered as he claimed her lips in a heart-stopping exchange.

"I will." She smiled sensuously at him and quietly left his room.

Lucia looked up, smiling brightly at her companions. "I think this will do it."

"Read it to me again," Malo demanded from where he lay on the bed.

"All right." She read:

My children,
   I know your father has told you that I'm dead, but I am not. As your mother, I'd like to have the chance to speak with you before I leave town. I am staying at the hotel.

                                        Eve McCaine

"How's that sound?" Lucia asked proudly.

"Fine. Now how do we get it out there without making anyone suspicious?" Pablo asked.

"I'll check with the man at the livery. He should know of someone who'd be willing to ride out there." Malo got up and took the letter from her once she'd sealed it in an envelope and addressed it to Jennie. "I'll be back."

He returned in less than half an hour with the good news that there had been an older man at the stable more than willing to deliver the message for a few extra dollars. Pleased that things were going so smoothly, they settled in to await the arrival of the McCaines in hopes that Rick would be accompanying them.

Jennie's heart was light as she practically floated back across the courtyard to her bedroom. She had never before been this happy, and she was totally unprepared for the sight that greeted her when she opened the door to her room.

She blinked twice in stunned confusion as she stared at the cluttered mess in the middle of the floor. The entire room was in a shambles. Everything she owned had been dumped unceremoniously together in a big heap, and even her bed had not escaped the vandal's wrath.

Shaken, Jennie lurched from the room to get Rick. Her first instinct had been to tell Hildago, but she realized that if she revealed the damage to her room to the other woman, she would know exactly where Jennie had spent the night. Upset and more than a little confused, she knocked softly at his patio door.

"Rick!"

Rick had had only enough time to pull on his pants when he heard Jennie at the door. Wondering at the nervousness he heard in her tone, he rushed to admit her.

"Jennie?" he asked as he opened the door, and she rushed in. "What's wrong? What happened?"

"My room." She was frowning, trying to understand why anyone would want to destroy her things.

"What about your room?" Rick took her by the shoulders and turned her to face him, reading in her expression all the bewilderment she was feeling.

"Someone was in there last night. They've wrecked everything—my clothes, my bed—"

"Are you saying that someone broke into your bedroom while you were with me?"

She nodded, casting a worried look in the direction of her room. "Come with me. I'll show you."

"Let me finish dressing first." He released her only long enough to pull on the rest of his clothes. I'm ready now. Let's go."

"I don't know who could have done it or why anyone would have wanted to," she remarked as she led the way back across the patio and opened the door to her room.

Rick followed her inside and looked around in disgust as Jennie knelt down and automatically started to straighten up.

"Can you tell if anything is missing?" Rick questioned, bending down beside her to help.

"I don't know. With everything dumped out this way it's hard to say. Who could have done this? We've never had this kind of trouble before."

"Lucia," Rick answered with a dreaded certainty.

"She must have seen me going to you last night."

Their gazes locked in understanding.

"I'll bet she's gone. Which room was hers?"

"The one right next door, and it opens onto the courtyard, too," Jennie told him, and Rick went outside to check.

"She's gone. The bed wasn't slept in."

"But where would she go?" she asked, pulling a riding skirt and a blouse from the jumble of clothing.

"I don't know, but as I recall, she wasn't all that enthusiastic about being sent back to Mexico with Chica tomorrow. I wonder if we should check on Pablo? If she's vindictive enough to do something this stupid, she might have tried to free him."

"Let me get dressed and we'll go together."

Rick held her close and embraced her for a long moment.

461

"I'm sorry about your things."

"It was just such a shock at first. I'm all right now." She smiled up at him bravely and then stepped away to shed her gown and pull on her riding clothes.

A few minutes later, they left her room and headed for the dining room. Jake and Chica were already there, but Todd had not yet made an appearance.

"Good morning." He greeted them brightly.

"Morning, Jake, Chica," Rick returned and then, deciding to dispense with the pleasantries, he asked, "Have either one of you seen Lucia this morning?"

"No, why?" Chica wondered quickly what Lucia had done for she knew the other woman's feeling about returning home.

"That's what I was afraid of. Some time during the night, she disappeared."

"What?"

"Her bed wasn't slept in," Rick told them.

"Have you checked on Pablo yet, Jake?" Jennie asked.

"No. Not yet."

"Then I think we'd better make sure he's still there."

"Do you think Lucia might have wanted him with her?"

"As cunning as she is, I wouldn't put anything past her."

"Let's go then." Jake was on his feet and heading for the front door. As he passed the gun case, he cursed long and loud. "She took some guns with her. It looks like two rifles and two sidearms."

With that news, they did hurry, and they were not surprised to discover that Pablo was indeed gone.

"We'd better check on the horses. I'm sure they didn't walk out of here."

One of the hands met them as they were approaching the stables.

"Jake, there are two mounts missing."

"Out of the stable or corral?"

"The stable."

"Thanks. We had a feeling that there might be. Get our horses ready for us. We'll be riding out in the next half hour," Jake instructed.

"Yes, sir." He hurried away.

"I guess we'll have to track them. I don't know if they'd head for Mesa Roja or not."

As they started back toward the house, Chica finally spoke: "I can probably tell you what's on her mind."

"Please do, Chica. It may help us to find them."

"I think they would go to town. Knowing Malo, if he's alive, he might be there, and she is probably trying to find him."

"But why? After all the things he's done to her?"

"Who knows? Lucia is not happy with a normal life. If she was she'd be going home with me."

"Then as soon as we're ready, we'll try to pick up their trail in that direction. Do you mind waiting another few days before you go home?"

"No. I am most comfortable here, and you've been very gracious."

"Good. We'd better wake Pa and tell him what's happened," Jennie remarked. "In fact, I wonder why he isn't up yet. It isn't like him to stay in bed so long."

They reentered the house, and while Jake and Rick went to get their guns ready, Chica went back to her room and Jennie went to awaken Pa, knocking loudly on the door to the master suite.

"Pa! We need to talk with you right away."

When there was no gruff reply as she expected, she knocked again.

Hildago woke at the sound of Jennie's call and she hurried to answer the door. "Jennie? Is there a problem?"

"Yes, is Pa up?"

"No. I mean yes, but he is gone."

"Gone?" Jennie could not imagine where he could be at this time of the morning.

"Yes, he left last night after you'd gone to bed. He'd received a letter while you were gone from an old friend who was in town, and he went to see him," she lied, uneasily.

"Last night? That late?" Hildago's story didn't ring true, but Jennie had little time to worry about it now. They had to start tracking Pablo or they would never be able to find him.

Hildago shrugged. "I told him to wait 'til daylight, but he was anxious to go. What is the trouble? Maybe I can help?"

"Some time during the night, Lucia stole some horses and guns and freed Pablo. They're both gone."

"Oh, no"

"Chica seems to think that they might have headed to town to try to locate Malo, so we're going to try to track them."

"Well, watch for your father. He told me he would be back early."

"I will, but if we should happen to miss him, tell him what's happened and where we've gone."

"Who's going with you?"

"So far, Jake, Rick, and me, although Jake will probably get a few of the hands to ride along, just in case."

"You be careful," she admonished, and for the first time that morning, Jennie realized how tired the older woman looked.

"Are you feeling all right?" she asked, concerned.

"Of course. I'm just a little tired after all the excitement yesterday, and then Mac's leaving at such an odd hour." Hildago smiled softly at her interest, but there was still a sadness reflected in her eyes that Jennie didn't understand.

"You're sure?"

"Of course, you go on. I'm just going to rest until Mac returns."

"All right," she said, anxious that they should be on their way. "I'll see you when we get back."

Jake and Rick were waiting for her in the hall near the gun case.

"Where's Pa?" Jake asked as he saw Jennie returning alone.

"He's gone to town."

"What?" He was astounded for their father never went anywhere unannounced. "When?"

"Last night, sometime. Hildago said that while we were gone he got a message from an old friend, and he went into Mesa Roja to see him."

"That doesn't sound like Pa. Taking off like that in the middle of the night."

"I thought it sounded strange, too, but she seemed to think that we'd probably run into him on his way home."

"I hope we do. I want him to know what's going on. Are you ready to ride?"

"Just about. Have you told Todd and Carrie where we're going?"

"Yes and Todd's coming with us," Rick told her. "Jake's enlisted the help of several ranch hands, too, so I don't think we'll have a problem."

She was about to reply when they heard a horse approaching out front. Expecting the rider to be their father, they hastened outside to meet him.

"It's not Pa." Jennie was certain it wasn't her father, but she couldn't make out who it really was.

Rick and Jake came to stand by her side, curious, too, as to who would be riding out to the ranch at this time of day. As the man reined in in front of them, they finally recognized him as one of the men who worked at the livery in town.

"Mornin'," the rider said.

"What brings you out to the M Circle C this early?" Jake took command of the situation as he stepped from the veranda. "Is there trouble in town?"

"No. No trouble. I just got a letter here for Miss Jennie."

"A letter?" Jennie was intrigued, and she stepped forward to accept the offered envelope with her name written on it.

"Who sent it?" Jake asked.

"Don't rightly know. They just paid me real good to bring it out here to ya."

"Well, thanks." She smiled up at him. "You have time for a cool drink?"

"No, ma'am. I got to be gettin' back, but thank you for the offer."

"You're more than welcome," Jennie answered.

"See ya," the messenger told them as he turned his mount and headed back toward Mesa Roja.

"Well, that certainly was a surprise." Jennie looked at Rick and Jake, bemused.

"Who's it from?" Her brother was growing more curious by the minute.

"I don't know. Let's go inside and I'll open it."

Leading the way, they reentered the house and went into the parlor. Jennie sat down easily on the sofa with Rick and Jake looking on expectantly as she tore the flap on the envelope and pulled out the single page.

She began to read it aloud, but suddenly her voice failed her as she skimmed ahead and she read the rest in silence.

"Jennie?" Rick noticed how pale she had become and he went to her quickly. "What's wrong, darling?"

Rick saw the wild disbelief reflected in her eyes as she glanced at him quickly, before looking to her brother.

"Jake?" There was a tremor in her voice, and her hand shook as she held the note out to him. "I think we'd better get Carrie."

"Why?"

"The letter." She swallowed in confusion. "It's from our mother."

Chapter Thirty-four

There was a stunned silence that followed her pronouncement as Jake looked from Jennie to Rick and then back again.

"What did you say?"

"Here—read it for yourself."

Jake snatched the letter almost violently from her and read it through twice before glancing back up, his handsome features contorted by a mixture of disbelief and anger.

"This has to be some kind of a cruel joke. We all know our mother's dead." He looked to Rick for some kind of affirmation. "She died when Carrie was still a baby."

"That's what Pa said," Jennie said and then paused as the seed of doubt had been planted. "Jake, you don't suppose he lied to us, do you?"

"No. Of course not. Not Pa," he answered fiercely.

"I'll go get Carrie." She stood up slowly, still dazed by the news the letter contained, and any thoughts she'd had of chasing after Lucia and Pablo were momentarily forgotten. "Even if this is all a hoax, I think she should know about it."

"All right."

Carrie had taken her time with her toilette that morning, wanting to look her best for Todd, and she had just finished dressing when she heard the knock at her bedroom door.

"Who is it?" Her tone was happy and quite carefree.

"It's me, Carrie, Jennie."

Carrie frowned as she wondered at the strained sound of her sister's voice, and she hurried to let her in.

"Good morning. I'm just about ready to come down for breakfast," she said as she went back to sit at her dressing table.

"Carrie." Jennie wasn't quite sure how to broach the subject.

"What's wrong, Jennie? You're acting awfully strange. Nothing's happened to Todd has it?" she asked, pausing in her primping.

"No, Todd's fine. It's just that I got a strange message this morning."

"A message? What kind of message?"

"A rider came out from town with a letter addressed to me."

"So?"

"So, it's supposedly from our mother," she finally blurted out bluntly.

For Carrie all motion seemed to stop as she stared at her sister in total astonishment.

"What?"

"The letter—It was signed by Eve McCaine."

"No," she denied quickly, turning back to the mirror. "Mother's dead. Pa said so."

"I felt the same way, but I thought I should tell you. Come and read the letter and tell me what you think."

Carrie slammed her brush down on the top of the dressing table. "I don't need to read any letter! She's dead, Jennie! She has to be!"

Jennie was surprised by her vehemence. "Well, come on down and join us when you're ready. We're in the sitting room right now."

As Jennie left the room Carrie sat, staring with unseeing eyes into the reflecting glass before her. When she heard the door close, she blinked in bewilderment, and her mouth twisted into a grimace of emotion. It was impossible. Eve McCaine, their mother, had died. Surely, this was some kind of trick, although, for the life of here, Carrie couldn't imagine what motive anyone would have for doing it.

Getting up, she nervously smoothed the skirt of her dress, and for just a brief instant, she wondered if what Jennie had told her was indeed true. The pain that accompanied the thought proved almost unbearable for Carrie. She quickly tried to dismiss it, but she knew in her heart that if it was the truth, it would mean that their own mother had been alive all this time and never once made any effort to contact them.

Wanting to know more, but afraid of what she might discover, Carrie headed slowly from her room. She hoped that Todd would be with the others when she joined them for she felt greatly in need of his supportive strength now.

Jennie and Jake were huddled together on the sofa, trying to decide what to do as Carrie entered the room. When she saw Todd standing off to one side looking decidedly uncomfortable, she went straight to him and was enveloped in the warmth of his embrace.

"They told you?" she asked, looking up at him after a minute.

"Yes, but I don't know if I believe it or not. It seems rather farfetched to me that Mac would tell everyone she was dead, if she really was alive."

"I know. It doesn't sound like something Pa would do—but—"

"Why don't we ask Hildago?" Jennie suggested. "I can't stand this not knowing. I'm sure if anyone knows the truth, it'll be her."

"I'll go and get her." Jake left the room, determined to find out the truth about the mysterious letter.

Hildago answered his call right away, and she wondered at his urgency. "What is it, Jake? Jennie's already told me about Lucia and Pablo. Is there something else wrong?"

"I'm not sure. We need to talk with you if we could?"

"Of course. Just give me a few minutes to freshen up and

I'll be right there."

Jake returned to the sitting room to await her coming, and it didn't take Hildago long to join them. Hildago sensed that something was terribly wrong as she entered the room and gazed at their expectant expressions.

"You said you had something you wanted to talk about?" she asked as she sat down on the sofa next to Jake.

"Hildago," he began hesitantly, "a rider came out from town earlier with a letter addressed to Jennie."

Her eyes clouded at this unexpected news. "Yes?"

Jake cleared his throat. "This may sound like a ridiculous question, but—Hildago, is our mother alive?"

"Why do you ask?" She tried to keep all emotions out of her voice, but deep within she was trembling.

"The letter," Jennie put in. "While it was addressed to me, it was written to all of us, and the woman who wrote it claims to be our mother—Eve McCaine."

Hildago caught her breath. What had happened while Mac was in town? Had he allowed Eve to contact them or was she being devious and trying to stir up trouble for him? Hildago wanted to back Mac in his struggle to protect Jake, Jennie, and Carrie, but she knew she couldn't deliberately lie to them about the other woman's existence, now that they were adults.

"Well, Hildago?" Jake pushed.

Girding herself for the scene that she knew her next words were about to provoke, she looked at him steadily and answered. "Yes. Eve McCaine is alive."

"What?" Jake, Jennie, and Carrie gasped in unison.

"It is a long—and sordid—story," Hildago told them defeatedly. "But I suppose you are old enough now to understand."

"You mean Pa has known all these years that Mother was alive, and he kept it from us?" Carrie was completely shocked.

"For a very good reason!" Hildago replied, almost angry in her defense of Mac. "Eve McCaine deserted this family

470

when you were just a baby, Carrie."

"She left us?" Jennie was wide-eyed in her amazement.

"That's right. Your father had been out working all day, and when he returned to the house, she was gone. All she'd left behind was a note telling him that she couldn't stand the ranch life anymore and that she wanted out."

"She deserted us," Jennie whispered, lost in a sea of conflicting emotions.

Her mother was alive! For a brief second her heart sang, but then reality came crashing in. Her mother was alive. So what? She was a woman who had run off and left a husband with three small children to care for, and not once in all this time had she made any effort to contact them. Now, years later, she was back, and Jennie couldn't help but wonder why.

"What do you suppose she's after Hildago?" Jennie asked so coldly that Rick glanced at her sharply.

"I wish I knew." Hildago sighed. "You know that friend I told you your father had received a letter from and went to visit in town?"

"It was her." Jennie's eyes widened as she now understood her father's haste to get to Mesa Roja last night.

"Yes, and in the letter she sent to your father, she said she was ready to attempt a reconciliation, but, knowing what I do about her, I find that terribly hard to believe."

"She probably heard that Pa was worth money now, and she came back to claim her share," Jake remarked cynically.

"We won't know for sure until we hear from your father."

"He told you he'd be back early, didn't he?"

"Yes, he promised me that he would return right away, but—"

"That's why you were looking so tired when I first talked to you."

Hildago smiled weakly. "It was a long night."

"Are they still legally married?" Carrie asked, stirring from the safety of Todd's arms.

"Yes, unfortunately."

"And that's what's prevented you and Pa from ever marrying?"

Hildago nodded sadly. "There was no way we could marry. If he filed for a divorce from Eve then everyone would have found out that she was alive, and Mac didn't want you to have to go through that trauma."

"Oh, Hildago, how awful for you," Jennie said sympathetically.

"It has not been easy." She sighed. "I have always loved you as my own, and I tried to pretend that Eve didn't exist. But, now that she is back—"

"Yes," Jennie said solemnly. "She is back and she wants to see us." She looked from Jake to Carrie. "Well? What should we do?"

"I'm not sure that Mac knows about this note you got from Eve, Jennie," Hildago put in quickly. "When he left last night, he was adamant that I not tell you anything."

"Do you think she might be trying to drive a wedge between us and Pa?" Jennie asked.

"I wouldn't be surprised," the older woman replied. "If Eve's trying to get something out of your father, she'd use any tactic she could come up with to get what she wanted."

Jennie imagined the strain her father had been under all these years, keeping up the pretense of being a widower, and she felt her admiration for him grow. She was sure that it had been a difficult time for him, and she could easily understand why he had chosen to lie to them when they were small.

"Maybe it's time we set the record straight. I think we should all go in to town and face her. She probably thinks that she'll be able to pit us against Mac, but we know where our loyalty lies," Jake said with firm resolve.

"I agree." Carrie wanted to see the woman who could so callously abandon her own family.

"I'll go have your horses brought up to the house," Rick offered, and he gave Jennie a reassuring look.

"Will you ride in with us, Rick?" Jennie asked quickly before he could leave the room.

"If you want me to."

"Please," she told him gratefully. "I'll need you with me."

"Hildago?" Jake asked as he stood up. "Would you like to go along?"

"No. I will stay here."

"But why? You have as much at stake as we do."

"Probably more," Carrie put in.

"That may be true, but I want to wait here for Mac. I am sure that he will come to me as soon as everything has been taken care of." She rose and made her way from the room.

"All right." He didn't understand her reasoning, but he respected her decision. "Todd? What about you? Do you want to come with us?"

"If it's all the same to you, why don't I take a few of the ranch hands and try to catch up to Pablo and Lucia? If what Chica said is true and they are heading for town, I'll probably meet up with you there."

"Good idea. Thanks. I'd forgotten all about them in all this confusion." Jake ran a hand nervously through his hair and looked over at Carrie. "I guess you'd better change, unless you'd like to take the buggy?"

"No. The buggy's too slow, and I want to get to town as fast as we can. I'm interested in seeing this *mother* of ours as soon as possible." Her tone was filled with bitterness. "I'll be ready to go by the time Rick gets back with the horses."

When everyone else had gone, Jennie looked at Jake. He seemed to have aged in these last few minutes, and she wondered how he'd deal with the shock of seeing Eve McCaine again. Jake was the only one who could remember their mother, and over the years his few memories of the fair-haired woman had been magnified by all of them into an almost cherished recitation of love. But now that had all been shattered, and in the cold, cruel world of adulthood, they were facing for the very first time the truth about the blond beauty they'd always referred to as their mother.

"Jake?" Jennie went to him and hugged him.

He returned her embrace warmly, resting his cheek

473

against the softness of her dark hair. "This is probably going to be the hardest thing any of us has ever had to do."

"I know. I'm afraid, and yet, I know we have to do this. We have to see her so we can come to understand why she didn't want us. Do you suppose it was something we did?"

"We were only children, for God's sake! There's no way we should feel guilty because she left, but can you just imagine what her desertion did to Pa?"

"I know. I don't know how he handled it. Thank heaven for Hildago."

They moved apart then and were silent as each meditated on the upcoming confrontation.

"What time is it?" Malo demanded gruffly as he moved to look out the window again.

"I don't know for sure, but it's probably after eight." Pablo supplied.

Grunting in reply, Malo said nothing but went to lie back down on the bed.

"How long has it been since the messenger got back?" Lucia asked.

"About half an hour. The McCaines should be arriving within the next hour, I'd say.

"Keep a close watch. I want to know as soon as they arrive in town."

Malo started to settle back on the bed when Lucia's whispered call brought him back to her side.

"Look!"

"What is it?"

"Mac McCaine's left the saloon.

"Where's he going? To the hotel?"

"No." Pablo looked at them both nervously. "He's heading in the direction of the sheriff's office."

"Relax, Pablo." Malo scoffed. "If Mac McCaine was after us, he wouldn't have waited all this time to go to the sheriff. I've got the feeling there's something else on his

474

mind this morning."

"Like his wife?"

"Exactly. Just keep watch for Rick Peralta. He's the only one I'm interested in right now."

"Malo?"

"What?"

"When this is over, then what?"

"We walk calmly out of here to where I've got our horses tied up out back."

"You don't think anyone will challenge us?"

"There'll be too much confusion. We should be safely away before they even figure out where the shots came from." His eyes were glittering at the thought of paying Rick back for his double-cross.

Lucia read the emotion in his gaze and smiled at him knowingly. "I am glad that we found you, Malo."

He turned to her then and, grasping her by the arm, pulled her up to him.

"Are you, Lucia?" he asked in a low, suggestive voice as his eyes roamed over her. "How glad?"

Thrilled that he was no longer ignoring her, Lucia wrapped her arms around his neck and pulled him down for a passionate kiss, paying no attention to Pablo. Malo released her abruptly.

"I am sorry for what I did," she told him, hoping she sounded suitably humble.

"We will talk of it later, when we are alone," he told her curtly and then walked away to lie down on the bed. "Let me know the minute the McCaines show up."

Lucia wondered at his indifference to her as he stretched out comfortably. She wanted to know if he was going to make her his woman again, but she decided not to push him. She knew how vicious he could be when he was angered.

As he left Dolly's, Mac inhaled deeply of the fresh morning air. The hours had been slow in passing, but at last it was time for him to act. Emboldened by the half bottle of whiskey he'd consumed, Mac knew that he was ready to deal with Eve this one final time.

Striding purposefully toward the stage office to speak with Silas, he couldn't help but wonder what she planned to do this morning. No doubt it would be something dramatic, but at this point Mac didn't really care. The only person she would be hurting, if she chose to make a scene, would be herself.

Silas Stratton had just finished unlocking the office door and bracing it wide with a doorstop when Mac entered.

"Good morning, Mac." Silas greeted him easily, having known him for a good many years. "I see you stayed in town all night."

"I had some more business to take care of," he said obliquely.

"Anything I can help you with?" Silas offered solicitously, all the while wondering if it had anything to do with that pretty woman who claimed to be his wife.

"I need to know your schedule for today."

"You going out of town?" He peered at Mac over the top of his glasses.

"No. I'm not, but I have a friend who is, and I need to know what you've got passing through today."

"Where is your friend heading?" he asked logically.

"Wherever your stage happens to be going," Mac said sternly.

Silas's eyes widened at his statement, but he knew better than to question Mac any further.

"Let me see." He bent worriedly over the ledger. "We've only got one due in and it's on a run to Yuma."

"That'll be fine. What time?"

"Hard to say. Probably some time early this afternoon, but if they have any trouble on the road, they'll be late."

"How much?" Mac asked, pulling out his money, and when Silas quoted him a figure, he handed over the cash without comment.

"I'll send Billy to find you and your friend when the stage comes in. Where should we look for you?"

"The hotel."

"Fine, Mac. Thanks." Silas looked up, hoping to draw him into a longer conversation and find out what was going on, but Mac had already turned and was walking out of the office.

Mac had one more important stop to make before he went back to Eve's room, and he started down a side street. He paused only a moment outside the small office and then, determined as ever, he opened the door and walked in.

"Mac?" John King was more than a little surprised to find Mac McCaine in his office so early in the morning.

"Good morning, John."

"What brings you to town so early in the day? Something I can help you with?" he said rising from his desk and movig to shake hands with him warmly.

"I hope so. This is very confidential, and you're the only person I can talk to about it."

"Please, sit down. Would you like a cup of coffee?"

"No. Thanks. I just want to get this over with as quickly as possible," Mac confided as he sat in the chair in front of John's desk.

"All right." The other man locked the door and pulled down the shade so that no one would be able to see them. "Now, why don't you tell me what's troubling you."

Mac waited until John had seated himself behind the desk before beginning. "I have some legal work I need for you to handle."

"Of course. I'd be glad to. What does it entail?"

"I need you to take care of divorce proceedings for me," Mac said harshly.

"What?" John was stunned. "Mac, I didn't know you were married."

"Well, I am, but I intend to remedy that as soon as you can draw up the papers."

"To whom are you married?"

477

"Eve." He said her name with such loathing that John could only stare at him in confusion.

"But you said that Eve was dead."

"I know what I said, but Eve is very much alive, and she's finally come back. In fact, she's staying at the hotel right now."

"You mean all these years—"

"That's right. I've been living a lie to protect my children."

"But why, Mac?"

"Eve deserted us, John. I didn't want Jake, Jennie, or Carrie to ever find out about it, so I'd told them that she'd died. It was that simple. I'm just sorry that she's shown up now, but at least it solves one of my problems."

"What's that?"

"Now that I know where she is, I can divorce her. So draw up whatever it is you have to draw up. I want her out of my life forever!"

"It's not quite as simple as you would have it, Mac."

"What does that mean?"

"It means that it takes time. I can file the proper papers, but it will be a while before it's final."

"What's a *while*?"

"Several months, at least."

Mac almost groaned at the news. "All right. Do whatever it is you have to do."

"I'll need some more information from you."

It was over a half an hour later when Mac emerged from the office feeling more satisfied with himself than he had in years. Soon his relationship with Eve would be legally terminated, and he would be free to marry Hildago!

Mac could hardly wait to tell Hildago the news, and it dawned on him then, as he started to the hotel to meet with Eve, that he had told Hildago that he would be back before dawn. He knew she would be upset, but he hoped the marriage proposal he had for her when he returned would ease any distress she'd been feeling.

478

Chapter Thirty-five

Since dawn, Eve had been anxiously awaiting Mac's return. Hovering by the window, she had kept constant watch over the street below, hoping to catch sight of him on his way back to the hotel.

During the long hours since he'd walked out so abruptly, she had struggled to find the solution to her dilemma in dealing with him. Mac had crudely proven to her that he was basically immune to her sensual prowess, and with that knowledge came a tempering of all her plans. No longer could she try to seduce him into giving her her own way; instead, she would have to face him with the facts and deal with him as logically as possible.

Determined to be in control of their meeting this morning, she had dressed with care. The gown she'd chosen was a sophisticated one that enhanced the fairness of her blond hair. She looked worldly and wise and totally at ease with herself. Pleased with her choice, she smiled warmly at her own reflection, feeling confident that, after today, all of her troubles would be over.

The knock at her door surprised her and she jumped, startled by the intrusion," Yes?"

"Mrs. McCaine?"

"Yes, who is it?"

"It's me, ma'am, Ace."

"Ace?"

"I'm the handyman around here, ma'am. Mrs. Bates sent me up. She said your door needed fixing."

"Oh, well, fine," Eve opened the broken portal to allow him to do his work.

"How are you this beautiful morning?" Ace asked as he set to work on the lock.

"Very well, thank you." She kept her tone deliberately aloof and, not wanting to encourage the little man in conversation, she turned her back on him and went to sit by the window.

But Ace, renowned in town for knowing everything about everybody, ignored her attempt to cut him off and kept up the flow of chatter, trying to break down her defenses.

"Glad to hear that. I'm feeling fine, myself, too," he told her, even though she hadn't asked. His eyes narrowed thoughtfully as he looked over to where she sat, and his boldness grew. "You know, folks around here have been mighty curious about you."

Eve was caught off guard by his brazen statement. "Oh, really? Why is that?"

"Well, we didn't know ol' Mac was married," he said cautiously.

"You mean he's never spoken of me?"

"Oh, yes ma'am. He talked about you but always in the past tense." Ace wondered if she knew about Mac's charade.

"I'm afraid I don't understand."

"Why, Mrs. McCaine. He told everybody you were dead!" He watched with interest as her features paled at the news.

"He what?"

"He told everybody years ago that he was a widower, even his own—pardon me, ma'am—*your* own children believe it."

"The children?" Eve was, at first, shocked by the news, but as she thought about it, it all began to make sense. It certainly explained why Mac was so determined to keep her away from Jake, Jennie, and Carrie.

"They've always thought that their mama died when Miss Carrie was just a baby. And you know, that's why everybody was so surprised when you showed up and registered as Mac's wife."

Eve smiled coolly, pleased with the position she found herself in because this new knowledge gave her a powerful weapon to use against Mac in her effort to force a settlement from him.

"How interesting," she told him drolly.

Ace went on easily as he continued to work on the door. "You know, you and Miss Carrie do look a lot alike. You sure can tell that you're related. She's one pretty little gal."

The thought struck Eve that, if indeed she and Carrie did bear a resemblance to one another, it might prove entertaining to meet her. She decided to ask Mac about the possibility, and she smiled as she imagined his reaction to the suggestion. Determined to use everything Ace had just revealed to her best advantage, Eve settled back calmly in the chair to await Mac's arrival.

"You were right, Malo," Pablo told him as he continued his surveillance from the bedroom window.

"About what?" Malo quickly rose from the bed to stand at his side.

"McCaine. He just went into the hotel."

"Has there been any sign of the rest of them yet?"

"No, nothing yet."

Malo nodded, growing more tense with each passing minute. He knew that they had to be ready to act as soon as they had Peralta in their sight for they might not get the opportunity to take a second shot at him. But, until he showed up in town, there was nothing they could do except wait.

Picking up his rifle, Malo sat down on the edge of the bed to check it once again. After making certain that it was loaded, he set it aside and leaned back against the headboard, waiting impatiently for word from Pablo that they were coming.

"Jennie?" Rick guided his horse closer to Jennie's so he could speak with her.

She looked over at him quickly. "What?"

"Are you sure you want to do this?" He posed the question she'd been asking herself for the past hour.

"Rick, I don't want to, but I know that I have to." The anguish she was feeling was clearly reflected in her eyes.

Rick wished that they were alone somewhere so that he could take her in his arms and comfort her, but he knew the time for that would come later.

"All right, sweetheart, but I'll be right there with you the whole time, if you need me."

Jennie gazed lovingly at him. "Thank you."

Rick gave her a reassuring smile. "There's no need to thank me, Jennie. I love you and I want to help."

"I just wish it was that simple."

"Well, we should be reaching Mesa Roja soon, and then it will all be over."

Jennie nodded tersely in response. Yes, very soon she would be face to face with the woman she'd thought long dead. Why had Eve done it? Why had she deserted her family? The questions tortured Jennie, and she knew she had to find the answers.

As Carrie rode silently alongside them, her thoughts, too, were tortured and confused. She was going to meet the woman who had given birth to her. Carrie supposed that she should be excited at the prospect, but instead she felt angry and resentful. Since she'd learned the truth from Hildago, her feelings for her mother, the beautiful Eve McCaine, had

482

changed from worship to hate. Carrie was not sure exactly why she felt it was necessary to see her, but she knew that she had to, just this once.

Although Jake was tense and on edge, his manner, as he rode with the others, was outwardly calm. She was back! He felt as if he was living a dream or a nightmare. How could this be happening? Since his childhood, he had fantasized that his mother would return, and now . . .

Learning the truth about Eve had hurt him badly. Jake realized now that all of his cherished memories of her had been a farce. A deep, abiding pain had been born within him, and he hoped he could keep his emotions under control when he finally met her. Determined not to let the woman know she had any power over him, he girded himself for the upcoming meeting as the outskirts of Mesa Roja came into view.

Mac took the hotel steps quickly, anxious to tell Eve about the divorce proceedings he'd just started. As he reached the top of the flight of stairs, he heard Ace deep in conversation, and he noticed that the door to her room was open. Knowing the fondness Ace had for gossip, Mac groaned inwardly and hoped the man had managed to keep his mouth shut.

"Yes, ma'am, you sure do look a lot like Miss Carrie. Why, if I was to see you together, I would think that maybe you were sisters instead of mother and daughter!" The little man chortled, but his amusement was cut short as Mac suddenly appeared in the doorway, his expression thunderous.

His eyes flinty, Mac stared at Eve, knowing she could have picked no better confidante than Ace if she wanted to start trouble, "You were serious, weren't you?"

"About what, Mac?" she asked with seeming innocence, but she knew full well what he meant.

Ace was avidly listening to their exchange until he felt

Mac's angry gaze upon him.

"You can finish that up later, Ace. I'd like a few moments of privacy with—"

"Your wife," Ace put in quickly, pleased at the look of fury that crossed Mac's face. "I can certainly understand that. Yes, sir, I sure can. I'll be going, but I'll come back later, Mrs. McCaine."

"Thank you, Ace," she called as he scurried from the room, and she turned her attention almost leisurely to Mac.

"Malo! There are riders coming, and I think it's them!" Pablo called excitedly from the window.

Malo snatched up his rifle and moved to join him, staring off in the direction he indicated.

"There's four of them, and two of them look to be women." He smiled evilly.

"I'm sure Jake must be one of the men." Lucia came to stand with them. "So, the other one will either be Peralta or Todd Clarke."

"Pablo, are you ready?"

"I've been ready for hours."

"Good. I want Peralta dead but don't fire unless you're sure you can hit him. I don't want any mistakes, because we're probably only going to get this one chance."

"Right," Pablo said solemnly.

"Can I do anything to help you?" Lucia offered.

"Here." Malo thrust a revolver in her hand. "Stand guard at the door. I want to know if you hear anyone coming."

Lucia nodded her understanding and moved to take up her post.

Jake glanced at his sisters as they entered the outskirts of Mesa Roja. "Ready?"

"As I'll ever be," Jennie replied, smiling weakly. "Where

do you suppose Pa is this morning?"

"I don't know, but as soon as we've finished talking with Eve, I think we'd better go looking for him."

She nodded. "It'll certainly be a lot easier on Pa once we tell him that we know the truth."

"It must have been difficult for him not being able to tell us everything," Carrie remarked.

"Well, it'll all be over real soon," Jake said as the hotel came into view.

"It's Peralta!" Pablo declared as the riders came within full view. "He's riding with them!"

Malo didn't answer. Intent only on wreaking vengeance on the other man, he levered his rifle into position and sighted down the barrel, as he waited for Rick to come within range.

Unaware of the danger that awaited them, they rode slowly into town, and as they neared the hotel, Rick urged his mount closer to Jennie.

"Do you want Jake and me to go up first and talk to her?" he asked, concerned about the upcoming interview.

"No, really, it's not necessary," she answered. "But I do want you to come with us."

"All right." Rick wanted to be there for her just in case she needed him.

"He's mine now! All mine!" Malo squinted as he took aim, but just as he would have pulled the trigger, Rick leaned toward Jennie, unintentionally blocking his perfect shot. Lowering his rifle, Malo swore loudly as he watched them dismount and enter the hotel.

"Damn! I had him in my sights."

"Don't worry, Malo." Pablo tried to cheer him. "He has to come back out sometime, and when he does, we will take him."

Malo smiled and took a deep breath. "You're right. Before this morning is over, Peralta will be dead and we will be gone from this town."

When Mac was certain that Ace was out of earshot, he stepped inside Eve's room. He attempted to shut the door behind him, but the handyman's ministrations had rendered it even more impossible to close and he was forced to leave it standing ajar.

Eve regarded Mac evenly as she gave a throaty laugh and stood up. "Was it necessary to send Ace away? He was a most delightful and *informative* little man."

"Really?"

"Really," she said calmly, keeping her manner precise as she approached him. "You know Mac, I've been thinking about the conversation we had last night, and it seems to me that we've left a lot of things unsettled between us."

"Hardly," Mac replied.

Jake hurried into the lobby and paused only long enough at the unattended front desk to check the register for Eve's room number before heading up the stairs with Jennie, Carrie, and Rick following immediately behind him. They had no trouble locating her room and were about to knock on the door when they saw that it was standing partially open, allowing them to hear the angry conversation going on inside.

"Everything has been settled between us—permanently this time, Eve. I've just come from my lawyer's office where I filed for a divorce on the grounds of desertion," Mac was saying

Jake looked questioningly to the others, wondering whether to go in or not, but Jennie and Carrie both shook their heads, knowing that this was not the time to interrupt their father.

"And what kind of settlement are you giving me?" Eve asked greedily, hoping she wouldn't have to fight him, but his next words killed that hope.

"The only thing you're getting out of me is a one-way ticket to Yuma," Mac replied smoothly. "I've already paid for it, and when the stage comes in early this afternoon, I'm going to see that you get on it."

"I don't think so," she told him with sly confidence.

"Oh?" Mac folded his arms across his chest as his cold-eyed gaze never wavered.

"I want to see my children," Eve announced calmly.

"I told you before how they feel about you and—"

"Mac, they don't even know about me! Ace told me the truth just now. He explained to me how you lied to everyone and told them that I was dead. Everyone including my own children!" Eve witnessed the play of emotions on his face, and she felt a surge of triumph. "I want to see them, Mac. Jake, Jennie, and Carrie. Ace seems to think that Carrie and I resemble one another. What do you think?" she taunted.

At her words, Carrie gasped audibly in the hall, but luckily Mac and Eve didn't hear her.

Mac's jaw tightened as he fought down the urge to strangle her. "I will not allow you to upset their lives. You nearly destroyed us once Eve, and there is no way I'd ever let you do that again."

"Try to stop me," she pushed daringly.

"But you know you don't care. You know you're just doing it for vengeance."

"Of course, why else?" She laughed lightly.

Jennie looked at Rick, her eyes filled with pain. "She's horrible," she whispered.

Rick put a comforting arm about her shoulders. "Don't worry, I'm sure Mac can handle her," he said softly.

"If I'd wanted a family," Eve went on, "I would have stayed with you after the youngest girl was born, but screaming babies and living in the middle of a desert are not

487

my idea of the good life."

"You're disgusting," Mac growled.

She shrugged, unconcerned with his opinion of her. "I know a lot of men who wouldn't think so."

Jake blanched at her words. His mother was no better than a whore!

"What do you want—to get out of our lives and stay out, permanently?"

"I want you to support me in the style to which I've become accustomed. You can either settle on me in full or send money every month. It doesn't matter how you do it, just as long as you do it."

Mac looked at her contemptuously. "And what if I refuse?"

"Oh? You aren't interested in working out an agreement? Would you rather I stay here and fight the divorce?"

"What guarantee do I have that you'll stay out of our lives, once I've given you the money?"

"Have your lawyer draw up whatever documents are necessary, and I'll sign them. Believe me, the last thing I want to do is stay here with you in this pitiful excuse of a town."

"And you'll make no effort to contact our children?"

"Heavens, no! If I didn't want to see them before, why should I now?" She shuddered at the thought. "I thought it might be amusing to see Carrie since Ace was so certain that we looked alike, but believe me, I can live without the thrill. No, you just go ahead and get the money for me, and I'll leave town very quietly right away."

"It'll take me a while to get the paper work drawn up and to get the money from the bank."

"I've got all the time in the world." She sighed contentedly and Mac cursed under his breath. "Come, come, Mac. It's not all that bad. Why, once I have all the money, I'll be gone and you can go on with your life as if nothing ever happened. Now, run along and get it for me." Her voice hardened toward the end, and it was that tone that spurred

Jake to action.

Violently, he pushed the already broken door open and entered the room.

"You don't have to pay her one cent, Pa," he declared, staring at the woman who stood so defiantly before his father.

"Jake! What are you doing here?" Mac was surprised to see his son and even more so when Carrie and Jennie followed him into the room. "Girls—I don't want you here."

"Never mind, Pa. It's too late. We know everything." Jennie went to him and put a comforting hand on his shoulder.

Carrie didn't speak but stood back, almost gaping at the beautiful woman who was her mother.

"Well." Eve looked at each of her children. "You must be Jake. And Jennie, you did have the dark hair, didn't you? And this must be Carrie." She moved closer to her youngest daughter and regarded her with open interest. "Ace certainly was right. We are quite alike. Your hair and figure—"

"I might resemble you physically, but that's where the resemblance ends." Carrie resented the implication after overhearing their conversation, and she suddenly understood Mac's attitude toward her all those years. "We're nothing alike. Believe me! You're selfish and money hungry and—"

Eve slapped her viciously. "You don't know anything about me! How dare you say such things?"

"We just overheard your entire conversation. So I think I know everything I need to know about you—now," Carrie told her with dignity. "I don't think we have anything else to say to one another. Jennie? Jake? Pa?"

Jennie and Jake joined her, and they walked slowly from the room as Mac turned to Eve in a rage.

"You'll be getting no settlement from me, Eve. Your little game is over and you just lost." He smiled crookedly at her as he thought proudly of how Carrie had just handled the confrontation. "I'll be back to get you when the stage arrives."

"Mac!" Eve pleaded, suddenly realizing that it was finished. "Mac, I have no money. I have no where to go."

"And you expect me to care?"

"Please, I'll starve."

Mac quirked an eyebrow at her. "Somehow, I truly doubt that." And then turned and left the room.

"Malo! Look! They're coming back out!" Pablo's call drew his attention down to the street below.

"I've got him now!" Malo gloated as he stood up to take better aim in Rick's direction.

They had paused on the sidewalk in front of the hotel to wait for Mac to join them, and Malo stood, finger on the trigger, waiting patiently for the perfect shot.

"I'm glad we got to meet her, but I'm sorry she slapped you, Carrie." Jake put an arm around her.

"So am I. I wanted her to be special—to be the woman we had always thought her to be, but I guess it was too much to hope for."

"We were all hoping for that." He hugged her gently. "But I guess it's time we put away our childish dreams."

"And face the truth," Jennie added as she went into Rick's arms.

"The worst is over. Mac will take care of it from here," Rick reassured them as he saw Mac coming through the lobby.

"Let's go to the restaurant and have something to eat. Silas said the stage isn't due until this afternoon, so it's going to be a while," Mac said calmly.

"All right," they said and they started off across the street.

Eve had never thought that things would turn out this way. She had been so sure of herself in the beginning, but now she knew that there was no future for her unless Mac helped her.

"Mac! Wait!" she cried, chasing after him into the street, uncaring that there were others watching. "I need to talk to you!"

Malo watched as they moved off the sidewalk and, after directing Pablo to start firing when he did, he took careful aim and pulled the trigger.

The instincts that had saved Rick's life many times before served him well again. He would never know what caused him to glance up as he stepped into the street, but he caught sight of the rifle barrel just as the outlaws began to fire.

"Get down!" he yelled as the first slug blasted into his shoulder, and he dove to the left, shoving Jennie safely out of the way behind a watering trough.

"How could he have seen me?" Malo screamed in agonized frustration as he realized that Rick had escaped. "Damn!"

"We'd better get out of here!" Pablo urged as he saw the townspeople running down the street in their direction. "The law will be coming any minute!"

"I want him dead!" He kept firing indiscriminately in Rick's direction, his actions seeming almost crazed. "He will not get away from me again!"

"Malo!" Lucia cried desperately as she heard a commotion below in the bar. "We have to go—now!"

With great reluctance, the outlaw turned from the window and followed the other two out of the room. Staying together, they raced down the back stairs, but just as they reached their horses, Todd came charging down the side street with the men from the ranch, blocking their escape route. Desperate, they tried to run back inside, but as Pablo reentered the building, shots rang out and he fell backward, dead, into the street.

Lucia dropped the gun she'd been clutching and looked around, fearful that one of the men would shoot her, but Todd reined in at the head of the small posse. "Don't move,

Lucia, and you'll be safe," he ordered. "Malo, drop the gun."

Malo was staring at the group of men who surrounded him, wildly contemplating trying to shoot his way out, when he heard the sound of Mac and Jake behind him.

"We've got him covered from this side. Drop your gun, real slow, Malo."

And with burning bitterness, Malo realized he was cornered. Knowing that they would hang him if he was taken alive, he made a run for it, dashing hopelessly away as he fired rapidly and haphazardly in all directions. Though they were surprised for a moment by his brazen move, it was only a matter of seconds before their return volley mowed him down, and he fell, crumpled and bloody, in the dust.

Mac and Jake were relieved to know that, at last, the ordeal with the bandits was really over, and they headed back to check on Rick, leaving Todd in charge. As they emerged from Dolly's, they were surprised to see a small crowd gathered by what looked to be an injured woman.

"Who was shot?" Mac looked worriedly for his daughters, and he was relieved when he caught sight of both of them, kneeling by the wounded woman.

"Pa, I think it was Eve," Jake told him as they drew nearer.

"Eve? Oh, God." Racing to her, with Jake at his side, he elbowed his way through the crowd. "Did anybody send for the doctor?"

"Yes, he's coming," someone answered quickly.

"Eve."

"Mac." She managed to say his name in a pain-filled whisper.

"Don't try to talk. The doc will be here in a minute."

"No." She gasped as agony pounded through her. "Mac, I'm sorry. So sorry."

"Please, Eve." Mac choked, trying to encourage her to hang on, but she somehow knew that the battle had already been lost.

492

"I'm sorry, Mac, but it just wasn't enough."

"Eve," he began, but it was too late. He stared down at Eve with disbelieving eyes. She was dead. A wave of pain rushed through him at the remembrance of their time together before she'd deserted them, and only Jennie's soft call penetrated his haze of grief.

"Pa?"

"She's gone, Jennie." He stood up and looked at her, his eyes dark with emotion.

"Oh, Pa." She sighed. "I'm so sorry."

"I think we all are," he answered dully, watching as the doctor quickly examined Eve and then, after pronouncing her dead, he covered her with a blanket.

"Pa, are you ready to go?" Jake came to him, sensing that Eve's death had been a blow to him and that he needed to get away.

"Yes," he answered, quietly. "Yes, I think I am."

Mac glanced to where Jennie stood with Rick. "How's your shoulder?"

"It's just a flesh wound, Mac."

"You're able to ride?"

"Yes."

"Good," he said as he turned away from the death of his past. "Let's go home, then. Hildago is waiting."

Thirty-six

One month later—El Rancho Grande

The moonbeams streamed through the unshuttered bedroom window, bathing the embracing lovers in pale, silver-kissed light. Wrapped in one another's arms, Rick and Jennie rested on the widespread coolnesss of the bed, replete in their love.

Jennie raised up on her elbows to stare down at her handsome husband admiringly. "I love you, Rick," she said simply as she bent to kiss him, her lips touching his in a fleeting pledge.

"I love you, too, Mrs. Peralta." His smile flashed in the darkness.

"That sounds so nice," she purred, shifting to lie against his chest.

The hard-tipped softness of her breasts pressed so intimately to him brought a low growl from Rick and he pulled her up, his mouth seeking hers in a passionate exchange.

"You're not sorry?" he questioned when they'd finally moved apart.

"About what?" she asked wide-eyed.

"About leaving the M Circle C so soon after our wedding. I know I rushed you more than a little—"

"No, I'm not sorry. My place is with you—my husband."

"I'm glad to hear you say that." He smiled at her tenderly. "Some women might not have enjoyed a honeymoon on the trail."

Jennie laughed as she remembered their trek to his home in the company of his grandfather and several ranch hands.

"It was—different—and our privacy was severely limited."

"Nonexistent, is more like it." He laughed.

"But you're worth the hardship." Jennie paused for effect as she added teasingly, "I think."

"You only think?" he said in mock outrage as his hands began to move arousingly over her. "Don't you know?"

"I know," she told him in quiet confidence as they kissed once more. "Do you think Todd and Carrie are as happily married as we are?"

"Nobody could ever be as happy as we are," Rick assured her as he pressed a heated kiss to the softness of her throat. "But I think they might come close."

"Mmmmm," she murmured sensuously as his lips moved lower in their continued foray. "Pa and Hildago will, too."

"They deserve all the happiness they can get after waiting so long to be married, but I'm glad things finally worked out for them."

"Me, too." Jennie smiled as she thought of the other woman's delight over Mac's marriage proposal. She paused for a moment as she remembered all the excitement of that fateful day, and she shivered at the thought of how close they had come to being killed. "I'm just sorry that things turned out the way they did with Eve."

"Sweetheart." Rick held her close. "She was responsible for the life she led, not you."

"I know, but—"

"No buts. Not tonight and not ever. All right?" He lifted

her chin and met her gaze lovingly.

"All right." She sighed as he kissed her tenderly, and the passion exploded between them again as they moved together in blissful union, seeking and finding, touching and holding, loving and being loved, until the flames of their desire consumed them, and they reached the peak of excitement together, sharing a love that would last for all time.